# Finding Us

## The Jade Series #6

# Finding Us

## The Jade Series #6

By

## Allie Everhart

Finding Us

By Allie Everhart

ISBN: 1942781008

ISBN-13: 9781942781004

# *Chapter 1*

**JADE**

The overfilled garbage bag fights with me as I try to pry it from the other bags wedged into the small trunk of my car. I probably should've listened to Garret and just used boxes for the clothes, towels, and sheets, but I didn't and now I'm left struggling with this stupid bag. I could ask Garret to help me but that would just prove he was right all along and I can't give him the satisfaction after I insisted, repeatedly, that garbage bags were better than bulky boxes.

I manage to pick up the bag, then try to hold it while shutting the trunk with my elbow, my keys dangling from my fingers. I take a moment to reposition it.

"Need some help with that?" I can't see Garret, but I can hear his voice and I know he's laughing at me.

"No. I don't need any help," I say, realizing we're now reliving the scene that played out last year when we met.

"It looks heavy," he says.

"I can handle heavy." I say it like I did last year, annoyed. "Besides I used better garbage bags this time. I went all out. Name brand. Double reinforced sides. Even has a handle on top."

"I see that. But that doesn't mean I can't be a gentleman and offer my assistance."

I feel his hands brush against my shorts as he reaches under the bag. I keep hold of it, my arms tightening around the middle causing two white towels to bulge out the top.

"Jade," Garret says calmly. "Let go of the bag."

"I'm perfectly capable of carrying it myself."

"I know you are, but I'm here and I need something to do."

"Then go unpack the boxes. That'll give you something to do."

"Jade, if you don't give me this bag, my hands will have no choice but to wander below the bag and do things that are not entirely appropriate given that our neighbors are watching us right now."

I glance behind him and see an older couple sitting on their porch. "You wouldn't dare. You know how embarrassed I would be if you—" I stop as I feel his hand extending beyond the bottom of the bag, his fingers touching my shorts.

"Fine. Take it!" I let go and he catches it, then easily transfers it to one arm.

He gives me a quick kiss. "That was easy."

I shake my head and take a box of kitchen supplies from the back seat and follow him inside. I set the box on the floor and assess our new digs. The house is about the same size as the townhouse we rented last summer but it's just one level instead of two. The bedroom is down the hall from the living room and looks almost exactly like our last bedroom.

It has a king-size bed with a nightstand on each side and a wide dresser along the wall that leads to the bathroom. It's a large room with lots of windows and a big walk-in closet.

The house has been completely renovated. The kitchen has new white cabinets, light-colored granite countertops, and stainless-steel appliances. The walls have all been freshly painted a soothing grayish-green color. The bathroom has a new countertop and sink and new tile on the floor and walk-in shower.

It looks like the owners bought all new furniture, too. It has a beachy feel like the furniture at our last place. The living room tables are the color of driftwood and have a distressed look. The overstuffed couch and two chairs are covered in a bright white canvas-like fabric. Light blue throw pillows add some color.

The real estate agent showed us what the place used to look like and it was pretty bad. The people who bought it fixed it up to use as a summer vacation home, but they didn't want it to sit empty the rest of the year, which worked out perfect for Garret and me. Of course we'll be homeless next summer, but I'm hoping we can spend the summer with Harper and Sean again, maybe on a different beach.

Most of the houses around us are also summer vacation homes and now that it's almost Labor Day, people are starting to leave. The neighbors on one side of us are already gone and the ones we just saw outside are moving back to their regular home in a few days, at least that's what the real estate agent said. So it'll be quiet around here, which will be good for studying.

"Hey." Garret comes up behind me, scooping me up into his arms. "Need a break?" He drops me on the couch and lays over me, brushing the loose strands of hair from my face.

"Let's get the rest of the bags from the trunk and then we'll take a break."

He smiles. "I think we should take a break right now. I'm kind of turned on at the moment and I don't think I should go back out there in my current state, you know, with the neighbors watching and all."

I smile back. "I have no idea what you're talking about."

He pushes his hips into me. "I think you do."

"How could you possibly get turned on while moving?"

"I probably shouldn't tell you this but…" He lifts off me little and slips his hand under my tank top. His lips touch my neck, kissing just under my ear, and he says, "There was this really hot girl out front just now. Round, little ass. Tan, perfect legs. And the most beautiful face I've ever seen. I couldn't take my eyes off her. Still can't. And now I can't help myself. I have to touch her." His hand moves down to my shorts, unbuttoning them and tugging the zipper down.

I was not at all in the mood for sex, all hot and sweaty and tired from moving. But now he's got me fired up and ready to go, as he always seems to do.

"And what would your wife think of you looking at this girl? And touching her?"

"I think she'd tell me to go for it. Because if I'm not mistaken, I think she was checking out the guy outside moving boxes. In fact I think when he took his shirt off, she was kind of staring. It was shameful, really. I mean, she *is* married."

He's right. I was totally watching him as he moved boxes; his muscles flexing, beads of sweat on his tan skin. And then he took his shirt off and I was staring. I know. It's crazy. I see him every day, with and without a shirt, and yet I was still staring at him.

"She really shouldn't stare." I bring his face to mine and kiss him, gently at first, then forcefully as I feel him press between my legs, his bare chest against my skin, which is now exposed since he managed to get my tank top off during this flirtatious interlude.

The blinds on the window flutter in the breeze and I look and see the back door open, the screen door allowing anyone walking by to get a glimpse of us on the couch, or more if they stopped and looked.

"Not here," I whisper. "Let's go to the bedroom." I latch my arms around his neck.

"What about your husband?" He sits up and I hang on to him, wrapping my legs around his waist. "And my wife?"

"I don't think they'll mind." I look him in the eye as he carries me to the bedroom. "It's not every day you meet someone you have this kind of chemistry with. That raw, uncontrolled passion that just takes over. You have to give in to something like that, you know?"

His eyes don't leave mine as he lays me on the bed, stripping my clothes off and then his own. His skin glistens with sweat, his hair wet from it. We're both hot from the late August heat and now we're even hotter from our short round of foreplay on the couch.

As if on cue, we both go at it like we really are two strangers who just met in the driveway and were instantly attracted to each other in such an intense way that we just had to give in to our desires.

Then we lie there, sweating even more than before, catching our breath. Moments later, we look at each other and say at the same time, "Shower?"

I laugh as he gets up from the bed and goes in the bathroom, starting the water. I yank the elastic from my hair and shake it out a little as I walk in there.

Garret's watching me. "After you." He holds the shower door open, guiding me in there with his body. As the water cascades over us, he turns me around and takes my face in his hands and kisses me.

And a few minutes later, we have officially christened the shower. I was thinking we would do this later tonight or maybe tomorrow, but who am I kidding? Garret and I are still crazy about each other. Marriage hasn't changed us a bit. In fact, we might even do it more now than before. I haven't really kept track, but it seems like we do. And I like that about us. I like that we still can't take our hands off each other. That I still think about him when he's not around. That I still get that little fluttery feeling inside whenever he walks in a room. I thought all that would change when we moved in together last May, and when it didn't, I thought it would change when we got married last month. But so far, it hasn't.

"What are you thinking about?" Garret asks. We're both lying on the bed, each wrapped in a towel, still wet from the shower.

"You." I stare up at the ceiling.

"What *about* me?" He reaches over and slips his hand around mine.

"About how you still get to me. How I still can't resist you."

"Still?" He laughs. "What does that mean? Did you think you'd be sick of me by now?"

"No. But I see you every day so you'd think by now I'd get used to your extreme hotness and somehow be immune to the effect it has on me."

"That almost sounded like a compliment, even though you expressed some annoyance with me toward the end there."

I flip on my side, my fingers trailing over his muscular chest. "My annoyance is not with you. It's with me, and my inability to control myself around you. This could be a real problem now that I need to focus on school again. I have a difficult class load this year."

He turns to face me. "I think you can make time for both this," he kisses me, "and your class work."

"I don't know. You can be awfully distracting. Look what you did just now. I would've been done unpacking if it weren't for you distracting me."

"It wasn't entirely my fault." He runs his hand over my shoulder and down my arm.

"I'm pretty sure it *was* your fault. It all started with you insisting on taking that bag from me."

He smiles. "It *did* all start that way, didn't it?"

"Yes, and now here we are, married, moving into a new place, and starting a new school. Just think how different everything would be if you'd let me carry that bag last year and—"

He kisses me before I can finish. "You'd still be in the same place, Jade. We'd still be here together. I would've made sure of it."

He releases the towel that's fastened around my chest.

"Garret," I say, the towel falling down around me.

"What?" He lowers me back down on the bed, kissing my neck, his hand on my hip.

"You're distracting me again. I need to unpack."

"You can't lie around in a towel on a bed and not expect this to happen. If anything, I would say *you're* the one distracting *me.*"

I laugh. "Okay, that's fair."

I unhook the towel from his waist and we let ourselves get distracted one more time. Then it's time to get back to work.

"I'll go get the rest of the bags." Garret takes a clean shirt from his box of clothes. He used boxes. He wouldn't use my garbage bags.

"Do you care if I turn the air on?" I slip on one of Garret's t-shirts because my bags of clothes are still sitting in the trunk. "It's so hot and stuffy in here and the breeze isn't helping much."

"Go ahead and turn it on. I'll close the windows."

While he does that, I locate the thermostat and turn the air conditioning on. Cold air blasts from the vents.

"They must've installed a new air conditioner, too. This air is freezing." I say it to Garret but notice he's already back outside, getting my bags from the car. I drag the other bag to the hall closet and take out the sheets and towels, arranging them on the wire racks.

We don't have much to unpack since the place is furnished but it still seems to take forever. Just hanging up clothes or stuffing them in dressers takes longer than you'd think. Then we unpack the boxes of bathroom stuff and cleaning supplies and kitchen items and it ends up taking the rest of the day to get everything put away. I guess we could've waited and unpacked later, but Garret's dad is coming here this week and I want everything put away and organized before he arrives.

I used to not care about things like that. I wasn't the most organized person when it came to household stuff. My dorm room was kind of a mess. When I needed to clean up, I just tossed whatever was lying around my room into a drawer or in the closet. But now I feel the need to put things where they belong and not be so messy. Garret's not messy so maybe I'm learning from him. Or maybe I'm just growing up and the sloppiness bothers me more than it did before.

"Let's go return the van, then grab something for dinner." Garret's standing in the kitchen, drinking a glass of water.

"Just a minute." I run back to the bedroom and rifle through a box, looking for a hair elastic. I can't find the one I tossed on the floor before the shower sex. It's probably under the bed.

I take one from the dresser and put my hair up while walking to meet Garret at the door.

"Ready?" He holds the door open. "Just follow me. The rental place is only a few miles from here."

I get in my car and he gets in the van.

We rented the van to move our stuff because our cars are too small to carry everything. Yesterday we drove Garret's car up here and dropped it off. Then this morning, he drove the van and I drove my car. Between all the packing and the driving the past couple days, it's no wonder we're both exhausted. We could've hired movers, but it seemed silly when we don't have that much stuff.

After we return the van, we stop at a fast food place for dinner. I'm really tired now and I just want to hurry up and eat so I can lie on the couch and watch TV for the rest of the night.

When we get back to the house, Garret puts his arm around me as we walk in the door. "So what do you think? Does it feel like home?"

I glance around at the living room and the kitchen. The boxes are gone and everything looks neat and clean.

"Not yet, but it will." I take his hand and lead him to the couch. "You're not having second thoughts, are you?"

"Second thoughts about what?"

"This." I motion to the room. "Living here. Going to school here. Living in California."

"Of course not. Why would you say that?"

"Because it's a big change. You grew up in Connecticut. And now you're on the opposite coast, really far away from your family."

"*You're* my family now. And this is a big change for both of us. This isn't exactly Iowa. And you're far away from your family, too."

"I guess. But after high school, I was ready to leave Iowa and I didn't want to go back. Not that it's a bad place. I just wanted a change."

"And so do I. I liked growing up in Connecticut and yes, I'm comfortable there, but I've moved on. I have a new life now. And I like that we're starting our life together someplace new. A place that neither one of us is from. It makes it seem more like ours."

"But what about the college? We kind of rushed into deciding to go there. Maybe we won't like it."

"You could say that about any college. We just have to go there and try it out. If we hate it, we can always transfer somewhere else. But I think we'll like it." He picks up the TV remote. "You want to watch a movie?"

"Let's just watch TV."

He clicks the TV on, then leans back on the couch and puts his arm up. "Come get in your spot."

I scoot under his arm, nestled against his chest. "You know I always fall asleep in this spot."

"I know. Go ahead and sleep. I know you're tired." He kisses my forehead. "I love you."

"I love you, too."

I fall asleep right away. Normally I wouldn't be able to sleep my first night in a strange place. But Garret makes everything seem familiar. As I told him not that long ago, I'm at home when I'm with him. It doesn't matter where I live, as long as he's there, I'll feel safe and at home.

# *Chapter 2*

**GARRET**

*I* wake up to the sound of a guy yelling "...just $19.95, plus we'll throw in this handy chopper AND this spiral-bound cookbook. It's a value worth—" I click the TV off, leaving the room dark except for the moonlight filtering in through the blinds that are still open.

I look down and see Jade sleeping soundly on my chest. She's looks so peaceful when she sleeps. A few times when I've been awake at night, I've heard her mumble something and I've looked over to see her smiling and it makes me wonder what she's dreaming about. I've asked her but she said she doesn't remember her dreams.

Tonight she's not smiling or mumbling. She's just sleeping contently, her face just under my chin and her arm tucked into her side and resting on my chest. I kiss the top of her head and watch her for a moment, noticing how beautiful she looks in the soft moonlight. Sometimes I still can't believe she's my wife. That she's all mine.

I love that she's mine. That she chose me as the person she wants to be with for the rest of her life. Sometimes I feel overwhelmed by the responsibility of that. I want to be the husband Jade deserves but I'm not quite sure what that means. All I know is that I want to make her happy. I want the pain and the sadness she had for all those years before I met her to go away, and I want all the years ahead of her, the ones we'll share together, to be filled with only good memories. I know that's not realistic. We'll have our ups and downs, but I want the good to far outweigh the bad and I'll do all I can to make sure of that.

I love Jade more than I thought it was possible to love another person. I finally know how my dad felt about my mom. I remember how my dad used to look at her and I know he loved her just as much as I love Jade.

I can't imagine how hard it was for him to lose my mom. How devastating it was when he got that call saying she was gone. It was bad enough for me, but it was different for him. I'm sure if I asked him, he wouldn't even be able to explain how he felt when she died. I'm sure that type of grief is something you can't put into words. I know I wouldn't be able to if something like that happened to Jade. And I've only known her a year. My dad was with my mom for 12 years. He loved her, like I love Jade, for 12 years and then she was gone.

I see my dad so much differently now. I understand him more. I don't approve of the way he turned his back on me after she died, but I kind of understand it. My mom and I are a lot alike, and to my dad, I was a constant reminder she was gone. So he avoided me. He kept his distance, spending all his time at work. At a time when I needed him the most, he abandoned me.

My grandfather deserves some of the blame for how my dad treated me all those years. After my mom died, my grandfather retired and forced my dad to take over the business. And he told my dad he had to be stricter with me. That's when our relationship completely fell apart. My dad started trying to control every aspect of my life, just like his father did with him. Even today, my grandfather still controls my dad. He's a master manipulator and he knows it and takes pleasure in that role.

As much as I complain about my dad, he's never treated me as badly as my grandfather's treated him. When my dad married my mom, my grandfather wouldn't speak to him for years. Then when he finally did, their conversations were nothing more than my grandfather telling my dad what a disappointment he was, how he'd disgraced the Kensington name by marrying my mom, and how he was a complete failure as a son.

I remember hearing those conversations when I was a kid and I had to tune them out. I loved my dad and I couldn't stand hearing my grandfather talk to him that way. And I didn't want to believe my grandfather was the type of person who would say those things. So I'd hide in my room and turn the TV on so I couldn't hear them.

For years, I pretended those conversations never happened. I pretended my grandfather was the person I wanted him to be. The kind, loving grandfather every kid wants. The kind who takes you fishing and buys you toy race cars and takes you to baseball games. But he was never that grandfather. He's always been distant and reserved, showing

little emotion, but not needing to because his words and his actions say enough.

Growing up, my grandfather didn't lecture me as much as he lectured my dad, but he did constantly remind me that being a Kensington is a privilege and that I always need to act in a way that protects and upholds our family name. So he was pissed last spring when I did all that stuff to ruin my image. Of course none of that was real, but my grandfather thought it was and he blames my dad for it. He blames Jade, too. He thinks she's destroyed my life and my future. That's why he acted the way he did last Fourth of July, refusing to speak to Jade and me.

I used to work my ass off trying to get my grandfather's approval but now I've given up. He'll never approve of me as long as I'm married to Jade. And if he's making me choose between Jade and him, I will always choose Jade.

I look down as Jade adjusts herself on my chest, her hand lightly gripping my t-shirt. I need to get her to bed. I can't see what time it is, but judging from the infomercial that was on TV, I'm guessing it's the middle of the night.

I sit up a little and rotate just enough so that I can reach under her legs and lift her up. Her head flops forward and one of her arms falls down under her, hanging there as I walk to the bedroom. I carefully set her down on the bed and slip her shorts off. She can sleep in the tank she's wearing. I pull back the covers and gently slide her over onto the sheet.

"Garret?" Her arm moves over the mattress like she's looking for me in her sleep. She always does this. If I get up

in the night to get a drink of water, I come back and find her arm sprawled over the sheet, trying to find me.

I drop my shorts to the floor, yank my t-shirt off, and slip in bed beside her. "I'm right here," I whisper.

She scoots closer until she finds my chest. I move my arm out and she lays her head just under my shoulder. Her leg hooks around mine and her arm drapes over my middle. It's not the most comfortable position, at least not for me. I'm basically trapped now until she moves. But I'll wait until she falls back to sleep, then I'll gently roll her off me and we'll lie together on our sides, like we always do.

"Goodnight," I whisper, pulling the blanket over us.

"I love you," she whispers back.

I don't think she's fully awake, but it's good to know she loves me in her sleep as well.

"I love you, too, Jade. More than you'll ever know."

It's true. I'll never be able to tell Jade how much I love her because there aren't words for it. But I plan to spend the rest of my life showing her. Maybe that's what it means to be a good husband. To not just tell your wife, but to show her how much you love her. I tried to do that in the time I spent as her boyfriend. And I will continue to try to as her husband because Jade means everything to me and I want her to feel loved. It's something she still struggles with sometimes because of the way she grew up. It took me forever to convince her she was worthy of being loved and to accept the fact that people love her. Frank. Ryan. Grace. Me. Even after I told her I loved her last November, I don't think she really believed it until months later.

Jade's come a long way since last year but she still has a ways to go. After what she went through with her mom, she still has trouble believing people actually care about her. It's just another reason why I need to always show her how much I love her. I don't want her to ever doubt that.

It's been a few minutes and I gently move Jade onto her side, then pull her into my chest and wrap my arm around her. Having her tucked safely in my arms, my mind and my body relax and I fall back to sleep.

When I wake up again, the sun is shining through the window, lighting up the entire room. I stretch my arms out and notice Jade's not there.

"Jade?"

She doesn't answer. Maybe she's in the bathroom. Sometimes she likes to brush her teeth before our daily tradition of wake-up sex. But the bathroom door is open and it looks dark in there.

"Jade?" I push the covers off and start to get up. "Are you in the kitchen?"

"Yeah, I was getting some water." I hear her voice, then see her come into the bedroom wearing running shorts and a sports bra, her skin slick with sweat, her hair in a ponytail and one of the headbands I gave her last Easter.

"Where were you?"

"I was out running." She climbs on the bed and kisses me. "I got up early and decided to go for a run on the beach. It was great. The weather's a lot cooler this morning."

"You shouldn't run by yourself early in the morning. There aren't enough people out. Wait until later. Or wake me up and I'll go with you."

"You hate running."

"Doesn't matter. I don't like you out there alone. If you want to run, I'll run with you."

"Garret, there are no crazy killers out on the beach. We're in a small college town and this is a private beach. I'm perfectly safe."

She doesn't get it. Jade doesn't get how much I worry about her. The world is not a safe place, especially for women, and especially for small, cute, young women who are barely dressed. I wish the world wasn't like that, but it is.

I also worry because what happened last spring is still fresh in my mind. The organization let me go, but what if they're still watching me? What if they're watching Jade? What if they decide to do something to her to punish me for ruining their plan?

My dad keeps telling me not to worry, but I know he only says that because he wants me to relax and enjoy college and my new life with Jade.

I don't believe him when he says we're safe. I don't trust the men from the organization or the people they work with. That's why I constantly keep a close watch around me. I keep a close eye on Jade. I always check to see if anyone's following us. I always lock the doors. I even check the cars for listening devices. Maybe it won't always be this way, but for now, it's what I need to do.

"Jade, please do not go running out there alone again early in the morning. I don't mind going with you. I really don't."

"I didn't want to wake you up. You needed your rest. I could tell you were tired from the move. What time did we end up going to bed last night?"

"I'm not sure. We both fell asleep watching TV. When I woke up I took you to bed."

"You got me to bed without waking me up? That's a skill."

"You didn't wake up?"

"I don't think so. Why? Did you think I was awake? Was I talking in my sleep?"

I smile. "A little."

"Garret." She pushes my shoulder back. "What did I say? Was it embarrassing?"

"You said something about how you wanted to have sex with me and couldn't wait until morning." I shrug. "I told you you'd have to wait. I was tired."

She looks like she really believes me. "You turned me down? Seriously? I can't believe you didn't wake me up."

I laugh. "You're right. If you'd said that, I totally would've woken you up."

"What did I really say in my sleep?"

"It doesn't matter." I gaze down at her neon green sports bra, then down to her flat, tan stomach still dotted with sweat. I get out of bed and haul her up over my shoulder, my hands cupping her tight little ass as I walk to the bathroom. "Let's get you in the shower, dirty girl."

"I'm not dirty. I'm sweaty."

"You're both. You're sweaty because you ran and you're dirty because you were having sex dreams last night." I reach in and turn the shower on.

"You just said you were making that up."

"Whatever. I know you dream about us having sex." I set her down and hold the shower door open.

"Maybe sometimes." She strips her bra and shorts off. "So you want to make my dreams come true?"

"Always." I follow her into the shower. And our morning tradition continues.

# Chapter 3

## JADE

After we shower, I search through the dresser trying to remember where I put stuff yesterday. As I find some shorts, Garret comes out of the bathroom, naked of course. The guy has no problem being naked. He'll walk right past an open window completely naked and not even give it a thought. Me? I never leave the bathroom without a towel around me or a robe or a long t-shirt. And the few times I'm not covered up, I at least make sure the blinds are shut.

"What's on the agenda today?" Garret joins me at the dresser.

I try not to look at his naked body. If I do, we'll end up right back in bed. I swear that's why he does it.

"I have to do some cleaning and then I need to go to the grocery store."

"Why do you need to clean? The place looks fine." He opens the top drawer and pulls out his boxers.

"Because your dad's coming on Thursday and I want our place to look nice."

"Don't worry about it. My dad doesn't care." Garret puts his boxers on, making him a little less distracting. But then my eyes drift up to his tan, muscular chest.

I go to the walk-in closet, distancing myself from him before I end up dragging him back to the bed.

"Are you kidding? Your dad's house is spotless. I'm sure he'll notice if ours isn't."

"Jade, I swear to you, my dad doesn't care. Katherine's the one who's obsessed with things being spotless. I mean, yeah, if we had day-old sandwiches sitting out and piles of dirty clothes everywhere, he'd notice. But a little dust or whatever else you're worried about? He won't notice."

"I still think I should clean at least a little." I put on a lightweight, button-up shirt because it's supposed to be really hot out again today.

"Then I'll help." He meets me in the closet, shirtless but wearing shorts. "What do you need me to do?"

"I can do it. Don't worry about it."

"I don't want you cleaning all day. I want us to go do something." He takes a red t-shirt from the hanger and yanks it over his head and through his arms. "So let's get this shit done. Tell me what you need."

"Could you make breakfast?" I adjust his shirt a little so that it sits right on his shoulders.

"I would, but we don't have any food."

"Then I guess we should start by going to the grocery store."

"Let's go out for breakfast and then we'll go to the store. We need to resume our pancake breakfast tradition."

"That's on Sundays."

"Yeah, but we need to find a place to go. Come on." He takes my hand, dragging me out of the closet. "We passed a

diner on our way back here last night. They probably have pancakes."

The diner is off on its own, about a mile from where we dropped the van off last night. It's an old building that needs to be painted. It reminds me of the truck stop restaurants they have back in Iowa off the interstate.

When we get inside, there's a sign that says to seat yourself so we find a booth in the back. The place isn't very crowded but it's 9 on a weekday so most people are at work.

"They only have buttermilk," I say, perusing the small menu. "They don't even have blueberry."

"You have to lower your pancake standards, Jade. There aren't many restaurants in this town." Garret turns my coffee cup upright, then does the same to his own as the waitress approaches.

"Coffee?" She pours it without waiting for an answer.

"Sure," Garret says, trying not to laugh.

"Ready to order?" The waitress looks hungover, her bleached-blond hair in a messy ponytail, her eyes tired and a little red. She's probably my age but she looks older.

"We'll both have the buttermilk pancakes," Garret says. "And I'll have a side of scrambled eggs. And bring two orange juice, please."

She glances at me. "That it?"

"Yes. Thanks." When she leaves I shut my menu and drop it in the holder at the end of the table. "Do you have to do that?"

"Do what?" Garret puts his menu next to mine.

"Order for me. It's embarrassing. Did you see how she looked at me?"

"I wasn't paying attention." He takes one of the little coffee creamers from the bowl and opens it, then pours it in my coffee.

"Now what are you doing?" I pull my cup back.

"Fixing your coffee." He reaches over and pours another creamer in. "Three creams, right?"

I glance toward the kitchen and see the waitress staring at us.

"Would you stop? Now she's watching us."

"What do you care?" He adds another creamer to my coffee.

"What if she goes to Camsburg? I don't want her telling people I'm so incompetent I can't order my own food and add cream to my coffee."

He smiles. "She won't say that. She'll tell people how you have the best husband in the world who takes care of your food and beverage needs."

I move my coffee out of his reach. "Thanks, but I got it. She's coming over here again."

"Do you want regular syrup?" She asks it only to Garret since she now assumes I have no say in the matter. Her jaw moves up and down as she chomps on the wad of pink bubble gum in her mouth.

"Jade, what would you like?" Garret's grinning at me from across the table.

The girl looks at me and waits, smacking her gum.

"Um, I don't know what that means. Are there different types of syrup?"

She sighs. "We have regular, light, sugar free, or blueberry. I can bring them all if you can't decide."

"Regular is fine. Thanks."

She takes off again.

I watch as she gets the syrup from behind the counter, then fills two glasses with orange juice. "I don't think I like this place."

"Yeah, something's missing. It doesn't feel right, does it?"

"It's definitely not Al's Pancake House. Maybe we could call Al and see if he could open a restaurant here."

"I think Al died 20 years ago. That place has been there for like 50 years."

A few minutes later, the waitress appears with our food, setting the plates down and walking off without saying a word.

"She forgot the orange juice. It's sitting on the counter back there." I see the girl take her apron off and walk out a side door. "And now she's on break. Or maybe she left."

Garret shakes his head. "I'll get it." He comes back with our juice. "So I guess we won't be coming here again."

"The pancakes are really bad," I say as I try them. "They're almost as bad as the ones in the dining hall."

He takes a bite. "These are worse. They aren't even edible." He shoves his plate aside. "Let's just go."

"What about breakfast?" I take a drink of the juice.

"We'll go to the store and make our own pancakes. A mix would be better than this."

As he gets his wallet out, a man stops by our table.

"Garret, I didn't know you'd be moving here this early."
The man is tall and thin with dark brown hair, wearing a navy
track suit. The jacket has the Camsburg College logo on it.

Garret looks up. "Hey. Yeah, we got here yesterday."

"How'd the move go?"

"It was fine." Garret drops some money on the table.
"This is my wife, Jade. I don't think you met her when we
were here in May."

Wow, that sounded weird. *My wife, Jade.* I think that's the
first time he's introduced me as his wife. I like it, but it's still
weird.

The guy looks at me. "Nice to meet you."

"Nice to meet you, too. Who are you again?"

He laughs. "I'm Keith Altman, the swim coach at
Camsburg. I guess your husband hasn't mentioned me."

Again, the husband term sounds strange. Since getting
married, Garret and I haven't been around anyone besides
Sean and Harper so the husband and wife terms haven't
really been used.

I look at Garret. "Um, no. He hasn't mentioned you."

"I did," Garret says. "I just called him 'coach.' I never
said his name."

"Congratulations on the marriage." Keith smiles at both
of us. "How was the wedding? Did the weather cooperate?"

"Yeah, it was great," Garret answers.

"Good. Well, I didn't mean to interrupt your breakfast.
I just wanted to come over and see if we could set up a time
to meet over at the pool. I'd like to watch you swim and see
if we can get you on the team this fall."

Garret hesitates, then says, "Yeah, sounds good. I'll give you a call."

"Can we just set a time? Are you free tomorrow? It wouldn't take long."

"I don't know." Garret looks at me. "I think we're busy tomorrow. We're going to the bookstore and then my dad's coming into town Thursday so—"

"That's great. I'd love to meet him. I always like to meet the parents and explain how the season runs. See if they have any questions."

"My dad doesn't have much time so that probably won't work." Garret acts like he's annoyed. I don't know why. Keith seems like a nice guy.

"Garret, you can go to the pool tomorrow," I tell him. "We'll just go to the bookstore after you swim."

Now Garret seems annoyed with *me*. He's giving me this look like I shouldn't be butting in. But I didn't know I *was*. I was just trying to be helpful.

He turns to Keith and forces out a smile. "I guess I'll see you tomorrow. Maybe around 11?"

"Yes, that's perfect. I'm looking forward to watching you swim. I think you'll be a great addition to the team. See you then."

He leaves and Garret quickly exits the booth.

I follow him to the car. "What's going on with you? You don't want to swim tomorrow?"

"No. I don't. I'm not ready to. I haven't even practiced." He gets in the car, closing the door a little too hard.

"You swam in the ocean all summer. You're in great shape."

"I didn't swim. I surfed." He backs the car up, then stops. "Put your seatbelt on." He waits until it's on, then continues backing out of the parking space.

"I saw you swim in the ocean at least a few times."

"It's not the same as swimming in a pool. I need to practice before I swim for that guy. And now I can't. I'm gonna suck tomorrow and he won't want me on the team."

"Are you mad at me?"

He sighs. "Yeah, kind of. But I'll get over it."

"Sorry. I didn't know you weren't ready to try out."

"Just forget it. I need to find a grocery store. Do you remember seeing one around here?" He picks up his phone and hands it to me. "See if you can find one."

"Garret, why won't you talk to me about this?"

"There's nothing to talk about. Just find a store, okay?"

He's mad and I can't figure out why. He loves swimming and I know he wants to be on the team so what's the deal? He's in better shape now than he was last year. And even though he hasn't been swimming in a pool all summer, it's not like he forgot how to swim.

He turns down a road and off to the right is a large grocery store. We stop and go inside.

As we're shopping, I notice that Garret's in a total daze. He usually takes the lead in the store but today he's straggling behind.

"Do you want to pick out some meat?" I ask him as we stand in front of the meat case. He always picks it out. I know nothing about cuts of meat and I have no interest to learn. I don't like handling raw meat or cooking it. Seeing

29

the bloody juice in the package makes me not want to eat it. I also don't like touching raw chicken. The slippery texture and the bones make me ill, which is why Garret always cooks it for me.

"Garret? Are you going to get anything?"

"Yeah." He tosses some packages in the cart. I don't think he even knows what he's putting in there.

It ends up being a short shopping trip. It should've been a long trip because we have no food at the house, but I didn't feel like shopping when Garret's acting so out of it.

When we get home, I put the groceries away while Garret disappears in the bedroom. He comes out wearing his work-out shorts and a t-shirt.

"I'm going to the gym on campus."

"Right now? I thought we were having breakfast."

"I'm not really hungry. You want me to make you something?"

"No. I'll just have cereal." I go over to him. "Are you going to the pool?"

"It's not open but the gym is. I just went online and checked their hours."

"We don't have our student IDs yet. How are you going to get in?"

"You just have to show a driver's license and they'll look you up in the computer. At least that's what their website said."

"I'll go with you. Let me change quick."

"Jade, you hate the gym. Just stay here."

I stare at him, trying to read his face. "Why are you acting so weird?"

"I'm not." He sits on the arm of the couch and puts on his gym shoes. "I just feel like I need to lift some weights. Maybe do some cardio."

"Okay." I decide not to push the issue. Maybe he'll be back to normal after he works out. "When will you be back?"

"I don't know. I'll call you."

"You said you wanted to spend the day together. You don't want to now?"

He walks up and kisses me. "I'll be back around lunch. Love you."

"Love you, too."

He takes his keys from the counter and leaves. I guess he just needs some time alone to deal with whatever's bothering him. He'll talk to me about it when he's ready to. At least I hope he will.

# Chapter 4

**GARRET**

*I* drive through town going way too fast, not slowing down until I reach the campus and spot a Camsburg cop at the security gate. It's not like the rent-a-cop could really do anything to me but I'd rather not start the school year with some stupid traffic violation.

I pull in front of the gym and turn the car off and just sit for a moment. I'm so pissed right now. If Coach would've just left me alone this morning, today would be going totally different. I'd be home making pancakes for Jade instead of feeling like shit that I left her there wondering what the hell's going on with me. But I can't tell her. I can't talk to her about this. I need to deal with this alone. This is my issue, not hers.

I did this to myself and now I need to face it.

I fucked my shoulder up. Big time. And I've been avoiding dealing with it for months now. It all started after I got shot by Royce last year. I got shot in the upper chest but the damage spread up to my shoulder. The doctor acted like it was no big deal. He injected something in my shoulder that speeds tissue growth so you heal faster. And it was working, but then I went back to lifting weights when I wasn't supposed to and my shoulder started hurting again.

Last January, I went in for some tests and the doctor said my shoulder had more damage than he originally thought. I didn't tell him I was the cause of that. I just let him think he misread the original tests. He injected more of that stuff into my shoulder but there wasn't anything else he could do for it. It's one of those things where you just have to give it time to heal. Something about tendons and tissue and how the blood flow to the shoulder isn't the same as other parts of the body.

I wasn't really listening to everything the doctor said. I probably should've had my dad there to listen for me, but I didn't. I wanted to handle this myself. I didn't want him, or anyone else, knowing what was wrong because if they knew, they'd force me to stop swimming and stop working out. And I didn't want to do that. I didn't want to rest. I just wanted to get back to normal.

I figured if I just worked out more, my shoulder would get better. But it didn't. It only got worse. It didn't help matters that I skipped out on most of my physical therapy appointments. The exercises they gave me didn't seem to do anything so I stopped going. The therapist told me the exercises work over time but I wasn't patient enough to wait. And I didn't want Jade thinking I was taking forever to heal. She already feels guilty about what happened. She blames herself for my injury, like it was somehow her fault that Royce came after us that day. Like it was her fault he tried to kill us.

I hate that she feels guilty about that. After it happened I had to constantly remind her that it wasn't her fault I got shot. I chose to push her to the ground when the gun went off. She had nothing to do with it. And there was nothing she could've done to stop my actions that day. I was prepared for whatever would've happened to me. As soon as I saw that gun in Royce's hand, my only thought was to protect Jade. I don't regret what I did. I'd do it again today.

But now I'm left with this injury that refuses to heal. If I told Jade, she'd blame herself. She'd say it's all her fault, which is not even close to the truth. If I'd just taken care of this like the doctor told me to, taking time to rest, going to physical therapy, my shoulder would be back to normal now. The doctor said it takes a year to fully heal so maybe it wouldn't be completely back to normal, but it would be a hell of a lot closer than it is now.

I get out of the car, slamming the door shut. My body is wound tight and I need to release the tension. Punch something. Kick something. I just need to get this out of me.

The gym is mostly empty except for a few guys over at the weight machines. I show my ID to the guy at the counter.

He doesn't even look at it. "Go ahead."

This college is supposed to have great security. After that little encounter, I'm not feeling like it's that secure.

I run on the treadmill to warm up my muscles. I can't stand the treadmill. I always feel like a hamster on a wheel, watching that belt move under my feet and running but not going anywhere. I don't like the feeling of not going anywhere. I like to constantly move forward. And now I feel like I'm moving backward, at least when it comes to my college swim career.

Maybe I should just forget the whole thing. Swimming consumed my life in high school. It doesn't need to consume my life in college. I'm married now. I have better things to do with my time. Besides, I knew the swimming would end once college ended. It's not like I'm training for the Olympics here. It's just a sport. A hobby.

Yeah, right. I can tell myself that all I want, but it's not true. Swimming isn't just a hobby. It's everything to me. It's part of me. My mom was a swimmer, both in high school and in college. She's the one who got me started in it. She had me in the water when I was just a baby and I've been swimming ever since.

My mom never pushed me to be on a team. She just wanted me to be able to swim. She said swimming is a survival skill and that everyone should know how to swim. She went to school with a kid who died in third grade because he fell in a lake and didn't know how to swim. She told me that story when I was really young and it still makes me sad. Who doesn't know how to swim? How could you be in third grade and not know how? As I got older I realized that not everyone grows up with access to a pool or swim instruction, so it makes sense but it sucks that people are dying because they don't have this basic skill.

But swimming was more than a basic skill to me. I liked doing it. It was fun and I felt at home in the water, probably because I spent so much time in the pool with my mom. I was five when I started racing other kids in the pool at the local Y. After my first race, I was hooked. I loved the competition and I begged my mom to teach me how to be a better swimmer. She taught me some stuff, but it's hard to teach your own kid how to do something, especially when she needed to get tough with me and point out my mistakes. So she hired a swim coach for me and that's when I got really good.

After my mom died, the pool became my sanctuary. I'd go to the pool at my school and swim for hours. My dad noticed how much time I spent there and that's why, when he built the new house, he put an indoor pool in there. I thought I was the only one who used it but sometimes I caught my dad in there in the middle of the night, just kind of floating. I think it's because the water reminded him of my mom. I didn't realize that back then, but I do now.

"Hey, could you spot me?"

I look over and see a dark-haired guy wearing navy shorts and a gray Camsburg t-shirt standing next to the treadmill. He's sweaty and his stench is filling the area around me. I really don't want to spot him but I notice the gym is empty now and I get the feeling the guy will keep bothering me until I do.

"I'll wait until you're done," he says, noticing my hesitation.

"That's okay. I'm done." I shut the treadmill off and follow him to the free weights.

"Are you new here?" he asks. "You don't look familiar."

"Yeah, I transferred in. I'm a sophomore."

He extends his hand. "Welcome. I'm Kyle. I'm a junior."

"Garret." I shake his hand.

"You play any sports?"

I almost say yes but then realize my mistake. "No. I played sports in high school but I don't anymore. How about you?"

"Football. I've got practice later. I come in here and do weights in the mornings."

"How's the team?"

He laughs. "We suck. But that doesn't mean we don't try."

"What position do you play?"

"Quarterback." He wipes his hand over his forehead, dropping sweat on the floor.

"Star of the team, huh?"

He shakes his head. "Hardly. I told you we suck, right?"

"I was quarterback in high school. Our team totally sucked, too." I smile. "But you still get the benefits of being quarterback, right?"

He smiles back. "Yeah, you do."

It's true. No matter how bad the team, the quarterback gets perks, like popularity and an endless supply of girls. And if your team is good, you get a lot more than that.

"I just need to do three sets." He lies down on the bench and positions his hands on the barbell. "Ready?"

"Yeah, go ahead."

I spot him, then wait for him to rest between each set. As he does, he tells me more about the football team and a little about himself. He's from LA and his parents are attorneys who handle high-profile celebrity cases. His parents always have the press following them around and Kyle hates it. He came to Camsburg to get away from the media circus that constantly surrounds his parents.

"You want to do some sets?" He wipes the bench down with a towel.

I haven't bench-pressed since last April but I'm here to work out so I might as well. "Yeah, I guess I could."

"You want me to change the weights?"

"No, what you've got on there is fine." I wrap my hands around the bar and lift it off the stand. The weight feels heavy. I used to bench 200 all the time but it's been a while and my muscles need time to adjust. My body feels strong and I know I'm in good shape from all the surfing I did last summer, but that uses different muscles than what I'm using now.

I do 10 reps and feel okay. I rest for a minute, then start another set and on the fifth rep my form gets off and I feel a sharp twinge in my shoulder. "Shit!"

Kyle catches the bar before I drop it. "You okay?"

I sit up and circle my shoulder, the pain now a dull ache. "Yeah. I think I'm done."

"Okay, well, I need to head out. Thanks for your help."

"No problem."

He starts to leave, then turns around. "I'm having a party tonight if you want to come meet some people. It's mostly guys from the team." He smiles. "And there'll be plenty of girls. This time of year it's mostly townies. Most of the Camsburg girls aren't on campus yet. But the townies can show you a good time."

"Yeah, I don't think so." I grab a towel from the stack next to the weights.

"You got a girlfriend?"

"Actually, I'm married."

He laughs. "You're shittin' me, right?"

"No. I'm married."

"How the hell old are you? I thought you said you're a sophomore."

"I'm 20."

He's staring at me like I'm the first alien to land on Earth. I hadn't considered that people might react this way to my being married. Sean and Harper didn't make a big deal out of it but I realize now that strangers might find it odd.

"You're seriously married? And you're only 20?" He nods, knowingly. "I get it. You knocked her up. So you did the right thing. That's good, man. I don't think I could do that."

"I didn't knock her up." I don't elaborate, but I shouldn't have to. He shouldn't make assumptions like that. A guy can get married without getting a girl pregnant.

My shoulder hurts now and this guy's starting to annoy me. I've lost all interest in working out.

"I need to go." It comes out sounding like I'm angry.

Kyle steps closer. "Sorry, man. I didn't mean to be rude or anything. I was just a little shocked by the whole marriage thing. Forget it. I'm sorry. Whatever works, right? Is she in school here?"

"Yeah, she's also a sophomore."

"So bring her to the party tonight."

"I don't think we can make it, but thanks for asking."

"Let me give you my number in case you change your mind."

We exchange numbers and he gives me his address. I go back to my car, not sure if I'm ready to go home yet. I'm starving because I skipped breakfast, so I drive through town and stop at a burger place. I take my food to the tables outside. As I'm eating, Jade calls.

"Are you still at the gym?"

"No, I'm done. I just stopped to get something to eat."

"Oh." She sounds sad and a little disappointed. "Okay, well, I'm done cleaning and since you already ate, I think I'll go for a run."

Shit. I told her I'd have lunch with her. I totally forgot. Dammit. Now she's going to think I'm avoiding her or rejecting her or hiding something from her. And I *am* hiding something from her but it doesn't have anything to do with her and she'll assume it does.

I have to be careful with Jade because there's still that part of her that doesn't trust people. And although I know she trusts me, I also know that her mind tends to conjure up scenarios that are nowhere near the truth. She always blames herself for shit. She always assumes she's the problem. She always thinks people don't like her or are rejecting her. She'd never admit that, but I know her better than anyone and to me it's painfully obvious.

"Jade. I'm sorry. I forgot about lunch. I just sat down. I won't eat. I'll come home right now and we'll eat together."

"It's okay. Don't worry about it. Just eat. I had a late breakfast so I don't need lunch. I'm going on a run. I'll see you when I get back."

"You sure?"

"Yeah. We'll do something later."

"You already ran this morning. Why are you running again?"

"I just feel like it. I didn't go that far this morning."

"I'm coming home right after I eat. Why don't you just wait and I'll go with you?"

"You don't want to run. Besides, you just worked out. I'll see you soon. Love you." She hangs up before I say goodbye.

Fuck. I've screwed this whole day up. I wanted to spend it with Jade, relaxing, checking out the town. But instead we're apart. I took off and left her there and now she's running because she's upset and doesn't know what's going on with me.

But I'm not ready to tell her. Maybe I'll tell her tomorrow, once I know for sure whether or not I'm on the team. Because who knows? Maybe my shoulder will be okay tomorrow and I'll be able to swim. It's not like that hasn't happened before. All last year I was able to fake it at practice. I just couldn't compete in the meets. Maybe if I just push through the pain, I can show the coach I'm good enough for the team and then I can work on getting my shoulder in shape for when the season starts.

I take a bite of the burger but I'm no longer hungry. I feel like shit. I keep hearing Jade's voice in my head, the disappointment in her tone. I don't like disappointing her. And yet I feel like I keep doing it.

# *Chapter 5*

**JADE**

*M*y feet hit the sand and I take off running. I don't even warm up. I just need to run. I need to feel the rhythm of my feet and arms working together. I need to feel my lungs gasping for air. I need to feel the burn of my muscles as they start to fatigue. I need to feel all of that instead of what I'm feeling right now, which is sad and confused and worried.

The day started out great, just like every other day since Garret and I moved in together last May. I can't remember a single day when we haven't been happy and in sync and excited to be together.

But today something's off and it all started at that diner. As soon as the swim coach showed up at our table, Garret acted strange and uncomfortable. Then after we left the diner, he just shut down. And now he's gone when we're supposed to be spending the day together.

I don't understand it. He's worried about swimming tomorrow but I don't know why he's worried. He'll easily make the team. He's a super fast swimmer.

So is he mad about something else? Did I do something to piss him off and not realize it? I can't think of what I did to make him mad. Is it because I talked to his coach? But why would he get mad about that?

I run faster, trying to do sprints but it's hard to run fast on the sand and my legs are starting to hurt. I keep running, lost in my thoughts as I try to figure out what's wrong with Garret.

I didn't bring a watch and I forgot my phone, so I have no idea what time it is or how long I've been running. I'm guessing I've been gone for almost an hour, which means it'll take that long to get back. I should probably head home, but first I take a moment to catch my breath.

I sit on the beach and look out at the ocean. I lie down and close my eyes and listen to the sound of the waves. It's so soothing that I drift off to sleep.

When I wake up it's not as hot out, the sun now hidden behind the clouds. I stretch a little, then start running back. After what seems like forever, I finally see our house. I'm exhausted. My feet hurt. My legs hurt. Basically everything hurts. Running on the sand is so much more tiring than running on pavement or a dirt trail.

As I approach the door, it opens and Garret's standing there. "Jade, what the hell?" He pulls me inside. "Where have you been? I was freaking out!"

"Why are you yelling at me? I was only gone a couple hours." I go in the kitchen and fill a glass with water and gulp it down.

"A couple hours?" Garret appears in front of me. "You've been gone for almost four hours, Jade. Four fucking hours! And you didn't bring your phone!"

I check the clock on the microwave. Shit, he's right. I *have* been gone that long.

"Sorry. I fell asleep on the beach. I must've slept longer than I thought." I refill my glass with more water. I'm still kind of pissed at Garret for his earlier behavior so I don't really care that he had to sit here wondering where I was.

Garret takes the glass from me and sets it on the counter. He turns me toward him, his hands on my shoulders. "Jade, I don't think you understand. I was freaking out here. I almost called the cops."

"You're overreacting. I was just running."

"Yes, and if we were a normal couple who didn't have to worry about shit, then maybe I wouldn't be so upset right now. But that's not us. So I can't have you run off like that and not tell me you'll be gone for four hours."

"We're not normal?" I reach around for my glass and drink some more water. "What does that mean?"

"You know what it means."

"No, I really don't. I need to sit down. My legs are killing me." I bring my water and take a seat at the kitchen table, putting my feet up on the other chair.

Garret picks my feet up, placing them across his lap as he sits down. "You know we have to be careful."

"Why? You keep telling me it's over. Are you saying it's not?"

"It's over. But I still worry. I don't want them to try and—"

I set my glass down. "Try what? What would they try?"

He shakes his head. "I don't know. I'm just paranoid, I guess."

"You told me you weren't worried about it anymore. The week of our wedding you told me to never think about the organization ever again. You said we shouldn't let them scare us or mess with our heads."

"I know, and I'm not doing that. I just—" He looks down, rubbing his forehead. "I just worry about you."

"Why?" I take my feet off his lap and set them on the floor. "What are you not telling me? Did they threaten to hurt me?"

He looks at me again. "No. That's not it."

"Then what is it?"

He's quiet and it's scaring me. I'm so sick of the organization and I'm tired of Garret not being able to tell me anything about them.

"Tell me, Garret. You're not keeping secrets from me. Just tell me why you're so worried about me."

He stands up, running his hands through his hair. "Because I love you, okay? That's why I'm worried. Because I don't want anything to happen to you. So you can't just fucking disappear for hours at a time without your phone."

"Why else are you worried?"

"Isn't that enough of a reason?"

"There's something else. I can tell. You think they'll come after me. You think they'll do something to me to get back at you for not going along with their plan."

He walks in the kitchen and leans back against the counter, staring down at the floor.

"Garret. Is that true?"

He sighs. "Yes."

I get up and go stand in front of him. "Why? What happened? Did your dad tell you something? Are they planning something?"

Garret shakes his head and pulls me into him. "No. I just—" He sighs again. "I can't stop thinking about it. I know my dad said this is just what they wanted. To make me live in fear, always wondering, always thinking they'll come back. And I know I said I wouldn't, but I can't help it. I think about it, Jade. I think about it all the time. I don't give a shit what they do to me, but I won't let them do anything to you. I can't. It's my job to protect you and I feel like I can't do a good enough job. I can't be with you 24/7. I can't always be there to make sure nothing happens."

I look up at him. "You don't have to be. I'm fine. Nothing will happen to me. I can take care of myself. I did before I met you and I can now."

"Before you met me you weren't involved in this. Now you are."

"You said it was over. So why do you keep acting like it's not?"

"I know it's over. I know I should stop worrying. But I don't trust them, Jade. They waited 12 years to go after my mom. Twelve fucking years. They waited until my dad was married and had a kid and 12 years had passed. He thought she was safe. And then they killed her."

He holds me closer, taking deep breaths.

"How long have you been worried about this?" My cheek's against his chest and I can hear his heart beating really fast.

"Since we got married. Actually, before that. Since Roth showed up at the restaurant that day."

"Why didn't you say anything?"

"Because this is *my* thing, Jade, not yours. I'm letting them fuck with my head and I need to get over it. And I'm trying to. I really am. But I haven't been able to yet."

"Garret." I speak softly. "They did that to your mom because your dad is a member. You're not. You never will be. They're not coming back for you. Your dad asked Roth and he admitted he only showed up at the restaurant to scare us."

"I know all that. But I also know what they're capable of. I know the type of people they are. And I don't trust them."

I pull back and look at him. "What are you saying? You really think they'd do something?"

"I think I just need more time to accept the fact that they won't. The whole thing is still too fresh in my mind. Maybe now that we're married and living in this town I'll get over it and accept that they're not coming back and that this really is over." He lifts my chin up and our eyes meet. "But until then, would you please not run off like that without your phone? And without telling me how long you'll be gone?"

"Yes. Sorry. I didn't mean to be out that long."

His eyes remain on mine, his face serious. "I love you. So much. I don't know what I'd do if anything ever happened to you."

"Nothing will happen." I pull back but his arms remain around my waist. "Garret, I need to shower. I stink. I can't believe you're able to be this close to me without gagging."

47

"You're sweaty, but it's not that bad." He gives me a kiss.

"Could you help me? I'm really tired after running for that long. I can barely stand up."

"Can I help you shower?" He smiles. "Yeah, I could do that."

He follows me to the bathroom.

"You know what?" I ask as he turns the shower on.

"What?" He peels the clothes off my sweaty body.

"I think we just had a fight."

"It wasn't a fight. It was a disagreement followed by a discussion."

"It was a fight." I undo his belt and shorts and let them fall to the floor.

He's still smiling. "Okay, I guess it was a fight."

"Which means we need to have makeup sex. *Shower* makeup sex."

"I don't think we've done that before." He strips off his remaining clothes and follows me into the shower. He grabs my hips and hauls me into him. Then he lifts me up and against the wall and puts his wet mouth over mine, his tongue pushing past my lips. Whenever we have sex after he's angry, he's more forceful and aggressive in the way he touches me and kisses me, like he is right now.

He pushes inside me and I gasp.

"Too rough?" he asks, his eyes aimed directly at mine.

I smile. "No."

"You want more?" He smiles back.

"Way more."

He continues, and the makeup shower sex is awesome. But I still feel like something is off with him. He isn't telling me something. I don't know why he thinks he needs to hide stuff from me. He should be able to tell me anything. So why is he doing this?

Later, as we're eating dinner, Garret's phone rings. He checks it and ignores the call. It rings again as I'm cleaning the dishes. This time he answers it.

"Hey. I can't make it." He listens, then says, "Maybe some other night. See ya."

"Who was that?" I close the dishwasher and dry my hands on the towel.

"Just some guy I met today."

"At school?"

"Yeah, at the gym."

"What did he want?"

"He invited us to a party tonight. I told him we couldn't make it."

"Why can't we go?"

"Because we don't go to parties." Garret walks over to the couch and sits down.

"Just because we didn't go to parties at Moorhurst doesn't mean we can't go to them here." I take a seat at the end of the couch, facing him.

"Jade, parties are just a bunch of people drinking. And you don't drink."

"You don't either. Do you?"

"I meant to say 'we.' *We* don't drink. Therefore we don't go to parties."

I tuck my legs into my chest, wrapping my arms around them. "Garret, you can drink. I don't care."

"Yeah, you do. But it's fine. I don't need to." He turns the TV on and starts flipping through the channels.

"Hey." I stretch my leg out and nudge him with my foot. "Can we talk about this?"

His eyes remain on the TV. "What's there to talk about?"

I don't like his tone. He sounds angry. What's his problem today? It's like he got up on the wrong side of the bed.

"Garret, what's going on with you?"

He doesn't answer. He found a sports show to watch and now he's not listening to me. I sit next to him and take the remote, turning the TV off.

"I was watching that." He tries to get the remote but I hide it behind me.

"Tell me what's wrong. You've been acting weird all day and I don't like it."

"Nothing's wrong. Can I have the remote back now?"

"On our wedding night, you said I could kick your ass if you're being a bad husband. Well, I'm officially kicking your ass."

"Why? I didn't do anything."

"Are you kidding me? You stormed out of here after we got back from the grocery store, then you yelled at me for getting home late from my run, and now you're mad because we're not at some party."

"I'm not mad about the party. I didn't want to go. I already told the guy that, so I don't know why he's calling me."

"Who is this guy?"

"Kyle something. I don't know his last name."

"Why is he on campus so early? Is he from around here?"

"He's on the football team. They get here early for practice."

"Was the whole team at the gym?"

"No, just him."

"Why don't you want to go to his party? Because of me?"

"Jade, why would we go to a party with a bunch of drunk people?"

"Not everyone drinks. And even if they do, it doesn't mean they'll get drunk."

"This is college. Everyone drinks. Everyone gets drunk." He reaches behind me for the remote but I bury it under the pillow.

"Garret, I want us to do normal things that college students do. Just because we're married doesn't mean we have to sit at home watching TV every night. This isn't Moorhurst. I can go to a party without having to worry about running into Blake or Ava or Sierra. We have a fresh start here. And I think we should get out and do stuff." I pick up his hand and thread our fingers together. "And if you want to drink now and then, I'm okay with that."

"Can we stop talking about this party?" He raises his voice. "I don't want to go. Just drop it."

I give him a moment to calm down. Why is he getting so angry? We're just having a conversation.

"I don't want you to be mad at me for missing out on stuff, or...or regret getting married when we did."

"Jade." His voice softens and he pulls me over onto his lap. "I'll never regret that. Don't you ever think that. I love being married to you. I don't care if we sit and watch TV or go out somewhere. It doesn't matter what we do. I just want to be with you."

"Are you sure?" I smile a little.

"I married you, Jade. I'd say that's a pretty permanent way to say I want to be with you."

"So you're not mad at me?"

He kisses me. "Why would I be mad at you?"

"I don't know. I just get this feeling that you are."

"It's not you. I'm just tired from the move. I guess it put me in a bad mood. I'm over it now. Let's just watch a movie." He lifts me off him and sets me on the couch, then gets up and goes to the metal stand that holds the movies. "You pick."

"Can it be a scary one? Like a horror movie?"

"Whatever you want." He stands there, waiting.

"Let's watch Carrie. The original, not the new one."

He shakes his head as he takes it from the rack. "I don't get why you like these movies. Don't they give you nightmares?"

"No. Never."

He puts the movie in, then slumps down on the couch. It's clear he's dreading this movie.

I kiss his cheek. "We can watch something else."

He puts his arm out. "Get comfortable. It's about to start."

I sneak into my spot under his arm. "Thanks for letting me pick the movie. I know you hate this one."

"I won't be watching much of it." He kisses my forehead. "You'll be asleep in five minutes and then I'll turn it off and watch sports."

"I'm not going to fall asleep. I'm wide awake."

"Good." He slides farther down on the couch, making my spot under his arm even cozier. "Enjoy the movie."

"I will." After the first few minutes I feel myself dozing off, then jerk awake.

"You still awake down there?" I hear Garret laughing.

"Yes. Why?"

"Just checking."

My eyelids get heavy and I can't help it. I fall right to sleep.

# Chapter 6

**GARRET**

*I* can't sleep. I've been up all night thinking about how it's going to feel to not have swimming in my life. I mean, yeah, I can still swim, but if I'm not competing on a team, then what's the point? I've been on a swim team every year since I was 12 and I'm not ready to give that up.

The other reason I can't sleep is because I keep thinking about Jade. I was a total ass to her today for no reason other than my shitty mood. I can't do that to her. I can't take my anger out on her for something she has no control over and knows nothing about. And I have no idea why I reacted that way about the party. I was practically yelling at her when she was asking about it which was completely out of line.

She would've gone to Kyle's party and she would've tried to have a good time. And she would've done all that for me. She keeps thinking that because we're married, I'm missing out on stuff.

I don't know why she thinks that. I never tell her I feel like I'm missing out on anything. It's true that I'd like to be more social but it doesn't need to be at a party. I'd just like to find some people we could do stuff with, another couple like Sean and Harper. But I'm not sure if Jade's ready for that. She didn't have many friends in high school and she's not really comfortable around new people. I'm hoping she'll make new friends here, but it's going to take a while. She doesn't take rejection well, so if she tries to make a friend and the person turns her down, there's a good chance she'll give up trying. Then she'll say she doesn't need friends and spend all her time doing homework and running.

Speaking of running, she nearly gave me a heart attack when I couldn't find her this afternoon. Who the hell runs for four hours? And if she insists on running for that long, she needs to at least tell me that and tell me where she's going. And she needs to bring her damn phone!

I know I sound overprotective and some might say controlling, but I feel like I have to be. I have to keep her safe. Right now, this thing with the organization doesn't seem final. Having Roth show up last July makes me think he has something planned. Maybe he doesn't and maybe I'm just being paranoid. But Jade's safety comes before anything else and if she, or anyone else, wants to think I'm being overprotective or controlling, I don't give a shit. Until I know for sure they aren't coming after her, I'm keeping a close eye on her.

"Garret?" I feel Jade's hand on my back. "Why are you up?"

"I was getting some water." I hold my glass up. It's 3 a.m. and I'm sitting at the kitchen table in the dark.

"Are you coming back to bed?"

"Yeah, in a minute."

She sits next to me. "I'll just wait. I can't sleep in there alone. That movie freaked me out."

I laugh. "You feel asleep after the first few minutes."

She leans her head on my shoulder. "Yeah, well, the first few minutes were really scary, okay?"

I kiss her forehead. "Let's go to bed."

As soon as we're in there, she tangles her arms and legs with mine and falls asleep within a couple minutes. I eventually fall asleep, too.

In the morning we go to campus for my swim team tryout. I just want to get this over with. I know the outcome.

"You sure you don't want me to go with you?" Jade reaches up to kiss me. "I love watching you swim."

"I know you do, but not this time. Some other time, okay?"

"Okay. So I'll meet you back here at noon." She holds her phone up. "It's on and fully charged."

"Good. You going anywhere besides the bookstore?"

"I might check out the library. I'm not sure yet. If you get done early, just call and we'll meet up. Love you." She kisses me again, then takes off for the bookstore.

I trudge over to the pool, nerves balling up in the pit of my stomach. I go in the locker room and quickly change into my swim trunks.

When I get to the pool, Keith is waiting with a clipboard and a timer. Great. Like I'm not already nervous enough? He can't even let me get some laps in before he starts timing me?

"Garret." He smiles. "You're right on time."

"Yeah. Can I do some warm-up laps first?"

"Of course. Go ahead. I have to make a phone call. I'll be back in a few minutes."

I stretch a little at the edge of the pool. My shoulder feels okay right now. After the bench press yesterday, I thought for sure it would ache when I got up this morning, but it didn't.

I dive into the pool and do some laps. The water feels good and I start to relax. Maybe this won't be so bad.

About five minutes later, Keith comes back. "You still warming up? Don't feel rushed. If you need more time, just say so."

"No, I'm good. What should I start with?"

He gives me the choice so I pick the backstroke. I swim to the end of the pool and back, then repeat that a few more times. I'm moving fast and my shoulder feels fine.

Keith stands at the edge of the pool. "That's excellent, Garret. Great form."

"How was my time?"

"It was good."

"What was it?"

"Let's not think about times right now. Let's focus on form. Try the breaststroke next."

*Good?* He describes my time as being 'good'? That means it sucks. Shit. I need to go faster. I do the breaststroke up and down the lane twice.

"Also very good form." Once again, Keith doesn't mention my time. "Show me the butterfly. Eight laps."

My shoulder is starting to ache but it's tolerable. I take off, doing the butterfly, which is my least favorite stroke because it's my weakest stroke.

"A few form issues to work on," he says, "but otherwise very good. Freestyle next?"

"Sure." I do the crawl, going as fast as I can. The ache in my shoulder is really bothering me now and it's pissing me off. I try to ignore it and swim faster.

When I'm done, I see Keith sitting on the bleachers, writing something on his clipboard.

"Come on over, Garret."

I grab my towel and meet him on the bleachers.

Keith sets the clipboard aside. "You're an excellent swimmer and I'd love to have you on the team."

My heart pounds harder in my chest because I sense a 'but' is coming.

"But I can't let you on the team with an injury."

"I don't have an injury." I sit up straighter. "I feel fine."

He nods. "I know this is hard. I've been in your shoes. I had an injury my junior year. Unfortunately it never recovered enough for me to compete again."

"That's not me. I promise you. I'm fine."

"I know you think you are, but I can see that you're not. Your form is off and I can tell it's from your shoulder."

"You just said I had good form."

"You do, but then it changes when your shoulder starts bothering you."

"I'm just tired from the move. Let me try again next week when I'm more rested."

He sighs. "I talked to your father. He told me about your injury last year."

I feel myself tensing up. "Why did you call my father?"

"I always call the parents when I'm considering someone for the team."

"And he told you I had an injury?"

"He didn't offer it up. I asked him and that's when he told me."

I wonder what exactly my dad told him. He couldn't tell him I got shot. He must've made up some story.

"What did he say?" I ask him.

"He didn't have much time to talk so he didn't go into details about your injury, but he said you healed quickly and didn't finish your physical therapy appointments."

"I didn't need to. Like I said, I feel fine."

"You don't need to lie to me. I understand what you're going through. When I injured my shoulder, I did just what you're doing now. I tried to ignore the pain and hoped it would go away. But it didn't. It just got worse."

I get up from the bleachers. "So I didn't make the team. I got it. Thanks."

"Garret, I didn't say that. I'd like to have you on the team, but I'd like you to see a specialist first and see what's going on with your shoulder. If the doctor gives you the okay, then I'll have you join us for practice and we'll go from there."

"Just forget it. I want to compete. If you don't think I'm good enough, then I guess we're done here." I walk off toward the locker room.

"Wait." I hear him trailing behind me. "Just hear me out."

I turn around. "What?"

"I'm not one of those coaches who puts their guys out there when they're in pain. And I don't shoot them up with painkillers or anti-inflammatories just so they can compete. I care about the guys on my team. I have two sons in high school who are also swimmers and I treat my guys here at Camsburg like I treat my own sons. Their health is more important than winning. I know a lot of coaches would disagree with me on that, but that's how I feel. I want you to see a specialist. I have someone I can recommend. His office is in the next town over, about a half hour from here. Maybe he'll say you just need to go back to physical therapy. If so, then let's get that started and we'll get you on the team."

"So if I do physical therapy I'm on the team?"

"Let's see what the doctor says first. Sound good?"

"Sure. Thanks."

"I'll send you his information. Try to get in to see him next week, then call me and let me know what he says. And if I don't hear from you, I'll be calling you myself. I really want you on the team, Garret, so I hope it works out."

I go in the locker room, not sure how I feel. Keith is a good guy and I didn't mean to yell at him, but I'm annoyed that he called my dad. I'm an adult and I'm married, so having him call my dad makes me feel like I'm 13 again. But at least my dad didn't make a big deal out of my shoulder. Then again, he has no idea how much it's been bothering me because I've hidden it from everyone.

I'm actually kind of relieved Keith is forcing me to see a specialist. I sure as hell wouldn't do it on my own, but now I have an excuse. Maybe this doctor can fix my shoulder and I won't have to think about it anymore.

I call Jade. "Hey, I'm done."

"How'd everything go?" She sounds excited for me and now I have to disappoint her. Again. I'll tell her later.

"It was fine. Are you still at the bookstore?"

"Yeah, I'm still here."

"I'll be there in a few minutes." I hang up and change back into my clothes.

Jade's shopping for a laptop. There aren't a lot of stores in this town so she's hoping she'll find a laptop she likes at the campus bookstore. They have a good selection and they give students a discount.

I see her when I walk in. She looks totally confused as she tries to compare the spec sheets.

"Need some help?" I come up behind her and wrap my arms around her waist and kiss her cheek.

"I don't know which one to get."

I lean over her shoulder and glance through the specs. "Get the more expensive one. It has more memory and it's faster."

"But it's $300 more."

"Jade, you have plenty of money. Just buy it."

"Grace is making me charge it on that credit card she gave me. She reminded me last week. She said she already got Sadie and her sisters new computers."

"Then get the more expensive one. Grace can definitely afford it."

"I feel bad making her pay for it. It's a lot of money."

Jade still does not understand that a lot of money to her is not a lot of money to people like Grace. The laptop Jade wants is $2000. That's nothing, but to Jade it's like $200,000.

"Jade, I guarantee Sadie spent way more than that on whatever computer she bought. I also know that Sadie racks up thousands of dollars a month on her credit card buying clothes and shoes. I'm sure her sisters do, too. Besides, Grace doesn't see the bills. They go to whoever manages her money for her."

I reach around Jade and grab the sales slip for the laptop and head to the register.

"Where are you going?" She races up behind me.

"I'm buying your computer." I hand the slip to the girl at the counter.

"I have to go to the back to get it," the girl says.

I nod and she takes off to the back of the store.

"Garret, I'm not sure I'm getting that one."

"You've been here for an hour and you narrowed it down to those two you were looking at. So do you like that one or not?"

"Yes."

"Then you're getting it. Decision made. It's a good laptop. You'll love it."

Even though she's worth millions now, Jade has a hard time spending money, which makes every decision monumental. So I've found it's easier to just intervene once I know what she wants. I can almost always tell when she wants something, but getting her to admit it is next to impossible.

I'm working on it, but for now I just need to take charge or a decision would never be made.

The sales girl returns with the laptop. Jade swipes her credit card and we leave.

"That was easy." I take Jade's hand as we walk to the car. I'm in a much better mood than I was earlier, which is odd because I was just told I didn't make the swim team. But I feel like Keith actually gave a damn and really wants me to get better so I can be on the team. And I like that. It's refreshing to have a coach care about his team more than his wins.

"I didn't think it was easy," Jade says. "I found it kind of stressful."

"Then it's a good thing I stopped by. You would've been in there all day." I open her door, then put the laptop in the trunk and get in on the other side. "I think we should get some sandwiches and take them to the park. What do you think?"

"That sounds fun. Where are we getting the sandwiches?"

"I'm sure there's a deli around here somewhere."

She reaches over and puts her hand on my mine. "Are we celebrating that you made the team?"

"No. I just wanted to eat lunch at the park."

"But you made the team, right? I mean, obviously you did. You were the best swimmer at Moorhurst until you got hurt."

I don't want to explain this in the car, so I pretend to put all my attention on the road. I spot a strip mall that has a sandwich shop and pull into the parking lot. "Let's try this one."

We get our sandwiches and some chips and soda and go to a park that's attached to the public beach.

While we're eating lunch, Harper calls Jade and they talk for a good 10 minutes. The two of them talk constantly, almost as much as when we were neighbors.

Jade says goodbye to Harper and sets her phone down. "Sorry, I didn't mean to talk for so long."

"It's okay. I was just checking out the views." I say it just as two girls in bikinis walk by. And yes, they're hot.

Jade hits my arm. "Garret!"

"What? I was talking about the ocean."

She rolls her eyes at me.

I toss out our trash, then come back and sit on top of the picnic table. It's time to tell Jade what's going on with me. I don't want to wait any longer.

"Jade, I need to tell you something."

# *Chapter 7*

**JADE**

That's one of the worst things you can say to a person. That you need to tell them something. Because why do you need to announce it like that? Why not just say what you need to say? The announcement implies it's going to be bad. Really bad. So bad you need to prepare yourself. Get ready, because here it comes. Granted, I've used this phrase many times myself, but I still don't like it. And I only use it for bad news.

"You sure you want to tell me here? At the park?"

Garret seems confused. "Yeah. Why? What's wrong with the park?"

"If it's that bad, I think I want to be home for this."

"It's not bad, but if you want to go home, we'll go."

"Forget it. Just tell me."

He turns toward me with a really serious look on his face. This can't be good.

I jump off the picnic table. "Okay, let's go. I don't want to do this here."

"You don't even know what I'm going to say."

"Then just spit it out. I can't take this long delay."

He waits for me to sit next to him again, then says, "Remember when I hurt my shoulder last year?"

"You mean when I got you shot and thought you were going to die? Yeah, I remember it. Every detail."

"You didn't get me shot, Jade. I got myself shot."

"No, it was my fault. If I hadn't been digging for info about my past and—"

"Jade." He holds my hand and looks me in the eye. "I can't tell you this unless you admit that what happened wasn't your fault."

"But it *was* my fault. You wouldn't have been hurt if—"

"Jade, stop. You can't keep taking the blame for that. It was my decision to get in front of you when he pulled the trigger. You had no choice in the matter. Just tell me it wasn't your fault or I'm not continuing."

"Okay, go ahead."

"Say it. Say it's not your fault."

I have so much guilt over that day and what happened to Garret. I still have nightmares of him bleeding and lying unconscious on the floor of the study. Sometimes they seem so real I wake up shaking and out of breath. It usually wakes Garret up, but I never tell him what I was dreaming about. I just say I can't remember.

"It's not my fault." I say it but I don't believe it.

"That wasn't at all convincing, but at least it's a start. Maybe if I get you to say it a few more times you'll actually believe it."

"Would you just hurry up and tell me whatever you wanted to tell me?"

"After I was shot last year, my shoulder didn't heal as well as I'd hoped it would. I tried to ignore the pain and sometimes it went away. But then it would come back. So I've kind of had this on-and-off pain for the past few months."

"Garret, why didn't you tell me?"

"We had a lot of stuff to deal with last spring. My shoulder was the least of our concerns. Anyway, it didn't heal and I made it worse by skipping out on my physical therapy appointments."

"You told me you didn't need them."

"Because I thought my shoulder was getting better. It was bothering me last January but then I got another one of those shots from the clinic and the pain went away. It didn't really start up again until February when I started swimming more and lifting weights. So long story short, I can't be on the swim team until this gets better. I thought the coach would tell me I can't ever be on the team, but today he said if I go see a specialist and get physical therapy that I might be able to compete again."

I don't know what to say. Why didn't Garret tell me this sooner? I guess I understand why he didn't tell me last spring, but why couldn't he tell me back in June or after we got married? I'm his wife. I vowed to take care of him and he's been suffering in silence for months.

"I need to go." I hop off the picnic table and walk to the car.

He follows me. "Jade. Wait."

"Could you open the door, please?" I stand next to the car. He clicks the remote and I get inside.

He goes around the car and gets in on the driver's side. "Why do you want to leave?" He puts his hand on mine. "Don't you want to talk about this?"

"There's nothing to say." I yank my hand back. "You've been dealing with this on your own for months now. You didn't need me then, and you don't need me now. I don't even know why you told me. It's not like I'm your wife or anything. Or yeah, that's right, I am."

"That's not what this was about. It didn't have anything to do with you."

"Your health doesn't have anything to do with me? So if I ever find out I have cancer or some other disease, I'll just keep it a secret because it has nothing to do with you?"

"That's not comparable, Jade. This isn't cancer. It's just some damaged tissue in my shoulder that's taking forever to heal."

"Can we please just go home?"

He starts the car and we ride in silence back to the house. I race inside to the bedroom and find a pair of running shorts and a t-shirt. Garret meets me in there.

"You're not running, Jade." He takes the clothes I just took from the dresser and tosses them on the floor.

"I'll only be gone for an hour." I go to pick up the clothes but he holds me in place, his hands on my shoulders.

"You're not going to start this again."

"Start what?"

"You're not going running whenever you can't handle shit. That was the old Jade. You're not her anymore. You're stronger than her and you face shit head-on instead of running from it. I taught you that, remember?"

"Yeah, but you also taught me to trust you and then you lied to me."

"I didn't lie to you." He sees my eye roll and says, "Okay, yes, a lie by omission is still a lie. And I'm sorry I didn't tell you. But I didn't think I needed to. I thought my shoulder would be better by now. I guess it just takes a long time to heal. I didn't realize that, and I made it worse by pushing it when it wasn't ready."

My body is aching to move. "Just let me run. I swear, I won't stay out that long."

"Why do you need to run, Jade?" He leads me to the bed and forces me to sit down with him.

"Because...I don't know. I just need to."

"Why?"

He knows why. He's already said it. Now he wants *me* to say it. Running to me is like a drug. Something I use to take the pain away when I don't want to deal with it. And right now, I have a lot of pain.

"Jade." He keeps his eyes on me but I won't look at him. "Why do you have to run?"

I swallow past the lump in my throat. "You hurt me. You hurt me by not telling me and now I have to run."

"Why? Why do you have to run? Why can't you just talk to me?"

"I don't know. I really don't. I'm sorry." Tears stream down my face and I quickly wipe them away.

Garret hugs me. "You don't have to be sorry. I'm just trying to figure this out. I want you to stop running every time you can't deal with your feelings. I want to help you."

"That's not fair!" I shove him away. "You want to help me but you won't let me help *you*."

"Because you couldn't. What could you have done?"

"I would've made you go to the doctor. I would've got you something for the pain. I would've been more careful around you so I didn't hurt you."

"You didn't hurt me. It doesn't work that way. It only hurts when I strain it by working out instead of letting it rest. I did this to myself, Jade. I didn't give it time to heal."

We sit there in silence. He's probably afraid to say anything, not wanting to start a fight. But this already feels like a fight and I don't want it to continue. I'm mad at him for not telling me, but I'm also worried about him. And I'd rather talk about his health than argue over the fact that he kept this from me.

"So when do you see the doctor?" I ask him.

"I'll try to get an appointment next week sometime. It'll probably be after classes start and his office is a half hour away. Do you want to stay here or do you want to go with me?"

I can't believe he even has to ask. It hurts me even more and I feel tears welling up.

"What do you want me to do, Garret? Just tell me what you need."

He holds my hands and looks me in the eye. "I'd like you to go with me."

"Good, because I would've had to run for the rest of the day if you told me I wasn't invited."

"Jade, about that. We need to talk about the running."

I shake my head. "No. I hardly ran at all last summer. There's nothing to talk about."

"You ran for four hours yesterday because you were mad at me."

"I didn't run that whole time. I fell asleep on the beach."

He studies my face, like he doesn't believe me. "Okay, but if you start this again, we're talking about it."

He needs to stay out of this. I need to run until I get used to my new life. I admit I run when I can't handle stuff, but it's better than doing something destructive, like drinking. And right now, I need to burn off some stress. I'm feeling overwhelmed starting a new school, losing Harper, trying to be a good wife. I just need to run until I can get control again.

I lie down on the bed, turning my back to him. "I think I'll take a nap. I'm tired."

He lies behind me and I feel his arm around my middle, tugging me into him. "Then I'll take one with you."

"You don't have to. Go watch TV or something."

"No. I want to be here with you." I feel him kiss the back of my head as he pulls me even closer. "I need you, Jade."

"If that were true, you would've told me about your shoulder."

"I'm sorry about that. I should've told you." His voice is soft, more intimate than before. "I was trying to be strong for you. And for myself. I hate feeling weak, and this thing with my shoulder made me feel like I wasn't as strong as I thought I was. So I kept fighting through the pain, trying to prove to myself that I was strong and could get past it. And I *will* get past it. I'll see the doctor and get this fixed."

"You don't always have to be strong for me. Sometimes you can let me be the strong one for you."

"I'm not there yet, okay? I don't know if I ever will be. Maybe it's a guy thing, but I need to be strong. I'm your husband and I love you and I will do anything to protect you. And I need to be strong to do that."

"That doesn't mean you can't go to the doctor when you're hurt. Or let me help you. Or at least tell me what's going on instead of dealing with it by yourself."

"I can't explain it to you, Jade. I just wasn't ready to tell you until today. I'm sorry for that but I can't change it."

"I want to be here for you, Garret. I don't want us to keep secrets from each other."

"I know." He says it quietly. "I don't either."

I turn and lie on my back. Our eyes meet and I get the feeling we're thinking the same thing so I just say it.

"What's going on with us? I feel like everything got messed up when we moved here."

He props himself up on his side and runs his hand along the side of my face. "I think it's just a lot of changes all at once. Moving here. Starting a new school. Having to make new friends. How are you feeling about all that?"

"Truthfully?"

He laughs a little. "Well, yeah. We just said no secrets, right?"

I nod. "I'm scared."

"What are you scared about?" He asks it with so much concern that it makes me wonder why I haven't talked to him about this. Garret's not just my husband. He's also my best friend. And I should talk to him about this stuff. If I don't, I'm being just like he was with his shoulder. Being secretive. Hiding stuff.

"Jade?" He's still looking at me, waiting.

"I'm scared I won't do well in my classes. I'm scared I won't make any friends. I'm scared I won't be a good wife to you."

He sweeps his thumb over my cheek, his hand cradling my face. "Listen to me. You never have to worry about being a good wife. You're already the best wife ever."

"I don't feel like I am."

"Why? What do you think you need to do?"

"I don't know. Maybe give you more space. Not make you feel like you have to take care of me. Let you do stuff other guys your age do."

"I have plenty of space. And I *want* to take care of you. I like doing that. And I don't feel like I'm missing out on anything being married. I don't miss going to parties and getting drunk. I did all that during high school. It's out of my system."

"Then what do you need from me, Garret? How do I do this wife thing?"

"You don't need to do anything. I don't want you to try to change into whatever you think a wife should be. I love you just the way you are. And I love being married to you. I'm happier than I've ever been."

"I am, too." I smile.

His face remains serious. "Jade, tell me why you're worried about school. You got all A's last year. You have nothing to worry about."

"The classes here are a lot harder than they were at Moorhurst. I looked online at last year's syllabus for one of the classes I'll be taking this semester and they move through the material really fast. What if I can't keep up?"

He rolls his eyes. "Are you kidding? You're super smart. I don't know how you get through those science classes. I can't understand any of that shit. All those diagrams of molecules in chem class? They look like stick drawings to me. They don't even make sense."

"I could teach you about them." I'm kidding, but I say it like I'm not.

"That's okay. I have no interest in science. The point is that I know you'll do well. And you don't have to get all A's. Stop putting that pressure on yourself. When you graduate, nobody will go back and look at your college transcript to see how many A's you got."

"If I want to get into med school, they will."

"You can get B's and probably even some C's and they'd still let you in."

I shudder. "Don't even bring up C's. I can't get a C."

"The world won't end if you get a C. Trust me. I've had plenty of them."

"Well, I haven't, and I don't want to experience it."

Just thinking about school makes me nervous. I declared a major this year and I picked chemistry. Most people who plan to go to med school major in biology, but I went with chemistry. I'm not even sure why. The advisor I met with last May suggested it, and at the time it sounded like a good idea. But now I'm panicking because I have to take two chem classes this fall in order to catch up on the requirements for chemistry majors. If you count the lab, it's three classes.

The thing is, I'm not sure I'm that interested in chemistry but I felt like I had to pick a major. Now I kind of regret it. I haven't told Garret this. I've decided to start classes first. Maybe once I'm taking the classes I'll find I like chemistry more than I thought I did.

"So I see that I need to keep working on this with you," Garret says.

"Working on what?"

"Keeping you from stressing out about your grades."

"Yeah, good luck with that," I mumble.

"Let's talk about the friend thing. What scares you?"

"That the girls here won't like me. That they'll already have friends they made last year and won't want any new ones. I'm not good at making friends, Garret. People don't like me."

"Stop saying that. It's a self-fulfilling prophecy. You assume they don't like you and people sense that and stay away. You need to be open to people. You need to stop assuming they don't like you before they've even met you. There's no reason for them not to like you." He tickles my side and nuzzles my neck. "You're cute. And sweet. And funny."

I laugh and squirm away from his tickling hands. "Yeah, that's what *you* think but you're blinded by love."

He stops tickling me. "You're wrong. I thought you were all those things before I fell in love with you, even with that tough act you tried to hide behind last year. Now you've let that go and it's even easier for people to see how great you are. People will want to be friends with you, Jade, if you let them."

"Enough about me. Now you have to tell me what *you're* afraid of."

"I'm afraid I fucked up my shoulder for good and may never be able to compete again."

"I know." I lean over and gently kiss him. "And I hope that's not true. I'm going to choose to believe that it's not and that you'll be okay." I smile. "So what else you got?"

"Nothing. I'm not worried about classes or making friends. That shit doesn't bother me."

"I'm jealous. I wish I was that way."

"You need to hang out with me more. My don't-give-a-shit attitude will eventually rub off on you."

I laugh. "You give a shit about *some* stuff."

"Yeah, you. You're basically all I worry about. Well, you and my shoulder." He kisses me. "You feel better now?"

"A lot better."

"Are we back to being us? And not whatever it was that we've been the past few days?"

"Yes. I'd say we're definitely us again."

"Let's go do something." He gets off the bed and holds his hand out.

I take it and let him pull me up. "What do you want to do?"

"Let's take a drive. We'll check out the area. See what's around here. And I'll get you some ice cream."

"Why would you get me ice cream?"

"Ice cream makes everything better. You'll see. You won't be worried about shit anymore once you have ice cream."

"I don't think that's true."

"It's true." He leans down and kisses me, cupping his hand around my butt. "And you're getting too skinny. All that running flattened your ass. I don't like a flat ass, Jade."

"My ass is not flat."

"It will be if you keep running for hours and not eating ice cream."

I laugh. "Okay, let's go."

He holds me in place. "I love you."

"I know you do." I smile, then break from his hold and walk off.

"Hey! Don't you have something to say to me?"

I keep walking. "Not after you told me I had a flat ass!"

I hear him laughing. "I was kidding. I love your ass!"

"Yeah, whatever. I'll see you in the car."

# Chapter 8

**GARRET**

That was a good talk Jade and I had. We needed it. I knew moving here would be an adjustment and I knew Jade would stress about it. And I only made it worse by not telling her what's been going on with me.

I don't like hiding stuff from Jade but for whatever reason I keep doing it. I tell myself I do it because I don't want her to worry, which is true, but not telling her just makes things worse. She senses something's wrong and ends up worrying even more. I need to be more honest with her and tell her when stuff's bothering me instead of trying to hide it. It's something I need to work on. Jade and I both have things we need to work on.

"Look what I found." I pull into the parking lot of an ice cream shop. It's not an actual restaurant. It just has a window where you walk up and order. There's a big wooden board on the side of the building with the menu on it.

"Did you see that menu?" Jade says as we park. "They must have 30 different sundaes on there."

I get out of the car and go around to open her door but she's already stepped out.

"Jade, why won't you just wait for me to get your door?"

"I don't need you to." She kicks the door shut with her foot.

I grab her around the waist. "I want to. So let me be a gentleman and open your door."

"I don't like waiting. I'm very impatient." She presses herself into me and gives me a long kiss that causes movement in my shorts.

"Jade. Not here."

"What?" She laughs. "It was just a kiss."

"You know what your kisses do to me." I press back into her.

She smiles. "I like what they do to you."

"I do, too, but we're in a parking lot and there are kids around."

She glances back at the kids in line at the window. "Then can we take the ice cream back to our place?"

"Let's take it to that park where we had lunch and then I want to drive around some more."

"Okay." She sighs, like she's upset that I turned her down.

I didn't really turn her down. I plan to find an out-of-the-way place at the park and see if she'll do it with me outside, just to mix things up a little.

"I don't know if I can wait until later." She whispers it in my ear as we walk toward the order window.

I love that Jade wants me that way. I always hear guys complain that, after a while, their girlfriends or wives don't want to do it anymore. That they lose all interest in sex. But not *my* girl. We've been together a year and Jade still wants to do it all the time.

79

Maybe that will change someday, but for now I'm enjoying every minute of it. I can't get enough of her. She turns me on like no other girl has. Sometimes just seeing her walk in the room makes my body react. If she kisses me or touches me and we're in public, I have to force myself to think non-sexual thoughts to keep things in line down there. I know she does it on purpose. I do it to her, too, sometimes. I get her all worked up in a public place. But she doesn't have to deal with the world knowing it, the way I, and all guys, do.

I peruse the menu board, holding Jade in front of me. "I'm getting you the Colossal Cookie Monster Mash-up."

"No, you're not." She laughs and leans back into me, her ass pushing into the front of my shorts. Damn. Think non-sexual thoughts. Some kid screams next to me and I see his mom wiping his nose. Thanks, kid. That did the job.

"You love cookies and ice cream," I say to Jade. "It's perfect."

"It has six scoops of ice cream and six cookies."

"I've seen you eat more than that."

She tilts her head back against my chest. "No, you haven't. I've never eaten that much."

"You need to." I hold her in place and whisper in her ear, "I don't like a flat ass."

She turns and swats at my chest and whispers back, "I do not have a flat ass. And if I eat that sundae, I will have a big, flabby ass, which is not what either of us wants."

We're next in line and before Jade can speak, I say, "One Colossal Cookie Monster Mash-up."

"You want two spoons with that?" the girl asks. She's probably around 15. Her eyes are glued on whoever's behind us. I turn to see a guy around her age, smiling at her.

I look back at Jade. "You didn't want to share, did you?"

She narrows her eyes at me, then turns to the girl. "Two spoons, please."

The girl rings up the order. "I need a name," she says.

I give her my name and pay, then Jade and I wait off to the side.

"Garret, why are you trying to make me look like a pig?"

"I'm not. I was just kidding." I kiss her, hugging her into my side. "Besides, that girl didn't even notice. She was too busy flirting with the kid behind us. I'm surprised she even heard. We'll be lucky if we get the right sundae."

As we're standing there I hear someone yelling my name. I turn to see a guy in a white Escalade pull up next to us. It's Kyle and some other guys. Their windows are down. There's a hot blonde in the front seat checking herself out in the visor mirror. Must be Kyle's girlfriend.

"Missed you at the party last night," Kyle says.

"Yeah. We were busy." I nod toward Jade, my arm still around her. "This is my wife, Jade."

The blonde hears me say 'wife' and immediately turns to look at us, as do the guys in the back seat.

"Hi." Jade smiles at Kyle. His eyes trail up and down her body. It annoys me, but shit, she's hot. Guys are always checking her out.

"Hey. I'm Kyle. This is Shandra." She gives us a weak wave. "And the guys behind me are Jason and Wes." They wave, too, then lose interest in us and look down at their phones.

"We're having a party over at Jason's place tonight," Kyle says. "You interested?"

"No. Sorry. We've got plans."

Jade nudges me. "We can go."

I give her a look telling her I don't want to.

"I forgot," she says to Kyle. "We *do* have plans."

"That's fine. I just saw you guys here and thought I'd ask. There's a party every night until classes start so just give me a call if you want to know where they are."

"Order for Kensington," the girl at the window yells.

I glance over and see the sundae sitting there. "That's ours. I'll see you later, Kyle."

As Jade and I are walking off, I hear a guy in the car say, "Kensington? That's Garret Kensington? As in Kensington Chemical?"

They take off. I wanted to keep a low profile at this school and now they know who I am. Maybe I could pretend I'm a different Garret Kensington. Then again, a quick Internet search and they'd know it was me.

We take the ice cream to the park we were at earlier, but this time I take out the blanket we keep in the trunk and spread it over the ground in a secluded spot tucked away in the trees, far away from the picnic tables.

"Why are we sitting back here?" Jade slips the plastic spoon in her mouth and slowly takes it out and that's all it takes to get me going again.

"I wanted privacy." I scoop up some ice cream, keeping my eyes on her.

"You wanted privacy to eat ice cream?" She takes another bite, then slowly licks the spoon.

Shit, that's hot. Major movement in the shorts.

"Yeah. I did."

She shrugs. "Okay."

"You have ice cream on your lips."

"Did you bring any napkins?"

"You don't need one." I take the spoon from her hand and toss it aside, then I lick the cold ice cream from her lips as I lean her back on the blanket.

She closes her eyes and I kiss her, my tongue tasting her mouth. I put my leg between hers and press myself against her so she feels what she's done to me.

She moans, which is one of my absolute favorite sounds in the world.

"What are you doing?" she asks, breathlessly.

"You." I say it forcefully as I reach down and unzip her shorts.

"Right here? Now? In the park?"

"You told me you're impatient." I run my lips across her cheek and over to her ear. "You said you didn't like to wait. And just so you know..."

"Yeah?" she whispers.

I slip my hand down her shorts and she moans again.

"I don't like to wait either."

I pull the blanket over us so we're completely covered, then get us both naked. And we do it. Outside. In broad daylight. Hidden, but still somewhat in public. It's fucking hot. And Jade thinks so, too. I know, because she's not exactly being quiet. She gets really loud at the end, like she forgot we're in public. Which means the sex was good. It was good for me, too. Actually it was freaking awesome. Maybe because we're outdoors. Something different than the bedroom. We'll have to do this again.

"That was..." Jade's struggles to catch her breath.

"Amazing," I answer for her.

"Yeah. That." She smiles. "I could do that all day. You're really good at that."

The comment makes me want to do it again. I love pleasing her, especially that way.

We lie there, listening to the waves. After a while, I assume Jade's sleeping because she's been so quiet. To wake her up, I lightly run my hand over her flat stomach.

"Don't," she whispers, her eyes still closed.

"Don't what?"

"Don't touch me like that or we'll end up doing it again."

I feel my body already preparing for it. "Is that a bad thing?"

She opens her eyes. "No, but we probably shouldn't do it here."

"Why? I like the great outdoors." I skim my hand along the curve of her hip and down her leg.

"I do, too, but we might get caught."

"That's what makes it exciting." I whisper it in her ear and see her smile as my hand moves up her inner thigh.

Her eyes close again as her lips turn up. "Okay, but just one more time."

I laugh a little, then kiss her and we do it again.

Afterward she sits up. "We forgot our ice cream."

I look over at it and see that it's now a soupy puddle in the bowl. "You could eat the soggy cookies."

"That sounds good actually." She wiggles into her shorts, then slips her t-shirt on. When she's fully dressed I flip the blanket off us and get up to dress myself.

"Garret! You're naked!" She practically yells it, which makes me laugh.

"Why don't you just announce it to the world, Jade?"

"What if someone walks by?"

"Then they'll be amazed." I grin. "And if it's a girl who walks by, she'll be very jealous of you."

Jade rolls her eyes and laughs as she digs her spoon in the bowl searching for the soggy cookies. She finds some and takes a bite, closing her eyes. "These cookies are so good. They're even better when they soak up the ice cream."

"My mom used to do that, too. She'd wait for the ice cream to melt into the cookies and then she'd eat them."

Jade smiles. "Your mom had good taste."

"Yeah, she did. I wish you two could've met. She would've loved you."

Jade looks down, her face sad and concerned. She knows how much I miss my mom. It's been 10 years but I still really miss having her in my life. It was hard not having her at my wedding last summer. And for a moment, I pictured her there, meeting Jade and telling me how happy she was that

I found the kind of love she had with my dad. I even pictured her and my dad together, dancing next to Jade and me. I really missed my mom that day. There's something about those big moments in life that remind you how much you miss the people who are no longer around.

"Hey." I lift Jade's chin up. "It's okay. I can talk about her. I like talking about her."

"I know. You just sounded sad."

I smile. "I'm not sad. I'm good." My phone rings. It's my dad. "Hey, Dad. You still coming tomorrow?"

"Yes, I'll be there around 4. Does that work?"

"Sounds good."

"Pick a place for dinner. It's your belated birthday dinner so it's on me. Are there any good restaurants around there?"

"No, not really. Shitty diners. Fast food."

"Is there someplace nicer that's near there?"

"I don't know. I'd have to check."

"Well, find a place. Wherever you want to go. I'll see you tomorrow."

"Bye, Dad."

I hang up just as Jade returns from tossing out the bowl of liquid ice cream. She joins me on the blanket. "We should probably go to the grocery store. We didn't buy much last time and now we're having a guest. We need to stock the fridge. What are your dad's favorite foods?"

"We don't have to get him anything. He's only here a couple days and we'll be going out to eat. I doubt he'll eat anything at our place."

"We should still have stuff for him, just in case."

"Why are you doing all this for my dad? First you want to clean the house and now you want to get his favorite foods? You weren't this way when he came to our place for the wedding."

"We're married now. It's different."

"How is it different?"

"I don't know. I guess it's not."

Jade's getting nervous about my dad's visit. She really wants to impress him, which is sweet, but totally unnecessary. He's already impressed by her. And after everything we've been through the past year, he sees her as his daughter. He's almost as protective of her as I am.

Jade has come to really like my dad, which is shocking given how he treated her last year. But the past few months, she's seen him step up and be a real father to me, and that's when she really started to like him. Then at the wedding, he took her aside and talked to her for several minutes. I don't know what he said to her, but after that, she liked him even more. She even talks to him on the phone when he calls. Sometimes she talks to him longer than I do.

"My dad likes you, Jade. You don't have to try to impress him. He's already impressed by you. You took his irresponsible drunk son and turned him into a respectable mature man." I smile. "I am respectable and mature, right?"

"Sometimes." She laughs. "Not always."

"Either way. He likes you, so stop stressing about his visit tomorrow. By the way, he wants us to find a restaurant for dinner. Remind me to check online later. There's no place here he'd want to eat at. We'll have to drive up the coast."

"Why don't you ask that football player friend of yours? He knows the area. He probably knows of a place."

"He's not my friend. I just met the guy."

"He seems to want to be your friend." Jade picks up my phone and hands it to me. "Just call him."

I scroll down to Kyle's number. When he answers, I put him on speaker.

"Hey, Kyle. It's Garret. You busy?"

"Not at all. What's up? You need directions for the party tonight?"

"No, I just called to see if you knew of any decent restaurants around here. Like a nice dinner place."

"There's nothing around here but there's a seafood place about 30 minutes north."

Jade scrunches up her face at the mention of seafood, so I ask, "Does the place have more than just seafood?"

"Yeah, it's a big menu. And the place is right on the water. There's a steakhouse next to it if you want that instead. I can't think of the name, but I'll text you later with it."

"Great. Thanks."

"Taking the wife out for dinner?" He chuckles.

"My dad's coming to town and he wants to take us out."

"Hey, I heard your name being called at that ice cream place. You're not Kensington as in *the* Kensington, are you?"

I hesitate, not sure if I should tell him. But he'll find out one way or another. "Yeah, I'm *that* Kensington."

"Shit, really? What the hell are you doing going to Camsburg? I mean, it's a good school and all, but it's not exactly Yale. Didn't your dad go to Yale?"

I nod, even though he can't see me. "Yeah."

"And Harvard business school, right?"

"You got a crush on my dad or something? You seem to know a lot about him."

"I'm just impressed. That's all. I'm a business major. I follow business leaders and your dad's someone I really admire. You think I could meet him while he's in town?"

"I don't think so. He's not here for very long."

"Okay, well, enjoy the restaurant. Oh, and your wife— Jade, was that her name?"

"Yeah. What about her?"

"Fucking hot."

I see the shocked look on Jade's face.

"Thanks. See ya, Kyle."

I hang up and Jade laughs. "He thinks I'm hot? I didn't even put makeup on today. He must've just said that to get you to be friends with him."

"You're hot, Jade. This isn't the first time a guy's told me this."

"Who else said it?"

"Practically every guy at Moorhurst."

"You're lying." She leans over and kisses my cheek. "But thank you. That's sweet."

"I'm serious. After a while I told them to shut the hell up. I don't like other guys checking you out, saying you're hot. They knew you were mine, so they shouldn't have been saying that shit."

"If that many guys thought I was hot, why didn't anyone ever ask me out during our break-up?"

"Because they knew I'd kick their ass. After Nic asked you out, I made it clear that no other guy was to ask you out."

"You did? They must've thought you were some possessive psycho."

"I didn't give a shit what they thought. I didn't want them bothering you."

"You could've told me that. Here I thought the Moorhurst guys had no interest in me. I wondered why not one guy besides Nic and Carson ever asked me out."

"Carson asked you out?"

"He said it wasn't a date, but he invited me to dinner and a movie. Everyone knows that's a date. I turned him down, of course."

"That guy's not even around anymore and I still hate him."

"Hey, I didn't know your dad went to Harvard and Yale."

"Yeah. And everyone who knows that always asks me why *I* didn't go to one of those schools."

"Why didn't you?"

"My dad practically forced me to go to Moorhurst. He wanted me close to home because he didn't trust me and he wanted to keep an eye on me."

"Yale isn't that much farther away."

"Yeah, but—" I lower my voice. "Presidents go to Yale. Now that I know what was planned for me, I understand why my dad never encouraged me to go there."

"But back then, he didn't know about the plan."

"Yes, but he didn't want me to start down a path for *any* type of political career. Politicians tend to go to Ivy League schools, not schools like Moorhurst. I actually wanted to go to Harvard for my MBA but when I mentioned that to my dad, he suggested other schools. At the time I thought he was trying to tell me I was too stupid to go there but it all goes back to this political thing."

"Did, um, Royce go to Yale?"

I need to get us off this topic. I don't want Jade thinking about this. Every time she thinks about Royce or the organization, her mind goes back to last year and I'm trying to get her past all that. Of course, I'm not really past it myself, so I guess I can't expect her to be either.

"Jade, let's not talk about him."

"I just wondered. I know Arlin went to Harvard, so maybe that's where Royce went."

"No, Royce went to Yale. He was there the same time my dad was. They actually lived in the same dorm, on the same floor."

"Oh. I guess I didn't know they'd been friends for that long."

"I don't know if they were friends back then, but they knew each other."

My dad's never admitted it, but I'm guessing he was forced to be friends with Royce. The Sinclairs are a powerful family and because of that, I'm sure my grandfather made my dad be friends with Royce, just like my dad picked my friends back in high school.

"Did your grandfather go to Yale, too?"

"Yeah. That's another reason he's unhappy with me. He expected me to go there. You should've heard him when my dad told him I was going to Moorhurst instead. It was March of my senior year. My dad didn't want me around when he told him so I went to my room, but I could hear my grandfather yelling at my dad. He told him he was ruining my future. After that, the two of them didn't speak again until they saw each other at my graduation."

"Do you ever wish you'd gone to Yale?"

"No." I kiss her. "If I'd gone there, I wouldn't have met you. And I *had* to meet you. You're the only person in the world for me."

"I am?" She smiles and her serious tone turns happy and lighter. "How do you know that?"

"*Everyone* knows that, Jade. You and I are meant to be together. So if I hadn't gone to Moorhurst, I would've had to spend the rest of my life looking for you. And you'd be left wandering around looking for me."

She laughs. "You really think I'd just be wandering around?"

"Yes. It would've been a sad, pathetic life for both of us."

She laughs again. "Sounds like it."

"Luckily, we found each other and everything turned out the way it was supposed to." I kiss her again. "You ready to go to the store?"

"Yeah." We get up and she takes the blanket and shakes it out a little. "We should go to some football games this fall. What position does Kyle play?"

"Quarterback." I take Jade's hand and walk toward the car.

She stops. "The freaking quarterback of the football team is trying to be friends with you?"

"I guess. Why?" I keep walking, taking her with me, our hands still attached.

"That's so annoying. You go to the gym for an hour and make friends with the most popular guy at our school."

"We're not friends. I don't even know him. And why is that annoying?"

"Because making friends is so easy for you. Can you give me lessons or something?"

"You don't need lessons." I open the car door for her. "You'll make friends."

We go to the store and then home. Harper calls Jade just as we pull in the driveway. I send Jade inside, telling her I'll carry the groceries in.

As I'm getting the bags from the trunk, I see a white car driving slowly by the house. It's an older model Toyota Camry with a dent in the front end. I noticed it parked on our street yesterday.

I take the groceries into the house and when I come out again, I see the car turning around at the end of the street. It looks like a guy's driving it. He drives back, going even slower than before.

Something doesn't feel right. Why is he going so slow?

As he approaches my driveway, I get a better look inside the car. The guy has dark hair and is wearing sunglasses and a black t-shirt. He looks like he's in his late twenties.

He turns his head and notices me watching him. He guns the engine and takes off down the street.

"Hey! Wait!" I run to the end of the driveway. I try to get a license plate number but he's too far away.

What the hell was that about? Why did he speed off like that when he saw me? Is he casing the place, planning to rob us? Or is it something else? My chest tightens and I inhale some deep breaths to loosen it up again.

I can't be this way. I can't live in a constant state of fear of what might happen. It's just a car driving down the street. The guy was probably just looking for an address.

But my gut tells me it's more than that.

# *Chapter 9*

**JADE**

"So you just got back?" I ask Harper as I plop down on the couch. She and Sean were in New Hampshire visiting Sean's parents.

"Yeah. I'm doing laundry at Sean's place. We're going out to dinner in a few minutes. Is Garret around? Sean wanted to talk to him."

"He's bringing groceries in from the car," I tell her as I watch him go back outside. "I still can't believe you spent all that time on a dairy farm."

They were only supposed to stay for a week but they were having such a good time they ended up staying for two.

"I loved it. It was quiet and relaxing. So different than LA. Did you show Garret the photos I sent? The ones from our hiking trip?"

"Yeah, and now he wants to take me hiking there."

"You should totally do it. It's really beautiful."

"So what'd you do yesterday? Anything fun?"

"I went to a movie with Sean's mom and then we went out for coffee. The guys stayed home and did stuff around the farm. I already miss Sean's mom. We got along great."

"My mom loves her." Sean takes Harper's phone. "She's making the wedding invitations as we speak."

"She is not." Harper's laughing in the background.

"Is Garret out surfing?" Sean asks.

"No, he hasn't surfed since we got here. We've been busy moving in and getting settled before his dad gets here tomorrow."

Garret comes in with more grocery bags.

"Sean's on the phone." I hand it to him.

"Hey, Sean. Can I call you later?" He listens. "Yeah, I haven't had time to get out there." He nods. "Okay, bye."

Garret gives me the phone and takes off again.

"Got any plans for when Garret's dad is there?" Harper's back on the phone.

"We're going to dinner tomorrow night. Friday we'll show him the campus. He has to leave on Saturday."

"Ask him if I can babysit Lilly."

"I'll ask, but I already know the answer. Pearce will be okay with it but Katherine will say no. She doesn't let anyone babysit Lilly."

"What is her problem?"

"I don't know. So are you staying with Sean until classes start next week?"

"I'm staying at his place through the weekend and maybe Monday night. But I'm moving my stuff in the dorms on Saturday. I didn't want to move in later, when everyone else is. It's too crowded." I hear Sean saying something to Harper in the background. "I guess we're heading out to dinner. I'll call you tomorrow."

"Okay, bye."

I end the call just as Garret walks in.

"Harper really liked hanging out at the dairy farm. Crazy, huh?"

Garret doesn't answer. He's standing there in a daze, holding a grocery bag in each hand.

I jump off the couch and take the bags. "I think she even misses being on the farm." I go in the kitchen and start unloading groceries. "How funny is that?" Garret still hasn't moved. "Garret? Did you hear me?"

"Yeah, it's funny," he says, still frozen in place.

"Why aren't you moving? Is something wrong?"

He finally snaps out of it. "No. Nothing." He comes over and unloads groceries with me. I tell him what else Harper said but he doesn't seem to be listening.

When the groceries are put away, I go in the bedroom and change into my running clothes. I have tons of energy and feel the need to burn some of it off. I feel really good today. Garret and I are back on track and I'm looking forward to seeing Pearce tomorrow. I wish Lilly was coming, too, but Katherine wouldn't allow it.

"Where are you going?" Garret walks in as I'm lacing my shoes.

"I'm going for a quick run." I look up and see the worry on his face. "Nothing's wrong. I'm not running from anything. I just want to be out on the beach and run for a half hour."

"I'll go with you." He says it really fast and goes to the dresser to get his workout clothes.

"Garret, I won't be out there long. You don't have to go."

"I'm going." He searches the top drawer, then shuts it and opens the one under it.

"Bottom drawer," I tell him.

He finds his clothes and changes, then sits on the bed to put his shoes on.

I take a seat next to him and kiss his cheek. "Thanks for going with me. This'll be fun. We can race."

"Sure, whatever you want." He's talking fast again.

"You're acting strange. You sure you're okay?"

He smiles and his tense shoulders relax. "Yeah, sorry. Guess I'm a little out of it."

After we run, it still seems like his mind is elsewhere. I ask him about it later and he says his shoulder's bothering him. At least he told me this time. We make dinner and stay in the rest of the night and go to bed early.

The next day Pearce arrives at the house at 4:30. Garret and I go out to the driveway to greet him.

"Hey, Dad." Garret gives him a hug. "How was the trip?"

"Very productive. I got a lot of work done on the plane." Pearce comes over and hugs me. "How's my daughter-in-law?"

Hearing him call me that makes me smile. "Good."

He keeps his arm around me. "How's my son treating you?"

"He's great. I still love him."

Pearce laughs. "That's important." He leans down and lowers his voice. "You didn't let him try to fix anything, did you?"

"No. I wouldn't risk it."

"Hey!" Garret acts offended. "I could fix shit if I really tried."

We go inside for a few minutes and show Pearce the house, then leave for dinner. We go to the seafood place Kyle suggested. It's nice, very upscale, just like he said. Garret offered to go to the steakhouse given my dislike for seafood, but I insisted on the seafood place because this is Garret's belated birthday dinner and he really likes seafood.

"How are Lilly's playdates going?" I ask Pearce after we order.

"She struggled at first but it's getting better now. She's become friends with a little girl who's even more mature for her age than Lilly. The girl talks like an adult and her vocabulary is impressive. It's very funny to watch the two of them interact." Pearce takes out his phone and swipes through some photos. "This is her."

He shows us a photo of Lilly sitting next to a girl with straight black hair and black rimmed glasses wearing a pink dress and a white cardigan sweater. She has a pearl necklace and little pearl earrings. She's sitting very straight with her hands in her lap.

"She seems very sophisticated," I say to Pearce.

"Her name's Jacqueline. And never make the mistake of calling her Jackie. I did that once and she nearly bit my head off."

Garret takes the phone to get a better look at her. "She looks kind of crazy."

"Garret, you don't even know her." I lean over to see the photo. "She's cute."

"She's one of those kids who looks all sweet and innocent and then goes crazy when she doesn't get her way. I knew girls like her." He gives the phone back to his dad. "Does Lilly have any other friends?"

"She had a group play date last week and made friends with a little boy in the group."

"You've gotta end that right now, Dad." Garret shakes his head. "No boys."

"Garret, he's only 7. I don't think we need to worry."

"I know how boys think. Even at 7, I had my eyes on girls. You got a picture of this kid?"

Pearce swipes through his phone, then gives it to Garret.

"Yeah, I don't like him. He's got trouble written all over him."

I'm laughing. "Let me see."

Garret holds the phone out in front of me and I see a photo of a little boy with bright blond hair wearing a suit with a bow tie.

"He has a bow tie, Garret. I think you can trust him."

"Decker wears bow ties and there's no way I'd let a guy like him date my sister." He points to the photo. "Look at the cocky smirk on this kid's face."

"You had a similar smile when you were that age," Pearce remarks, taking his phone back.

"Yeah, and I was bad news. Parents should've been watching their daughters around me."

Pearce laughs. "You were harmless, although the candy for kisses incident did concern your mother."

"What's candy for kisses?" I'm laughing just saying it.

"Garret started a business in the second grade in which he gave out candy to any girl who would kiss him. He even made up flyers and handed them out at school."

I can't stop laughing. "Did you really do that, Garret?"

He shrugs. "It worked."

"His mother was mortified, but I thought it showed a strong entrepreneurial spirit and a mind for business. But after that, I encouraged him to use his business skills to find alternate ventures that didn't involve young ladies."

"How long did this business of yours last?" I ask Garret.

"About two recesses. By then I'd gone through all the girls in my class." His cocky smile appears. "But I *did* have some repeat customers."

"Must've been some really good candy," I tease.

"Leftover Halloween candy." His cocky smile remains. "Three months old."

"He never ate all of his Halloween candy," Pearce says.

"Because he was saving it for his shady business."

"Probably true," Pearce says as he picks up his water glass.

"It wasn't shady," Garret insists. "I was providing a service. The point is that you can't trust 7-year-old boys. So keep bow-tie boy away from Lilly. I'd rather have her hang out with crazy Jackie."

"It's Jacqueline," I say, smiling. "You better say it right in case you ever meet her. You don't want to screw up and have her throw her pearls at you."

Our food arrives and as we eat, Pearce gives us more updates on Lilly. She starts private school in a week and is starting to get excited about it. Crazy Jackie will be there so at least Lilly will have a friend. I get the feeling bow-tie boy will be there, too, but Pearce doesn't want to upset Garret so he doesn't mention it.

The entire dinner is great. The more time I spend with the new, improved Pearce, the more I like him. And I like how he talks about Garret's mom now instead of pretending she never existed.

The new Pearce seems more like the dad Garret grew up with before his mom died. It's really sad that Garret lost that dad for most of his teen years. It's almost like he lost *two* parents after the plane crash instead of one. I blame Katherine for that. She came into their lives and destroyed everything. Pearce should've stood up to her and not let her take over and push Garret away. I don't know why he didn't.

I can't believe Pearce got stuck marrying Katherine. I still think Holton is the one who picked her, but I don't know why he'd pick her over someone else. Maybe he's friends with her dad. Or maybe Holton knew Pearce wouldn't like Katherine and chose her as punishment for Pearce marrying Garret's mom. It sounds like something Holton would do.

On Friday, we take Pearce to campus and show him around. Garret hasn't said anything about the swim team or his shoulder and I wonder if he will. It's not my place to tell his dad so I'm not going to say anything.

But at lunch, the topic comes up.

"I talked to your swim coach the other day," Pearce says to Garret.

We're at a sandwich shop across from campus, sitting in a small booth.

"Yeah, I heard." Garret takes the salt and pepper shakers and moves them back and forth between his hands.

"It seemed like he really wants you on the team."

"He does." Garret clears his throat.

"Did you swim for him?"

"Uh huh." Garret's eyes remain on the salt and pepper shakers.

"And? What happened?"

I'm prepared for Garret to lie to his dad, but instead he says, "I didn't make the team. At least not yet."

"Not yet? What does that mean?"

The salt and pepper shakers slide even faster between Garret's hands. "I'm having problems with my shoulder and Coach won't let me compete until it's better."

Pearce takes the salt and pepper shakers from him. "When did this happen?"

"Tryouts were the other day. Like two days ago maybe?"

"Not the tryouts. When did you start having problems with your shoulder?"

"Oh, um, it started in January, but it got worse in February."

"And you didn't tell anyone?" Pearce sounds both mad and concerned.

"I thought it would go away. But it didn't so I'm going to see a specialist next week."

"Who? Who are you going to see?"

"I don't know. Some guy the coach recommended."

Pearce sighs. "Garret, you should've told me this. You should've told me as soon as you were having pain." Pearce checks behind our booth to see if anyone's listening. Nobody's around us, but he still lowers his voice. "You could've gone to the clinic. You know they're better than any specialist you'll see elsewhere."

He means in the real world, where the rest of us don't have access to fancy doctors with treatments only the rich and powerful are allowed to have. The "clinic" is code for the secret medical group I learned about last year. I still don't know that much about it.

"Yeah, well, it's too late now," Garret says. "I'm sure this guy is good enough. I don't need the clinic for this."

"You don't know that, Garret. You don't know what's going on with your shoulder. This wasn't a sports injury. Your coach doesn't know that, so sending you to a specialist who treats sports injuries is not going to help you. Is that who this specialist is?"

"I think so. I think he handles all kinds of injuries, but there was some stuff about sports injuries on his website."

"And what do you plan to tell this man? You can't tell him the truth about what happened."

"I'll tell him I shot myself cleaning my gun. It's the story we told everyone else."

"When he runs the tests on your shoulder and assesses the damage, he'll know it wasn't from a self-inflicted gunshot wound."

"Maybe he won't be able to tell."

"Even so, he'll ask for your medical records. And you can't give him those."

Pearce is right. We can't tell this doctor what really happened. We can't tell him about the clinic. We can't tell him anything.

"So what are you saying, Dad?"

"How bad is your shoulder? How bad is the pain?"

Garret stares down at the table. "Pretty bad. It's not continuous but when it hurts, it really hurts."

I wrap my arm in Garret's and scoot closer to him. "You didn't tell me that."

Pearce sighs again and rubs his chin. After a long silence, he says to Garret, "Cancel your appointment for next week."

"What? Why?"

"I'll get someone out here to take a look at your shoulder and run some tests."

"Someone from the clinic?"

"Yes."

"You can't do that. It's not allowed. I lost all privileges."

"Don't worry about it. I'll take care of it."

"They'll find out. They'll punish you."

"Garret, how many times do I need to tell you that I don't care what they do to me? You're my son and you come first. When you become a father someday, you'll understand."

"What exactly are you going to do?"

"I'll send Cunningham out here. He's familiar with your injury and how you got it and he owes me some favors. He paid back most of them by taking care of Frank last year but he owes me a couple more."

That explains it. I could never figure out how Pearce was able to get Cunningham to help Frank.

Why do all these people owe Pearce favors? I can't ask but I still wonder. And does *he* owe people favors, too? He must. It can't be all one-sided.

"Are you sure you want to do this?" Garret asks his dad.

"Garret. This is what we're doing. Call that doctor right now and cancel your appointment."

Garret gets his phone out and steps out of the booth. He goes outside to make the call.

"Thank you," I say to Pearce.

"You don't need to thank me, Jade. I'm taking care of my son, like any father would do. I just wish he'd told me this sooner."

"He didn't tell me either until just the other day. He didn't tell anyone."

"He keeps things like this to himself. He always has. And knowing that, I should've kept a closer eye on him during his recovery. I should've noticed what was going on with him."

"It's not your fault. I see him every day and I didn't notice."

"It's always your fault when you're a parent. You always think you could've done a better job taking care of your child. And believe me, I know I could've done a better job with Garret."

He's not just talking about Garret's shoulder. He's talking about all the years before this when he sucked at being a dad.

There's such sincerity in the way he says it, and so much regret for the past, that I realize that the new Pearce isn't just temporary. He isn't going to return to the way he used to be. He's truly committed to being a better father.

I like Pearce even more now.

# Chapter 10

**GARRET**

*I* shouldn't have told my dad about my shoulder. Now he's going to send Cunningham out here and someone at the organization will find out and my dad will get in trouble. This is why I don't tell him shit like this. He always takes over the situation and makes a bigger deal out of it than it needs to be.

Except in this case he might be right. I can't tell this new doctor what really happened to me. And he can't see my medical records. So I guess Cunningham is my only option. Maybe I should've tried calling him myself without getting my dad involved. But it's too late now.

After I cancel my doctor's appointment, I go back in the restaurant. We finish lunch, then return to campus.

My dad arranged to have a meeting with the president of the college. It's so embarrassing. My dad's sudden interest in my life is a good thing, but this is going too far. Unfortunately, I couldn't talk him out of it. He does what he wants. The meeting started at 2 and Jade and I are hanging out on campus until he's done.

"Your dad's been in there an hour," Jade says, as we sit on a bench in front of the bookstore. "What do you think he's talking to him about?"

"Who knows? He's probably quizzing him about the business school. Seeing if it's good enough. And now that he's got you as his daughter, he'll be asking about their science program, too."

"I'm sure he's not doing that. I'm not his daughter."

"You're family now, Jade. He takes care of his family."

Jade gets this glazed-over look on her face.

"What's wrong?"

"What you said just now. It reminded me of something your dad said after you were shot."

"What did he say?"

"After it happened, he welcomed me to the family. I didn't know what he meant by that."

"He meant that he'd look out for you."

"But I'd only been friends with you a few months, so why would he look out for me?"

"Because you saw something you shouldn't have. And knowing shit like that could put you in danger."

"But nobody else knows what I saw."

"All kinds of people know. The people who cleaned it up. The doctors. Listen, we can't talk about this here. We shouldn't be talking about it at all."

Jade's quiet for a moment, then says, "What if your dad decides this school isn't good enough?"

"He'll donate a shitload of money and demand they hire new business professors or science professors or get new equipment for your labs."

"Seriously? He can do that?"

"If you have as much money as he does, you can do whatever the hell you want. Before I started at Moorhurst, he got rid of one of the business professors and replaced him with a guy he thought was better."

"All because you were going there?"

"I know, it's crazy. The guy he hired was my finance professor. I had him for two classes last year. He's really good. He should be teaching at Harvard, not Moorhurst. Now I don't even go there and the guy's still stuck working there, although I'm sure he gets paid a fortune so he really can't complain."

I see my dad exiting the building where the president's office is located. Right behind him is Dr. Adler, the college president. He's in his early sixties but has a full head of white hair so he looks older than that.

"I think they're done." I stand up as they approach us. Jade does as well.

"Garret. Jade." Adler smiles at us. "Pearce and I were just discussing some possible improvements to the business program and the science department."

"Dr. Adler is going to give me a quick tour," my dad says to me. "Would you like to come with us?"

"No, we'll wait here. What kind of improvements?" I direct the question to Adler.

"Your father has offered to fund a lecture series that will bring top business leaders from various industries here to campus to talk to our business students. And he's creating two new summer internships at Kensington Chemical just for Camsburg students."

My dad waits for my reaction. I'm sure he thinks I'll get mad at him for interfering like this, but instead I just smile and say, "That's great."

Adler nods. "And we also discussed some improvements to the science labs. We're going over there now."

My dad follows him toward the science building. He looks back at Jade and me. "We shouldn't be long."

Once they're gone, Jade turns to me and says, "I'm surprised you're not mad at your dad for doing this."

"I *would* be if it were just about me. But now it's about you, so it's different."

"I don't get it."

"I made you change schools. Moorhurst had a good science department and now you're stuck going here and I don't know anything about the classes or the professors."

"I told you they had a good science department."

"I want you to have more than good. I want you to have the best. My dad does, too. So I don't mind that he's doing this. I'm actually happy about it."

"What if other students find out? They'll think we're getting special treatment, like better grades, because of what your dad did."

"They won't find out. Since we're trying to keep a low profile here, my dad will make sure his donation is anonymous."

A half hour later, Adler appears again with my dad. They walk back toward the middle of campus.

"Give me a call and we'll set up a time," I hear my dad say.

"Will do," Adler says. "Enjoy the rest of your day."

My dad walks over to Jade and me. "Sorry that took so long. Ready to go?"

As we're driving back to the house, Jade says to my dad, "So what did you think of the science building?"

"It could use some improvements. They need some new equipment. It'll be ordered next week." My dad's sitting up front with me. He turns back to Jade. "If you need anything else, don't hesitate to call. I'll have it taken care of."

I check the rearview mirror and see Jade sitting there stunned that my dad is doing this. She's not used to the way he just steps in and does stuff like this. I don't think anything of it.

We go out for dinner again that night. Then on Saturday morning, my dad stops by the house to say goodbye before he leaves. He brings over a big box of donuts he picked up at a bakery.

"Thanks for the donuts." Jade hugs my dad.

He gives her a funny look. He has no idea how excited she gets over donuts.

"You're welcome." He sits down at the kitchen table.

I hand him a cup of coffee. "You just made her day. Jade loves donuts."

"I'll keep that in mind for future visits." He sips his coffee.

Jade takes the seat next to him and grabs a donut. "When do you think you'll come back here again?"

He sighs. "Probably not for a while. Work is getting busy and I have—well, you know. Other commitments to take care of."

He means stuff for the organization. I think they're making him do even more for them now because they blame him for fake Garret's bad behavior last spring.

"Do you think you two will make it out to Connecticut this fall?" He looks at Jade when he asks it.

"Um, I'm not sure yet." She glances at me to answer.

"We'll talk about it and let you know."

"Have you made plans for the holidays?" My dad looks at me this time.

"We're going to Des Moines for Thanksgiving. I'm not sure about Christmas."

My dad nods. "I understand."

He seems hurt. I didn't mean to make him feel bad. This isn't about him. It's about the rest of my family. I know Jade doesn't want to go back to my house for Christmas. That's the absolute last place she'd want to spend the holidays and I don't blame her. She shouldn't have to endure being treated like shit from both Katherine and my grandparents.

"Dad, it's not like we don't want to. It's just—"

"You don't have to explain, Garret."

"We'd love to come to your house for Christmas," Jade says to my dad. "I mean, if you want us to. We'd love to be there."

There she goes again. Jade just made me love her even more. This is not at all what she wants to do but she'll do it for my dad. And for me. And for Lilly, who Jade knows will be crushed if we don't show up for Christmas.

"Are you sure?" My dad is just as surprised as I am.

"Absolutely." Jade takes another donut. "Could we stay there a week or is that too long?"

My dad smiles. "A week would be perfect."

Jade's phone rings. "It's Harper. I'll be right back." She goes in the bedroom and shuts the door.

"So I guess you're coming home for Christmas." My dad's still smiling.

"I guess we are."

"You two haven't discussed this?"

I laugh. "No. She just decided for us."

"Well, I'm very happy you'll be coming. And I know Lilly will be as well." He reaches in his suit pocket and pulls out an envelope. "While Jade's in the other room, I want to talk to you about something."

"Okay, what?" I'm concerned that he doesn't want Jade to hear this.

He hands me the envelope. "Open it."

I rip it open and inside is a check for $2 million. "What the hell is this?" I lower my voice. "You can't give me your money. Are you insane? You know what they'd do to you if—"

"It's not mine. I guess technically it is, but it doesn't have any connection to the company or the organization. That's the insurance money from when your mother died. I kept it in a separate account all these years. I'm not sure why but now I'm glad I did. I wasn't sure if I could give it to you, but I checked the rules and found a loophole. Since this money didn't come from the company or my parents or the financial rewards of membership, I'm allowed to give it to you. I want you to have it, Garret. It's not anywhere near the amount you would've received in your inheritance but at least it's something."

"Dad, I don't need it. Jade has money, now."

I haven't told my dad how much money is in Jade's trust fund, but he knows she has one.

"I know Jade has money, but I think it's important for you to have your own. If it were me, I wouldn't want to be living off my wife's money. I don't want this to become an issue in your marriage."

"It's not an issue. We don't talk about it."

"Does it bother you that she's paying for the house and not you?"

"It doesn't matter to me."

"I don't believe you. You've always had money, Garret. And I know you don't like relying on other people. I also know you want to take care of Jade and you don't feel like you're doing that when she's paying for everything."

I didn't think my dad knew me that well, but he's exactly right. I don't like not being able to support Jade the way I feel I should.

"How are you paying for your other expenses?"

"Grace gave Jade a credit card to use. It's the same deal she made with Sadie and her sisters. Grace pays for all expenses for her grandkids until they graduate college."

"I see. So you're using the credit card as well?"

"I usually take money out of the ATM. Jade put some of the trust money into a bank account so it's easier to access whenever she needs cash. And if we don't pay cash, then Jade uses her credit card."

"Garret, I know you're not okay with that."

I sigh. "I'm not, but what am I supposed to do? I tried to get a job last summer but Jade wouldn't let me. I didn't want to fight about it before the wedding so I just let it go. I've been looking for something around here but there's nothing. This town's too small. And it's not like we need the money so it seems stupid to get a job."

"Take this." He picks the check off the table and hands it to me. "Put it away and talk to Jade about it later."

I take the check and fold it up and stuff it in my pocket. I don't know when I'll tell Jade about it. It's not a conversation I want to have. She won't understand why I took it. She'll say we don't need more money. And we don't, but I feel like I need my own. I don't need $2 million. A few thousand would've been plenty, but my dad doesn't deal in thousands. He deals in millions.

"Garret, I want you to use some of that money to install a security system. You need cameras set up around the outside and an alarm system."

"Why?" I'm almost afraid to ask. I keep having this feeling that we're not safe and now he's just made it worse.

"You should always have security. You know that. You're a Kensington. People come after us. You could easily be robbed."

"Is that it? You're worried about us getting robbed? Or is something else going on?"

He checks that the bedroom door is still closed. "There was a meeting last week and I heard one of the members mention your name."

"Shit." I check the bedroom door again myself, then turn to my dad. "Who was it?"

"It was Ezra Jamison. He was talking to Loran Harlow."

"And what did he say?"

"I only heard your name. I went over and interrupted the conversation and Jamison became agitated. It was obvious he didn't want me overhearing. I told him I heard him talking about you and he said he was talking about Garret Bancroft, Martin's son. But I know what I heard. He said Kensington, not Bancroft."

"What do you think he was saying about me?"

"I don't know, but I didn't like the fact that he was talking about you and didn't want me knowing about it."

"Shit. I knew it. Ever since Roth showed up last July I've been thinking this isn't finished. And now it sounds like I was right. They're going to come after me again. Force me to be a member."

"No. That's not going to happen. My concern when I heard Jamison talking is that they might try to scare you, like Roth did by showing up before your wedding."

"Why would they do that?"

"That's just how they operate. Like I told you last summer, they're all about power and control and you took that away from them when you didn't go along with their plan."

"Did you ask Grandfather about this?"

"Yes. I talked to him the day after the meeting and asked him if he'd heard anything about you. He said he hadn't. Then he told me I was being paranoid and lectured me about how I shouldn't be eavesdropping." He lets out a short laugh. "You know your grandfather. He can't have a conversation without including a lecture."

"Did he ask about me?"

"No. I'm sorry, Garret. He's going to need more time before he comes around."

"What about Grandmother?"

"She's not upset with you. She never was. She wishes you had chosen to marry a girl with your background instead of Jade, but she's accepted it now." He pauses. "Garret, I'm sorry things have to be this way with your grandfather."

"It's not your fault. Like you said, he'll eventually come around."

He nods. "Going back to the security system, if you're not sure who to call, I'll take care of getting it done for you."

"If you could, that would be great. I don't know anything about that and I don't have time to research it with classes starting." I lower my voice. "And do it soon. Maybe I'm over-reacting, but the other day when I was in the driveway, I noticed a white car driving by. It went really slow and when the driver saw me looking at him, he took off. I couldn't get a license plate number."

"When did this happen?"

"A few days ago."

He thinks about it, then says, "I'm sure it's not them. That's too obvious of a move. They wouldn't do something like that. They're far more discreet. Which means the man in the car could've been a burglar casing the place. I'll get the security system set up right away."

Jade comes bursting out of the bedroom and sits at the table, grabbing another donut.

"Sorry I took so long but it's hard to get Harper to stop talking." She turns to my dad. "I know you'll say no, but Harper's making me ask you this. She wants to know if she could babysit Lilly sometime. I told her Katherine would never allow it."

"I think it's a good idea, actually."

"You do?" Jade sets her donut down. "What about Katherine?"

"She's been gone a lot lately. Garret probably told you that she's seeing someone."

"Yeah. I heard."

"Lately she's made more time for him than she has for Lilly, which has left me taking care of her. And I'm happy to do so, but I also have to deal with work and it's been difficult to watch Lilly and get my work done. It would be great to find a sitter we could trust. And I definitely trust Harper."

"But Katherine won't. She's never met Harper."

"She knows the Douglas family. They've been to our house several times. And Katherine's been on charity committees with Kelly. I'm sure she'd be okay with Harper watching Lilly, as long as they stayed at the house and didn't go anywhere."

"Harper's going to be so excited. Can I tell her or do you need to talk to Katherine first?"

"Let me talk to Katherine, but I'm sure she'll be fine with it." He stands up. "I should be going."

Jade and I walk out to the driveway with him. He gives Jade a hug. "Goodbye, Jade. Good luck at school. I'm sure you'll excel as you always do."

"Bye. Thanks for coming."

He gives me a hug next. This hug thing is all new for us. My mom was a hugger but my dad isn't, so it's still a little awkward.

"I love you, son." It's another new thing he does that feels awkward. But it's good.

"Love you, too."

"Dr. Cunningham will be in touch with you in the next day or so. I called him last night. And I'll call about the other thing before I get on the plane."

Jade looks at me, confused about what he meant by 'the other thing.' I sigh, because now I have more stuff to tell her that I know she's not going to like.

# Chapter 11

**JADE**

"What did your dad mean by 'other things'? What was he talking about?"

Garret and I walk back inside and sit on the couch.

"He's installing a security system for us."

"Why do we need one?"

"Because once word gets out that we're Kensingtons, we'll be a target for criminals. They'll think our house is full of expensive shit, like jewelry and electronics. So my dad's setting up cameras and an alarm system."

"You really think someone might try to rob us?"

"The other day I saw a guy driving by our place. He was going really slow and when he saw me watching him, he drove off. It seemed suspicious."

"Why didn't you tell me?"

"Because I wasn't sure what he was doing. I thought maybe he was just looking for an address, so I didn't tell you because I didn't want to scare you. But Jade, you've gotta be more careful. You need to stop running by yourself and you need to always lock the doors and windows when we're gone and whenever you're alone here. I know you like the windows open but keep them closed unless I'm home with you."

"You didn't tell me to do that last summer."

"Because you had Sean and Harper next door. Someone was always around. Now we're alone out here. Most of our neighbors are gone, so we're basically by ourselves. You know, now that I think about it, this seems like a bad place to live. Maybe we should move to an apartment where there are more people around."

"I'll just keep everything locked, like you said."

I don't agree to stop running because I think Garret's being overly cautious. Even though our neighbors next door are gone, the houses a few down from ours still have people living there. And the beach usually has people on it, so I'm not really alone when I run.

"I have something else to tell you."

I groan. "Do you have to say that every time you give me bad news?"

"It's not bad news."

"It still makes me nervous when you announce that you have to tell me something. Just say it."

"My dad gave me some money. A lot of money."

"He can't do that. He'll get in trouble."

"He found a loophole that allows me to have it. And this money isn't really his. It kind of is, but not really. It's the insurance money he got after my mom died. He kept it in a separate account ever since he got it and now he wants me to have it."

"How much is it?"

Garret reaches in his pocket and hands me a check made out to him for $2 million.

"Wow. That's a lot of money."

"It's not even close to what my inheritance would've been. And it's a lot less than I had in my trust fund."

"It's still a lot of money, Garret."

He takes the check and stuffs it back in his pocket. "I'll go put it in the bank today."

"We don't have a bank here. So you're opening an account?"

"Yeah, I'll have to. I'll just go do it right now. It shouldn't take long. You can stay here."

"But I have to sign stuff, don't I?"

His eyes shift to the floor and he doesn't answer. It takes a moment but then I get it.

"You don't want me on the account."

He looks up at me, his brows raised. "Are you okay with that?"

"Um, yeah. I guess."

"I just thought since your trust fund and credit card are only in your name, I would get an account of my own."

"I could ask Grace to add your name to those accounts. It's not like I was intentionally leaving you off them. I just didn't think about it."

"That's okay. You don't need to do that."

This money conversation is causing tight knots to form in my stomach. This is the first time we've really addressed the money issue and I wasn't ready to do it right now.

"Garret, I'm okay with you having your own account, but I get the feeling there's a reason behind it. Like you're not telling me something."

He doesn't say anything.

"You're mad that I'm the one paying for stuff, right? You liked being the one with money and now you don't like that I have it."

"It's not that, Jade. I'm happy you have money. I just want some, too."

"You already have it. What's mine is yours."

"It's not the same as having my own." Garret sounds calm, but I see his chest rising and falling.

"Why not? What's the difference?" I hear the anger in my tone and I need to get control of it. I don't want to fight about this, although I think we already are.

"Because I need my own money." Garret's voice is raised. "Don't you get that?"

"No. I don't." There's that angry tone again. I can't seem to stop it. "Is this some sexist guy thing? The girl can't have money? Only the guy can?"

"I told you. I don't care if you have money. But that doesn't mean I can't have it, too. And yeah, maybe I feel like less of man when I can't buy you anything. Or when I have to ask permission to do so."

"I've never once made you ask permission for money. You take cash out of the ATM all the time."

"Yeah, and you always check my pockets for the receipts, like you want to make sure I didn't take out too much."

"I clean out your pockets before I do laundry. I'm not checking your stupid receipts."

"Jade, I've seen you look at them. You don't just toss them in the trash."

"So? I'm not allowed to do that?"

"You do it right in front of me! I get the message, Jade. You're telling me not to spend too much."

"I'm not telling you anything. I'm just looking at a damn receipt!"

"It's not just the ATM receipts. I feel like I can't buy anything unless it fits within your approved price range. I went all summer without buying stuff because I knew if I did you'd tell me I spent too much."

"That's not true."

"You can't even buy *yourself* anything. You agonize over even the smallest purchases. You have millions of dollars, Jade. You just need to buy shit and stop worrying about how much it costs."

"I'm not used to having money, okay? So yeah, it's hard to spend it. And I'm sorry you think I'm trying to control your spending. I'll never do it again."

"You won't have to, because I have my own money now. I'm not using that ATM card or the credit card. They're all yours."

"They're *ours*. We're married, remember? We don't have his and hers."

"Married people can have separate bank accounts. This isn't a new idea and it doesn't say anything about our relationship. It's just separate accounts. That's it."

I get off the couch and pace the floor because I need to move. "Why do you need $2 million? You told me the night of our wedding that you didn't care about expensive watches and clothes and all that other stuff. Did you change your mind? Did you decide you need a $50,000 watch or a better car?"

"No!" He stands up. "I didn't ask for $2 million! That's just what some insurance company thought my mom's life was worth! I don't even want the fucking money knowing that's where it came from. But it's my only option if I want my own money. So I took it, okay? I would've been happy with a few thousand. I just needed something that was my own. I'm sorry if you think it's wrong of me to want my own money but it is what it is. And I know I didn't earn the money so it's not really mine but—it's not yours."

That last statement hits me hard. I never knew he felt this way. I thought he was okay with how things were. And now I find out he's been hiding his feelings from me.

I stop pacing and look at him. "I can't believe you went all summer and didn't say a word about this."

He goes to the kitchen and takes his keys from the counter, then walks to the front door. "I'm going out. I'll see you later."

"Wait!" I meet him at the door. "We're not done here."

"Yeah. We are." His tone is gentler now, his voice quiet. "We're both angry. We're not ready to talk. I need to calm down. And so do you."

I nod, unable to find the words that will make him stay. I don't want him to leave. I need him here. I need him to stay. So why is he leaving?

I feel my throat getting dry and pressure building behind my eyes as I try to hold back the tears. But then one slides down my cheek.

Garret notices and gives me a hug. "We'll talk later, okay?"

"Yeah." I whisper it.

He kisses the top of my head, then lets me go and takes off. I hear the car engine and the sound of him driving away.

Another fight. This past week it seems like all we've done is argue. We went all summer without a single argument, but then we moved here and everything changed.

I feel myself slipping into the old Jade. I fight it. I really do. But the feeling is overwhelming. The trust I thought I'd built with Garret feels like it's crumbling into pieces. He keeps saying he'll be honest with me, but then he hides stuff from me, like he doesn't trust me enough to tell me. And truthfully, I hide stuff from him, too. Why are we doing this? Why are we hiding things from each other?

My mind is racing and it's making me jittery. I can't be here right now. I need to get out and move. I need to run.

I race into the bedroom and change into my running shorts and a t-shirt. I grab my shoes, keys, and phone, then go back to the living room and straight out the door. I sit on the steps and put my shoes on, then take off sprinting down the beach.

My feet keep sticking in the sand and my legs are already aching, but it's the type of pain I crave. The type I need to take over so the emotional pain melts away, or at least gets buried so deep I can't feel it anymore.

I run and run, and soon I'm at the place where I was the other day when I was late getting home. But instead of turning around, I keep running. Garret would be mad if he knew I was out this far, but at least today I have my phone. Not that I would answer his call right now. I can't talk to him yet. I need to figure out what's wrong first. Not what's wrong with him, but what's wrong with me.

I don't know why I'm reacting this way. It's just money. I don't care about money and I know Garret doesn't either. Yes, he likes money, but I believe him when he says he would've been fine with a few thousand dollars. He just wanted some money that was his own.

Now I get why he kept insisting on finding a job last May. We had just moved in together and one day I found him looking online for jobs. I asked him why he wanted a job and he said he just thought he should get one. I told him I didn't want him to, that he didn't need to. But he *did* need to. He needed his own money. I just didn't understand why.

I'm still not sure I understand it. But maybe I don't have to. Maybe I just need to accept that he feels this way. It's not like I don't have my own hang-ups about money. I have plenty of them. Garret's right. I *do* check his ATM receipts. And if it were the other way around, and it was *his* money and he was checking *my* receipts, I'd be mad, too.

I stop running and sit down on a large rock jutting out of the sand. I get my phone out. I need to talk to someone about this. And I can't talk to Harper. She doesn't know about my trust fund or that Garret lost his.

I could call Frank, but he'll worry if I tell him Garret and I are fighting. And I'm not sure what advice Frank could give me.

When he was married, he and his wife didn't have any money to fight about. Whatever money they had went to pay bills.

The only other person I could call is Grace, but I don't think she'd understand the situation. She and Arlin always had money. They both came from wealthy families. She was just as wealthy as him when they met.

I find her number and call her anyway. She always has good advice. Her phone goes straight to voicemail.

Damn. I really need to talk to someone.

I scroll through my phone, stopping when I see Pearce's number. Before I can figure out why I'm doing this, I call him. He answers on the second ring.

"Hello, Jade. Did I leave something at your house? I tend to leave sunglasses lying around."

"No, I um...I just wanted to know if you had a minute to talk. I know you're busy so if you can't, that's fine. I probably shouldn't have—"

"Jade, go ahead. I have plenty of time. I'm at the airport and my pilot is ill. I'm waiting for his replacement and it could be a while."

What am I doing? I can't talk to Garret's dad about this! Why did I call him? Now I don't know what to say. I could just tell him to have a safe trip and hang up. Or I could tell him the truth.

"Jade? Are you still there?"

"Yes." My heart's beating really fast and I'm tempted to just say goodbye and end the call. But for a reason I can't explain, I change my mind. "I wanted to talk to you about that check you gave Garret."

"I'm guessing it caused some issues between you two."

"Yes. It did. And he left and now I'm not sure what to do."

"What do you mean he left?"

"He was mad and he won't talk to me when he's mad."

"It's not just you. He does that to me, too. His mother did the same thing. She needed time to calm down before she'd talk to me. It's frustrating, isn't it?"

"Yeah. It's *really* frustrating. I just want to talk it out and end it."

"I'm the same way."

I'm so relieved at how this is going. Pearce's voice is calm and soothing and I feel myself relaxing.

"I assume Garret wants the money in his own account," Pearce says. "Is that why you're fighting?"

"Yes. That's part of it."

"He's not doing this to hurt you, Jade. Or to exclude you. It has nothing to do with you, at least not directly. I don't mean for that to sound harsh. I'm just trying to explain where my son is coming from. He loves you. He loves you very much. And he has a strong need to take care of you. It's what men do when they love a woman. I know that may sound sexist but Garret doesn't mean it that way. He respects women and he respects you more than anyone. You have more money than you'll ever need and Garret knows that. And he's okay with it. But he also needs money that is just his own. If he wants to buy you roses, he doesn't want to have to use your money for that. Or maybe he wants to take you to dinner and doesn't want to have to charge it on Grace's card."

I sit there quietly, taking in what he's saying. He's right. Garret wants to take care of me. It's important to him. He's old fashioned that way. He knows I'm capable of taking care of myself, but he still feels the need to take care of me. And this past year, I've learned to let him do that. It's hard for me. I'm all about independence and being strong and not relying on anyone, especially a guy. I used to think it was sexist for a guy to even hold a door open for me, like he thought I was too weak to open my own door. But Garret doesn't think I'm weak. He tells me all the time how strong I am and how I can do anything. So he doesn't do this stuff because he thinks I can't. He does it because it makes him happy. He likes opening a door for me or taking my hand when we cross the street. And he likes surprising me with things like flowers and chocolates. That's just how he is.

Pearce continues. "Jade, Garret didn't take the money because he wants to go out and buy himself expensive things. He's not like that. He's never been one to flaunt his wealth. But he might want to use the money in other ways, such as investing in the stock market. He's always been interested in finance and last year he built up a portfolio of investments that was doing quite well. But then it was taken from him. I'm sure he wants to try investing again. Or someday he might want to use that money to start his business. But if his business or his investments didn't do well, he'd feel bad that he used your money."

"I hadn't thought about that, but yeah, that makes sense."

"Jade, I'm sorry if I caused problems by giving him that check, but I really felt that Garret should have it. If you two decide you don't want it, I'll take it back. But I want you to consider what I said before you make a decision."

"I don't want him to give it back. It's his, and I want him to have it. That's not what this is about. I mean, it kind of is, but it's really more about him not telling me how he felt."

"Well, that's something you'll have to work out your-selves. But Jade, keep in mind that all couples struggle with this, not just you and Garret. Spouses don't always tell each other everything."

"Yes, but this is something we should've talked about. It's important. It's not something he should keep to him-self. All summer, he acted like he was okay using my money. Why would he do that? Why wouldn't he tell me?"

"Because he couldn't fix the situation. And if he can't fix it, there's no use complaining about it. He was broke all summer. He had no choice but to rely on you. He told me he tried to get a job."

"Yeah, and I told him not to."

"You probably should've let him get the job."

"I know that now. I just didn't understand why he thought he needed one. That's why he should've told me how he felt."

"He's not good about expressing himself when he feels weak or vulnerable. That's why he didn't tell anyone about his shoulder."

"I'm his wife. He has to tell me this stuff."

"He will. Just give him time. He's still young." Pearce pauses, then says, "Jade, how did you feel when Garret was the one with money back when you had none? How did you feel when he was the one always paying? I'm just curious."

"I didn't like it. Actually, I hated it. I felt like I had no control and—"

Wow. Pearce should be a psychologist. It just hit me that Garret is feeling the same way I felt last year.

"I think you're ready to talk to Garret," Pearce says.

"I am. Thank you for talking to me. I feel a lot better now."

"Anytime, Jade. And on a less serious note, if you ever need a laugh I have plenty of stories about Garret to share."

"Are they as funny as his candy for kisses business?"

He laughs. "Yes, his childhood was full of stories like that."

"Then we'll definitely have to talk later. I need to go. I'm probably like six miles from home right now and I have to run six miles back."

"You're running?" His tone turns serious. "Alone?"

"Yeah, why?"

"Where are you?"

"I'm on the beach." I look around. "I'm not sure where exactly. The beach goes on forever so it's easy to lose track of where you are."

"Go home. Right now." His voice is stern, forceful.

"Yeah, I'm going. I'll see you later." I'm about to hang up but then I hear his voice again.

"Jade, wait. Is there anyone near you? Are there people on the beach?"

"No. I'm pretty far out. I'm way past where the houses end."

"Where's Garret?"

"I told you, he left. I don't know where he went."

"Are you running back now?"

"No, I'm walking. I can't run and talk at the same time."

"Then I'll let you go, but keep your phone on. And start running."

"Um, okay. Bye." The phone is silent. "Pearce?"

He hung up without saying goodbye.

That was odd. My phone call with Pearce went great and I was feeling really good, but now I feel like he's hiding something from me.

# Chapter 12

**GARRET**

*M*y phone rings as I'm sitting at the stop light. I pick it up and see that it's my dad.

"Hey, Dad. Shouldn't you be on your plane by now?"

"The pilot got sick. It's delayed. Where are you?"

"Driving home. Why?"

"I just talked to Jade and she's—"

"You talked to Jade? Why were you talking to Jade?"

"It doesn't matter. Listen to me. She said she's six miles from your house. You need to go get her. She can't be out there alone."

"What do you mean six miles? What's six miles away? Did she go to the store?"

"She's on the beach. She went running and she thinks she's about six miles from where you live. It sounds like it's a very isolated area. She said there was nothing around and that she was the only one on the beach."

"Shit!" I step on the gas as I round the corner. "I told her to stop running alone! I've told her that repeatedly!"

"Are you almost home? Maybe you could drive down to where she is."

"I can't. The road ends." I turn onto the small dead-end street that leads to our beach house. Two kids walk out in front of me and I have to slam on the brakes. They take forever to cross. "Why are you freaking out about this?"

"Because I worry about her. I worry about *both* of you."

"Why? Tell me." The kids in the street finally move and I speed forward.

"I just have a feeling. I don't know anything for sure."

"A feeling? What the hell does that mean?"

"It means I want you two to take some precautions. And Jade should never be running alone, at least not until we know she's safe."

"Why wouldn't she be safe?"

"I don't know. Again, it's just a feeling I have. Maybe it's nothing. Or maybe my father's right and I'm being paranoid."

"Does this have anything to do with Roth? Have you seen him lately?" I park the car and run inside to the bedroom. The clothes Jade had on earlier are scattered all over the floor.

"I've seen him, but we didn't talk. Your grandfather attended a dinner party at his house last week. I was invited as well but I was out of town for work. Perhaps that's why I'm paranoid. I couldn't understand why Roth would invite me *or* my father to his estate. Everyone knows Roth isn't happy with the Kensingtons after what happened with you last spring."

"Maybe Grandfather knows something you don't. Did you tell him what Roth told you last July?" I grab my running shoes and put them on. I don't have time to change my clothes.

"Of course not. I was never supposed to ask Roth those questions. It's not allowed. My father would be furious if he found out what I did. And he'd be even more furious if he knew I got Roth drunk that night so he'd talk. Listen, Garret. I may be worrying about nothing so don't get too worked up about this. I just want you to be careful."

I race back outside. "I'm on the beach now. I have to go."

"Call Jade. And keep her on the phone until you see her."

"I will."

When I call her phone, it goes straight to voicemail. What the hell? She better have it turned on. It's probably out of battery. She never charges the damn thing. I call her again and she answers.

"Garret, I'm out running but I'm heading back. Where are you?"

"I'm on the beach. I'm coming to get you. Why are you running alone? I told you not to run alone!"

"Why are you getting so angry? I'll be home in a half hour."

"I'm not angry. I'm just concerned." I try to remain calm. I don't want to start another fight. "Do you have any idea where you are?"

"No. There's tall grass lining the edge of the beach. I can't see over it but there's an opening up ahead. I'll check it out. Maybe it's a parking lot. There's a car there that—"

"No! Jade, don't go over there!"

She doesn't respond.

"Jade? Are you still there?" The phone is silent. "Jade?" I check my phone to make sure we're still connected. We're not. I call her again. I get her voicemail. What the hell's wrong with her phone?

She said she saw a car, but a car should not be there. There's no road where she is. It doesn't go down that far.

What if the car she saw is the white car that was driving by our house? What if that guy is following her? Watching her? Planning to do something to her? Shit!

I'm trying to get to her as fast as possible but my feet keep sinking in the sand, slowing me down.

I call her phone, and again it goes to voicemail. Why isn't she answering? I try to come up with an explanation that doesn't involve Jade being attacked or kidnapped. Or worse. Fuck!

I run faster.

My phone rings and I answer it mid-ring. "Jade?"

"Yeah." I hear her voice and relief washes over me. "Sorry. We got disconnected."

"Where are you?"

"I still don't know. I checked and I couldn't see any landmarks beyond that tall grass. There was just an open field and a car sitting there."

"What did the car look like?" I stop running and hold the phone closer to my ear so I can hear her better.

"It was just a white car. It looked kind of old. Why?"

"Did it have a dent in the front end on the driver's side?"

"Yeah, how'd you know that?"

Shit! I take off running again. "Was there anyone in the car?"

"Just a guy. He was on his phone."

"What did he look like?"

"I don't know. Dark hair. Maybe late twenties."

It's the same guy who was on our street the other day. I know it is.

"Jade, are you running?"

"No, I'm walking. I can't run and talk."

"Don't hang up. Just hold on to your phone while you run. Start running right now."

"What's going on, Garret?"

"That guy in the white car is the same guy I saw the other day. The one I thought might be planning to rob us."

"Seriously?"

"Yes, and he could be dangerous. So run. Run as fast as you can."

She doesn't respond, but I hear the swishing of her shorts as she runs with the phone in her hand.

I wonder if that guy saw her. She was right there next to him. If he wanted to hurt her, he had his chance. So if he *did* see her, maybe he has no interest in her. Maybe he's just a burglar and he's casing the entire area. These beach houses are very expensive and most are owned by people who only live here in the summer. A lot of the houses are vacant now that summer's over, so it's the perfect time for a criminal to try to rob one or more of them.

"Garret?" I hear her voice again.

"Jade, are you okay?"

"I'm around some people now. There's a family with some kids. So I'll hang up and call you when I'm closer."

"No! Don't hang up."

"Garret, you're scaring me."

"I'm sorry. I'd just feel better if you didn't hang up."

We both keep running. I don't know how she can run so far on this sand. I'm in great shape but I'm freaking dying here and I've only gone a mile, if that. My legs are burning so damn bad I want to stop, but I can't. I have to get to her. Every few seconds I bring the phone back to my ear and listen for her swishing shorts.

I finally see her off in the distance. When I reach her, I hug her tightly against me. "Do NOT go that far ever again. Promise me, Jade."

I feel her nod against my chest. "I won't. I promise."

I take a moment to catch my breath. "I'm sorry I left you like that. I need to stop doing that whenever we have a fight."

"I ran away, too, so it's not like you're the only one."

"I'm gonna work on it. I swear. You may have to tie me down the first few times but eventually I'll stay there on my own." I pull back and hold her face in my hands. "I love you. And I don't care about the money. It's not worth fighting over. We'll talk it out and we'll come up with something we both agree on."

She nods, then looks at me, her face tired and sweaty. "Can we go home now?"

"Yes." I hug her again because I need to feel her and make sure she's okay. Because for just that brief moment, when she was miles away and I couldn't hear her voice on the phone, a part of me thought something had happened to her. Something bad. And I'd blame myself for that.

Jade's part of my world now. She's so far in it she'll never get out. And it's not always a good world to be in.

My dad is right. As a Kensington, there will always be people after us. And not just my dad's enemies, or the organization, but criminals. People trying to get our money. We're never completely safe. I don't have access to my dad's money anymore, but criminals don't know that, which means they'll come after me. Or Jade.

I don't know if that guy in the white car is watching us, planning to rob us, or do something else to us. But it doesn't matter. Even if he isn't, someone else might be. That's why I have to protect Jade, and today, I didn't do that.

We walk back, neither one of us speaking. I hold her hand the entire time and she keeps brushing against me, trying to get closer.

When we get home, she goes in the bedroom and I go in the kitchen and get us both some water. I bring it to her, then go turn the shower on to warm it up. I go back to the bedroom and help her take off her shoes and her clothes. She looks exhausted, which you would be after running 12 miles in the hot sun.

We say nothing. Not one word. And the room remains quiet as I lead her to the shower and open the door for her to walk in. I kick off my shoes and rip my sweaty clothes off and join her. I pull her into me and let the hot water fall over us as we stand there in silence.

It's one of those times when we don't need to say anything to know what the other person is thinking. Right now, we're both saying we're sorry. She can tell by the way I hold her. When I'm sorry, I hold her head against my chest, keeping it there until I feel like she's forgiven me.

I can tell when Jade's sorry by the way she puts her arms around me, tighter and higher up on my back, and by the way she tucks her head down against my chest. It's different than her other hugs and I'm the only person in the world who knows that about her.

It's these little things we share, the way we touch, the unspoken language we have, that prove to me time and time again that we're meant to be together. That fights like we had today will never break us apart.

Jade will test that theory in the months ahead, maybe even the years ahead. She already has many times and I'm prepared for her to do it again. Her tendency is to run. To hide her feelings. To push people away. Those were the skills she learned growing up in a home with a mom who abused her. And one year with me isn't going to erase the 15 years she had with her mom. I knew that when I fell in love with Jade.

She has so much pain that I haven't even begun to address with her. I'm trying to take it slow and let her heal on her own timeline. But I get the feeling she's going to need a little push to get past some of the stuff she's dealing with. This running thing she's doing really concerns me. I feel like we're going back to last year, when she ran every time something bad happened.

And today was bad. It was a bad fight and I could've handled it better. But Jade needs to learn to handle things better, too. She can't run every time I get mad at her.

I can't run either. I shouldn't have left in the middle of our fight. But I did because I was afraid if I stayed, I'd say something I didn't mean. I needed to calm down. I can't be around Jade when I'm that angry. When we fight I feel like I have to censor every word so she doesn't think I don't love her anymore. Because that's where her mind goes. Every damn time. If I raise my voice, if I curse, if I storm out of the room, she thinks I don't love her anymore. And when we argue, she's not good at fighting back. She shuts down and turns off all emotion and then gets quiet. Or she runs.

The hot water is raining over us, steam hovering in the air. We haven't moved. I'm still holding Jade against my body. Her eyes are closed and her ear is pressed over my heart, which is still thumping hard in my chest.

I take my hand off her back and reach for the pink soap she uses. It's the same soap she used when we first showered together back in my room in Connecticut. I don't even know where it came from. Maybe the maid put it in there. Anyway, it was pink, girly soap that didn't seem like something Jade would like, but she used it because she didn't want to use my guy soap. That was the first time we had shower sex and I was surprised how much she liked it. I mean, she really, really liked it.

The next week, as a joke, I went to the store and bought her five bottles of that soap, so that every time she showered in the dorm she'd think of the shower sex we had. And ever since then, she only uses that pink soap.

I pour the soap in my hand and put it on her warm skin, starting with her back and working my way down her arms. I see her smile, her face still plastered against my chest, her arms now dropped to her sides. When I'm done with the back of her, I peel her off me and turn her around and wash the front of her. It's totally turning me on, but I don't want this to be about sex. I want it to be about us getting past this fight and getting back to the place we were before we moved here, because for some reason, things have seemed off between us ever since we arrived.

Jade grabs my bottle of soap and pours some in her hand, then flips around and does to me what I just did to her.

Okay, so maybe the no-sex thing isn't going to work because this is killing me. To distract myself from what she's doing to me, I take her shampoo and wash her hair. It doesn't help. I'm even more turned on as she continues to slide her hands up and down my body. She stops and tips her head back, rinsing the suds from her hair. Then she pulls me under the water, rinsing the soap off me.

She's hurrying this up. She wants to do it, but she doesn't want to do it here. Once again, I know what she wants without us even talking. I shut the water off and grab towels for each of us. After we're dried off, I pick her up and she wraps her legs around me. When our eyes meet, I can tell she's as desperate to be with me as I am to be with her.

I throw her on the bed. And we have our best makeup sex yet.

# Chapter 13

**JADE**

That was not what I thought would happen when we came inside from the beach. I thought we'd clean up and then talk, but instead we made up without words. Not a single word was spoken and yet I knew what Garret was thinking and how he felt.

After we showered he took me to the bed and it was amazing. Beyond amazing. The sex was hot. Urgent. Uncontrolled. It's like we were both filled with adrenaline from what happened on the beach, which made the sex over-the-top intense. And then we fell asleep, our bodies wrapped together.

Now I'm awake but Garret's still sleeping. I check the clock. It's almost 3 and my stomach's growling. All I've had to eat all day are a few donuts, and after that long run I'm so hungry I feel lightheaded. I need to get something in my stomach, but first I sneak out of bed and go use the bathroom. As I walk back through the bedroom, headed for the kitchen, I hear Garret.

"Jade, come here." He's on his side, with the covers pulled back.

I go and lie beside him. "Hi." I smile and run my hands through his hair. "I was just going to get something to eat. It's 3. We missed lunch."

"I'll make you something." He places his hand on the back of my neck and gently massages it. "What would you like?"

"You don't have to make me anything. I'll just have a bowl of cereal."

"Let's go out. I'll take you to that steakhouse up the coast."

"Because you can buy me dinner now?" I meant it jokingly but he doesn't take it that way. His face is serious.

"That's not what I meant. You can pay. I don't care."

"Garret, no. I was kidding. I'd like you to take me to dinner." I smile again, trying to keep the mood light.

But he remains serious, his eyes on mine. "When I was out earlier, I opened a bank account in both our names. I brought the application home for you to sign."

I was hoping the money discussion would wait until later but I guess it's happening now.

"I don't need to be on the account. Just keep it in your name."

"Jade, you were right. There is no his and hers. It's our money and you should be on the account."

"I don't think I want to be. I thought about it and I'd rather have that money just be yours."

"Why?"

"Because I want you to buy me roses. And take me to dinner."

"What are you talking about? What does that—"

"Never mind. The money is yours, Garret. Just put it in your own account. I was thinking that maybe I'll tell Grace that I'm not going to use that credit card anymore. It's nice of her to offer it to me but I'd rather just have us take some money and open an account in both our names and use that to pay bills or buy stuff."

"We can do that with the money I just got. I'll just put some of it in a joint account."

"I don't care where it comes from. It doesn't matter. I just don't want to fight about this. We have millions of dollars and the last thing we should argue about is money."

"I know. I was being stupid. I'm so used to being the one with money that when we switched roles I wasn't prepared for it. I wanted to be able to do stuff for you, like buy you chocolates or surprise you with flowers, and I felt like I wasn't able to do those things anymore."

"I get that now. That's why you need your own account. We both do."

He smiles. "Did you talk to my dad about this?"

I feel my face heating up. I didn't want Garret to know about that. "How did you know I talked to your dad?"

"He called me before I found you on the beach and told me he'd just talked to you."

"I called him. Sorry. I didn't know who else to talk to."

"It's okay. You can talk to him." Garret's still smiling. He likes that I get along with his dad. "What were you guys saying about me?"

"Who said we talked about you? Maybe we talked about something else."

He moves his hand to my lower back and pulls me closer. "I know you talked about me. So what did my dad say?"

"I can't tell you."

"So you admit you talked about me?"

"Okay, fine, we talked about you, but I'm not telling you what he said. Except I did forget to ask him about something."

"Why don't you just ask *me*?" He laughs. "If it's about me I should be able to answer."

"He said you invested some money last year and that you did really well."

"Yeah, that's true. So what about it?"

"You invested in the stock market? How did you know how to do that?"

"My dad taught me some stuff and the rest I learned on my own. I read a lot and I keep up on business news."

"I didn't know that. I mean, I know you read business articles but I thought that was just because it's your major. I thought you did that for school."

"Some of it's for school, but a lot of it's to help me make investment decisions."

"So how much did you make?"

"A lot."

"What's a lot? Like a few thousand?"

"More like a million."

"Holy crap! You seriously made that much money?"

"When you have a lot to invest, you can make a lot more back. Or you can lose a lot. But I didn't lose very often. I mostly came out ahead."

"What did you do with the money you made? Reinvest it?"

"I used it to buy your engagement ring and all the other stuff I bought you last year. Then I invested the rest."

"So that was your money. It wasn't your dad's money." I don't ask it. I say it aloud to myself as I think about what he said. I had no idea Garret was doing that. I just assumed he used the money from his trust fund.

"That's why I started investing. I wanted to be able to buy you stuff using money I'd earned. Obviously, the money I invested came from my dad by way of my trust, but I felt like the money I got back from my investments was mine. My dad didn't have anything to do with that. I'm the one who did the research and picked the stocks. And because of that, I felt like I earned the money. Like it was really mine and not his."

"And then the organization took it away."

"They didn't take it. They gave it to my dad. It was part of the deal. My dad tried to get them to let me keep it, but they wouldn't allow it."

I smile. "I'm really impressed."

"With what?"

"I'm impressed that you did all that. That's amazing. That investment stuff is really hard and you were able to figure it out and make money. A lot of money. That's really impressive, Garret. Why didn't you tell me you were doing that?"

"I didn't think you'd be interested."

"I'm *very* interested. In fact, I think it's really hot."

He laughs. "You think investing is hot?"

"I think it's hot that you know how to do it and that you're good at it. You should invest some of that money you just got."

"I will. But right now I want to use some of it on you." He kisses me. "So can I take you out for dinner?"

"I'd love that. But I'm really hungry, so I'm telling you right now it's not going to be cheap. I'll probably order the biggest steak they have."

"I think I can afford it. I'd spend every last dime of that money on you if you'd let me."

"I know you would."

"I love you, Jade."

"I love you, too."

He looks like he's going to say something else, but then he doesn't.

"Oh, and uh, thanks for the makeup sex." I kiss him. "It was really good."

"I thought so, too."

"I'd do it again but I'm too hungry. Maybe later."

He keeps his eyes on me as I get up and go to the closet. "You should walk around naked more often."

I laugh. "I know where that would lead. We'd never get anything done. Come on. Let's go eat."

On the way to dinner, we stop at the bank and Garret turns in the paperwork for his individual account. Then we use some of Garret's money to open the joint account, and later, when we need to add money to it, I'll take some out of the trust. That way we feel like we're both contributing.

Garret thinks I should keep the credit card Grace gave me and use it for small stuff, like clothes and other things that aren't living expenses but are just things I want. He said I'd hurt Grace's feelings if I gave her the card back. And he's right. The grandma in her feels the need to buy me things and this is her way of doing that. She's always telling me to go shopping and buy stuff because she knows I never had the opportunity to do so growing up. So I'll keep the card, but will use it differently.

For dinner we go to the steakhouse Kyle suggested. It's next to the seafood place we went to for Garret's belated birthday dinner. The steakhouse is right on the ocean and the food is really good. It's an expensive place so the atmosphere is upscale; white linen tablecloths, low lighting, and candles on each table.

I feel like Garret and I are on a date, and I like that. I like that he asked me out and took me to a nice place and I even like that he's paying. Since I got the trust fund, we haven't gone out like this. We usually get take-out or go to a pizza place or some other casual restaurant. Now I realize that's probably because Garret didn't feel like he could take me to a place like this because he'd have to use my money and I have a hard time spending it. I never even thought about that and probably wouldn't have if we hadn't had that fight today.

We take our time eating dinner and when we get home, we have sex again, but this time it's not the intense, throw-me-on-the-bed, makeup sex. It's a gentler, slower, loving type of sex that reconnects us in a different way than what we did earlier.

Later, as I lie in bed with Garret asleep next to me, I think about the fight we had and realize that I still have a hard time fighting with him. I don't handle it well. As soon as I feel my anger rising, I shut down. I get quiet. And then I run to get rid of the anger. I don't notice myself doing this during the fight. It's not until I think about it later that I figure it out.

I think I act this way because growing up, fighting with my mom was really bad. So bad that I learned to stop doing it when I was around 10. I'd just shut down and refuse to fight with her.

Before that, when my mom and I would fight, she'd stay mad at me for days, screaming and yelling and throwing things at me. Or sometimes she'd just leave and not come back for hours. I remember her doing that when I was really young, maybe 4 or 5, and I didn't understand. I thought she'd left me for good. I was so scared I'd get in my bed and hide under the covers.

So sometimes, when Garret and I fight and he leaves in the middle of it, like he did today, I panic and think he won't come back. I know he would never do that, but I still have that fear in the back of my mind.

And if we argue I try to end it as soon as possible. If the argument starts to escalate, I get the urge to shut down. And Garret gets the urge to leave. I guess we both have our issues to deal with when it comes to that.

The mattress moves as Garret rolls onto his side. I snuggle into his back and wrap my arm around him. He wakes up a little, notices my arm there, and picks up my hand, holding it in his and tucking it into his chest, just over his heart.

It makes me smile and I whisper, "I love you."

He brings my hand to his mouth and kisses it, then lays it back on his chest. He whispers back, "I love you, too."

We may still need to work on how we fight, but we definitely know how to end one.

On Sunday morning, I wake up and Garret isn't in bed. I smell coffee brewing and hear him in the kitchen. I go in the bathroom and brush my teeth and slip on the short, silky robe Garret gave me last New Year's.

I wander into the kitchen and see him standing by the stove, a spatula in his hand. He's shirtless and wearing his white cotton pajama pants which hang low on his hips.

"Hey." I go up to him and leave soft kisses over his bare chest, letting my hands roam below his waist. "What's up?"

He laughs. "Me, if you keep doing that." He leans down and gives me a slow, sexy kiss as he slips his hand under my robe. "You've got nothing on under this."

"Because I just got out of bed." I glance over at the stove. "What are you making?"

"Pancakes." He sets the spatula down and turns the stove off. "Let's go."

"But I want the pancakes."

"They'll be there when we're done." He kisses me and walks forward, forcing me to walk backward.

"But they'll be cold."

"We'll reheat them."

"Let's just eat and we'll do this later."

He stops. "You already started it." He glances down at his tented pants. "And I can't walk around like this."

I laugh. "Nobody's here. And for the record, I didn't do anything. I just gave you a kiss."

"That's all it takes. And for the record, you did more than that." He unties my robe, then shoves his pants to the floor.

"Wait. We're doing this here?"

He picks me up and backs me into the wall by the kitchen.

I tighten my legs around him. "Don't you want to go to the bedroom?"

"No. Here is good." He hoists me up a little.

"But the bed's right—"

"Jade." He kisses my neck.

"What?"

"Stop talking."

Before I can utter another word, his lips meet up with mine and we kiss in a hot, urgent way. He brings us together and we do it, hard and fast against the wall.

When we're done, he sets me down and puts his pants back on. "I made you pancakes."

"Yeah, I see that." I tie my robe, laughing at the way he just goes back to what he was doing, like we didn't just have smoldering hot sex against the kitchen wall. "Your pancakes smell delicious."

"They *are* delicious. I got the recipe from Charles."

"When did you do that?" I follow him to the sink to wash my hands.

"He emailed it to me yesterday." Garret grabs a towel and dries his hands, then dries mine as his face dips down to give me a kiss. "I'm starting a new tradition."

"What's the new tradition?"

"Sundays at Garret's Pancake House. It starts today."

"So you're going to make pancakes every Sunday?"

"I don't have a choice. They don't have a decent pancake place in this town."

"Will there be different types of pancakes? Or just basic buttermilk?"

"The menu here isn't as extensive as Al's, but it's not bad." He hands me a sheet of paper. It looks like an actual menu with 'Garret's Pancake House' written at the top. Below it he's listed five different types of pancakes. The first one is buttermilk and next to it he's written 'Five Kisses.'

"What's with the five kisses?" I ask him.

"That's how much it costs. This is a restaurant, Jade. You don't eat for free."

He's very serious and it makes me laugh. I review the menu again. Blueberry pancakes are listed next, with the payment being sex.

"You go from kisses to sex? That's a huge price increase from buttermilk."

He shrugs. "Blueberries are expensive and they're hard to work with. You have to be careful not to squish them when you stir the batter. Otherwise you get those blue streaks in your pancakes." He points to the skillet. "And just so you know, those are blueberry pancakes."

"You didn't even let me order."

"Not this week. Next week you can."

I refer back to the menu. "Shower sex for apple cinnamon?"

"You love apple cinnamon and you love shower sex so that's a bargain. It's like getting them for free."

"Wall sex for chocolate chip?"

"Yeah. But it can be any wall. Doesn't have to be in the kitchen."

"And outdoor sex for strawberry-lemon pancakes?"

"Those are seasonal, so you should take advantage when they're available. They won't be offered in the winter."

I take a seat at the kitchen table. "I really like Garret's Pancake House and I haven't even had the pancakes yet."

"They're coming." He warmed them on the stove and now he's stacking them on a plate. He brings the plate and the bottle of syrup to the table and sets them in front of me.

"Do I have to leave a tip?"

"It's an expected practice at most dining establishments, but it's up to you." He lifts my chin up and leans down and gives me a slow, deep kiss, then backs away, smiling. "If you think the service is good, you should tip your server accordingly."

"The service is excellent, so I'll be tipping well."

He goes back to the kitchen to get his own plate.

"These pancakes are amazing," I say as he sits across from me. "They're light and fluffy and almost as good as Al's. Can I see the recipe?"

"Charles said I'm not allowed to share it."

"He did not say that."

"He did." Garret pours syrup over his pancakes. "So are you gonna pay for these after we eat?"

I laugh. "I already paid for them last night."

"Payment is due on Sunday. You can't retroactively pay."

"Then I paid for them just now. Actually, I paid for chocolate chip but got blueberry."

"Yeah, I wasn't expecting we'd do that and it was too late to change the order. But it doesn't matter because payment is due after the meal, not before."

"Geez, there are a lot of rules at Garret's Pancake House."

"It's a business, Jade." He takes a bite of his pancakes. "There have to be rules."

I read his menu again. "So just regular sex for these?" I point down to my pancakes.

"Sex with me is never regular." He gives me his cocky smile.

"You know what I mean. Sex in the bed. No crazy places."

"It seemed appropriate for blueberry. They're kind of your basic, traditional type of pancake. The kind everyone likes." He takes the menu back. "I'll also be offering specials throughout the year with payment being buyer's choice."

"That sounds fun. When do these specials begin?"

"You'll just have to show up every Sunday to find out. I don't announce the specials early."

"Well, I must say this is an excellent substitute for Al's Pancake House."

We finish our pancakes, which are so good I can't wait to have them again next week. And I love Garret's menu. The prices are as good as the pancakes. After we eat I make sure to pay him, including a really big tip.

Later that day we go to the campus bookstore and get the books we need for class, as well as some other school supplies. Then I spend the evening getting myself organized, printing out all the schedules and other stuff the professors have already posted online.

On Monday, which is Labor Day, Garret and I go out and buy a small gas grill so we can have a cookout. He spends half the day putting it together while I read magazines out on the deck.

He grills burgers and hotdogs for dinner and we eat outside. Then we go to that ice cream stand again and order the same sundae as before but this time we actually eat it.

We haven't seen that white car driving around since that day I was running on the beach. I'm hoping that guy's gone for good.

The security system was installed yesterday. I'm still learning how to use it. The outside cameras link to our phones so we can check the views remotely. Pearce's private security team in Connecticut can also access the cameras if they log into our account. It's not like they'll be watching us all the time but Pearce wanted them to have access, if needed.

The cameras are placed all around the outside perimeter. We had to contact the real estate agent who found us the house and have her ask the owners if it was okay. Luckily, they were fine with it. The real estate agent told us the area where we're living is very safe, but even so, I feel safer knowing we have a security system.

Now it's Tuesday, our last day of freedom before classes start. I always like to figure out where my classes are before the first day, so Garret and I go to campus so I can locate all the rooms.

Freshman orientation is going on and it reminds me of last year. The day of orientation at Moorhurst was the day I found out Garret was a Kensington. I went to dinner at his parents' house and there he was, sitting across from me. Now a year later, we're married and living on the opposite coast. It seems crazy when I think about it.

"We should go out for dinner tonight," I tell Garret after we get back from campus. We're sitting on the deck, looking out at the ocean.

"Where do you want to go?"

"Someplace fun. I need a new memory of this night."

"Why?"

"Because last year on the day after Labor Day, we had dinner at your parents' house and I found out who you were and we had that big fight and didn't talk for days."

"Jade, just forget about that. You ended up marrying me so everything worked out."

"I still want to do something. It's our last night without homework. We could just get fast food and take it to the park."

He turns to me and smiles. "The park, huh?"

I roll my eyes. "I wasn't thinking we'd have sex at the park. Just dinner."

"And then sex." He says it like it's a given.

"No. Just dinner this time. The Camsburg students are back. There'll be more people hanging out at the park."

"Yeah, drunk people. They'll probably be doing it, too."

"Let's go. I don't want to be out too late. I need to get to bed early. I have class at 8." I stand up and pull on him to move.

"I don't have class until 10. I can sleep until 9:30."

"Great, good for you."

I'm jealous of his schedule. His business classes always start late in the morning. Science classes start early because they usually have lab after the lecture.

I'm feeling nervous about classes tomorrow. I always seem to get this way before the first day. I was this way in high school, too. Tonight I'm even more nervous than usual and I'm not sure why. But I'll get over it. I always do.

# Chapter 14

**GARRET**

Jade and I pick up some sandwiches for dinner and take them to the park. It's more crowded than before so I'm unable to talk Jade into the outdoor sex. It's too bad. I like doing it outside. I'll have to entice her into it some Sunday with my strawberry-lemon pancakes.

When we get home, Jade packs her backpack for class. She's like a little kid. She takes it so seriously. She puts pens and pencils in the little slots in the front of the backpack, then packs extras in a zippered pouch. Then she opens another zippered pouch and tosses in a calculator and a protractor.

"Why are you bringing a protractor?"

"Because it's a mathematical supply," she says, as if that should make sense.

"Those are for geometry. You're taking calculus."

"I still should have one."

"You're not going to use a protractor, Jade. You're not going to be measuring angles."

"Maybe not, but I need the calculator."

"What does that have to do with the protractor?"

She sighs and points to the pouch. "This is the mathematical supply pouch. I can't just have a calculator in there and nothing else."

"Why not?"

"Because then it wouldn't be a supply pouch. It would just be a calculator pouch and that doesn't make sense."

I give up trying to understand her logic and watch her fill up another pouch, this time with miniature Kleenex packets, some lip balm, several headbands, hand lotion, some aspirin, cough drops, and after that I lose track of what she's tossing in there.

"Jade, why are you bringing all that shit to class?"

"You have to have this stuff in case something happens."

"Like what? A hair emergency? Dry lips? You suddenly develop a cold in the middle of a 50-minute class?"

"Yes, those are all possibilities," she says very seriously. "What's in *your* backpack?"

I motion to it. "Take a look."

She picks it up and sets it on the kitchen table. Inside I have my laptop and the one book I need for tomorrow.

"You haven't packed it yet."

"It's packed and ready to go." I yawn and stretch out on the couch.

"There's nothing in here. Where are your notebooks and pens?"

"I don't use that stuff. I take notes on the laptop."

"What if your battery dies?"

"I'll charge it. Hey, could you throw the cord in there? That's what I forgot to pack."

Jade appears in front of me, holding my backpack. "Garret, I can't let you go to class like this. You need supplies. You want some Kleenex?"

I laugh as I imagine myself sitting in class, pulling out one of those tiny packets. Yeah. Not gonna happen. "No, Jade. I'm not bringing those."

"What if you have to blow your nose?"

"I'll go to the bathroom and do it."

"You can't just get up and leave during class."

"Sure I can. I did it all the time last year."

"At least let me put some pens in here. I have extras."

"I know you do, but I don't need one."

Jade has a ton of pens. She pretends it's a collection but it's really just a bunch of freebie pens she picks up at various locations. Frank and Ryan bought her some better ones last year and she guards them with her life. I don't dare use them because I always lose pens and she'd kill me if I lost one. For Christmas I've decided I'm going to buy her an assortment of nice pens so she'll toss out those freebie ones that never work.

"I'm going to put a pen in here, just so you'll have it."

"Okay, Jade. If it makes you feel better, go ahead."

I watch as she returns to the table with my backpack and starts searching through her pen box for just the right one. This is more entertaining than watching TV.

"Were you always this way?" I ask her.

"What way?"

"Do you always pack like this for class?"

"Usually, but I didn't last semester and it was a complete disaster. I went to the first day of class totally unprepared and it was all your fault."

"What did *I* do?"

"You kept luring me to your room for sex and because of that, I didn't get myself organized for class."

"I don't think that was my fault."

She finally picks a pen and sticks it in one of the pen slots in my backpack. "It was totally your fault."

"How so?"

She sighs and looks over at me. "Like you don't know this already? You're really hot. And you smell good. It's completely distracting. I'm lucky I got anything done last year." She unzips one of the pouches on the front of my backpack. "You still need more supplies, Garret. You want some cough drops?"

She's so serious about it, I have to laugh. "I don't want any cough drops."

"At least we see each other between classes. I can loan you stuff if you need it. Hey, you're taking accounting. That's a math class, which means you'll need a calculator. And you don't have one. Ha! I told you you weren't packed."

"I'll use my phone. It has a calculator app and so does my laptop."

She comes over and slumps down beside me. "Okay, I think I'm done."

"You didn't pack your laptop or your books. The two most important things."

"Damn!" She bolts up. "I knew I forgot something."

I'm laughing again. I should've got this on video.

Now that the Jade show is over, I pick up the remote to watch some TV. Before I turn it on, someone knocks on the door. It's several hard, fast knocks.

I get up, glancing back at Jade. Nobody ever comes to the door so this is strange. The knocking starts again. Any normal person would just answer the door but I don't have a normal life. I'm always watching my back, expecting trouble. I look out the window and see a cop car.

"It's the cops," I say quietly to Jade. She meets me at the door but I step in front of her and open the door just a crack. An older guy with white hair is standing there. He's wearing his uniform.

"Can I help you?" I ask him.

"Yes, I want to talk to you about an incident in the area."

"Can I see your badge?"

He has a jacket on and it's covering his badge. He seems annoyed, but moves his jacket aside just enough to give me a quick flash of the badge.

"I need to look at it, please."

He sighs and takes his jacket off.

I inspect the badge. It seems legit. "So what do you need?"

"Can I come inside?"

"We'll come out there." I step outside with Jade right behind me.

I don't want this guy in our home. I don't trust cops. I never have. I've seen them abuse their power on more than one occasion and I know how easily they can be bought off. My dad pays them off all the time. I've even witnessed it.

The guy does the typical wide-legged cop stance with his arms crossed over his chest. "I don't know if you heard, but there was an incident at your neighbor's house last night. They were robbed."

"What neighbor?"

"The people who live in that yellow one." He points to the house that's three down from ours. "Do you know them?"

"No, we've never met them."

"They weren't home at the time. They were away for the Labor Day weekend. The incident happened around 7. The guy broke in and cleared out the electronics and took some watches and jewelry along with some cash."

"Did you catch him?"

"Yes, we apprehended the suspect at a gas station not far from here."

I almost laugh. Whenever cops say things like 'apprehended the suspect' I always think they sound like some bad actor on a cop show.

"How did you know it was him?" Jade asks the cop.

"A couple kids saw the guy carrying some items out of the house and they knew he didn't live there so they had their parents call us. The kids gave us a description of the guy's car and one of our officers found it at a gas station just outside of town."

"What did the car look like?" I ask him.

"White Toyota Camry. About 10 years old. Has a dent on the driver's side. That's why I'm here. I wondered if you'd seen it driving around. We think this guy might've been planning several burglaries in the area."

"I think I—"

I interrupt Jade. "No. We didn't see anything."

The cop nods, his eyes darting from Jade back to me. "So I hear you're Pearce Kensington's son."

"Where did you hear that?"

"It's a small town. Word spreads fast." He points to the roof. "Plus, with a security system like that, it's clear you have money. You're almost making yourself more of a target with all these cameras."

"And why is that?"

"When criminals see this, they'll assume you have valuables you're trying to protect." He glances at Jade. "Or people you need to protect."

I don't like the way he said that. Or the way he looked at Jade just now.

"Are we done here?" I step in front of Jade.

"Yes. But keep in mind that the guy who robbed your neighbors could have friends. I suggest you keep your place locked up, even when you're home." He turns to leave. "Have a good evening."

"Wait. Do you have a card?"

He hesitates, then takes one from his wallet and hands it to me. "Goodnight."

As he leaves I follow Jade back in the house, locking the door behind us.

"That's really scary," Jade says. "That could've been us, Garret. I bet that guy would've robbed us if we didn't have all the cameras outside."

"At least they caught him." I check the window to make sure the cop's gone.

"Why were you so rude to that guy?"

"I wasn't rude. I was just making sure he was a real cop. Bad people impersonate cops all the time so you always have to check their badge. And even if it's a real cop, you can't always trust them. There are a lot of bad cops out there."

"Why did you lie to him? Why didn't you tell him we saw that car?"

"I don't want us to be called in for questioning. I want to stay out of it." I bring her over to the couch to sit down.

"Do you think he's right about the security cameras? Does it make us more of a target?"

"No. If it did, that guy would've robbed *us* instead of the neighbors. And besides, everyone who lives on this beach is rich. They all have expensive shit. Criminals know that. It's not a secret." I hand her the remote. "Let's watch TV."

I need to get Jade's mind off this. I know it's freaking her out. It's freaking me out, too. That guy was hanging around our place just last week. He definitely would've robbed us if we didn't have the security cameras. And what if he'd done it while Jade was home and I wasn't? What if the cop is right and the guy *does* have friends?

"I'll take you to class tomorrow," I say, as she flips through the channels.

"Why? I thought you were sleeping in."

"I don't need to. We both have afternoon classes so it'll work out better this way anyway. We can ride home together. We don't need two cars on campus."

"Okay." She positions herself in her spot under my arm.

"You're going to fall asleep if you lay there."

"No, I won't."

A few minutes later, she's out cold.

The next day, I drop her off at class, then go to a coffee shop near campus. I get out my laptop and take that card the cop gave me and search online to make sure he's a real cop. He is. His name is listed as being on the local police force. But that doesn't make me feel better.

Something about that guy bugged me. It was the way he looked at Jade and that comment he made, insinuating that she needed protection. And then he hesitated to give me his card, like he didn't want me to know his name.

I get my phone out and call my dad. I haven't talked to him since last Saturday. I'm sure he's busy at work and won't pick up but I'll leave a message.

"Hello, Garret," he answers.

"Hey. I thought you'd be in a meeting or something."

"I'm working from home this morning. Katherine had to go out so I'm watching Lilly."

"Did you do anything for Labor Day?"

"We went to your grandparents' house. I was hoping to have a quiet day here at home and have Charles grill out like he did on the Fourth of July, but my father insisted we go to his house."

"Which means you didn't get a cookout."

He laughs. "Can you imagine your grandfather eating food cooked on an outdoor grill? Or eating outside?"

"So what did you end up having?"

"A formal dinner, as usual."

"Why did he invite you over? You don't usually go there on Labor Day."

"He wanted to tell me some news."

"What news?"

"Are you someplace private? Is anyone listening to this? Is Jade with you?"

"Jade's in class. I'm at a coffee shop but nobody's around me. Tell me what he said."

"Your grandfather is getting a promotion."

My mind immediately thinks of Kensington Chemical but that doesn't make sense. He owns the place. And he's retired. Then I get it. He's being promoted in the organization.

"Garret? Are you there?"

"Yes. So how much of a promotion?"

He sighs. "All the way to the top. Same level as Roth."

This isn't a good thing. Being at the top means making decisions. Big decisions. The kind that affect millions of people. I don't know what those decisions are, but I assume they're not good. My grandfather always talks about making sacrifices. He's always saying how only a few people can be leaders because most people aren't strong enough to make the tough calls that need to be made for the greater good.

When I heard him say those things in the past, I always thought he was talking about Kensington Chemical. I thought he was referring to how hard it is to find good managers, people who are willing to fire employees who aren't performing. But now I realize that wasn't what he meant.

It makes sense that he would be promoted like this. He's exactly the type of person they need at the top. He's someone who can always find a way to justify doing bad things. So I see why they picked him. I'm just surprised they would, given how I acted last year.

I ask my dad about it. "Why would they choose him after what happened with me last spring? He had to have lost some respect among the members."

"I wondered the same thing, but apparently they put all the blame on me. They assume I wasn't strict enough with you. My father has given them a multitude of reasons why you acted that way and they all come back to me."

"So he threw you under the bus to make himself look good."

"Yes, but it's true. Your behavior had nothing to do with him. If anything, they should be blaming him for how *I* turned out."

"Why? You didn't do anything out of line, at least not that they know of."

"Everyone knows about my involvement with your mother. That was a huge embarrassment to my father. That's why after I married her, he pretended I didn't exist. But now that I think about it, doing that gave him some clout. It proved where his loyalties lie. Garret, we really shouldn't be talking about this. Is there a reason you called me?"

"Yes. I wanted to tell you that some guy robbed one of the houses next to ours. It was that guy I told you about. The one in the white car who kept driving by our place. And Jade saw him last Saturday when she was out running."

"Did they catch him?"

"Yeah. A cop came to our house last night and told us they got the guy. The cop was acting strange. He knew I was a Kensington and he told me the security cameras were making us a target for crime. It was almost like he was encouraging us to take them down."

"Who is this man? Did you check him out?"

"Yes, and he's on the force. I just wanted you to know what was going on in case anything happens."

"Don't talk like that. Nothing's going to happen. Send me the officer's name. I'll do some more digging. It's probably nothing to worry about. You know how those small town police are, always trying to scare people, make you think you need them around."

"Yeah, that's probably it."

"Garret, you need to talk to Jade about getting a gun. I know she's opposed to the idea but you need to explain to her that being a Kensington means needing protection."

"She'll never go for that, Dad. She doesn't like guns."

"She needs to get over it. Explain to her how you can't count on others for protection. She should know that after the incident with her father."

It's true. Royce walked right up to our property that day and killed our security guys. My dad and his gun were what saved Jade and me from being shot dead by Royce.

"I'll talk to her."

"I need to go. Good luck on your first day of classes. Tell Jade I said hello."

"I will. Bye."

As I set my phone down, I notice a text from Jade. *Class ends at 9:30. Meet me outside the building.*

I text back. *Want a coffee?*

She texts, *Yes! Dying for one! Ur the best husband EVER!!*

I text back. *I know.*

I'm sure she's either laughing or rolling her eyes at that.

"Want a refill?"

I look up and see a girl holding a coffee pot. She's small, a few inches shorter than Jade. At first I thought she was a kid. She has short black hair that's angled to her chin and is wearing jeans and a red t-shirt with the coffee shop logo on it.

I look down and see that she filled my coffee cup before I could even answer. "I didn't know you guys gave refills here."

"It's a new thing we're trying. You get one refill, but if you order food you get unlimited refills. We have a whole breakfast menu if you're interested."

"No, thanks. I just ate, but maybe some other time."

"We have lunch, too. Do you want to see the menu?"

She seems eager to show it to me so I say, "Sure. I'll check it out."

She reaches in the apron that's around her waist and hands me a menu. "The tuna salad is really good. Actually all the sandwiches are. They're served on homemade bread. We make it here every morning. I can bring you a sample if you want to try it."

I smile at her. "You're quite the salesperson. Are you related to the owner?"

"No." Her cheeks blush. "Sorry, I didn't mean to be pushy. It's just that business has been kind of slow and if it doesn't improve, I'll lose my job and I really need this job." She cringes. "Forget I said that. I shouldn't have told you about business being slow. Dammit!" She cringes again. "And I should NOT have just cursed in front of a customer. I'm so sorry. Please don't tell my boss."

"I won't. It's fine." I give her the menu. "Maybe I'll stop by for lunch sometime. You sold me with the homemade bread."

Her shoulders relax. "Do you go to Camsburg?"

"Yeah, and I need to get going. I have class soon."

"Maybe you could tell your friends to stop by for lunch?"

"Sure, I can do that." I don't bother to tell her I have no friends here.

The girl walks off and I put my laptop away and get up to leave. As I'm walking out, I go past the girl as she's cleaning one of the tables. There's a guy in a suit talking on his phone next to her. He swings his laptop bag over his shoulder and it knocks into the girl and the tray she's holding. The coffee cups fly off the tray and hit the floor, shattering and making a loud noise.

The guy in the suit whips around. "Can't you see I'm trying to talk here?" He storms outside.

The girl looks like she's about to cry as she picks up the fragments of broken cups.

I kneel down to help her. "Hey, it's just some cups, right?"

"What are you doing?" She keeps her head down, but I see a tear running down her cheek.

"I'm just trying to help. That guy was a total ass."

"He comes in here all the time. He works at a law firm down the street. Sometimes they meet here before work."

"A lawyer, huh? That explains it."

She takes a towel from her apron and sweeps the mess away from me and toward her. "I got this. Really. Get to class."

"You sure you're all right? You seem really upset over a few broken coffee cups. I'm sure you have more around here."

"We do." She wipes her cheek. "But I have to pay for these. It comes out of my check."

"Why?"

"That's just the rules, okay? Would you please go before my boss sees you? I'll get fired if she sees a customer cleaning up my mess."

"Sorry." I stand up and check my phone. There's another text from Jade. *Don't forget the cream. Love you!*

When I look down, the girl is gone. I notice she's back at the counter, so I go up to her. "I forgot that I need a coffee to go. Can I get one quick? And if you could add cream to it, that'd be great."

"Sure." She's flustered and her eyes are all red. She gets the coffee and sets it down on the counter near the register. "It's $2 even."

I pull out a $5 bill but don't give it to her. "How much are the cups?"

"What?"

"How much do you owe for the coffee cups?"

"No, don't. It's fine."

I put the $5 bill back in my wallet and take out a twenty and set it on the counter.

"Consider it a tip for good service." I leave before she can give it back.

I normally don't just give out money to strangers like that, but I feel really bad for that girl. I don't know what her situation is, but I've never seen someone get so upset over broken coffee cups.

# *Chapter 15*

**JADE**

*I* wait for Garret on the bench outside of the science building. It's warm and sunny today with a light breeze. I'm looking forward to having weather like this year-round instead of freezing for half of the year. I've had enough long, cold winters in my life. I don't need to experience any more of them. I *will* miss having snow but Garret's promised me trips to the mountains whenever I need a snow fix. That's what's great about California. You get sunny beaches and snowy mountains all in the same state.

I spot Garret walking toward me and I get that fluttery, excited feeling inside. I see him all the time and he still gets to me this way. He has on light-colored shorts and a navy polo shirt, his backpack hanging off his shoulder and sunglasses on his face. He looks like an ad for an Ivy League college, a little preppy but also super hot with his tan skin and muscular arms.

"How was class?" He leans down and gives me a kiss.

I kiss him back, lingering a bit. Okay, a lot. What can I say? I love kissing him.

When I let him go, he's smiling at me. "Did you miss me or something? I just saw you two hours ago."

"Sorry, I won't do it again." I take my coffee from him and grab his hand and drag him to the bench to sit down.

"I'm kidding. I like it. I'll take another one." He puts his arm up behind me on the bench.

"Maybe later." I sip my coffee.

He rubs my shoulder. "How's the coffee?"

"It's really good. Where'd you get this?"

"At a place just down the hill, right by campus. Campus Brew or Cafe Brew. Something Brew. Anyway, we should go there for lunch. They have a lot of different sandwiches and they're made with homemade bread."

I look at him funny. "Did you study the menu or something?"

"One of the servers was trying to get me to eat lunch there and she mentioned that the bread was homemade."

"I don't have much time for lunch today. I have lab at 1 and I need to get there early. But you could go there for lunch. We don't have to eat together. I'll just find something on campus."

"I'm eating lunch with my wife." He turns my face toward his and kisses me. "So stop trying to get rid of me."

"I'm not. I'd love to have lunch with you. I just don't have much time. There's a place to eat in the student union. We could go there, and we'll try your coffee shop tomorrow. Maybe I'll go there after class while I'm waiting for yours to end. By then I'll need more coffee. I'm really tired."

"Didn't you sleep last night?"

"I did, but I kept waking up thinking someone was trying to break in. I woke up every time I heard a noise."

"Jade, I need to ask you something."

"What?"

"What do you think about us getting a gun?"

"No way. Forget it. I don't want one in our home. It's too dangerous."

"It's dangerous *not* to have one. I'll teach you how to use it. We'll find a shooting range and you can practice."

"Practice killing someone? No, thanks."

"Jade, it's just a precaution. Criminals have guns. If *they* have them, we should, too. It only makes sense."

"I don't want a gun. We already have a security system. That's all we need."

"My dad's house in Connecticut has the most sophisticated security system available. It cost a fortune. He also has security guys guarding the house. But did any of that stop your father?"

I don't like Royce being called my father. I try to pretend he's not. But I know Garret's saying that because he doesn't want to say Royce's name. He always avoids saying it, like he thinks someone's listening to us.

"Fine, but that was a special circumstance. It's not like that's going to happen again."

"You never know what's going to happen. That's why you need to be prepared. Just think about it, okay?"

"I don't need to. I don't want us to have a gun. I think it's a bad idea." I check my watch as I stand up. "Class starts soon. I should walk over there."

Garret gets up. "Are you mad at me now?"

"No. As soon as that cop told us about the robbery, I knew you'd bug me about getting a gun." I reach up and kiss him. "I'll see you at lunch. Love you."

"Love you, too."

As I walk to class I think more about the gun. I'm not as opposed to it as I was last year but I'm still not ready to agree to it. Guns scare me, and the thought of having one sitting in a closet or in a drawer or under our bed totally freaks me out.

I go inside the social sciences building and stop at the vending machine to get a Coke. I already finished my coffee and I need more caffeine to make it through my next class, which is developmental psychology. It was one of the few electives that was still available since I enrolled so late. I took psych 101 last year and found it interesting, so I'm hoping this class will be, too. It's about how your mind and behavior change over your lifetime, starting from when you're a baby and going until old age. Even if it's not that interesting, it'll be an easy class—much easier than my science classes.

I go in the classroom and sit next to a girl with red hair, wearing ripped jeans and a wrinkled t-shirt. This school is very expensive so the students come from wealthy families, but from the way they dress you wouldn't know it. Some of them look like they just rolled out of bed. It's totally different than Moorhurst where people showed up to class wearing designer clothes and looking like they spent hours getting ready.

Camsburg is known for academics, not sports or partying or whatever else schools are known for. Moorhurst was known for academics, too, but the students here seem way more serious about their classes. In my organic chemistry class this morning, some of the people had already read the first three chapters of our book even though it wasn't assigned. And they were already asking questions about the material they read. I felt like an idiot. I had no idea what they were talking about.

If that wasn't bad enough, I decided to try to make friends in that class and my first attempt went horribly. After the lecture, I asked my new lab partner, who was assigned to me by the professor, if she wanted to get coffee after class and she completely ignored me like she didn't hear me. I asked her again and she informed me that being her lab partner does not mean we're friends and that I should stop trying.

I didn't tell Garret that because it would piss him off, and knowing him he'd probably go yell at the girl.

She seemed like kind of a loner so maybe she just doesn't like people. I was that way in high school after my mom died so I understand.

After I get my laptop set up, I turn to the red-headed girl next to me. "Hi, I'm Jade."

She was staring straight ahead, but she turns a little and says, "Hi."

It wasn't an enthusiastic 'hi' and she didn't give me her name.

"Do you know anything about this class? I kind of got stuck in it because I enrolled late."

"It's a psych class. Aren't they all the same?" She gets her phone out and starts swiping through it, a sign she doesn't want to talk.

Strike two in my attempt to make a friend today.

I turn to the girl who's sitting on my left. She looks a little like Harper, with blond hair that's pulled up into a ponytail. She's flipping through the first chapter of our psych book.

"Did the professor assign some reading?" I ask her. "I forgot to check."

It's a lie. He didn't assign anything but I'm trying to make conversation.

"Did you say something?" She looks at me, annoyed.

"I was just asking if the professor assigned reading for today's class?"

"No. I just read ahead. I always do. I like to be prepared." She flips to page one of the book and starts reading.

And there's strike three.

I face forward again and notice three girls huddled around the desk in front of me with their phones out.

"What time do you want to get together tonight?" the one girl asks.

The girl next to her says, "I have biochem study group at 7 but I could do 9."

"That works for me," the third girl says. "So psych study group at 9 every Wednesday."

They agree, then take their seats.

People are already having study groups? Classes just started. What's there to study?

I feel like an idiot again. I'm used to being one of the smartest people in class and now I feel like the dumbest. How hard are these classes? Obviously really hard if people are studying this much. Maybe developmental psychology won't be so easy after all.

When I meet Garret for lunch I give him a huge hug. I'm ecstatic to see a friendly face and someone who will actually talk to me.

He laughs at my over-the-top hug. "You miss me again?"

"Yes. A lot. You sure you don't want to switch your major to chemistry? You'd be in all my classes and it'd be nice to have someone there who'd actually talk to me."

"You don't like the people in your classes?"

"They're not exactly friendly."

We take our trays and find a place to sit.

"Yeah, I noticed. The people here really stress out about school, although I met some guys who are more laid back. They invited me to lunch but I told them I was busy."

"You already have friends? Damn. How do you do it?"

"Just give it time. People are always uptight on the first day. They'll loosen up after a week or so."

"I don't think so. Some of them are already having study group tonight."

"Well, *I'm* not studying tonight." He leans over and lowers his voice. "I'm having dinner with my hot wife and then I'm taking her into the shower with me and I'm going to—"

"Mind if I sit here?" A tall, muscular guy with messy blond hair sets his tray down across from us.

Garret sits up straight again and says to the guy, "No, go ahead."

I'm annoyed by the interruption, my mind left wondering what exactly Garret planned to do to me in the shower.

The guy puts his hand out toward Garret. "I'm Tyson. We just had class together. I sat in the back so you probably didn't see me."

Garret shakes his hand. "Hi, I'm Garret."

I swear. I don't understand this. Garret has people coming up to him, trying to be his friend, and I can't even get someone to talk to me. I must be doing something wrong.

"Are you new here?" Tyson asks.

"Yeah, I transferred here."

"That's cool. You from California?" The guy takes a big bite of his burger. He has two burgers and a pile of fries.

"No. I'm from Connecticut. This is—" Garret was about to introduce me but the guy interrupts.

"I'm from Orange County. Born and raised there. You surf?"

"Yeah."

"We should go surfing sometime. You want to go tonight? A bunch of us are going. Like eight guys. We have a spot we like just north of town."

"Thanks, but I'm busy tonight."

"Garret, it's fine." I say it quietly to him. "Go ahead."

Tyson looks at me. "Are you the girlfriend?"

"This is Jade," Garret answers. "She's my wife."

The guy laughs. "You're joking, right? Wife. That's hilarious."

I hold my hand out and show him my ring. "He's not kidding. I'm his wife."

"Holy shit. What are you, like 19?" he asks Garret.

"I'm 20." Garret's angry. I can hear it in his voice. "Maybe you should go sit somewhere else."

He gets up, still laughing. "I think I will. No offense, man. You can do what you want, but I'm not interested in hanging out with married people."

Once he's gone, Garret says, "So we're probably not going to have many friends here."

"We need to find a couple to hang out with, like Harper and Sean. I really miss them. Maybe we could convince them to move here."

Garret puts his arm around me. "It's only the first day. We'll find people to hang out with. It just takes time. And if we don't, we always have each other."

The tables around us are filling up with people and I see that it's getting close to 1. I need to get to chem lab, so I leave Garret there, telling him I'll meet him after class at that coffee shop he went to this morning. I'm done at 2 today but he has class until 3.

Organic chem lab is uneventful. Emily, my lab partner, does all the work while I just stand there and watch. Every time I try to help, she takes over again. I can tell she thinks I'll screw up the experiment. She informed me that she wants an A in this class and when I told her I did, too, she acted like she didn't believe me. Since it's only the first day, I didn't want to argue with her so I just let her do the experiment.

After lab, I walk down to the coffee shop. It's right by the entrance to campus. It has a bright red awning out front that says 'Campus Brew' and a sign on the window that reads 'Students welcome. Show your ID for a discount.'

The inside of the place has an open, loft-like ceiling with exposed pipes. There are lots of different seating options;

booths, small tables, long high tables with stools, and some lounge chairs scattered around. I take one of the soft chairs. They look relaxing and I need to relax. I feel tense. I sink into the chair and close my eyes for a moment.

"Long day?"

I open my eyes to see a girl standing there. She's tiny, maybe 5 feet tall, with short dark hair and deep brown eyes. She has a t-shirt on with the coffee shop name so I'm guessing she's a waitress. I didn't know they had waitresses. I thought you just ordered at the counter.

I sit up a little. "Yeah. The first day of class always kind of sucks."

"Can I get you something? The smoothies here are really good. We make them with fresh fruit."

It's hot out today and an icy cold smoothie does sound good. "Okay, I'll have a smoothie."

"What kind would you like? We have lots of different ones. I'll get you a menu."

"Just pick whatever's good."

"They're $4. Is that okay?"

"Yeah, that's fine."

She smiles, then takes off for the kitchen. Finally, someone who's friendly. I know she's just doing her job, being nice to a customer, but I still appreciate the friendly greeting.

A few minutes later, she comes back with the smoothie. "This one has blueberries, bananas, strawberries, and vanilla frozen yogurt. It's my favorite, but if you don't like it I'll make you a different one."

I taste it. "It's really good. Thanks!"

"Do you want anything to eat? We're done serving lunch for today but we have pastries or pie."

"No, thanks. The smoothie is enough."

"Just let me know if you need anything."

She leaves, then comes back with a rag and a spray bottle and begins wiping down the tables next to me. She's fast, yet thorough. She even wipes down the chairs.

"Do you go to school at Camsburg?" I ask her.

"No." She laughs.

I'm not sure why that's funny. Maybe she's still in high school. She has a young-looking face and she's so small.

"Are you in high school?" As I ask it, I realize that if she was, she'd be in school right now.

"High school?" She laughs again. At least she's not insulted. "I'm 21, almost 22. Do I really look like I'm in high school?"

"Kind of. Actually, yeah, you do. You look really young."

"Well, that's good I guess. It's better than looking old." She spritzes cleaning solution on the tall table across from me. "I'm guessing you go to Camsburg?"

"Yeah, I transferred here from another college. I'm a sophomore."

"How do you like it?"

"I haven't found the students to be very friendly. I guess I shouldn't say that because I really haven't met many of them yet."

"They're all like that. They're either popular and cliquey or they're academics who want to be left alone. At least that's what I've decided after watching them in here the past year." She sets her spray bottle down and extends her hand. "I'm Sara, by the way."

"I'm Jade." We shake hands. "So you've worked here a year?"

"Yeah. I'm trying to find other work but there aren't many jobs in this town and I need a flexible schedule."

"Because of college? Where do you go?"

"I'm not in college. I have a kid."

"Oh." I didn't expect her to say that. I'm flustered, which means stupid things are about to come out of my mouth. "What kind? I mean, a boy or a girl?"

She smiles. "What kind? That's funny. I have the crying, diaper-wearing, constantly-needs-to-be-fed kind. A boy. His name is Caleb. He's six months old."

"Do you have a picture?"

Her face lights up as she reaches in her pocket and pulls out her phone. "He was five months when this was taken. He has a little more hair now."

She shows me the photo. He's a cute baby; chubby with pink cheeks and a tuft of brown hair sticking up on the top of his head.

"He's cute."

"Thanks." She puts her phone away. "I have to pick him up at day care at 3. It's going to be a long night. He just started teething and I can't get him to stop crying. I was up with him all last night."

"Do you have family around here?"

"No. My mom left town last year. I don't even know where she lives. She ditched me and moved in with her boyfriend after I got pregnant. She didn't want another mouth to feed. She'd rather spend her disability checks on alcohol and cigarettes, not her grandson."

"She's disabled?"

"No. She faked a back injury years ago so she wouldn't have to work. She basically just drinks, gambles, and hangs out with loser guys. She's got some issues."

"Sounds like my mom."

"Oh, yeah?"

"Not exactly, but she also had some issues. She died a few years ago."

"I'm sorry."

"So where's Caleb's dad?"

"He graduated from Camsburg last May and now he works in San Francisco. He doesn't want anything to do with Caleb or me."

"Does he at least send you child support?"

"No, and I don't want to fight him for it. His parents are rich and they'd make my life hell if I went after their son for child support. They think I purposely got pregnant to get their money." Sara rolls her eyes. "I was on the pill when I got pregnant. Everyone knows it's not 100%. And I always told Caleb's dad to use a condom as backup but he wouldn't do it." She wipes down another table. "I always pick the wrong guys." She stops cleaning and smiles. "There was this guy who was here earlier and he was so hot I was actually nervous around him. I figured a guy that hot would be a real jerk, but he was really nice. Why can't I find a guy like that?"

"You should ask him out."

"Who?"

"That guy you met. The one you were just talking about."

"Yeah, right. No guy our age wants to date a single mom."

"You never know. You said he was nice. I bet he'd go out with you."

"You really think so?"

"You won't know unless you ask. Next time you see him, ask him if he wants to go to dinner."

"I can't. I don't have anyone to watch Caleb."

"I could watch him. I know you don't know me, but I'm very responsible. I don't know that much about babies but I think I could handle him for an hour or two. And my husband could help. He's good with kids."

She sits in the chair across from me. "You're married? How old are you?"

"I'm 19. We got married last July and now we're both going to Camsburg."

"You wanted to get married at 19?" She blushes. "Sorry, that sounded bad."

"It's fine. We get that reaction a lot."

"I didn't mean anything by it. Really. I was just surprised. But it doesn't matter how old you are. You seem really happy so that's all that counts, right?"

"Finally, someone who isn't judging me for being married this young. People on campus act like we're crazy."

"I'm 21 and single with a baby and a crappy job so I can't judge." She gets up. "I gotta go but it was nice meeting you. Stop by again. Maybe we could talk some more. I miss having a real conversation with someone. Caleb's not much of a talker." She smiles as she walks away.

I think I just made a friend. I never thought it'd be a single mom I met at a coffee shop but hey, a friend's a friend.

# *Chapter 16*

**GARRET**

*I* walk in the coffee shop and see Jade reading one of her textbooks.

"Ready to go?" I ask her. "I have the car outside but I'm in a no parking zone so we need to hurry."

She jumps up from her chair, grabbing her backpack. "No parking zone?" She takes my hand as we walk out the door. "You're breaking the law?"

"Today I am."

She smiles. "I like this bad boy side of you."

"I can be as bad as you want when we get home." I kiss her as I open the car door.

As we're driving away from campus, I look over at her and say, "Did you go through a lot of Kleenex today? Have any hair emergencies to use up those headbands? Or how about that protractor? Did you measure any angles?"

She hits my arm. "Someday you'll need those things and you'll be sorry you don't have them."

"Yeah, I'll be sorry I don't have a pink headband and cherry lip balm."

"Maybe not those things but the other ones. Hey, I met this girl at the coffee shop. We talked a little and she seemed really nice. I think we might become friends."

"You guys should go do something. Maybe you could have lunch with her this week."

"She works during lunch. And she can't do anything after work because she has a baby. The dad took off and she doesn't have any family around."

"That sucks. So the dad doesn't see the kid?"

"He doesn't want to. He doesn't want anything to do with Sara or the baby. He went to Camsburg and graduated last May and now he works in San Francisco. He's rich. Well, his parents are rich. But he won't help her with money. He won't even pay child support."

"What an ass. Who leaves their kid like that?"

"A lot of people do. My dad left me. Her kid is basically me. He has a rich dad who wants nothing to do with him. Anyway, I told her I'd babysit if she needed me to."

"Babysit? How old is this kid?"

"Six months."

Somehow I can't see Jade watching a baby. Jade doesn't like loud noises and babies are very loud. And I can't imagine her changing a diaper. "Have you ever taken care of a baby?"

"No, but I'll have you there to help me out." She gives me the smile she uses when she wants me to go along with something. "You took care of Lilly when she was a baby."

"That doesn't mean I should be babysitting someone else's kid."

"Then I'll just do it. I already told her I would. And she may not even need me to."

"Hey, before I forget, Dr. Cunningham won't be here until tomorrow afternoon so my appointment is at 4. We can go right after class. Your calculus class ends at 3:30, right?"

"Yes. Ugh, another semester of calculus. I am not looking forward to that."

We're home now and as we get out of the car I scan the outside of the house. Everything appears to be okay. While we were gone, I used my phone to check the views from the cameras. I didn't see anyone lurking around, but I only checked the cameras a few times.

I follow Jade inside and check for anything that looks out of place. Ever since that burglar showed up, I haven't felt safe. I feel like we're open targets out here with no protection. No gun. No security guards. No locked gate keeping people out.

I hate to admit it, but I kind of wish I lived closer to my dad now. When I went to Moorhurst, I didn't worry about shit as much because my dad was just a half hour away. Even after Jade's room was broken into last year, I felt safe because we were in the dorm. There were always people around and the doors were locked at night. And if we needed to, Jade and I could always go stay at my dad's house and feel safe. Now we can't do that. We're out here all alone and there's nobody here we can trust. And I can't run to my dad for protection. It's just me now and I have to take care of Jade.

Over the summer I didn't have to worry. Harper was always with Jade and even when she wasn't, the beach we lived on always had people on it. We didn't know our neighbors that well but we'd introduced ourselves. Our neighbors were mostly families or older couples and I felt like Jade could go to them if she ever needed help. Living there felt much safer than here, where we rarely see anyone.

My phone rings and I see it's my dad.

"Hey, Dad." I go outside on the deck.

"Hello, Garret. I don't have much time to talk but I wanted to give you an update regarding the robbery in your neighborhood. I've been trying to locate the police report."

I don't know how he does it, but my dad is somehow able to get access to police reports. This isn't the first time he's done this. When I used to get in trouble with the cops back in high school, my dad always got copies of the reports they made about me. I never asked how he got them.

"So did you find it?"

"No. I even had someone go to the station and look, but it wasn't there. I don't think they ever filled one out."

"That doesn't make sense. They arrested the guy."

"Yes, and I checked on that. He's still in jail but not for the robbery. They picked him up on charges related to drug possession."

"How did you know who he was without having the police report?"

"I had one of my security experts check the footage from the cameras at your house. He was able to zoom in and identify the man in the car as a man who was already in the police's criminal database. He has a long record, including charges for rape and attempted murder."

"So there was a rapist killer hanging around my home? That's just great."

"He was never convicted on either of those charges. It sounded like he was almost convicted for the murder but he got off on a technicality. The point I'm trying to make here is that the police want to get this guy locked up for good, so it's in their best interest to file a police report about that burglary."

"What are you telling me here, Dad?"

"I want you to be careful. I'll keep working on this, but until I figure out what's going on, I need both of you to be careful."

"What does this have to do with Jade and me? The guy robbed the neighbors, not us, and if he's in custody now, why are you so worried?"

"When police reports are missing, it means someone's trying to hide something."

That's all my dad needs to say for me to understand. It means the organization might be involved. They're always trying to hide things. The question is, why would they be involved in this?

"I'll let you know if I get any updates," my dad says. "As of now, I wouldn't tell Jade about this. There's no use worrying her until I know for sure what's going on."

"Yeah, okay."

"Goodbye, Garret."

"Bye."

I almost wish he hadn't told me that. He told me because he wants me to be alert. Check for anything suspicious. Keep an eye on Jade. But it's just another thing to worry about and I don't need the stress. I have enough of it with moving and starting a new school and dealing with my shoulder.

This missing police report could be nothing. The cops could've just misplaced the file. Or whoever my dad hired to find it may be looking in the wrong place. I hope that's all it is.

My phone rings again. It's Sean. I haven't called him since we moved here. I kept meaning to and then I'd get busy and not do it. I need to call him more. We became really good friends over the summer and I want to make sure we stay friends. From the way things are going, I don't think I'll have many friends here.

"Hey, Sean." I try to relax and get that conversation with my dad out of my head. I can't worry about it. If I do, Jade will notice and then she'll ask questions.

"Hey, how it's going?"

"Good. Sorry I haven't called. It's been busy with the move, and then my dad was here, and classes started."

"Don't worry about it. So how's the new place?"

"It's great, but one of the houses a few down from ours was broken into the other day so I'm not feeling too safe about the area."

"Yeah, Harper told me. That sucks. You'd think you'd be safe in a small town like that."

"I don't think you're safe anywhere anymore. So what's new in your life? Work going okay?"

"Not really. My boss didn't like me taking the summer off so he's being a real ass about it. Giving me the worst shifts. Not giving me time off when I ask. I need a different job."

"Doesn't seem like you have many options around there."

"I don't. That's the problem. If I want to work somewhere decent, and not some shit diner, I need to go out of town."

"Meaning you'd have to move?"

"Yeah."

"Have you told Harper this?"

"No. And I'm not going to. As much as I hate my job, I love Harper and I'm not willing to risk our relationship for a job somewhere else that I may not even like. I might as well stay where I am."

This is one of those times when it sucks to have inside information. Jade's told me that Harper isn't sure about her future with Sean and yet Sean is putting his career on hold for her. But I can't tell him what Harper said. He needs to hear it from her. The two of them need to work this out themselves.

"So you're going to stay at that job until she graduates? That's three more years, Sean. You sure you want to do that?"

"I don't have a choice."

"You could try dating long distance. Where were you thinking of moving to?"

"Don't tell Jade this, okay?"

"Sean, you know I'm going to tell her."

"Fine, but ask her not to tell Harper."

"Okay, so what is it?"

"The guy I worked for last summer called and offered me a job at his flagship restaurant in LA. He said he was really impressed with me and could see me working as head chef at one of his restaurants someday. He's got places all up and down the coast."

"Sean, that's a great opportunity. You can't pass that up."

"I already told him I couldn't do it. I can't lose Harper."

"She goes back to California all the time to visit her family. And she'd live with you in the summers. You guys could make this work."

"Not for three years. That's too long."

"You have to tell Harper about this. She has to know what you're giving up to be with her."

"If I did that, she'd tell me to take the job."

"Yeah, so what's the problem?"

"I don't want us living on separate coasts. I'm hoping we'll be engaged in a few months and I don't want to live 3000 miles away from my fiancé."

"You're proposing to her?"

"Yeah. I told you that last summer."

"You haven't said anything since then so I wasn't sure if you still planned to."

"I'm going to. I'm just not sure when. I'm trying to save up for a ring. I've been shopping around but shit, they're expensive. How much did you pay for Jade's?"

"You don't want to know."

"Yeah, that makes sense. Sometimes I forget you're loaded."

That's another reason I like Sean. He treats me like I don't have money. He doesn't know I lost my trust fund and he doesn't know about Jade's money. But none of that matters. To Sean, I'm just his friend and he doesn't even think about the money. He's so different from the fake friends I had back in high school who only hung out with me because of whatever benefits they thought they could get from being friends with a Kensington.

"If you're not proposing right away, you don't need to buy a ring yet."

"I know. I'm just shopping around."

"Does Harper know you're proposing? Did you drop any hints?"

"I thought I did, but I don't know if she picked up on them."

"You should drop some more hints. Make it clear to her this is what you're planning. She may not be ready for this. She's still in college."

"So are you and Jade. What's up with you, man? Are you trying to talk me out of this? Or did Jade tell you something? Did Harper say she didn't want to marry me?"

Shit. Now I have to lie. But I can't get in the middle of this.

"I just think you might want to make sure you two are on the same page. Maybe she'll want to wait to get married. Like wait until after graduation."

"That's fine. We can just have a long engagement."

"Are you going to ask Harper's dad before you propose?"

"I'd like to, but the guy hates me and I really don't want him telling me I can't marry his daughter. I don't know what his problem is. He's nice to everyone except me. I must've done something to piss him off."

"You didn't do anything, Sean."

"Then what the hell's his problem? Even her mom hates me now. It doesn't make sense. The only thing I can think of is that they want Harper to marry someone who's rich. But her parents grew up without money so you'd think they'd be okay with her marrying someone like me."

"Hollywood people are strange. Don't worry about them. You don't need Kiefer's permission to marry her."

"I'd still like to ask him. And I know Harper would want me to. She's really close to her dad and it would mean a lot to her if he gave us his blessing. But I know he's not going to, which really pisses me off. I don't care how he treats *me*, but I care how he treats Harper and right now he's hurting her by acting this way. Last week I caught her crying right after she talked to him. She said it wasn't about us but I know it was. I mean, is that really what her dad wants? To hurt his daughter like that? Would he rather have her dating some rich asshole who treats her like shit?"

"Just give it time. My dad didn't like Jade when we first started dating. I told you how he kept trying to break us apart. My stepmom still hates her, but she hates everyone, including me. Anyway, the point is my dad eventually came around and now he loves Jade."

Just as I say it, Jade comes walking out on the deck wearing her bright green bikini and sunglasses. Damn, she's hot. It causes movement in my shorts, which is awkward when I'm trying to talk to Sean.

"Who loves me?" Jade asks, hearing the tail end of the conversation.

"My dad." I put the phone on speaker. "Sean's on the phone."

"Hey, Sean, how's it going?" Jade reclines back in the chair, putting her feet up on me.

"Good. How was the first day of class?"

"It sucked. The only good part of the day was eating lunch with this really hot guy."

"Does Garret know?"

"Asshole," I mumble.

Jade laughs.

Sean laughs, too. "I need to go, but I'll call you guys later."

"Sounds good. See ya, Sean." I put my phone away.

"What's new with Sean?"

My eyes are fixed on the cleavage spilling out of Jade's bikini top. Harper gave her that bikini last spring, along with a few others, but this one's my favorite. It hugs her ass perfectly and the top pushes up her breasts.

"Garret? What did Sean say?"

"You need to cover up if you want to talk."

"I came out here to get some sun. I'm not covering up."

"Then we need to go have sex and then come out here and talk." I take her feet off my lap and yank her chair toward me. "This suit drives me crazy. You know it does."

She tries to play innocent. "Actually, no, I never knew that."

I put my lips to her ear. "Bedroom. Now."

"Tell me what Sean said first."

"Jade." I lick the skin just below her ear and her breath catches.

"What?" She closes her eyes as I kiss the area I just licked.

I talk low but forceful. "Get your hot little ass in that bedroom or I'll do you right here."

"No, you won't. There are cameras out here."

"Do you really think I give a shit?" I run my hand up her inner thigh and right before I slip my finger under her suit, her eyes pop open and she stands up.

I laugh. "Going somewhere?"

She grabs my hand and yanks me inside. I scoop her up and take her to the bed. She rips her suit off before I can do it. Yeah, she knew what she was doing wearing that thing. It works every time.

Right after we have sex, she says, "Now will you tell me what Sean said?"

I'm still on top of her. "Really, Jade? You can't wait a few minutes?"

"Why? What's the problem?"

"We just had sex. I'm trying to enjoy the moment here. I don't want to talk about Sean."

"Oh, sorry. Get off me and we'll go back outside."

I sigh as I get up. "Just use me for sex, then move on, huh?"

"The sex wasn't my idea," she insists, putting her bikini back on.

"Yeah, that wasn't at all what you had in mind when you came outside wearing that."

She just smiles as she walks away. "I'll see you out there."

I throw my shorts on and grab my sunglasses and meet Jade outside. "So if I tell you what Sean said you can't tell Harper." I set my chair next to Jade's, facing the ocean.

She reaches over and holds my hand. She always links our hands when we're next to each other. It's so automatic I don't even think she realizes she does it.

"I won't tell her. So what did he say?"

"He said that guy he worked for last summer offered him a job. The guy owns a bunch of restaurants up and down the coast and he wants Sean to work his way up to head chef at one of his restaurants."

"What's Sean going to do? Did he take the job?"

"No. He won't take it because of Harper. But you can't tell her that. He doesn't want her to know. He still plans to propose to her in a few months. He's been looking at rings."

"But she's not ready for that. Why doesn't he know this? He needs to be dropping hints to see her reaction."

"I told him that and he said he already did, but it sounds like she didn't pick up on them."

"Did he mention Harper's dad? Because I'm sure he knows her dad's not going to be happy about the proposal."

"I don't think he cares. I mean, he cares, but he'll still propose."

"So Sean's giving up a huge job opportunity all because of Harper and she doesn't even know. This really sucks."

"If he told her, do you think she'd break up with him?"

"She'd tell him to take the job, which would basically mean they're breaking up. They can't live on separate coasts and still date. They could try it, but doing that for three years? It wouldn't work."

"She could move to California with him. She'd be closer to her family."

"I don't think she'd do that. She likes being on the tennis team at Moorhurst and I don't think she'd change her whole life like that for Sean. She still sees him as just a boyfriend, not a future husband, so if he proposes, she'll say no. She isn't ready for that kind of commitment."

"Then I guess he's stuck there." I squeeze her hand. "Look what you girls do to us."

"What do we do?"

"Make us love you so we end up doing stupid shit we shouldn't do."

"You guys do the same thing to us."

"You girls are way worse. You know we're weak when it comes to your womanly wiles."

She laughs. "Womanly wiles? Did you suddenly step back into the Victorian era?"

"That green bikini." I point to it. "Prime example of using your womanly wiles to get what you want."

"I did not want anything. I was just sunbathing."

"Whatever, Jade." I lean over and kiss her cheek, then we both recline back in our chairs and let the sun bake into our skin.

I hear the waves and am reminded of the invite to go surfing with those guys. I'm glad I didn't go. As much as I like to surf, that guy who invited me seemed like an ass, which means his friends probably are, too. I'd much rather spend the rest of the day hanging out with my hot wife in her green bikini, which by the way leads back to the bedroom an hour later.

# Chapter 17

**JADE**

The alarm goes off and I hit the button to make it stop. I forgot to turn the alarm off last night. Garret and I don't have class until 10 today and it's only 6:30.

I'm tired because I kept waking up in the middle of the night thinking about Sean and Harper. I know I should stay out of it but part of me thinks I should tell Harper what's going on. She's still not sure about her future with Sean, so it doesn't seem fair for him to miss out on this great job opportunity. Besides, maybe some time apart would be good for them. It might help Harper make a decision about Sean instead of her constant wavering. And if she decides she wants to break up with him, at least he'll be left with a good job that has a future. Sean is going nowhere in the job he has now and I know he doesn't like working there. He's only staying there for Harper.

I have to talk to her. I won't say anything about Sean, but I need to get an update on where she stands with him. I know I'm butting in and Garret will lecture me about it later but hey, that's what friends do, right? Give you advice even when you don't ask for it? Harper did it to me all last year. I lost count of how many times she lectured me about Garret and how I needed to let him know how I felt about him. And look how that turned out? I'm happily married. So I figure I'm just returning the favor with my subtle match-making moves.

Garret's still sound asleep beside me. He didn't even notice the alarm. He has the sheet shoved way down by his ankles because he gets hot when he sleeps, probably because my arms and legs are always draped all over him. He only wore boxer briefs to bed, meaning he's practically naked. It's a nice view to wake up to.

He's lying on his side facing me. I lean over and gently kiss his cheek. I love him so much. Every day I tell myself I can't possibly love him any more and then every morning I wake up and feel like I love him even more than the day before.

"Jade?" he mumbles.

"Go back to sleep," I whisper, kissing his cheek again. "It's still early."

He shifts onto his other side as I sneak out of bed, closing the door behind me. I go in the kitchen and make some coffee, then take my phone to the couch and call Harper. With the time difference it's 9:30 there, so I'm sure she's awake but she could be in class. She hasn't sent me her schedule yet.

She picks up on the third ring. "Why are you calling so early? It's the crack of dawn there." She's laughing. She sounds happy.

"It's 6:30. It's not that early. And I missed my best friend."

"Jade, don't start. You know I cry every time you say that."

208

"Sorry, we'll talk about something else. How was your dinner last night?"

Harper went to dinner with her tennis team. They do it every year to welcome everyone back and introduce the new team members.

"It was fun. We didn't get back until late so I didn't call you because I wanted to get to bed. I have an 8 a.m. class on Tuesdays and Thursdays. It sucks but it's the only time it's offered."

"So did you get the same dorm room this year?"

"Yeah. Basically, everything's the same except you and Garret aren't here. Oh! Guess who else isn't here this year?" She uses the tone that implies she's got juicy gossip.

"Katy? Or maybe Jessica?"

"No, it's not someone on the tennis team. Sorry, I should've said that. It's someone else you know. Guess."

"Um, Sierra?"

"No, she's still here. She's in my French class. Guess again."

"Ava?"

"No, unfortunately she's still here. I saw her yesterday."

"I'm out of guesses. Just tell me."

"It's someone who really annoyed you last year. Actually, last semester. Someone Garret hated."

I think for a moment. A lot of people annoyed me but Garret only hated Blake and he wasn't there last semester. Then I remember who else Garret hated.

"Carson?"

"Yes! A girl on my tennis team wanted to go out with him and she looked him up and found out he doesn't go here anymore."

"That's weird. He always said he liked it there and that he liked living in Connecticut. Do you know where he transferred to?"

"I have no idea. I just know he doesn't go here anymore. So how was your first day of class? Do you like Camsburg?"

"It's okay." I try not to be too negative since Harper's dad recommended it.

"You don't like it, do you?"

My tone must've given me away. "It's too soon to tell. I think the classes will be challenging, which isn't a bad thing. I like being challenged. But I haven't found the people to be very friendly."

"I forgot to tell you, one of my friends from high school just transferred to Camsburg. She was a year ahead of me so she's a junior. Her fiancé, who's the guy she's dated since she was 17, got a job in the marketing department there. He graduated last May and this is his first real job. Anyway they moved there a month ago. I haven't talked to her for like a year, but my mom ran into her mom at a charity thing last week and that's how I found out she's going to Camsburg. You have to meet her, Jade. You guys would totally get along. And I think Garret would get along with her fiancé."

"Give me her number and I'll see if we can meet for dinner or something. Garret and I could really use some couple friends. People here act like we're freaks because we're married. We were just saying how hard it's going to be to make friends."

"I'll send you her number as soon as we get off the phone. Her name is Brook and her fiancé's name is Dylan.

210

I'll call her and tell her about you and give her your info if that's okay."

"Yeah, that'd be great. Thanks!"

"Jade, can we talk later? I didn't realize how late it was. I have to get to class."

"Yeah, okay. Bye."

I get up and go into the kitchen just as Garret walks in.

"What are you doing up so early?" He looks half asleep.

"I called Harper."

"You didn't tell her what Sean said, did you?"

"No." I grab some mugs. "You want coffee?"

"Sure." He yawns.

I pour the coffee in the mugs, then hand him one. "I was up during the night thinking I should tell Harper about Sean. Or at least push her to make a decision about him."

"It's not your place to do that, Jade."

"Yeah, but—"

"Just let them deal with it." Garret leans against the kitchen counter and takes a sip of his coffee. "Besides, I told Sean you wouldn't say anything to her."

"Fine, but I'm still going to ask her about their relationship. She asked about ours all last year. It's a thing girlfriends do. Guys don't understand."

He shakes his head, smiling. "So what else did she say?"

"Oh! Guess who isn't at Moorhurst this year?"

"You know I don't like the guessing game thing. Just tell me."

"Carson. He didn't come back. Isn't that weird?"

"Maybe he decided it was too far from home."

"That's the thing. He used to say how he went there because he wanted to try living someplace new. He said he liked living in Connecticut."

"Maybe he changed his mind. I don't want to talk about Carson. I'm trying to forget about that guy."

"She also said her friend from high school goes to Camsburg now and the girl's fiancé works in the marketing department. Harper's going to send me her phone number. I thought we could meet them for dinner some night. We might have a new couple to hang out with."

"How long did you talk to Harper?"

"Not long. But you know Harper. She can tell you a lot in a short amount of time." I sip my coffee. "Since we're up early, would you go on a run with me?" I set my coffee down and put my arms around him. "Just a short one?

"Yes." He kisses my forehead. "I just need a few minutes to wake up first."

"You'll really go with me? I thought you'd say no."

"You're not running alone, Jade. I told you that. So if you want to run, I'll be going with you."

"And you don't even like to run. You must really love me."

"Either that or I'm looking forward to the shower that comes *after* the run." He smiles, then drinks his coffee again.

"Yeah, I'm looking forward to that, too."

"But I need to eat something before we go." He sets his coffee down and takes some cereal from the cupboard. "You want some?"

"Sure." I grab the bowls and spoons while Garret gets the milk.

We pour our cereal and take it over to the couch. Garret turns on the TV. A morning news show is on and the woman at the news desk is talking.

"...at the upcoming debate. Now that Kent Gleason has secured the nomination he's putting all his focus on preparing for the debates in the hopes that he can boost his poll numbers in some of the swing states. Gleason's poll numbers overall have gone up significantly since he resuscitated a six-year-old boy on a beach in La Jolla last Friday."

A video shows Kent Gleason running up to a little boy lying on the sand with his mother next to him, crying out for help.

They cut to the mother being interviewed on the beach. "My son was swimming and the current just took him away. When I got him out of the water, he wasn't breathing."

"Garret, does she look familiar to you?"

He's eating his cereal, not really watching. "Who?"

"That lady. Look."

He glances at the TV. "I don't know her. Why? Should I?"

The mother is still talking. "Thank God Mr. Gleason came along when he did. He saved my son."

The camera pans out to the beach and shows the kid again, this time on a stretcher with Gleason and the paramedics around him. I spot an oddly shaped, large rock off in the distance behind them.

They cut to the newswoman again. "The boy was taken to a nearby hospital and is expected to make a full recovery. In other news..."

I take the remote and turn the volume down.

"That was weird," I say to Garret.

"What was weird?"

"I know I've seen that woman before."

"The mom of that kid?"

"Yes. I know I've seen her somewhere." I take a moment to think. "I saw her last summer at Kiefer's party. I think she was one of the servers. I remember because she kept offering me shrimp even though I kept telling her I didn't like shrimp."

"Huh. Well, that's too bad about her son. I hope he's okay."

"And that beach they were at. Didn't that look familiar to you?"

Garret sets his cereal bowl down on the table. "No. Why? Are you trying to tell me something here?"

I set my bowl next to his. "We've been on that beach, Garret."

"What are you talking about?"

"That was Harper's beach. It was the private beach behind her house."

"Jade, it wasn't the same beach. They said it was in La Jolla, not Malibu."

I jump up and get my phone and bring it back to the couch. I swipe through my photos until I find the ones I took of the beach behind Harper's house. "Look at this." I show it to Garret. "The slope of the sand, the red buoy in the water. It's the exact same as what they just showed. That kid was lying right here." I point to the spot on the photo.

"It's similar, but it's not the same beach. They have those red buoys all over the place."

I swipe to a different photo. "See that rock? It's the same one that was behind the kid when he was on the stretcher. When we were eating lunch with Harper's family out on the patio, I told you how I thought that rock looked like a mini volcano."

"Yeah, I remember you saying that, but I didn't see the rock in the video they just showed."

"It was there. I'm telling you, it was the exact same rock."

Garret gets up and takes our empty bowls to the sink. "What are you trying to say here, Jade?"

I meet him by the sink. "Gleason saved that kid on the beach behind Harper's house. Why would Kent Gleason and that server from the party be hanging out behind Harper's house? That's a private beach. And you can only access it from their backyard."

"Maybe Kiefer had a fundraiser at his house for Kent Gleason and maybe that woman was working as a server that night."

"Then why was her kid there?"

"Maybe it was a barbecue and people were allowed to bring their kids."

"They wouldn't let the hired help bring their kids. And why would the news say this happened in La Jolla if it really happened in Malibu?"

Garret hesitates, then says, "Because it's probably a fake story."

"What do you mean?"

"If you're right, and that video was filmed behind Harper's house and that woman was a server, then that whole story was fake. Kiefer filmed it just like he'd film a movie scene. That woman and the kid were probably actors. That whole thing was just a made-up story to make Gleason look like a hero so people will vote for him." Garret walks off toward the bedroom. "Come on. If you want to run, we need to get going."

I stand there, thinking about what he said. I guess I should've known it was a made-up story. I've seen Gleason being interviewed on TV and he doesn't seem like the type of guy who would save a kid on a beach. He seems completely self-absorbed, not interested in helping anyone but himself. I can see why he's not appealing to voters. That's why the organization needed that fake story. They need to get Gleason ahead in the polls so they can rig the election and have him win without people questioning it.

"Jade, let's go." Garret's yelling at me from the bedroom.

I meet him in there. "So if Kiefer made that video, it means he's involved with the organization and he knows about the election fraud."

Garret's in his shorts and t-shirt and putting his shoes on. "We already knew that about him."

"Not really. Before we were just guessing. Now it's confirmed."

"Jade, it doesn't matter what Kiefer's doing because we're staying out of all that shit, so stop thinking about it." He walks out of the bedroom. "I'm getting some water. You want some?"

"No, I'm good."

Sometimes I wonder if Garret knows more about Kiefer than he's telling me. Pearce knows what's going on with Kiefer and maybe he told Garret. If so, he'd tell Garret not to tell me because he'd worry I'd tell Harper. I'm sure she doesn't know what her dad is involved in. I wonder if Harper's mom, Kelly, even knows.

I hear Garret open the back door that leads to the beach. "Jade, we have to go."

"Yeah, I'm coming. Hold on."

Garret and I go on a short run, then shower and head to class. I have chemistry this morning. I took chemistry last spring but this is part two. I should've taken it last year, but back then I hadn't declared a major so didn't know what classes to take. I also had calculus last year but have to take another semester of it. So now I'm stuck taking chem 2, organic chem, and organic chem lab, along with advanced calculus and my psych class. I'm not looking forward to this semester.

After class, I go to the coffee shop, which is where Garret and I are meeting for lunch. He's not there when I arrive, so I find us a table and sit down.

I see Sara behind the counter. She looks really tired.

"Were you up all night?" I ask when she comes over.

"Yeah." She lets out a laugh. "You know what's funny? For most people my age, that question would refer to partying. But for me it means I spent the night massaging baby gums with teething ointment."

"So he's not getting any better, huh?"

"The stuff I put on his gums seemed to help. Poor little guy. I feel bad he's in so much pain. I went online and found some other things to try. I kind of figure it out as I go, you know?" She frowns. "That makes me sound like a terrible mom, doesn't it?"

"Not at all. I'm sure there's a lot to learn about taking care of a baby."

She sighs. "There's so much to learn. I have some books but they don't tell you half the stuff you need to know."

The door to the coffee shop opens and Garret walks in. Sara straightens up and smooths her apron as he approaches the table.

"Hey." He smiles at Sara, then sits next to me, putting his arm around the back of my chair. "I see you met my wife."

She looks confused. "Your wife?"

"That's who the coffee was for yesterday. This is my wife, Jade."

"Um, yeah, we've met." Sara says it slowly.

I look at Garret. "I didn't know you'd met Sara."

"I didn't know I had. She didn't tell me her name." He turns to her and extends his hand. "Hi, Sara. I'm Garret. Now we've officially met."

"Hi." She weakly shakes his hand.

"Jade was telling me you have a son."

"Yeah. His name's Caleb."

"She also said she volunteered us to babysit."

"Actually, I don't need you to now."

"Why not?" I ask her. "That guy said no to dinner?"

Sara's cheeks are bright red. She's probably embarrassed to talk about guys in front of Garret. That's girl talk.

Garret gets up. "I need to use the restroom. I'll be right back."

Sara waits for him to leave, then says, "I didn't ask that guy out. And I'm not going to."

"Why not?"

Sara slumps into the chair Garret was just sitting in. "Because you're married to him."

"Garret's the guy you were talking about?"

She nods.

I laugh. "I should've guessed that when you said it was a hot guy who was also nice."

"I'm so sorry. I didn't mean to say all that stuff about your husband. I swear, I thought he was single. I didn't see the ring."

"Don't worry about it. I think it's kind of funny."

We see him coming out of the bathroom. She grabs my arm. "Please don't tell him. I'm already so embarrassed."

"I won't tell him. I promise. It's our little secret."

She stands up and gives Garret his chair back. Her face is still red as she pulls out two menus. "I'll give you some time to decide what you want." She hurries off to the kitchen.

"She seems nervous or something," Garret says as he reviews the menu.

"She's just tired. Her baby is teething so she was up all night."

He shuts his menu. "Grilled ham and cheese. That's what I'm getting. What do you want?"

"I think I'll get the turkey."

"I'll go order at the counter so she doesn't have to come back here."

"I'll do it." I move around him and go up to the counter.

Sara's hiding in the back. She comes out when she sees me. "You didn't tell him, did you?"

"No. And I won't. So stop worrying about it. I wanted to give you our order."

She takes the order, then says, "I understand if you don't want to be friends with me now."

"Sara, it's fine. Really. I'm sure I'll be spending a lot of time here between classes and I'd like us to be friends. And if you ever find a single guy to take you to dinner, the baby-sitting offer still stands."

She smiles. "Thanks. Your order will be right up."

When Sara brings out our food later, she won't even look at Garret. I think she's afraid I'll get mad, which I would never do. It was just a misunderstanding and it's not like this hasn't happened before. I know other girls check out Garret and some of them probably flirt with him. They did at Moorhurst and they will here, too. That's what I get for marrying someone as hot as him.

After lunch Garret and I go to our afternoon classes, then we go to his doctor's appointment. I've avoided talking about his shoulder ever since he told me about it. He's already worried enough about it so I didn't want to keep bringing it up.

The appointment is at a small hospital 20 miles away. He has to have tests run on his shoulder and the hospital is the only place that had the equipment.

When we arrive, Dr. Cunningham is waiting for us in an office at the hospital. The office belongs to some other doctor and has diplomas on the wall and family photos on the desk.

I still don't know how Cunningham does this. How does he just step in and borrow someone else's office? And how is he able to use the hospital's equipment when he doesn't even work here?

"Garret. Jade." He greets us as we walk in, shaking our hands. "Congratulations on the marriage."

"Thanks." Garret's trying to act normal but I know he's nervous. He thinks these tests will tell him he can't swim anymore which is the last thing he wants to hear.

Cunningham takes a seat behind the desk and we sit in the chairs across from him.

"So the shoulder isn't getting any better," Cunningham says, his eyes on Garret. "I'm not going to lecture you here, Garret, but I will say that waiting this long to address this could mean you've done permanent damage. And you may need surgery."

"Yeah. I know."

Surgery? I'm already holding Garret's hand but I hold it even tighter after hearing that. I don't want him having surgery. Surgery is dangerous. Things can go wrong. Anesthesia can kill you. It's not likely, but it happens.

"We'll do some tests and go from there. The best case scenario is that we just have to get you back in physical therapy and this time you actually have to go."

Garret nods. "I will. What about swimming?"

"We'll have to see, but given what you told me on the phone about the pain you're having, I'm guessing you can't compete this year."

Garret doesn't respond. He just nods again, like he knew that would be the case.

Cunningham continues. "You also shouldn't be surfing until we get this healed. And weight lifting should be limited to whatever exercises the physical therapist gives you." He stands up. "Well, let's get you down to radiology."

I sit in the waiting room while they run whatever tests they're doing on Garret's shoulder. Then we leave and go out for dinner while we wait for the results. Normally we'd have to wait a few days, but Cunningham is able to consult with the radiologist right away so we don't have to.

Even this short wait is making me anxious because I have no idea what they're going to find. Last year on the news I saw a story about a teenage girl who had pain in her leg and thought she hurt it playing soccer, but when she had tests run they found out she had some kind of rare cancer.

Of course I would remember this now. I hadn't even thought about that in months. Why does my mind even go to these places? Garret does not have cancer. And he does not need surgery. He'll be fine. I know he will.

# *Chapter 18*

**GARRET**

*A*round 7 Jade and I go back to the hospital to get my test results. Jade's been really great about this whole thing. Ever since I told her about my shoulder, she hasn't forced me to talk about it or lectured me about how I should've taken care of this last year. She's just been there for me and I love her for that. It's exactly what I need right now. When I'm ready to talk about it, I will. But I can't until I know what's going to happen.

I didn't say much during dinner and I hardly touched my food. Jade talked a little about school and current events, trying to keep my mind off the test results. It was sweet of her to try, but it didn't work. I couldn't stop thinking about those tests and how the results could end my swimming career. I don't know what I'll do if I can't swim. Swimming is such a huge part of who I am and I can't give it up.

We meet up with Dr. Cunningham back in the office we met him at earlier. I have to know the results, so as soon as he sits down I say, "Just tell me how bad it is. Bottom line. Can I swim again?"

He shakes his head. "Not at a competitive level, at least not this year. But if you follow the treatment plan this time, I think you might be able to compete next year."

I sit back in my chair, relieved. I was holding Jade's hand really tight, but I relax my hold and thread our fingers together.

"So what's the treatment plan?"

The doctor opens up a folder and shows me a diagram of my shoulder and outlines the injured areas. The good news is that there isn't any new damage. The problem is that the old damage never healed because I didn't do what I was supposed to do to make it better.

"You'll have physical therapy for at least six months and then we'll reassess. I'm assigning you to a different physician and that's who you'll see going forward. He has ties to me but he's not part of the clinic. He already knows about your case and he'll be contacting you in the next week or so to check in. I'll give you his information. If you have questions, you'll need to call him, not me. He'll also contact your swim coach and tell him the plan."

"Does this plan involve any swimming?"

"Yes, you'll be given exercises to do in the pool and the weight room. This will take some time and effort on your part if you really want to compete next year."

"I'll do whatever it takes. I'm just happy I don't need surgery."

"I wish I could speed up the healing but I'm not allowed to—you know, give you anything."

He means he can't give me the shot like I got last year. Whatever was in that shot speeds healing and it seemed to work, at least until I injured the tissue again with my aggressive workouts.

The shot isn't available to the general public, which is what I'm part of now. I can no longer get the treatments offered by the clinic. I'm okay with that for myself, but I wish Jade could get their medical care. If she got sick someday, I'd want her to have the best possible care and the most innovative treatments, which is what she'd have if we still had access to the clinic. And if we had kids, I'd want them to have access, too. But it's not possible. I just have to accept that.

We get all the information we need, then say goodbye to Cunningham and head home. I don't talk much on the ride back but I feel a lot better than I did on the way to the hospital. At least now I have hope.

"So do you want to talk?" Jade asks when we get home. "I understand if you don't, but I'd like you to."

"We can talk." I bring her in for a hug, kissing the top of her head. "You've been great through all this, Jade. It meant a lot to me that you let me deal with this on my own timeline. I wasn't trying to shut you out, but I didn't want to discuss it until I knew the outcome."

"How do you feel about what he said?"

"Relieved. I thought for sure he'd say I could never compete again." I pull her over to the couch to sit down. "I'm so damn stupid. If I'd just done what they told me to do last year I'd be competing this season."

"You're not stupid. I would've done the same thing. When I hurt my knee I kept trying to jog on it so I could get back to running. We're both impatient when it comes to stuff like that."

"We are, aren't we?" I turn and face her on the couch. "Okay, so here's the deal. Now that we know this about ourselves, we need to help each other out. When you get hurt or sick, I'll make sure to keep you in line."

"Keep me in line? What does that mean?"

"It's a nice way of saying I'll kick your ass if you don't follow the doctor's orders. And you do the same for me. Because if we don't, we'll both have useless, broken-down bodies by the time we're 30."

She laughs. "Okay, I can do that. I'll even go to the pool with you when you do your workouts." She moves closer and smiles. "I miss our pool time."

"I do, too." I kiss her.

She pushes me down on the couch and straddles me. "I was looking in your treatment plan and it said frequent sex is recommended for faster healing."

I smile. "You said the same thing last year when you hurt your knee."

"Then it must be a common treatment for injuries because it was definitely in your plan."

"I didn't even see that."

"You didn't read it close enough. But it's in there. And since I have to force you to follow orders..." She leans down and kisses me as she undoes my belt.

I talk against her lips. "You gotta do what you gotta do."

"I'm such a good wife." She says it kiddingly, but it's true.

She's more than a good wife. She's the best, in so many different ways. And today just proved that, once again. Jade knew how nervous and anxious I was. When we got those test results, my mind was all over the place. I could barely concentrate. At times I wasn't even listening to the doctor. But Jade was fully absorbed in everything he had to say. When Cunningham went into detail about my treatment plan, she asked more questions than I did. She made the doctor explain everything and she even took notes. She wouldn't let us leave there until she was sure we had all the information we needed. She could've just sat there, but instead she took over when I wasn't able to. And I love her for that. It just shows how much she cares about me.

Later, as Jade and I are watching TV, my dad calls to see how the appointment went. I tell him the basics but then he starts asking me questions I can't answer.

"You'll have to ask my wife that stuff," I say to him. "She's taken over my health."

She laughs as she takes the phone. "I have not. I just listened better than your son did."

The two of them talk about me for a good 10 minutes and then she gives me the phone back.

"It sounds like she has your whole treatment plan memorized," my dad says. "She takes good care of you. You're lucky to have her."

"I know I am." I smile at Jade as she goes in the bedroom.

"Garret, I wanted to let you know I still haven't been able to locate that police report for the robbery at your neighbor's house."

"Maybe you just couldn't find it."

"It's a small police department and there isn't a lot of crime in that town. It should be easy to find the report."

"So what does this mean?"

"Nothing, at least not yet. It's just unusual and I'd like to look into it some more."

"Well, let me know what you find out."

"I will. By the way, Lilly started school today and she wants to tell you about it. I know you've been busy, but can you give her a call tomorrow?"

"Shit, I totally forget she started today. Yes, I'll definitely call her. How did her first day go?"

"I'm not sure yet. She was quiet when she came home. She didn't tell me much. She said she wanted to talk to you about it."

"Okay. I'll call her. Bye, Dad."

I go in the bedroom. Jade's already asleep. It's been a long day and she has class early tomorrow.

I get into bed. Her back is to me so I lean over her shoulder and whisper, "I love you. Thanks for taking care of me."

Her eyes are closed, but I see her smiling. "I'll always take care of you," she whispers back. "I love you, remember?"

I move her hair back and kiss the side of her face and she rolls over into my arms and falls back to sleep.

When we get home from class on Friday, I call Lilly. I used to be able to call her on her cell phone but Katherine took it away because she doesn't want me calling Lilly. Then I tried doing a video chat with Lilly but Katherine found out and took the computer away.

Things have gotten worse between Katherine and me ever since she and my dad broke up. She used to tolerate me because of him, but now she doesn't need to so she's being even bitchier than before. And since she has to pretend to be married to my dad, she's still living at the house. My dad tries not to fight with her for Lilly's sake, which means he avoids talking to Katherine at all. Talking just leads to fighting.

"Jade, I'm calling Lilly," I yell into the bedroom.

"Yeah, I'll be there in a minute."

The phone rings several times and then I hear Katherine's voice. "What do you need, Garret? Your father's not home yet."

"I need to talk to Lilly."

"She's busy. She has homework."

"She's only had school for two days and she's in second grade. I highly doubt she has homework."

"Goodbye, Garret."

"Put her on the damn phone, Katherine!"

"You think you'll get your way speaking to me that way?"

"She's my sister. I have a right to talk to her."

"And I'm her mother, which means I have the right to control who she speaks with."

"Your husband, Lilly's *father*, has asked me to speak with her. And you don't want to piss off my father, do you? You know how he gets when he's angry."

She hesitates. "You get five minutes. That's it."

I hear her heels clicking on the tile. "Lilly, Garret would like to speak with you."

"Garret?" It's Lilly. She sounds excited.

"Hi, Lilly. How was school?"

"Can I talk to him alone?" Lilly asks her mom.

"You know that's not allowed," I hear Katherine say.

I want to reach through the phone and strangle her.

"Lilly, put your mom back on the phone."

Katherine picks up again. "Four minutes, Garret."

"I have video," I say calmly.

"Video of what?" Katherine spits out.

"Of you. And you don't even want to fucking know the damage I could do with these videos. I've been saving them for when I need them and I think now is a damn good time to bring them out of storage."

It's true. When I was 15, I was coming down the stairs one day and I heard Katherine talking to someone in the living room. I went in there and saw she was alone but on the phone. She had her back to me so she couldn't see me. I stayed there and listened and figured out she was talking to her mom. Katherine was saying all this bad shit about her so-called rich friends, so I hid off to the side and got video of her saying all this stuff.

I continued to record these conversations until just last year, so I've got a lot of videos. The people she was gossiping about are rich, powerful, and well-known. If they found out she was saying these things about them, Katherine's reputation would be destroyed. She'd never be invited to another dinner party or charity ball. She'd be kicked out of the country club. It would be her worst nightmare.

I've considered putting these videos online for the world to see, but then I changed my mind because I didn't want to hurt my dad's reputation or the company's. But I don't think it would if I was strategic about it. I'd have to go back and review the videos to see which ones would be most damaging to Katherine but have the least effect on my dad.

"I don't believe you, Garret. I know how you lie to get your way."

"No, Katherine. That's what *you* do. So I guess I'll release the first video to the press tomorrow. Or maybe tonight."

"You have nothing."

"You really want to call my bluff? Good. I can't wait to see your face when you see the morning paper. I'll tell Dad to make sure he gets a picture."

There's silence and then, "What do you want?"

"I just want to talk to Lilly. Alone. Without a time limit. And if that's not acceptable to you, then get ready for some damage control. I'd suggest you lawyer-up."

"You're blackmailing me?"

"I'm a Kensington. What do you expect?"

"Lilly, take this and go to your room." Her voice sounds distant as she hands Lilly the phone.

I hear Lilly running up the stairs and down to her room and the door closing behind her.

"So how's everything going?" I ask her.

"I miss you, Garret." She says this every time I call and she always sounds sad. It breaks my heart.

"I miss you, too."

Jade comes running into the living room. I put the phone on speaker.

"Hi, Lilly," Jade says.

"Hi," she mumbles. It's not her usual enthusiastic response.

"You don't want to talk to Jade today?" I ask her.

"I don't know. I guess it's okay."

Jade frowns.

"What's wrong?" I ask Lilly. "Did you have a rough time at school?"

"I don't like it. I got in trouble."

"Why did you get in trouble?"

"Because I went to the bathroom."

"Did you ask your teacher first?"

"No."

"You have to ask the teacher first. You can't just get up and leave."

"Nobody told me that. I don't like those rules."

"I know, but school has lots of rules. I have rules at my school, too."

"Do you have to ask the teacher if you can go to the bathroom?"

"Yes." I smile at Jade. "And Jade does, too. It's a rule for everyone."

"Oh. Okay."

"Besides that, did you like your teacher?'

"Yes. She has blond hair and today she wore a pretty dress with flowers on it."

"Did you make some friends?" Jade asks her.

"Nobody wants to be my friend. They already have friends."

Jade gets closer to the phone. "It takes time to make friends. I haven't made any friends at my school either."

"Really?"

"Really. And today was my third day at school. You've only had two days. You need to give it more time. What about Jackie? I mean Jacqueline. Isn't she your friend?"

"I guess she is, but I don't really like her."

Jade's laughing and she motions me to talk.

"Then she's probably not your friend. You should like your friends, Lilly."

What am I saying? For most of my life, I didn't like my friends. They were chosen for me. Knowing Katherine, it wouldn't surprise me if she forced Lilly to be Jacqueline's friend because of whatever connections her parents have that Katherine needs or wants.

"Jacqueline doesn't like my dolls," Lilly says. "She says they're for kids. And she doesn't like to swim because her hair gets wet."

Jade's giving me the thumbs down and shaking her head.

"Maybe you should find a different girl to hang out with," I say.

"I like to play with Max."

"Max? Is that her nickname?"

"Max is a boy. His name is Maxwell, but everyone calls him Max."

I feel heat rising in my veins as I think of Lilly with some boy.

"Does he wear a bow tie?" Jade asks.

"Yeah. He has different colors. Today he wore a blue one."

"You shouldn't hang out with boys." I say it a little too forcefully.

Jade shakes her head at me. "What he means is that you should find some girls to play with. Boys are messy and loud and they smell bad."

"Garret doesn't smell bad."

"I don't *now*, but I used to smell *really* bad." I overemphasize the 'really.' "All boys do at your age. They don't grow out of it until they're *my* age. So stay far away from Max. And if he comes near you, spray him with air freshener."

Jade's laughing so hard she has to leave the room.

"I have to go," Lilly says. "I hear Dad downstairs and I want to see him before I go to bed."

"I'll talk to you later. Call me whenever you want."

"Okay, bye."

"And stay away from Max."

She already hung up.

I go in the bedroom. "What so funny?"

Jade's sprawled out on the bed, laughing. "You. Talking to Lilly."

"I had to say something to get her away from that kid. And you're the one who told her that stuff about boys."

"Spray him with air freshener?" Jade's got tears in her eyes, she's laughing so hard. "She'll get kicked out of school if she does that."

"Good. It'll get her away from Max." I lie on the bed, leaning against the headboard, my arms crossed over my chest.

Jade wipes her eyes and sits next to me. "Garret, Lilly's only 7. She's not interested in boys that way. She's just friends with him."

"Time's have changed, Jade. Boys start going after girls much younger now."

She laughs again. "You sound like an old man. We're not that old. Times haven't changed that much."

"That kid, Max, needs to back off and stop making moves on my sister."

"Seven-year-old boys don't have moves."

"*I* had moves at that age. Shit, I had moves in kindergarten."

Jade uncrosses my arms and hugs me, pressing her cheek against my chest. "If we have kids, and we have girls, is this how it's going to be? You're going to chase every boy away?"

My mind leaves Max and Lilly and all my focus turns to Jade. This is the first time she's ever brought up kids. She usually won't even talk about them. Sometimes I'll make a comment about us having kids and she tenses up and gets really quiet. I know she said 'if' just now but even that is a huge step for her. It's like she's actually considering maybe having kids someday.

I really want that. I want us to have kids and I still want three of them. I don't want them right now. We're not ready for that. We need to get through college and have a few years to get our careers going, but after that I want to start a family. I was beginning to think Jade would never agree to it, but now I'm thinking maybe it's a possibility. A distant possibility, but still a possibility.

# Chapter 19

**JADE**

"Garret, did you hear me?"

"Yeah, I was just trying to think of the various torture devices I would need if a guy ever got near my daughter."

"So you're saying she could never date? Not even when she's 16?"

"Sixteen? Hell, no! She can date when she's 40 or 50 or whenever I'm dead and not around to see it."

"You're terrible." I keep my arms around him. "If we have kids, you better hope they're not girls. I think they'd give you a heart attack."

"I'd take girls," he says quietly.

He smooths my hair as I close my eyes. It's been a stressful week and it feels good to just lie here as his hand moves down my back and up to my hair again, repeating the pattern.

I probably confused Garret just now with my comment about us having kids. I didn't mean to say it. It just kind of came out when we were talking about Lilly. Maybe because I've been thinking more about kids ever since we got married. I haven't told Garret that. I don't want to get his hopes up and then tell him I don't want them.

The thing is, I think I do want them. But as soon as I think that, I question it. I tell myself that maybe I only want them because Garret does. I love him so much that I don't want to deny him something he really wants. But I can't make a huge decision like that based only on what *he* wants. I have to make sure it's what I want, too, and that changes from day to day.

I haven't spent much time around kids so how do I know if I could even take care of one? What if I couldn't? Lilly is the only kid I've really been around. And I love her, and I love being her big sister, but it's not the same as being a parent.

As much as I've tried to get over it, I'm still scared to death of being a mom. I have been ever since Garret started bringing up the topic. Before I met him, I never even thought about it. I didn't think I'd get married so I definitely didn't think I'd have kids. And I was okay with that. I didn't feel like I was giving up anything. But falling in love with Garret changed all that. In my head, I can see him being a dad. I can imagine us playing outside with our kids and putting them to bed at night. And those images make me happy. Really happy. Then my internal panic button hits and I tell myself it'll never happen. That it *can't* happen because I don't trust that I'd make a good mom. I still fear I'll become the mom who raised me.

My mom's influence on me is more than I care to admit. As much as I've forgiven her, part of me still hates her for what she did to me. I hate how much she's affected me as a person. I blame her for my indecision over having kids. I should want them, right? Doesn't everyone? I guess some people don't, so maybe I'm just one of those people. But I don't think I am. When I saw that photo of Sara's baby, I got this warm feeling inside. He looked so sweet and tiny and I just wanted to pick him up and hold him. I thought that was a sign I should be a mom, but then I realized everyone feels that way about babies.

I'm so confused. I don't know what I want. I need to think about it some more. I don't have to decide right now. Garret wouldn't want kids for years. He wants to get through college and maybe get his MBA or start his business. So I have time.

"It's Friday night." Garret's voice startles me. "You want to go out?"

"Where do you want to go?"

"Let's go to a movie. Friday night's date night, right?"

I look up at him. "Do you have a date?"

"Are you saying I don't?"

"You should *ask* a girl on a date, not just assume she'll go out with you. I bet even Max knows that."

"Hey, don't start talking about bow-tie boy. I'm trying to forget about him."

"Are you going to ask me out or not?"

He tucks my hair behind my ear and says very formally, "Jade. Would you go out with me this evening to the local cinema?"

"Do I get to pick the movie?"

"Yes."

"Do I get popcorn?"

"Yes."

"Do I get a cold beverage of my choice?"

"Yes."

"What about candy?"

"No, just popcorn."

"Why can't I have candy?"

"Movie, popcorn, a cold beverage, and me. I think I've offered enough here, Jade."

He always makes me laugh when he's so serious.

"Just one more request before I'll go on a date with you."

"You can ask, but there's a good chance I'll say no."

"You won't say no." I kiss him.

"What is it?"

"Can I take you home after the movie and have my way with you?"

"I think I'll need you to define what that means before I agree to it."

I rub my hand over the front of his jeans and whisper over his lips. "I'd like you to strip me naked and—"

He kisses me before I can finish. "Forget waiting until after the movie. We're doing it right now."

We end up going to the late show. Date night heated up fast and the sex portion of the night went on a little longer than planned.

I love date night. I hope Garret asks me out again.

Over the weekend I force myself to do homework and study. It's really hard to stay focused when the sand and the ocean are right outside my window and I just want to lay out in the sun. And then Garret keeps breaking my concentration by watching TV or doing stuff in the kitchen or kissing me or luring me to the bedroom for sex.

It's Sunday and I asked for buttermilk pancakes this morning because the price of five kisses was more affordable timewise than the price of the other pancakes. But then we ended up doing it this afternoon so I didn't really save any time.

Now it's 7:30 and we just finished dinner and I know I should study some more but I can't. I'm too tired. I can't believe how much work my professors assigned the first week of the semester.

"Why do I have so much homework and you don't have any?" I ask Garret as I wash the last pan in the sink. Garret made spaghetti and since he made the meal, I'm on clean-up duty. That's the deal we have, but he always ends up helping me.

"I have homework. I just don't have as much as you." He takes the pan from me and dries it. "Speaking of that, I need to do some reading before class tomorrow."

"Then while you're doing that, I'm going to call Frank and Ryan before it gets too late there."

"Tell them I said hi."

I take the phone out to the deck and call Frank. Ryan answers. "Hey, Jade. Sorry I missed your call the other day."

"It's my fault. I called at the wrong time. I keep forgetting the time difference."

"Dad told me about your classes. Sounds like a tough schedule."

"Your schedule is just as bad."

"I know, but I had to cram in all those classes so I can graduate this year. At least I don't have to work. That's a huge relief."

It's a relief for me, too. Last year, I was starting to think Ryan would never go back to school. Even with his job, the bills were piling up. But after I gave Frank that money, everything changed. Ryan quit his job, took summer classes, and now he's back on track to graduate in May and start med school next fall. He's already been accepted to the same school Chloe goes to. Taking last year off means Ryan will be starting med school a year later than he planned, but at least he's going. Without that money, I don't know if he would've been able to.

"Go tell Frank to get on the phone so I can talk to both of you."

"He's um, busy." Ryan sounds weird, almost like he's half-serious, half-laughing.

"Busy doing what? Is he in the bathroom or something?"

"No, he went out."

"What do you mean he went out? It's Sunday night. And it's 9:30 there. He never goes out that late."

"Well, he did tonight." There's hidden meaning in Ryan's tone but I'm not getting the message.

"Just tell me, Ryan. What's going on there?"

"Dad is, um, out having dinner with a friend."

"A friend? What friend? Like a friend he used to work with?"

"No, like a lady friend." He laughs as he says it.

"Yeah, that's funny, Ryan. Where's he really at?"

"I'm not joking. Dad's on a date."

I jump up from my chair. "No freaking way!"

Ryan's full-out laughing. "I know, right? I reacted the same way when he told me he was going out with her."

"Wait—where did he meet this woman? He never leaves the house except to go to his doctor's appointments."

"That's how he met her. He's been going to his appointments without me since he can drive now. And if he gets there too early or has to wait for test results, he goes over to the hospital next to the clinic and has coffee in the cafeteria. This woman he's out with tonight is a nurse, and one day last summer they got to talking in the cafeteria and that led to getting coffee at a restaurant and now dinner."

"What's she like? Have you met her?"

"I've met her a couple times. She's nice. I think you'd like her. She's around 50. She doesn't have kids. Her husband died 10 years ago in a car accident."

"What does she look like?"

"Tall, like 5'9, with short, blond hair. She's thin. She runs half marathons."

"So Frank has a tall, blond, athletic girlfriend?"

"When you put it that way, damn, I guess he did pretty good, didn't he? And he didn't even ask her out. She asked *him* out."

"Are you serious?"

"Yeah. I think she got tired of waiting for Dad to ask her out so she asked him out instead. He hasn't dated for a while. He's out of practice."

"She doesn't know about his money, does she?"

"No. She has no idea. Even if she knew, I don't think she'd go after his money. She's got her own money. Her parents sold their farmland and made a boatload of cash and gave her and her sister a big chunk of it. And I'm sure she got an insurance settlement when her husband died."

"Where did they go on their date?"

"Some Italian place downtown. She picked him up in her Lexus. He was all dressed up. I felt like I was sending my kid off to prom."

Ryan and I shouldn't laugh but we do anyway.

"Do you think they'll go on another date?"

"Probably. They should've been home an hour ago, so if the date's still going on, then I'm guessing it's going well."

"This is so strange. I don't know if I can handle Frank dating."

"You? You're not the one living with him. What if he brings her back here and they go in his room? You know how thin the walls are in this house. I can't listen to that. They'll have to go to her place if they want to do stuff."

"Ryan, don't talk about it! I can't think about Frank that way. We need to get off this topic. How's Chloe?"

"Good. Did I tell you I bought a ring?"

"No! What the hell is going on there? Frank's dating? You're buying engagement rings?"

"Just one ring. Not plural," he kids.

"You know what I mean."

"I'm not proposing to her anytime soon. I just saw this ring that I knew she'd like and I didn't want the store to not have it when I'm ready to propose. So I bought it. It was expensive but it didn't cost six figures like the rings some people have." He says it jokingly.

"How do you know what my ring cost?"

"I asked Garret when I was out there in July. It's a nice ring and I wanted to know how much something like that cost."

"I didn't want you to know."

"Why? Garret's loaded. It's not like that was a lot of money to him."

Ryan doesn't know that Garret lost his trust fund and I can't tell him because telling him would mean explaining why he lost it, which is a huge secret.

"You should marry Chloe next summer. You could have the wedding here in California on the beach like I did."

"Chloe's family is in Iowa so I'm sure we'll be having it in Des Moines. But maybe a honeymoon in California."

"So what do you think? A summer wedding?"

"Stop rushing me into marriage. Let me enjoy my bachelor years a little longer."

"Fine. But Chloe may get tired of waiting and go find someone else. Then you'll be stuck trolling the hospital cafeteria for women."

"Worked for Dad. It could work for me, too."

"I better let you go. You need to check on Frank and his date. You know how kids are on prom night."

"I know. And I forgot to give him condoms. We might be getting a sibling out of this date."

I laugh. "I'll talk to you later, okay?"

"Yeah, and hey, don't say anything to Dad about this. I don't want him knowing I told you. He'll tell you himself when he's ready to."

"I won't say anything. Bye, Ryan."

As I'm getting up to go inside, I hear a noise out front. It sounds like the garbage can fell over. It's a windy night and it tends to tip over since we never have much in it. I walk around to the driveway and see it lying on its side, empty. I turn it upright and wheel it closer to the garage.

"What was that noise?" Garret asks as I'm walking into the house.

"The wind blew the trash can over. We should put something in it to weigh it down. Otherwise it'll just tip over again."

"I took the trash out twice this week. There are at least two bags in there."

"No, there's nothing in there. I just checked."

"That can't be right. I know there were two bags in there."

"Maybe the garbage guy came early."

"They don't pick up garbage on Sundays." Garret gets his phone out. "Did you see anyone out there?"

"No. Nobody."

He swipes through his phone. "These are all fuzzy. The wind must be shaking the cameras."

"What are you looking at?"

"The video from the security cameras."

"Why? You think someone stole our garbage?"

"Yeah. I do."

"Why would someone want our garbage?"

"To get our bills, our receipts, anything else that has personal information on it. Like that cop said, that robber might have friends. They could be searching our garbage trying to find out who we are to see if we're worth stealing from. Or they could be looking for stuff that would let them steal our identity." He sets his phone down. "You're sure there was nothing in the trash can? Not anything?"

"You can look for yourself but I know it was empty."

He goes outside to check. I follow him and watch as he opens the lid. He pulls out a black garbage bag. And then another. "Jade, there are two bags in here. Just like I said."

"I see that, but I don't understand. I was just out here and it was empty."

"It's a deep garbage can and these were way at the bottom. You just didn't see them."

"Okay, well, anyway, let's go inside. I've gotta tell you what Ryan said."

When we're back in the house, Garret asks, "So what's new with Ryan?"

"You gotta sit down for this." I push him down on the couch. "Frank, as in the-man-I-consider-my-father-Frank, went out on a date tonight!"

I wait for Garret's reaction.

"Good for him." He says it casually, like this happens every day.

"Garret!" I climb on his lap, straddling him. "You're supposed to have more of a reaction. This is Frank we're talking about. The man who hasn't been on a date the entire time I've known him. And get this—she asked HIM out!"

"Did Ryan tell you anything about her?"

"Yeah, she's a tall blonde who runs half marathons. She's a nurse, widow, no kids. He met her at the hospital. She picked him up for their date tonight." I'm talking fast so I stop to take a breath. "This is so crazy."

"Why is it crazy? Frank's a good guy. I'm sure a lot of women would want to go out with him."

"It's crazy because he never acted like he was interested in dating."

"Because he didn't have anyone he wanted to date. Now he does."

"Do you think they kissed? They had to have, right? I bet they're home now and kissing on the front porch like a couple of teenagers."

Garret laughs. "Now who sounds like an old person? What do you care if they kiss? You're not their parent."

"Well, they better not take it beyond kissing. They have to wait until they're married, or at least engaged."

"Yeah, because that's what *we* did, right?" He brings my face to his for a kiss.

"We're young. We lack self-control. I *still* lack control when it comes to you."

"Maybe Frank loses control when he's around the hot blond nurse."

"I didn't say she was hot. I just said she's blond."

"I bet Frank thinks she's hot," Garret says, smiling.

"Okay, enough about Frank. Here's the other news. Ryan bought an engagement ring."

"Oh, yeah? When is he proposing?"

"At his slow pace, probably not for 10 years. He found the ring he wanted so he bought it. I told him he should marry her next summer and he yelled at me for trying to take away his bachelor years." I sit back and look at Garret. "Do you ever regret not having more time as a bachelor?"

"No. What's so great about being a bachelor? You go out and get drunk and hit on girls every night. I already did all that in high school. I'm over it."

Garret says that, but sometimes I wonder if he thinks he's missing out on stuff being married at this age. I don't mean getting drunk and hitting on girls, but just going out. He likes being social way more than I do.

I wouldn't mind if Garret went and hung out with some of the guys from school. But I think he stays home because he feels bad leaving me here alone. He did the same thing last year when we were at Moorhurst. He went out with me instead of his guy friends. But at least back then he had his swim team. Now he has nothing but me, and I think he needs more than that. I know he does.

The rest of the night Garret watches TV while I force myself to study some more. I wasn't going to, but I have two quizzes next week and I'm not ready for either one of them. It's only the first week of the semester and I feel like I'm already way behind.

Monday morning after class, I go to the library to study. Then I meet Garret for lunch, go to my afternoon classes and then the library again. To keep up with my homework and get decent grades, I'm going to have to study a lot. The classes here are definitely harder than the ones at Moorhurst.

I've been at the library for hours now and I can't be in here anymore. I pack up my backpack and go outside. I'm meeting Garret in 15 minutes. I could just wait on one of the benches but that would mean more sitting and I can't sit any longer. I'll just take a short walk to stretch my legs. I have time to make a quick loop around campus.

It's a really beautiful campus. I should study out here under a tree instead of in the library. The campus is full of big shade trees along with some smaller trees that have brightly colored flowers on them. There are also flowery bushes along the outside perimeter, concealing the fence.

The campus is surrounded by a tall, black iron fence that looks nice but also provides security. Camsburg is known for having good security, which is one of the main reasons Garret and I picked it. They don't let just anyone walk on campus. You have to enter and leave through the front entrance gate, which is monitored by a guard station. I always thought the only way off campus was that front entrance but I just saw a guy going out a side gate. I never noticed it before because of all the bushes that hide the fence. Nobody else seems to notice it either because there aren't any students anywhere near it, other than the guy I just saw.

If I'd known that gate was there, I could've saved myself a lot of time getting to my car. I always park on the side street and to get there I have to go out the front entrance of campus, down the main street, then back up the side street. This would be a huge shortcut.

I walk over to the gate to find out exactly where it leads, but I can't see anything other than a small green building with a sign on it that says 'maintenance.'

I'm guessing the street is just beyond that maintenance building. I go through the gate and notice a faculty parking lot to my left. I walk around the maintenance building and straight ahead I see the street where my car is parked.

This is way shorter than my usual route. I'm glad I found this. Garret will be happy about it, too. He's always saying how the campus should have more than one exit.

I hear some commotion in the faculty parking lot and look back and see the guy I spotted earlier, the one I saw going through the gate. He looks a few years older than me, like a grad student. I bet he's a teaching assistant and that's why he gets to park in the faculty lot.

There's another guy with him and they seem to be arguing. The grad student has a small bag in his hand and is passing something to the other guy. It's money. Wait—is this a drug deal? I don't want to be around this!

I start walking back toward the gate. The two guys are getting louder and I glance over and get a look at the drug dealer. I do a double take when I see his face.

It's the burglar. The guy who robbed the house just down from ours. He's supposed to be in jail. That cop said they caught the guy and arrested him. They must've let him out of jail.

This is bad. I need to get out of here.

I walk faster toward the gate. I don't want to draw attention to myself by running. I keep my head down, not looking at them. I can still hear them arguing and they're getting louder. It's making me nervous.

The maintenance building is just a few feet away so I speed up and duck behind it. I'm thinking I should wait here until they go away. I don't want them seeing me.

I hear one of the guys yell, "What the fuck?"

I peek out the side of the building and see the burglar/drug dealer's body on the ground. Did he pass out? I see a line of blood coming from his head, pooling on the ground. Oh my God. I think he's been shot.

Shit! This is bad. Really, really bad.

What is going on here? Did the grad student shoot him? I didn't even hear a gun go off. Maybe he has a silencer on it.

My heart's racing, my breathing shallow. I remain hidden behind the maintenance building.

"Somebody help!" I hear the grad student yell.

I peek out again and see him holding his phone in the air, like he's trying to find a signal. Why is he calling for help if he shot the guy?

As I'm watching him, I see the phone drop from his hand and he staggers back. He falls to the ground, blood streaming down his face.

Holy crap! He just got shot, too!

Who shot him? Is someone hiding in the bushes? Or maybe behind a car?

I get my phone out. I need to call the police and get someone out here as fast as possible.

My phone is on, but when I dial 9-1-1 nothing happens. I check my phone. The battery's charged but there's no signal. How could there be no signal? I always have a signal on campus.

I have to get out of here. But what if the shooter's close to me? What if the person is on the other side of the maintenance building?

The gate that leads back to campus isn't that far away. If I ran really fast, I might be able to make it before this person sees me. But if the shooter *does* see me, he'll shoot me. And I'll be dead like the two guys in the parking lot.

I can't believe this is happening! I just wanted to take a quick walk before meeting up with Garret. And now I might end up getting killed! Shit!

My eyes are still on the gate. I have to do it. I have to make a run for it. I'm a runner. I can sprint to the gate.

I take off and in four long strides I'm there. But the gate won't open! I try the handle over and over again, checking behind me to see if someone's there. I don't see anyone, but I didn't see the shooter when he took down those guys either.

The gate is at least eight feet high. I don't think I can climb it. And even if I could, I'd be making myself an even more obvious target and get shot for sure. I wiggle the handle on the gate, then yank on it repeatedly. It still won't open. And then it hits me. The gate is locked. It's another security measure to keep unauthorized people from getting on campus. The faculty who use this parking lot must have a key or some other way to open it.

Now my only option is to turn around and walk back to the street, so that's what I do, hoping the shooter doesn't notice me. I walk at a normal pace and reach in my backpack and pull out my headphones, pretending I'm just a college student headed to class, having no idea what just happened.

I make it all the way down the side street, then turn onto the main street and keep walking. There are people all around me and I'm finally able to breathe. I pick up my pace and when I reach the front entrance of the campus, I stop at the security guard station.

"I heard some guy's fighting up by the library," I say to the campus cop. "You should go check it out. They sounded really angry."

"Can you show me where?"

I didn't want to get involved in this, but I have to get help. Maybe one of those guys is still alive.

"Yeah, it was up the hill, behind the fence," I say as the campus cop follows me.

As we're walking, I get my phone out and check the signal. It's back. What the hell? I see Garret up ahead, waiting for me in front of the library. I text him because I don't want to tell him about this with the campus cop next to me.

My text reads, *Something happened. Can't explain. I'm walking toward you with a campus cop. Meet up with me. Go along with what I say.*

"So you said you heard a fight?" the cop asks.

"Yeah. It was really loud." I shrug. "But maybe it was nothing."

Garret walks over to us, a worried look on his face.

I smile at him, but my body is shaking. "Hey. Sorry I'm late."

I give him a look, reminding him to pretend everything's normal.

"Hey." He gets my message but he still looks worried because he can feel that I'm shaking. He puts his arm around me as we walk.

"Are you her boyfriend?" the cop asks.

"He's my husband," I say.

"Oh." The cop looks at us, like he's trying to guess our ages.

I point to the gate. "So I saw a guy go out this gate and then I heard the fighting. I didn't even know there was a gate here until today. Where does it go to? The street?" I try to play dumb so he won't think I was anywhere near the crime scene.

"It's not meant for students," the cop says. "It goes to the faculty parking lot. And there's a maintenance building back there." He opens the gate.

"Okay, well anyway, that's where I heard it." I turn to leave, taking Garret with me.

"Wait." The cop stops us. "Come here. I might need you to identity the guy you saw going through the gate. The one you think was involved in the fight."

Garret squeezes my hand. He's giving me a look like he wants an explanation but I can't give him one. Not right now.

I'm realizing this was a really bad idea. I never should've said anything to the campus cop because now I'm going to be involved in whatever this is. I'll be interviewed by the real cops and then there'll be an investigation. And whatever comes after that.

"We really have to be going," I tell the cop.

"It'll just take a minute. You made me come all the way over here. You need to at least show me where to look." The guy sounds annoyed. Seriously? Like he really has anything better to do? He just sits in the security guard station all day.

I hesitate because the killer might still be out there, although I'm sure he's left by now. Why would he stick around?

"Are you coming?" He holds the gate open.

"Yeah. Okay." I follow him through the gate with Garret right behind me.

"It sounded like they were over there." I motion to the parking lot as we walk past the maintenance building.

"Nobody's out here," the cop says, walking ahead of us and scanning the lot.

"Maybe they're in their cars."

The cop checks some of the cars and as he does, Garret leans down and whispers, "What the hell's going on?"

"I'll tell you later," I whisper back.

"They must've left." The cop turns and walks back toward me.

I take a few steps to the right so I can see the area where the two bodies are lying. But they're not there. I know they were between two cars but I wasn't really paying attention to what the cars looked like. Maybe I have the wrong spot.

I walk around a little, checking between the other cars.

"What are you doing?" I hear the cop ask.

"Nothing." I turn and smile. "I saw a cat running under the cars but she ran off. I really like cats."

Garret's looking at me like I'm crazy.

"Whatever fight you think you heard, it's over now." The cop motions us back to the gate. "Let's go."

He uses a key card to unlock the gate and when we're back on campus, he just walks off.

"What the hell was that about?" Garret asks when the cop is gone.

"I'll tell you when we get home." I'm shaking even more now. Even my voice is shaky.

Garret notices and leads me to a bench to sit down. "What's wrong?"

I lean over and talk in his ear. "Two guys were shot in the parking lot. I was there, hiding behind the maintenance building. I saw them drop to the ground. I saw the blood. They were shot in the head. They weren't moving. I'm almost positive they were dead. And now the bodies are gone."

Garret squeezes his eyes shut, then opens them again. "Fuck."

"What does that mean? Are you just upset or does that mean something?"

He takes my hand and gets up from the bench. "Let's go."

When we're back home I tell him what happened, including how my cell phone signal was gone but then appeared again a few minutes later.

We're sitting on the couch and Garret's quiet, his eyes on the coffee table.

"What is it, Garret? Why aren't you saying anything?"

"I'm just trying to figure this out. It could've been a drug deal that got messed up. Like maybe a rival drug dealer got pissed off this other guy was taking his customer. Or—"

"Or what?"

He sighs. "Or it could've been they wanted it to look that way, in case someone walked by and saw what happened and reported it."

"What are you talking about? Who's 'they'?"

He gives me that look. The one that tells me the organization is involved.

I shake my head. "No. You're wrong. Why would they be here in this town? And why would they care about a drug deal?"

"It's not about the drug deal. It's about those two guys. They wanted one of them dead so they waited for the right time. Maybe they knew that guy was a drug dealer so they followed him and took him down during a deal, so if anyone saw what happened it'd just look like a drug deal gone bad."

"But what about the other guy? You're saying they'd kill an innocent guy just to kill the drug dealer?"

Garret nods, his gaze back on the table. "Or maybe they wanted both of them dead."

"I don't understand. Why would they care about either one of those guys?"

Garret shrugs. "I don't know."

"Why do you think it was them? Maybe some other drug dealer killed those guys because they owed him money or something."

"It's possible. But getting rid of the bodies like that? It sounds like them. They clean up their messes."

My stomach feels sick and my head's starting to throb. I can't handle the idea of the organization being here. They're supposed to be gone. Out of our lives. Far away, on the East Coast.

"Maybe drug dealers clean up their messes, too."

"Yeah. They might. Maybe it's not them." Garret's tone is not at all convincing.

"The phone." I take my phone out and hold it up to him. "The way my phone had no signal. Did they do that? I mean, is that something they do?"

"Anyone could do that if they had the right equipment."

"My phone had no signal that first day I met Arlin. After he took me to that office, he sent me home and had the signal disabled in the car so I couldn't call you. Or anyone."

"Yeah. I remember."

Garret doesn't elaborate but I'm sure we're thinking the same thing. The pieces all seem to point to the organization.

"It can't be them, Garret. I can't handle dealing with them again."

"Whatever happened today, it doesn't have anything to do with us. We have no connection to either one of those guys." He holds my shoulders. "You sure nobody saw you there? Like absolutely sure?"

"I don't know. But if they saw me, they would've done something, right?"

He brings me into his chest, holding me tightly in his arms.

He doesn't answer my question, but he doesn't need to. I know the answer. They would've killed me.

# Chapter 20

**GARRET**

*I* spent the past hour trying to calm Jade down. I think I've convinced her what she saw was a drug deal that didn't go as planned. I told her the burglar who was dealing drugs probably had his boss hiding in the bushes and something went wrong with the deal and he shot the two guys. It's not like this doesn't happen and it's possible that's what she saw. And I think Jade believes that now. I just can't convince *myself* of it.

After I calmed her down, Jade was tired from all the stress so we went in the bedroom and I laid down with her. Now she's asleep so I get up and go in the living room to call my dad.

"Hey, I need to tell you something," I say when he answers. "Can you talk?"

"Yes. What is it?"

"Shit, I probably shouldn't say this over the phone. I wasn't even thinking of that when I called you."

"I'm on a secure line."

"Yeah, but I'm not sure if mine is secure."

"They shouldn't be tracing you anymore. Technically it's against the rules. So go ahead."

"Jade saw something today. Something she shouldn't have seen."

"Go on."

"She went out a side exit on campus and it led to a parking lot where she saw two guys doing a drug deal. One of them was the burglar."

"The one who robbed your neighbors?"

"Yeah. I guess they let him out of jail."

"That's not what my sources say."

"Then your sources are shit because Jade's sure it was him."

"It's possible they let him out last night or this morning. He must have got out on bail."

"Who would pay his bail? I thought—"

"Just continue, Garret."

"The burglar, the guy selling the drugs, got shot. And then the guy *buying* the drugs got shot and Jade doesn't know who did it. She was hiding behind a building and she saw the guys fall to the ground but she didn't hear any shots and she didn't see who shot them. She tried to call the police but her phone couldn't get a signal. She went back to campus and told one of the Camsburg cops that she heard some guys fighting and to check the parking lot. The cop made us go with him and when we got there, the bodies were gone."

There's silence on the other line.

"Dad, are you still there?"

He lets out a heavy sigh. "Yes."

"Do you think it's them?"

"I'd have to look into it. If they were involved in this, they'd have to be somehow connected to the burglar. Or the other man. Does Jade know who the other man was?"

"No, but she thinks he might be a grad student. Dad, you've gotta find out what's going on here. Jade's freaking out and so am I."

"Listen, Garret. This didn't involve you or Jade so you shouldn't have anything to worry about."

"But Jade saw what happened. So now it *does* involve us. If they saw her—"

"She wouldn't be with you right now. She would've been taken care of at the scene."

My chest tightens when I hear him say 'taken care of' because I know what that means. I've overheard my dad use those same words when talking about other people. People I don't know. People who saw stuff they shouldn't have and who my dad had to 'take care of' by order of the organization. I try to forget he does that stuff but then he says things like that and I'm forced to think about it.

"Garret, it's quite possible that what Jade saw was simply a drug deal that didn't go as planned. Maybe it involved gangs. Or organized crime. In either of those cases, it would make sense for the bodies to be taken and disposed of so that all evidence is destroyed."

"I know, but you'll still check on this, right? See if you can find anything out?"

"Yes. Of course. Try to get Jade to calm down. If whoever did this suspects Jade saw something, he might be watching her, and she'll appear even more suspicious if she walks around looking fearful and anxious."

"Yeah. I'll talk to her."

"You know, it's not too late to move back here."

"What are you talking about?"

"You and Jade might feel better living closer to home. You wouldn't have to live in Connecticut. You could live in Boston. There are some excellent colleges there and you'd be much closer to—"

"Dad, no. We're not moving. We just need to figure out what's going on here. Like you said, maybe it's not them. Maybe we're just paranoid and making this into something it's not."

"Even so, I think you'd feel safer if you lived out here. You've never been this far from home before."

"Yeah, I have. You sent me to boarding school in London."

"That's right." His tone lightens. "You almost burned the place down. Cost me a fortune."

"Sorry about that." I laugh, then get serious again. "Dad, I'm not a kid anymore. I can't run home whenever there's a problem. I can handle being out here. And everything would be fine if I knew they weren't going to bother us."

"They won't. I'll make sure of it. Don't worry about this. Just focus on school. And Jade. Let me worry about the rest."

"I need to know if you find out anything."

"Yes. I'll keep you informed."

"Okay. Call me soon."

"I will. Goodbye, Garret."

I feel a little better after talking to him. He's right. There are a lot of bad people out there who have nothing to do with the organization. And they could've easily disposed of the bodies. Tossed them in the trunk of a car or the back of a van and been gone within a minute. As for the cell phone signal? They sell shit online to disrupt signals. Any criminal could access that equipment.

When Jade wakes up I tell her what my dad said. I tell her his theory that it could be a crime ring or other drug dealers and that he doubts it's the organization. But it's not completely true. I know my dad thinks there's a strong possibility they're involved, but he's trying to downplay it until he knows for sure. He doesn't want to worry me. And I don't want to worry Jade. Like my dad said, she needs to play it cool and not act like she knows shit she shouldn't know.

She seems more relaxed after we talk. But I'm not. I still don't feel safe. I'm starting to think I never will.

The next few days I'm on high alert, paying extra attention to our surroundings and the people around us. But I don't notice anything suspicious. Nobody seems to be following us and we haven't had any strange phone calls or people hanging around our house or parked on our street.

The thing that concerns me is that I never heard anything on the news about those two guys being missing. Maybe nobody would care about the criminal, but the other guy? The grad student? I'm sure he has family or friends who are looking for him, but I didn't hear anything about him on the news or on campus. There haven't even been any missing person signs posted. It's like the whole incident was covered up and people were silenced, which is exactly what the organization does.

But my dad did some investigating and he doesn't think they're involved. He didn't tell me exactly what he did to find this out. I'm guessing he talked to some of the members and got information without actually saying why he needed it. He's good at that. He can ask questions without the person realizing why he's asking.

So I guess this didn't have anything to do with the organization. It was just a random crime. But I still find the whole thing really strange.


Three weeks have passed and Jade's been so busy she hasn't had time to worry about the shooting. She's completely consumed with school, to the point I'm starting to get concerned. She studies all the time and then says it's still not enough.

I feel like we barely see each other anymore. I see Jade when we're in the car riding to and from campus, then sometimes at lunch, and then when we're in bed at night. That's about it.

Jade's been struggling to keep up with her classes and it's totally stressing her out. The other day she yelled at me just for walking in the room when she was studying. She apologized to me later but I wasn't mad at her about it. I know she didn't mean to yell at me. She's just really stressed and I'm worried about her. I've never seen her like this. She wasn't this way last year.

She's taking really hard classes and she has tougher competition here so her grades aren't as perfect as she'd like them to be. I tried to tell her she doesn't have to get all A's but then she accused me of thinking she's not smart enough to get A's. That's not what I meant but I didn't argue with her. I have to be careful what I say around her now. Every little thing seems to set her off.

As for me, my classes are harder than the ones I had at Moorhurst, but unlike Jade, I don't obsess over getting A's. I'm fine with a mix of A's and B's and the occasional C. I strategically place my efforts on the classes and assignments I'll get the most out of, or what interests me the most. For example, I'm interested in finance and entrepreneurship so I put a lot of effort into those classes. I have zero interest in accounting so I slack off a little in that class. I'll never remember that stuff anyway. And when I have my own business someday, I'll hire someone to do my accounting.

Jade doesn't think that way. To her, every class is important, even if it's not in her major. She's taking an elective psych class and she's already stressing about a paper that's not due until November.

When we're home, Jade's constantly studying. We only have dinner together a couple times a week. Instead of eating a meal, she just snacks all night while she studies. Our sex life is suffering, too. I think she wants to do it, but she's so tired from studying she falls asleep as soon as we get into bed.

I've been tired, too. In addition to classes, I have physical therapy three times a week. I usually have it noon to 1, which is why Jade and I haven't been eating lunch together. And the therapist has me doing exercises in the pool and weight training at the gym. So it seems like I'm never home, and when I *am* home, I try to spend time with Jade but she tells me she can't because she has to study.

Things can't keep going on this way. I need to intervene somehow but I'm not sure what to do. Jade doesn't want to go anywhere on the weekends, or go out for dinner during the week, or watch TV at night. She's completely focused on school. She hasn't even talked to Harper much.

A few weeks ago Harper emailed Jade the phone number of the friend she went to high school with who lives here now. Her name is Brook and Jade was supposed to call her but she hasn't. She doesn't think she has time for friends, although she *is* friends with Sara, but she usually only sees her at the coffee shop between classes.

Actually, Sara's coming over tonight for a couple hours and bringing her baby along. Jade's getting a short lesson in baby care because she agreed to babysit for Sara next week. Sara has a job interview at an architecture firm and she needs someone to watch Caleb. She's interviewing for a secretary job that pays a lot more than the coffee shop. Jade really wants to help Sara out so she's willing to give up her study time to babysit.

"She's here," Jade says as she looks out the window. "Are you still going to the gym?"

"Yes." I kiss her cheek. "I just need to pack my gym bag and then I'll go. I won't bother you."

"You're not bothering me." She rests her head on my shoulder and sighs. "I'm sorry. I promise we'll spend more time together. I just have so much to do."

She says this almost every day and then we never spend time together. I know she feels bad about how things have been the past few weeks but she's not doing anything to change it.

The doorbell rings and Jade goes to answer it. Sara comes in with a baby carrier and a diaper bag. I go over and take the bag from her. "Hi, Sara."

"Hey, Garret. You staying for the baby lesson?"

"No, I'm going to the gym."

"I'm the one who needs the lesson," Jade says to Sara.

"Well, thanks for doing this."

"I'm happy to," Jade says. "I know you want to get a better job."

"I just hope I get it." Sara takes Caleb out of his carrier. She sits down on the couch, placing him on her knee. "So this is Caleb." She kisses his cheek. "Caleb, say hi to Jade and Garret and thank them for helping us out."

He's chewing on his fingers and rocking back and forth on her leg. Drool is dripping down his chin.

Sara notices the drool. "Can one of you hold him while I get a towel?"

Jade freezes. She's never held a baby.

"I'll take him." I pick him up, holding him face out, one hand under his chubby legs and the other around his middle. I bounce him up and down. He takes his hand out of his mouth and starts to laugh, more drool dripping off his fingers onto the floor.

Sara quickly wipes it up. "Sorry about that."

"Drool happens." I smile at Sara. "I saw that on a bib one time."

She laughs. "I've seen that bib. I should get it for him. He drools a lot because of the teething."

Caleb keeps giggling as I bounce him while walking around the room.

Sara watches me. "You've done this before, haven't you?"

"I helped out when my sister was a baby."

"I've never done it before," Jade says. "I've never even been around babies."

Sara turns to Jade. "You won't have to watch him for very long so you don't need to know too much."

I bring Caleb over to Jade. "I have to get going so here you go."

From the expression on Jade's face, you'd think I was handing her a live hand grenade.

"Jade, just take him." I hand him to her and she takes him, holding him out in front of her with his feet dangling.

"Set him on your hip," Sara says. "And if he gets fussy just bounce him a little like Garret did."

I go in the bedroom as Sara continues to give Jade instruction. I'm not sure Jade's ready to babysit. She seems scared of the kid, although knowing Jade, she's probably just afraid she'll screw up and do something wrong.

As I'm packing my gym bag, I hear Caleb crying. That's not good. It'll make Jade even more nervous. I take my bag and go back out to the living room. The crying has stopped and Jade's now sitting on the couch with Caleb on her legs, facing her. He's laughing as she bounces him.

"See?" Sara says to Jade. "You're a natural."

"I think he's just a good baby." Jade seems more relaxed now.

"I'm heading out," I tell her as I walk to the door.

"See ya later." Jade doesn't even look at me as she says it. Her attention's all on the baby.

Jade won't admit it, but I know she wants kids. She's just afraid to have them. She thinks she'll be a bad mom and I can't seem to convince her otherwise. I keep reminding her that her mom was a drunk and addicted to pills and that's why she acted that way. Jade knows this, but she's still scared to death to have kids. And I don't know how to help her. All I know is she needs to figure this out. Her fears are holding her back. And eventually they'll hold us *both* back because we'll never have the family I know we both want.

When I get to the gym, the weight room is packed. Everyone goes there at night which is why I usually avoid going at this time, but I wanted to give Jade and Sara some time alone.

The physical therapist gave me a series of exercises to strengthen my shoulder and I have to do them in a certain order. I go to the lat pull machine first. I have to move the pin way up to the 40-pound weight because I'm not supposed to use heavy weights. It's so embarrassing. I notice a guy staring at me. I drop the lat pull and consider adding more weight, but I know that's stupid. I'm trying to heal my shoulder, not make it worse.

"You hurt yourself?" The guy who was staring at me stands next to the lat machine.

"Yeah, I tore my shoulder up."

He nods and motions to his leg. "I tore my knee up a little over a year ago. It's still not 100%. You doing physical therapy?"

"For the next six months."

"I did it for almost a year. And I still can't play football."

"You play any other sports?"

"No, just football. I had a scholarship to Ohio State but busted my knee during practice freshman year. There went my scholarship. I ended up going here because my uncle works in admissions."

"So you're a sophomore?"

"Yeah. Business major."

"Where are you from?"

"Phoenix. My dad still lives there. My mom moved to LA after the divorce. Now she lives with some Hollywood writer." He laughs. "Sorry, didn't mean to give you my whole life story while you're trying to work out."

"That's okay." I hold my hand out. "I'm Garret."

"Nate." He shakes my hand. "I think you're in my accounting class."

"Yeah, I thought you looked familiar."

"I'll let you get back to the weights. Hey, if you're not doing anything Saturday night, I'm having some guys over to watch the game. You're welcome to come."

"I don't know. I think I have plans Saturday."

"If you don't, then just stop by. I'll give you my address when I see you in class."

Another guy comes up behind Nate. "Hey, I could use a spotter on the bench."

"Dylan, this is Garret. He might come over and watch the game with us on Saturday."

"Hey." The guy nods at me. He's too sweaty to shake hands. "Dylan Matthews. Nice to meet you."

I step aside to let another guy use the lat machine. "That name sounds familiar. Did we meet already?"

"I don't think so. I'm not a student here. I work in the marketing department."

"Do you have a fiancé named Brook?"

Dylan gives me a strange look. "Yeah, how'd you know?"

"Her friend, Harper, is best friends with my wife."

He smiles really wide. "So you're the mysterious Garret. Brook keeps saying we need to meet you and…Jade? Is that your wife's name?"

"Yeah. Jade and I used to go to Moorhurst with Harper. We transferred here this fall."

"Brook said she's called Jade and left messages but she didn't get a call back. We figured you guys weren't interested in meeting, which is totally fine. Don't feel like you have to."

"No, we want to get together. We just haven't had time."

"Don't worry about it. Whenever you get time, just give us a call. If you're coming over to watch the game on Saturday, maybe Jade and Brook could do something together."

"I'll check with Jade. She's really buried in homework right now."

Dylan jabs Nate. "What's with you? You haven't said anything this whole time." Dylan looks at me. "Nate never shuts up. This is the longest he's gone without talking."

"You're really married?" Nate asks me.

"Yeah."

"You've made him speechless," Dylan says. "He can't imagine being married. It's too grown up for him. Nate lives in a state of delayed adolescence. He lives on pizza and plays video games five hours a day."

"Two hours," Nate says. "Maybe three."

"Let's go." He motions Nate to follow him. "See ya, Garret."

They go to the bench press and I continue on the weight machines. Then I run on the treadmill. I shower at the gym to use up more time. I'm not sure how long Sara will be with Jade and I want to stay out of their way.

When I get back to the house, Sara is gone and Jade's on the couch watching TV. Jade hasn't watched TV in three weeks so this is strange.

"What are you doing?"

"Watching a movie. Come watch with me."

I sit on the couch. She moves over and settles herself under my arm.

"No studying tonight?" I'm almost afraid to ask but I want to know what's going on.

"I need a night off. I'm tired. I think it's Caleb's fault. He fell asleep and he looked all cozy and sleepy and it made me feel the same way."

She's in a way better mood than she was earlier. After hanging out with a baby. Very strange.

"So you like Caleb?"

"What's not to like? He's adorable."

"You seemed a little nervous when he got here."

"I've never held a baby before. I didn't want to drop him."

"He seemed to like you."

"He did. And he *really* liked you. Did you see how much he laughed when you were holding him? Sara said she's never seen him laugh like that."

"I didn't do anything special. I think he's just a happy kid."

Jade wraps her arm around my chest and looks up at me. "I liked seeing you with him."

"Why?"

"You were just so good with him. It made me think—" She stops, and looks down.

"It made you think what, Jade? Finish what you were going to say."

"It made me think of you and me and—"

"And what?"

She looks at me again. "Garret, could you see us with a baby? I mean, do you ever picture it?"

"Of course I do. You know I want that. Not like right now, but when we're older."

I can't believe Jade's saying this. I thought I'd come home from the gym and find her sitting at the kitchen table with her books spread out, yelling at me to be quiet. But instead we're watching a movie and discussing kids. What the hell?

"I think about it, too." She puts her head on my shoulder and looks down at my chest, her finger outlining one of the buttons on my polo shirt.

"What do you think about?"

"Sometimes in my head I see us with kids. Sometimes they're babies and sometimes they're older. I've had dreams about it, too." She laughs. "I had this dream where you were teaching our daughter how to drive and you were being really patient but I could tell you just wanted to take over the wheel."

I'm trying not to react and to just pretend this is something we talk about every day. But seriously, where is this coming from? She's never once told me she's imagined us with kids or had dreams about it.

"So you saw us with a daughter?" I ask her.

"For that dream, yes. It depends on the dream. I had a different dream where we had a son. He was in high school and you coached his football team. He looked just like you."

"I hope he was a swimmer, too."

"I woke up before I could find out, but I'm sure he was."

This is so strange. Jade's been dreaming about us having kids and she's not freaking out? I'm not going to ask her any more about it. If she wants to say more, fine, but I don't want to pressure her in any way.

She hugs my chest, keeping her head down. "I'm sorry for ignoring you the past few weeks. These classes I'm taking are tougher than I thought they'd be and I feel like I can't keep up."

And here's another topic she refuses to talk about, so I'm a little surprised she's bringing it up.

"You're burning yourself out, Jade. You need to take some breaks."

"I know, and I'm going to try to."

"Hey, when I was at the gym I met that guy, Dylan, the one that Harper knows. Brook's fiancé."

"Oh, yeah? That's weird. He's not even a student. Why was he at the gym?"

"Staff and faculty of the college can use the gym, too. Anyway he said Brook called you a few times and you didn't call her back."

"I got busy and forgot."

"Jade, you shouldn't blow her off like that. If you don't want to meet her, just tell her you're busy."

"I *do* want to meet her, just not right now."

"Dylan and some of his friends are watching a football game Saturday night. They asked if I wanted to come over. Do you care if I go? I'd rather take you out on Saturday night but if you don't want to then—"

"I have a calculus test on Tuesday so I need to study. You should go hang out with the guys."

"Are you sure? Because I don't have to go. I can stay here."

"You're going. Now let's watch the movie."

Jade falls asleep 10 minutes later. I carry her to bed and she's so tired she doesn't even wake up. It's still early so I go back in the living room and watch TV.

I'm not sure what to make of Jade tonight. She sounded like she wanted kids, but was that just because she spent time with Caleb? I'm not getting my hopes up. But at least it's a step in the right direction.

# Chapter 21

**JADE**

*I* wake up at 2 a.m., my heart racing because I just had a dream that I forgot to study for a test and ended up failing it. I had a similar dream last week, but it was one in which I forget to turn in a paper.

I sit up a little and lean against the headboard as my heart rate returns to normal.

The past three weeks I've been completely overwhelmed. My classes are more than I can handle. I feel weak for saying that, but it's true. It's too much math and science all at once. I desperately want to drop a class but then I'd feel like a failure. And I'm afraid Garret, Frank, and Ryan would think I'm a failure, too. I don't want them thinking I'm not smart enough to get through the semester. Because I know I'm smart enough. I just don't have enough hours in the day to complete all the homework and study for tests.

Two weeks ago I had my first quiz in advanced calculus and I got a 75. With the grading curve it turned out to be a B minus, but for me that's failing. I've never had a 75. I didn't tell Garret about it. He'd tell me I'm overreacting but he doesn't get how much I worry about this stuff. I won't get into med school if I keep getting 75's on my tests.

That's the other thing. Lately I've been rethinking the med school idea. Even though I'm good at science and math, I don't really like them that well. I just always thought that if you're good at something, you should pursue it as a career. And I always wanted a job where I could help people, so the doctor idea made sense. But I don't have to be a doctor to help people. I could do something else. I just don't know what.

This is why I never wanted anyone to know I was thinking about med school. I was never 100% sure about it, but now I feel pressured to continue down this path. Frank, Ryan, Grace, and Garret will all think I'm a failure if I don't pursue this, especially since I don't have an alternative in mind.

For now I just need to get through this semester. Maybe after that I'll make a decision. Unfortunately I don't know how I'll make it through the next few months. To keep up, I'll have to study even more, which means spending even less time with Garret. I already feel like I never see him. Every time he asks me to do something, I turn him down. I don't like doing that, but I need to study. He's been really understanding and supportive, but I know he's getting tired of this. I am, too. I miss him. We live together and yet I miss him. How messed up is that?

That's why I finally took tonight off and watched a movie. Being with Sara and Caleb earlier gave me some perspective. Here I am complaining about being overwhelmed with classes, and poor Sara is trying to raise a baby on her own. Talk about being overwhelmed. It makes my stressing over homework seem completely stupid.

I can't imagine what Sara's going through. I know she struggles to pay her bills and I wish I could help her but she won't let me. Last week she said she was running out of diapers but that she couldn't buy more until payday which wasn't for two more days. I gave her a twenty and she gave it right back. She hates taking money from people, just like I do. She wants to be able to support Caleb by herself, and she's really trying, but her job at the coffee shop doesn't pay enough, which leaves her struggling to make ends meet.

I told her to take the money I offered her and to pay me back later if she felt she had to. She still refused and said she'd try to get an extra shift at work. She's as stubborn as I am. Now I understand why Garret was so frustrated with me last year when I wouldn't accept his help.

After Sara told me about her money problem, I snuck in the coffee shop later that day and left a $20 bill on a table that was waiting to be cleaned. There was some money already there to cover the check but the people who left it didn't include a tip. People always forget to leave a tip because most people order at the counter. But the waitress still brings your food and fills your drink so you're supposed to leave a tip.

Anyway, after I left the tip, I stood outside and watched as Sara cleaned the table. When she saw the money, she covered her face and I saw her shoulders shaking. She was so relieved to get the money, she was crying. I was glad she didn't know it was from me. I'd rather have her think it was from some random customer, someone who thought she did a good job or who thought she could use some extra money.

Sara needs that. She needs to have faith in people so she doesn't turn into the person I was before I met Garret. Someone who thinks nobody cares and that you can't rely on anyone but yourself. Sara's not there yet and I'm hoping that tip she got will act as a gentle reminder that she can count on people.

"Jade, what are you doing?" Garret notices me sitting up in bed. "Why aren't you sleeping?"

"I was thinking about Sara." I lie down beside him. "Last week I gave her some money because she really needed it, but I didn't tell her the money was from me. I made it look like it was a tip from a customer. That wasn't wrong, was it? I mean, it's not considered lying, is it?"

"No. Not at all. Sara's stubborn and she doesn't like taking help from people. She's just like you that way."

"It's totally frustrating. She needs money but she won't take it from me."

"Believe me, I know how frustrating that can be." He pulls the blanket over me and kisses my cheek.

"I was a real pain in the ass last year, wasn't I?"

"Let's just say you were frustrating." He hugs me into his chest. "You still are, but I love you."

"I love you, too."

He goes back to sleep, but I can't. I keep hearing noises in the house and think someone's trying to break in. I'm still freaking out about seeing those guys get shot in the parking lot. I keep thinking the shooter saw me and is going to come after me. Three weeks have gone by and nothing's happened so I probably don't need to worry, but I still do.

Garret keeps telling me it's over and to relax, but at the same time he's been super cautious ever since it happened. He takes me to and from class and calls and checks on me whenever we're not together. So despite what he says, I know he's worried about it, too.

I finally fall asleep, and a few hours later the alarm is beeping. I dread getting up because getting up means going to class and getting even more homework on top of the stuff I haven't even finished.

The talk I gave myself last night about needing to take time off and not work so hard is all forgotten when I go to organic chem and get my test back with a giant C written on it. I spent forever studying for that test so I wasn't expecting to get a C. But I'm finding organic chemistry is more difficult than regular chemistry. Or it could just be that my professor sucks, because he does. He's not good at explaining things in simple terms. He uses so much chemistry jargon that I have to keep referring to the glossary in the back of the book to make sure I'm understanding him correctly.

The bad grade I got pushes me to return to the nonstop studying that I told myself I wasn't going to do. I was supposed to take some breaks and not stress out so much, but I can't seem to make myself do it.

I study constantly for the rest of the week, including Friday night and all day Saturday. Garret leaves me alone. He can tell I'm in a crappy mood. He just doesn't know it's because I got a bad test grade.

Saturday night, Garret goes over to his new friend's apartment to watch a football game. I haven't met this Nate guy but Garret seems to like him. He said there will be about 10 other guys there, including Dylan.

While Garret's gone I study for my calculus test. I never know how to study for math. It's not like you can memorize anything. You just have to keep doing practice problems and hope they put similar problems on the exam. When I'm done with calculus, I read a chapter in my organic chemistry book. It's so boring.

This is not how I want to spend my Saturday night. Everything in my life just seems so out of balance right now and I don't know how to fix it.

When Garret gets home at 10, I'm angry, frustrated, and exhausted. He has no idea what he's walking into. I shouldn't be around him, or anyone, right now. I'm so tense I just want to scream.

"Hey." Garret comes over and kisses me. "Did you get your studying done?"

"I never get my studying done. As soon as I get caught up, they pile on more."

"Why don't you quit for tonight and hang out with me?" He pulls me up to standing.

"I told you, I'm not done yet." I back away from him.

"Jade, it's late and I think it'd be good if you took a break."

"Stop telling me to take a break! I can't take a break!" Shit. I did not mean to yell at him like that.

"Why can't you take a break?" He steps closer to me.

"Because I'm failing my classes. That's why."

"What do you mean you're failing?"

"I got a 75 on my calculus quiz a few weeks ago."

"Yeah? So? That's probably a B with the grading curve. And it's just a quiz. You're not failing the class."

"I studied really hard for that quiz, Garret, and I still got a 75. And then I got a C on my organic chem exam and it's a big part of my grade."

"That's not failing. You're overreacting here."

"I'm NOT overreacting! You don't understand!" I'm yelling at him again and I don't mean to. I really don't. I should've locked myself in the bedroom before he got home. I can't talk to him when I'm like this. This has nothing to do with him. He didn't do anything wrong. I'm just really cranky and really tired and really stressed right now.

"Jade, it's okay." He holds my shoulders and says calmly, "We're only a month into the semester. You'll have plenty of other quizzes and exams."

As he talks I smell the beer on his breath. I'm not used to that smell on him. He hasn't drank since last fall, other than some sips of champagne, which he had with me. "You were drinking?"

He tenses up but his voice remains calm. "I just had a few beers."

"What's a few?"

"Three or four. I don't know."

"And then you drove?" I shove his hands off my shoulders. "What the hell? Are you trying to kill yourself? Or kill other people?"

"I'm not drunk. I finished my last beer like an hour ago."

"So are you going to do this all the time now?"

"Do what?"

"Are you going to start drinking again?" It comes out harsh and accusatory.

"Why are you freaking out about this? I just had a few beers!" Now he's getting angry. "You're the one who keeps telling me to hang out with other guys and you've told me repeatedly that it's okay if I drink. And I've promised you I won't get drunk."

"Well, I was wrong. I don't want you to drink, okay?"

"No, it's not okay. I should be able to have a few beers without being accused of being an alcoholic."

"I didn't say you were."

"You sure as hell act like it."

"You know my past, Garret. You know I can't be around alcohol or people who drink."

"You need to get over it. People drink. You can't avoid it."

"Maybe not, but I should be able to avoid it in my own house."

"Jade, you can't tell me I can do something and then get mad at me for doing it!"

He's completely right and I don't know why I'm saying these things to him. I'm not mad at him for having a few beers. I'm happy he went out and had fun with his friends. But I'm also jealous that he got to do that while I had to spend the whole night studying, feeling like a failure, and feeling trapped in this stupid major. I need to get away from him before I do more damage.

"I can't talk right now, Garret. I'm going in the bedroom and I'm closing the door and I need you to leave me alone."

"Why? What's going on with you?"

"I just need time to myself. Can you sleep on the couch?"

"Why the hell would I sleep on the couch?"

"Then I'll sleep on the couch. You take the bedroom." I go to the hall closet and pull out a pillow and a blanket.

Garret takes them from me and throws them on the floor. "What the fuck is going on here?"

My patience is completely gone and I'm about to explode. "Just leave me alone!" I run in the bedroom, slam the door, and lock it.

Garret tries to open it. "Jade, open the door."

I'm slumped on the floor, hugging my knees, tears pouring from my eyes.

"Jade." He jiggles the door handle again. "Open the door. Right now."

"Please, Garret. Please just leave me alone."

I hear him sigh, then walk away from the door. I hear his fist slam against something. And then I hear the TV, the volume turned way down.

I take off my shorts and get into bed wearing my bra and t-shirt. I'm too tired to change into pajamas. I'm still crying because I feel horrible for treating Garret that way. But I'm not ready to talk to him yet. I need to calm down and figure out why I'm such a mess right now.

I get up and unlock the door, just in case he wants to come in later. But I'm sure he won't. He needs a break from me after I yelled at him like that. He probably won't even talk to me tomorrow. I get back in bed and eventually fall asleep.

Two hours later I wake up. My head is pounding and I'm sweating but I have goosebumps everywhere. I draw the blanket up to my chin but it doesn't help. I'm still freezing to the point that I'm shivering. My stomach starts to churn and my throat is hot and dry.

I know this feeling. I haven't had it for a long time but it's something you don't forget. I have the stomach flu and it's coming on fast. I rip the covers off me and race to the bathroom and throw up everything I ate earlier. Afterward, I want to rinse my mouth out but I can't make it to the sink. My head is spinning so bad I can't tell where I am in relation to the sink. I take off my sweaty t-shirt and bra and lie down on the tile floor. It's cold and feels good on my hot skin.

I lie there until that sick feeling in my stomach rises to my throat and I throw up again. Based on past experience, I know this is how it'll be for the next few hours. It's like clockwork. My body will give me a little break and then I'll get sick again. I really hate the stomach flu.

After my third time throwing up, I crawl out of the bathroom and back into the bedroom. I accidentally run into the nightstand and knock something off it. It makes a loud noise and I cringe because the sound makes my head hurt even more. I collapse on the wood floor.

"Jade?" I hear knocking. "What was that noise?"

"Nothing," I mumble.

"Jade." I hear the door open and the sound of Garret walking toward the bed. "Jade, where are you?"

"Down here." My voice is weak and hoarse and my throat burns when I talk.

"Down where?" I feel his foot hit my leg and he almost trips. "Jade, what the hell are you doing on the floor?"

"I'm sick."

"You're what?" He kneels down and feels for me in the dark. His hand is like ice on my skin. "Shit. You're burning up."

"I have the flu." I reach my arms up trying to find him. "Would you help me?"

He lifts me up onto the bed. "Why didn't you come get me?"

"I didn't want to wake you up."

"If you get sick in the night, you wake me up. That's the rule. Got it?"

I nod, weakly.

He turns the light on by the bed and a sharp pain shoots through my already-pounding head. I cover my eyes with my hand. "Too bright."

"I need to get a cold washcloth. You need to cool down."

I'm completely delirious. I'm not even sure Garret's there. This could all be a dream. I reach for him and find him in the dark. "Don't leave."

"I'll be right back." He goes to the bathroom and returns with the cold washcloth, spreading it over my forehead. "What do you need? Did you take anything? Should I—"

I yank on his shirt. "I think I'm going to be sick again."

# Chapter 22

**GARRET**

Jade climbs out of bed and stumbles to the floor, crawling back to the bathroom, barely making it there in time. She's really sick. I never get sick like this, but Lilly's had the flu a few times so I'm familiar with the symptoms. When Lilly had the flu, I had to take care of her because Katherine refuses to be around sick people, especially if it involves vomit. I don't like vomit either, but you just have to get over it. Besides, it's way worse for the person who's actually vomiting.

Back when Lilly had the flu, Katherine wanted to hire a nurse to take care of her. I didn't want some stranger taking care of my sister when she was sick, so my dad and I took care of her and Katherine kept her distance. What kind of mother doesn't take care of her sick kid? Jade's mom didn't take care of her either when she was sick. I don't understand it.

Jade's now crumpled in a heap on the bathroom floor. The place reeks and I need to get her out of here. I take her back to the bed, then wet the washcloth again and place it over her forehead. Her skin is scorching hot and yet she's shaking and shivering and her teeth are chattering. Lilly was never this sick but I've heard the flu can sometimes be worse for adults.

I get her pajamas from the drawer and put them on her. Then I cover her with blankets and keep watch over her. She gets sick every hour for the rest of the night.

Now it's 9 in the morning and she's gone almost two hours without a trip to the bathroom. She can't possibly have anything left in her stomach. During the night I kept trying to get her to drink water so she wouldn't get dehydrated but the water came right back up.

The alarm goes off. I don't know why it's going off on a Sunday. I reach over and turn it off.

"Garret?" Jade's voice is hoarse. She reaches over trying to find me.

"I'm right here." I move over a little.

She rests her head on my stomach, and curls herself into a ball. "Thank you. For staying."

"You don't have to thank me." I move the damp strands of hair off her cheek. "I'm taking care of you. I'm not going anywhere."

"She always left." Jade says it softly, in almost a whisper. "She never stayed."

"I know. But I'm not her."

Jade's talking about her mom. The last time Jade had the flu was when her mom was alive. Her mom used to get mad at her for getting sick, like it was Jade's fault. She'd force Jade to stay in her room with the door closed until she was better. And if Jade had the stomach flu like she has now, she had to clean the bathroom if she made a mess. Her mom would yell at her until she did it.

I guess that's why Jade didn't come and get me on the couch last night. She probably thought I'd get mad at her or yell at her. Jade still has irrational thoughts like that. She thinks I'll treat her like her mom did. It makes no sense, but then again, I didn't have that kind of traumatic childhood so I can't really understand where her head is sometimes.

"Will you stay here until you have class?" she whispers.

"I'm not going to class. It's Sunday."

She lifts her head. "It is?"

"Yeah." I feel her face. It's still burning hot. "And if you're like this tomorrow I'm not going to class."

She mumbles something, then her head drops down on my stomach again and she falls asleep.

Her phone is on the nightstand and I pick it up and see several messages from Sara. I normally wouldn't check Jade's phone but Sara doesn't usually send this many messages so I'm wondering if she needs something. I check the first message. It says she's sick and that it might be contagious. The next message says the flu was going around at Caleb's day care and that he's sick, too. Then the other messages are all Sara asking Jade to call her because she'll feel terrible if Jade's sick.

So that explains it. Jade must've got sick when Caleb and Sara were here the other night. It takes a few days before it hits so the timing is right.

I put the phone back on the nightstand and let myself sleep a little.

When I wake up three hours later, Jade hasn't moved, which means she hasn't been sick for a few hours now.

I need to use the bathroom so I try to gently slide her head off me but she wakes up. "Are you leaving?"

"Just to go to the bathroom. I'll be right back."

The bathroom is a mess but I'll clean it up later.

When I get back in bed, Jade lays her head on my chest and says, "I really wanted pancakes today. And now I can't have them."

"We'll have them next week. I won't even charge you for them."

"That's why I wanted them," she says weakly. "I wanted to pay for them."

I smile. "You did?"

"Yeah." She tilts her head up and looks at me. A tear's running down her cheek. "I miss you."

I wipe the tear away with my thumb. Her skin is still so hot. "Jade, why are you crying?"

"Because my whole body hurts really bad. And because…" More tears trail down her face.

"What, Jade?"

She gazes down at the blanket. "Because I'm a mess. Everything's a mess and I don't know what to do."

"What's a mess? What are you talking about?"

"My classes. My major. I'm stressing out, Garret."

"I know you are. We're going to work on that, okay?"

She nods. "I don't want to lose you."

"You'll never lose me. Don't even think that."

"I never see you anymore. All I do is study and I still can't keep up."

"Which is why I think you need to drop a class. You're killing yourself trying to keep up and you're not having any fun. This is college. You should be having at least a little fun."

She looks up at me again. "You'd let me drop a class?"

"*Let* you? Jade, you don't need my permission to drop a class."

"But it means I failed. It means I'm not smart enough."

"That's not at all what it means. Everyone drops classes. It doesn't mean they're not smart enough. They're just balancing their class load better. Sometimes you sign up for a class and you don't know how much work it'll be until you're in it."

"You're not mad? I thought you'd be mad."

I don't know why the hell she thinks this way. I seriously don't. I rarely get mad at her and I definitely wouldn't get mad at her for dropping a class. This is what I mean when I say she still needs to deal with stuff from her childhood. Everything she did made her mom mad. Even the tiniest things. So then she thinks I'll react the same way, even though she knows it's not true.

"Jade, I would never get mad about that. I don't like seeing you so stressed out all the time. You don't eat right. You don't sleep. And now you're sick. So the decision's made. You're dropping a class."

She groans and rolls onto her back. "I think I might be dying. I don't remember ever feeling this bad. Every part of me hurts."

"You think you can drink some water now? Because you need to. You're really dehydrated and if you keep throwing up, I'm taking you to the hospital."

"I'll try to drink some."

I go in the kitchen and get some water and bring it to her. She takes two tiny sips.

"You need to drink more than that."

She shakes her head. "That's all I can do. I'll try again later."

"You should go to sleep. I'll wake you up in an hour to drink some more."

"Can you stay? Please?"

I wanted to take a shower but she sounds so desperate for me to stay that I get back in bed with her.

She lays on me. "Garret?"

"What?" I lightly rub her back.

"I'm so sorry I've been mean to you."

"You weren't mean. You were just tired and stressed out from class."

"I need to fix this. And I need help. I need you to help me."

"You know I will. Whatever you need."

"We'll talk later?" Her eyes are shutting.

"Yeah, we'll talk later. Get some sleep."

I'm so relieved Jade finally admitted she's struggling with her classes and is willing to do something about it. And given how stressed she's been, I think she's struggling with other stuff, too. I've been trying to get her to talk to me for weeks but she wouldn't. Maybe now, or when she feels better, she'll finally tell me what's going on.

In the afternoon, I try to get Jade to eat some crackers and she does, but they come right back up. Looks like we'll be sticking with liquids for now.

When Jade falls asleep again, I call Grace to ask her what else I should be doing for Jade. I didn't know who else to ask. My dad doesn't know about this stuff and I don't think Frank and Ryan would either. Grace raised two kids and I'm sure they got sick so I figure she knows what to do.

"Hi, Grace. It's Garret."

"Garret, this is a surprise. Usually Jade's the one who calls."

"Yeah, she's sick. That's why I'm calling. Sorry, I should ask how you're doing. How are you doing, Grace?"

She laughs. "I'm doing well. Thank you. So Jade is sick?"

"She has the flu and I'm not sure what to do for her. I'm trying to keep water in her but she can't eat and she has a high fever and chills. I figured since you're a mom you might have some experience with this."

"I've had a lot of experience with it, with my sons as well as my granddaughters."

Grace goes through a list of things I should try. I take notes as she talks. I'm glad I called her. She knows a lot more than I do about this and I trust her advice more than I trust the advice on the Internet.

"Thanks," I say when she's done. "I'll try that stuff and hopefully she'll feel better."

"You have to let it run its course but this will help with the symptoms. So how have you been, Garret?"

"I'm okay."

"Garret." She says it like she knows I'm lying. I barely know Grace but sometimes I think she understands me better than my own family does.

"Things have been a little stressful around here. Jade's classes are taking up all her time and there was a burglary at a house just a few down from ours."

"And your father told me about your shoulder."

"Yeah, there's that, too."

"Jade hasn't called me for a while. Is it because of her school work?"

"Yeah, she's feeling overwhelmed with everything. I think she took too many classes this semester."

"Is there any way I can help? I'm not sure what I could do, but if you think of anything, please let me know."

"Actually, is there any way you could make it out here for her birthday? Frank and Ryan will be here so I'm planning to have a small party for her."

"I would love to be there. Thank you for inviting me."

"It would be great if you could spend the weekend. I know Jade would like that."

"I'll plan to arrive Friday morning and leave Sunday afternoon. Does that work?"

"Sounds perfect. Maybe we should make this a surprise."

"Yes, I think that would be nice."

"Great. Well, I should go check on Jade."

"I know I've said this before, but you're a nice young man, Garret. We should talk more. You should at least get on the phone when Jade calls me so I can say hello."

"Okay, I will."

"Tell Jade I hope she feels better soon. Have her call me when she does."

We say goodbye and I quietly walk back into the bedroom. Jade's huddled up in the blankets, shivering. I feel so bad for her.

"I'm so cold," she says, her teeth chattering.

I feel her forehead. She's still burning up.

"I just talked to Grace and she gave me some things to try that might make you feel better."

"You talked to Grace?"

"Yeah, I called her and she gave me a list of stuff to get, so I need to go to the store."

"Can you wait until tomorrow? I don't want you to leave. I seriously think I might be dying here."

"You're not dying. It just feels like it. Oh, I forgot to tell you that Sara and Caleb also have the flu."

"Did I give it to them? I hope not."

"You didn't. It's going around. Caleb's day care had it last week and Camsburg sent out an announcement saying half the campus has it now. Two of your classes and one of mine are canceled tomorrow because the professors are sick."

"Why aren't *you* sick?" She's curled up in a ball and her eyes are struggling to stay open.

"I don't get sick. I did when I was a kid but I don't anymore. I haven't been sick since I was 15. I must have a strong immune system."

She's not listening. I think she's falling asleep.

"Jade, I'm gonna run to the store."

"I don't want to be alone," she mumbles.

I get up from the bed. "I won't be gone long."

"It's worse when you're alone," she whispers, her eyes now closed.

"What's worse?"

"Sick, alone, nobody would help." Her eyes are still closed and I'm not sure if she even knows what she's saying. "I wanted to die."

She says it quietly, but I hear every word. And it kills me to hear those words. I wish I could take away her past. Get rid of those memories she still holds on to.

She's shivering again so I pull the blanket over her.

"It's worse when you're alone." She says it in just the faintest whisper.

I take my phone out, keeping my eyes on her as I walk to the other side of the room.

I call Dylan. "Hey. It's Garret. I know we don't know each other that well but I'm wondering if you could do me a favor." He agrees and I read off the list of stuff I need.

Then I get back in bed. "I'm right here, Jade." I lean down and kiss her forehead. "You're not alone."

# Chapter 23

**JADE**

When I wake up, it's dark again. I must've slept all day. My head is still pounding and my muscles still ache but at least the nauseous feeling isn't as strong as before.

I turn over and see Garret lying next to me, wearing the clothes he was wearing Saturday night. He probably hasn't left my side since I got sick. I kind of remember him helping me off the floor and I know I talked to him a little but I don't remember what I said.

He's sleeping now. He's on top of the sheet with no blanket on him. I've got all the covers wrapped around me, yanked out of the bottom of the bed. I unwrap myself and place part of the blanket over Garret. Then I lay on his chest and fall back to sleep.

I have no idea what time it is when I wake up again, but bright sunshine fills the room. I look over and see that Garret is gone. I feel a little bit better so I get up to use the bathroom but my vision blacks out on the way there. I drop to my knees until it passes, then crawl the rest of the way and run right into Garret's legs.

"Where are you going?" he asks.

I look up and see him wearing yellow cleaning gloves.

299

"I have to use the bathroom."

"I just finished cleaning it so it's all set." He takes his gloves off and reaches under my arms. "You need some help?"

"Yeah, I blacked out."

"You need to eat something. I made Jello and I have some soup if you want it."

He helps me into the bathroom, then waits in the bedroom until I'm done.

"I think I'll take a shower," I tell him.

He comes back in and turns the shower on. "I'll go in with you. You can't shower alone. You can barely stand up."

I'm so lightheaded I have to hold on to Garret as he washes my hair and then the rest of me.

Part of me can't believe he's doing all this. You understand love even more when someone's there for you when you're sick. I've never had that before. I've never had anyone help me when I was sick.

"I love you," I say to Garret as he helps me get dressed after the shower.

He smiles as he tries to get my arm through the sleeve of my shirt. "I love you, too. But you're really hard to dress. Undressing you is a lot easier."

I laugh.

"I got you to laugh. That must mean you're feeling better."

"I feel better. I'm just weak."

"I can fix that. I've got a whole assortment of get-better foods."

"When did you go out?"

"I didn't. I had Dylan go get them."

"Harper's friend?"

"Yeah. He's a good guy. I talked to him at Nate's apartment on Saturday. The game was kind of boring so Dylan and I went out on the deck and had a—" He stops before he says 'beer.' "Anyway, I think you'd like him."

"Garret, I didn't mean to yell at you about the beer. That had nothing to do with you. I was just tired and really cranky."

"Don't worry about it. Let's get some food in you, okay?"

I nod.

He tucks me in bed and disappears into the kitchen, then comes back with soup, crackers, and Jello arranged on a tray.

"I can't eat all that," I say, eyeing the tray.

"It's a sampler platter. Just eat what you can. For beverages, I have water, juice, Sprite, 7-Up, and those sports drinks that have electrolytes."

"Any of those is fine."

He comes back with Gatorade.

I take a few sips of it, then eat a cracker, and a few spoonfuls of soup.

"Okay, that's all I can eat."

"You didn't even try my orange Jello. I worked really hard on that." He smiles as he takes the tray away. "I had to boil water and everything."

"Sorry. I'll try it later. My stomach is full."

"At least you ate something." Garret sits beside me. "Are you going back to sleep?"

"No. I'm not tired right now." I check the clock. It's 10 a.m. "What day is it?"

"Monday. Why?"

"Don't you have class now?"

"It's canceled because the professor is sick. And I'm skipping my afternoon classes."

"Garret, you can go. I'll be fine."

He kisses my forehead. "You still have a fever and you're blacking out. I'm not leaving you until you're better."

I smile. "You're an awesome husband. Have I told you that?"

He smiles back. "Once or twice. But I don't mind hearing it again."

I reach up and kiss him. "I love you."

"I love you, too. Do you want me to bring the TV in here?"

"Um, no. That's okay. I kind of wanted to talk."

"What do you want to talk about?"

I don't want to tell him this, but I have to. I can't do this anymore.

"I'm having trouble keeping up with my classes."

"That's why you're dropping one. I checked online for how to do that and I already—"

"Wait. How did you know I wanted to drop a class?"

"You told me yesterday."

"I did?" I have no memory of that. I wonder what else I told him.

"Yeah, and I told you it was a good idea. Anyway, I printed out the form you have to fill out. Do you know what class you want to drop?"

He doesn't care that I want to drop a class? I thought he'd be mad at me or tell me I'm not trying hard enough.

"Um, I'm not sure yet. I need to tell you something else. I'm—" This is so hard to tell him. He was so proud of me for wanting to be a doctor. Everyone was, and now I have to disappoint them.

"Go ahead, Jade. You can tell me."

"I don't think I want to be a doctor." I say it really fast, then shut my eyes so I don't have to see his reaction.

"Then don't be a doctor." He says it so casually that I think I must've heard him wrong.

I open my eyes and stare at him. "What did you say?"

"If you don't want to be a doctor, don't be one. Do something else."

"You're okay with this? You're not going to try to talk me out of it?"

"Why would I do that? It's your life. Your career. You should do what you want to do. Something you have a passion for."

"But being a doctor makes sense. I'm good at math and science."

"So find a different career that involves math and science."

"The problem is, I don't really like math and science. I mean, they're interesting to learn about, but—I don't know. It's just not what I want to do. And being a doctor means I'd be working all the time and I don't want to spend my life at work. I don't need to, now that I have money. It's not that I don't want to work. I just don't want it taking over my life, especially if I'm in a job I don't even like."

I wait for Garret to respond. He doesn't, and I get nervous again.

"What is it, Garret? Why aren't you saying anything?"

"Because I'm trying to figure out why you do this to yourself."

"Do what?"

"Make yourself miserable."

"I didn't say I was miserable."

"Jade, I live with you. I see you every day. And since the first week of classes you've been miserable. I just didn't know how to help you because you wouldn't talk to me."

"I didn't say anything because I thought if I could just do better in my classes I could still go to med school."

"But you just said you don't want to be a doctor."

"Yes, but I told everyone I would."

Garret moves so that he's sitting across from me. "Jade, you don't have to do something you don't want to do just to please other people. Nobody said you had to be a doctor. You can be anything you want."

"But I don't know what I want to do. And what if I make the wrong decision?"

He takes my hand and looks me in the eye. "Then you'll try something else. You can try 10, 15, 20 different things. Just keep trying until you find something you like."

"So you won't be disappointed in me if I don't go to med school?"

"I'd be disappointed if you *did* go, now that I know how you feel about it. Listen, Jade, if this really isn't the path you want to go down, then drop *two* classes or *three*. Stop wasting your time studying calculus and organic chem. Spend the rest of the semester figuring out what interests you instead of suffering through classes you don't even want to be in."

"I don't know. I'd have to think about that."

"Then think about it. But don't let other people affect your decision. Don't worry about what Frank thinks or what Ryan thinks or Grace."

"I don't even want to tell them. I know they'll be disappointed."

Garret laughs. "Jade, do you know how much I disappointed my dad and my grandfather when I told them I wouldn't take over the company? And they didn't hide their disappointment. They made sure I knew how they felt. And that's just one thing. I constantly disappoint them, especially my grandfather. If I did what he and my dad expected me to do, I'd hate my life. You can't worry about what other people want. You'll never be happy if you do."

I'm so relieved Garret reacted this way toward my news. I feel a million times lighter. It's like all that pressure I felt is gone. I didn't think I had options. I was convinced I couldn't change my mind about med school. I told myself I had to be a doctor to make everyone happy. I'm not used to making *myself* happy. I don't even think about it.

"You know what?" I ask Garret.

"What?"

"Sometimes I forget what a great friend you are." I smile at him. "You have really good advice. I should talk to you more often."

He smiles back. "Yeah, you should."

"Hey." I pull on him to sit closer. "Thanks for taking care of me through this whole flu disaster."

"It wasn't that bad."

"Are you kidding? I don't remember everything that happened yesterday, but I'm sure it was disgusting. You didn't see too much, did you?"

"What do you mean?"

"You didn't see me get sick, right?"

"Of course I saw it. I was in the bathroom with you."

"Ugh." I bury my face in my hands. "You weren't supposed to see that. Now you'll never have sex with me again."

"Why wouldn't I?"

"You'll have that image in your head and you'll never want to do it with me again."

He laughs. "Where do you come up with this shit? I'm not sitting around thinking about you throwing up. I've already forgotten about it."

"Really? Then I shouldn't have brought it up."

"And as for sex, we're doing it as soon as you're better. It's been way too long."

"I know. This dry spell of ours has gotta end."

"I think it's time for you to transition to the couch. You want to go watch some TV? I could put a movie in."

"I would love that. I've missed watching movies with you. I've missed doing a lot of stuff with you. This Garret-free month has really sucked."

He helps me off the bed. "It ends now. We're spending more time together whether you want to or not."

"I want to." I kiss his cheek. "I really want to."


On Tuesday Garret goes back to class but he only has one class. The others were canceled due to so many people being sick. I stayed home Tuesday and again today because I'm still feeling weak.

As bad as it was to have the flu, I'm almost glad it happened. It forced me to stop working so hard and to figure out why I was doing it in the first place. Getting sick was like hitting rock bottom. I knew things had to change. And I knew I had to talk to Garret about it. Now that I have, I feel like everything's starting to come into focus. Being a doctor was never right for me. I just couldn't see that before because I was too busy thinking about what I *should* do instead of what I *wanted* to do. And if I hadn't gotten sick, I'd probably still be on that path.

I've now missed three days of classes and although I'm a little stressed about it, it's not even close to how stressed I would've felt before I got sick.

I decided to drop organic chemistry and the lab that goes with it, so technically that's two classes. I filled out the paperwork this morning and Garret dropped it off for me. It was such a great feeling just filling out the form. If I wasn't so tired I'd be doing a happy dance around the living room right now.

My remaining classes are chem 2, advanced calculus, and my psych elective. It's a much more manageable schedule. In fact, I'm actually looking forward to class now instead of dreading it. I don't like calculus but my chem class is okay and I really like my psych class.

Around 2, I decide to go to the coffee shop. After being cooped up in the house for days, I needed to get out for an hour or so. Plus, Sara went back to work today and I want to see her.

"Feel any better?" she asks as I sit on a stool along one of the long tables.

"I'm still tired."

"Yeah, me, too."

"I shouldn't complain. You're tired *and* you have to work *and* take care of a baby. How's Caleb doing?"

"He's better. Another tooth came in. With his chubby face and his partial teeth he's starting to look like a Jack-o-lantern." She shows me a photo. We both laugh.

"So what happened with your job interview? Did they reschedule it?"

Sara's interview was on Monday but she was too sick to go.

"No, they hired someone else."

"Sara, I'm sorry. I know you were hoping to get that job."

She shrugs. "It's okay. I'll find something else. You want something to drink?"

"I'd take one of your smoothies."

"What kind?"

"Surprise me. Make it a different one this time."

She takes off and an older man joins me at the long table. He sits across from me a few seats down and puts his glasses on to read his newspaper.

I see this guy a lot. He's usually in here the same time I am. He always wears casual pants, button-up shirts, and a tie, which is how a lot of the professors dress so I assume he's a professor.

"Have you had this flu that's going around?" He points to the front page of the paper. The flu is the main story.

"Yeah, I just had it. I got it last weekend."

"I haven't had it yet." His eyes roam the front page, then he opens the paper and scans page two. "But it seems to be spreading around campus."

"Are you a professor?"

He glances at me. "No. I'm a consultant. I'm working on a project for the college. Since I don't have an office on campus I come here to work. Are you a student?"

"Yes. I'm a sophomore."

"What's your major?"

"Chem—I mean, I'm not sure yet."

"It's an expensive school to go to if you're unsure about your major." He scans his newspaper again.

"What do you mean?"

"Once you decide on a major you'll have to make up all those required classes you didn't take your first and second years. So you'll probably be in school for five or six years instead of four. That's a lot more tuition money."

"I guess." I get my phone out and check for messages. There's one from Garret asking how I'm feeling. He asks every hour. I text him that I'm at the coffee shop.

"What's your name?" the guy asks.

"Jade."

"No last name?" He chuckles. "Your generation never gives a last name. I'm Walter Payson. I go by Walt. And you are?"

He looks at me, waiting for my last name. Do I tell him? For some reason I feel like I shouldn't, but then it just comes out. "Jade Kensington."

He sets his paper down. "You're not one of THE Kensingtons are you? I know it's a common name but given the cost of tuition at Camsburg, it's a possibility."

"No, I'm not one of *those* Kensingtons." I'm not sure why I lied. The man seems normal but his insistence on knowing my last name raises a red flag. And I'm kind of getting a weird vibe from him.

Sara comes back with a dark blue drink. "Here's your smoothie."

I taste it. "Blueberry and banana?"

"And orange juice. Do you like it?"

"I love it. This might be my new favorite."

Sara walks over to Walt. "Hey, Walt. You want the usual?"

He smiles. "Yes, but give me the blueberry muffin today. Thank you, Sara."

She goes back to the kitchen.

I follow her in there. "Do you know anything about that guy?"

She whips around, startled. "What are you doing here? You can't be back here. I'll get in trouble."

"Sorry. I'll wait out there."

When she comes out of the kitchen, I ask her again. "What do you know about that guy?"

"Walt? He's one of my favorite customers." She takes some milk from the mini fridge under the counter. "He always orders a muffin and coffee. He's really nice to me. He asks about Caleb all the time. He has a grandson the same age."

"Does he work at the college?"

"Yeah, he's some kind of consultant. He's only here for a few more weeks."

So his story checks out. Maybe I'm just being paranoid. Sara makes him sound like a normal guy. I go back to the table to drink my smoothie.

The guy notices me there but keeps his eyes on his newspaper. "You ever wish you WERE that Kensington?"

"What are you talking about?"

"Do you ever wish you were part of that family? You know, the *other* Kensingtons."

That's a strange question but I answer it anyway. "No. I don't."

"They're one of the richest families in America. Who wouldn't want to be part of that? You'd have an endless supply of money."

"I don't need all that money. I don't think anyone does. If I had that much money, I'd give most of it away."

He peers out the side of his newspaper. "I find that hard to believe."

I'm insulted by his comment. I see him eyeing my large diamond ring and I quickly hide my hand under the table.

"Why do you say that? Do I look like someone who's materialist? Because I'm not. I grew up without—"

His eyebrows rise. "Grew up without what?"

"Never mind." I'm not telling this guy about my past or anything else about me. I don't know why he's so interested anyway. I don't even know him.

Sara brings him his coffee and muffin. "I warmed the muffin for you."

"Thank you." He folds his newspaper up. "How's Caleb doing?"

Sara smiles whenever someone even mentions Caleb. "He's doing okay. He had the flu, which is why I wasn't here the past couple days."

"That's too bad." Walt pulls his phone out of his shirt pocket. "I just got a new picture of Adam." He gives her his phone.

"Aww, he's so cute." She brings the phone over to me. "Jade, look. Isn't he cute? That's Walt's grandson, Adam."

The photo shows a baby around Caleb's age, wearing jeans and a blue hooded sweatshirt with baby sneakers.

"Yeah, he's cute," I say.

"His father is the basketball coach at a small college in Minnesota," Walt says. "He likes to dress Adam the same way he does. Jeans and a sweatshirt. That's what my son wears to work every day. It's his dream job. He doesn't have to dress up and he gets to watch basketball all day."

Sara gives him his phone back. "I have some other customers to help. Enjoy your muffin, Walt." She races off to another table to take an order.

Walt sips his coffee. "Adam is my only grandson. My son and his wife don't plan on having any more children. People don't have large families these days. I came from a family of 10 kids. I grew up on a farm in North Dakota and all us kids had to help out. We never had money. I left home when I was 16 to get a job so I could finally have some money. It was stupid of me to drop out of school, but when you want money you'll do just about anything to get it. You know what I mean?"

The way he asked the question and the way he's staring at me right now, I feel like he's accusing me of something.

"I should probably be going." I fish through my purse for my wallet.

"I didn't mean to bother you. Don't feel you need to leave on my account." He picks up his newspaper and starts reading again.

I don't have anything smaller than a $20 bill. Sara will insist on giving me change back but she's with a customer right now and I don't want to wait for her. I just want to leave. I drop the $20 bill on the table.

As I'm putting my wallet away, I feel a hand wrap around my shoulder.

"I got your text." I turn to see Garret behind me. "What are you doing here? You should be home resting." He leans down and kisses my cheek.

Walt's eyes leave his paper and a smug grin appears on his face as he sees me with Garret. He recognizes Garret. He knows I'm one of *those* Kensingtons. I've been caught.

# Chapter 24

**GARRET**

"*I* was just leaving," Jade says. She holds on to my arm as she gets down off the high stool.

"Are you okay to drive? You said you felt dizzy this morning."

"That was before I ate breakfast. I just needed to eat. I feel fine now. I drove here without any problems."

"Excuse me, but are you Garret Kensington?" An older man asks it. He's sitting a few seats down from where Jade was sitting. I've seen him in here before.

"Yeah, why?"

Jade squeezes my arm. I look over at her but her eyes are on the old man.

"I'm Walt Payson," he says when I look back at him. "I'm a business consultant and I've been following your father for years. The way he's grown Kensington Chemical since he took it over is truly impressive." Walt glances at Jade, then back at me. "You two know each other?"

"This is my wife, Jade."

Jade squeezes my arm again. That time it hurt.

"We need to go," she says, taking my hand.

"Nice to meet you, Jade," Walt says.

Jade ignores him. She grabs her purse and pulls me toward the door, not stopping until we're outside and a few feet down the sidewalk.

"What are you doing? Why'd you yank me out of there like that?"

She points to the coffee shop. "That guy in there—Walt whatever—was trying to get all this information out of me. I didn't like him."

"What kind of information?"

"He wanted to know my last name. And after I told him, he asked if I was one of THE Kensingtons, and I said no."

"Why did you say no?"

"Because he was being nosy and it was a weird thing to ask."

"No, it's not. People ask me that all the time."

"Whatever. I didn't like him. I mean, he seemed like a nice guy but I don't trust him."

"What else did he ask you?"

"I don't remember. He just bugged me. And now he knows I lied to him. He's always in there when I go to get coffee so now he'll be asking me why I lied."

"Just ignore him. You don't have to answer his questions."

We're at Jade's car now. I click the key remote to unlock it and open her door. "You sure you're okay to drive? I could run you home quick."

"I'm okay." She gives me a kiss. "I'll see you tonight. Love you."

"Love you, too. If you need me to stop and get you anything on the way home, just let me know."

She gets in the car. "Would you bring home some ice cream?"

"Sure, what kind do you want?"

"I want a sundae from that ice cream shop."

"What do you want for dinner?'

"Just the ice cream. With my stomach all messed up, ice cream is the only thing that sounds good."

I lean into the car and kiss her. "Then I'll get you ice cream. Maybe we'll both have ice cream for dinner. See ya tonight."

She drives off with a huge smile on her face. Jade's smiled more in the past few days than she has in weeks and it's all because she dropped those two classes. Last Saturday when we had a fight and she kicked me out of the bedroom, I was lying on the couch thinking I needed to convince her to drop a class. I knew she'd get mad at me for even suggesting it, but I was going to do it anyway. Luckily, she came to that conclusion herself.

But I didn't know she felt that way about med school. That was a surprise. Truthfully, I never felt that being a doctor was the right choice for her. I knew she could do it and I knew she'd be a good doctor, but I didn't think she'd be happy doing it. When she talked about it, she never seemed that excited. And she seemed unsure. She'd never commit to going to med school. She'd always say she was still thinking about it. I should've taken that as a sign she didn't want to do it.

I've found that I have to really push Jade to figure out what she wants. Most of the time she won't even let herself *think* about what she wants because she doesn't think she can have it, or that she's *allowed* to have it.

It goes back to her childhood again. As a kid, she wanted the things all kids want, and I don't mean toys and bikes and stuff like that. I mean things that should be a given, like love, a safe home, parents who'd take care of her. When she never got those things, she learned to stop wanting them. She learned to stop trying to get them. Then her mom made her feel like she didn't deserve those things. Like she was a bad person for even wanting them. Because of that, Jade has a hard time figuring out what she wants and when she finally does figure it out, she tries to deny herself from having it because she doesn't think she deserves it.

It took me a while to learn this about her but I gradually figured it out last year when she kept pushing me away. I knew she wanted us to be together. I knew she was happy when I was around. But she kept pushing me away because she didn't think she deserved the friendship and the love that I kept trying to give her, or the happiness she felt when we were together.

It's such a foreign concept to me that I have to keep reminding myself that she thinks like that. And now that I know that about her, it's my job to push her into doing what makes her happy. As odd as it sounds, she's much more comfortable making herself miserable than making herself happy. It's something I have to continually work on with her. It's not easy because she's good at hiding what she really wants. I should've picked up on her clues about not wanting to go to med school but I didn't. I'm just relieved she opened up to me now instead of waiting years from now to tell me this.

I have 10 minutes until my next class starts so I'm sitting by the fountain in the middle of campus and soaking up some sun. I'm freaking exhausted after missing so much sleep last weekend taking care of Jade. I should go to the pool later and work on my shoulder, but I'm too tired to do it.

My phone rings. It's Harper. Usually she calls Jade, not me, so this is surprising.

"Hey, Harper, what's going on?"

"Hey, how's Jade? Is she any better? I didn't want to call and wake her up."

"She's a lot better. She's going back to class tomorrow. You can call her. She's not sleeping."

"Okay, but before I do I wanted to ask you something. Sean and I want to fly out there next week for Jade's birthday. Moorhurst doesn't have classes Friday and we really want to see you guys."

"We'd love to see you guys, too. How long can you stay?"

"We'd fly home Sunday night and take the red eye back. Is that okay?"

"Yeah, it's great. Frank and Ryan will be here, too. And I invited Grace but I'm making that a surprise."

"I want Sean and me to be a surprise, too. Don't tell Jade we're coming."

"I won't."

"What are you planning for her party?"

"I rented a private party room at a restaurant just up the coast. It's a steakhouse I took Jade to when we first moved here. She really liked it. The private room overlooks the ocean."

"Do they let you decorate or bring your own cake in?"

"I'm not sure."

"Give me the number and I'll call and ask. Or do you not want me to? Sorry, I kind of took over, didn't I? I couldn't help myself. You know how much I love planning parties."

Once Harper gets an idea, she runs with it.

"If you want to take over the party plans, I'm totally fine with that. I'm sure you'd do a better job than I would. I'll send you the phone number for the restaurant."

She squeals. "This is going to be so much fun! I can't wait! And I can't wait to see you both. Sean and I really miss you guys. I wish we lived out there."

If Sean would just tell her about his job offer, maybe they *could* live out here.

"I'll let you go, but I'll call later with any party updates. Bye, Garret."

Jade is going to be shocked when Sean, Harper, and Grace show up next Friday. She's already excited about Frank and Ryan coming. She thinks we're just going out for dinner here in town, but I wanted to do something special since Jade's never had a birthday party. That's why I reserved the private room at the restaurant. But I didn't plan to decorate it. I knew I wouldn't have time with everyone flying into town that day, so I'm glad Harper offered to take care of that.

On the way home from class, I stop and get two big ice cream sundaes. Jade won't be able to eat all of hers but I got her the big one anyway.

As soon as I walk in the door, Jade runs up and gives me a hug.

"You brought me ice cream!" She takes the sack from me and sets it on the kitchen table.

"Didn't you ask me to?"

"Yes, but I wasn't sure if you'd remember." She comes back over and kisses me. Like really kisses me.

I smile. "You must be feeling better."

"A lot better. I finally have some energy." She pulls me to the table and takes the sundae containers and spoons out of the paper sack. "We're having ice cream for dinner. Isn't this great?"

"It's a perk of being a grown-up. Dinner can be whatever you want."

"Tomorrow we should have donuts for dinner. Like all different kinds. A donut smorgasbord."

I laugh. "I don't think that's a good idea. I'll get you donuts for your birthday breakfast. How does that sound?"

"I get a birthday breakfast?"

"Of course. The celebrating starts as soon as you wake up."

"I thought we were just going out for dinner."

"A birthday is an all-day event, Jade. Last year you screwed everything up by not telling me it was your birthday. If you'd told me sooner I would've planned out the entire day. But instead I had to try to salvage the last few hours with a movie and ice cream."

"That was a great birthday." Jade takes a bite of ice cream and sits back in her chair. "Except you almost ruined it when you gave me that lame kiss on the cheek."

"Hey." I kick her foot. "I was respecting your friends-only rule."

"Yeah, well, I needed more than that." She sets her spoon down and leans over the table. "I *wanted* more than that."

"And I gave it to you." I keep my eyes on her as I eat my ice cream.

"You could've made it longer. Or kissed me more than once."

"I didn't know that was an option. You said you wanted a birthday kiss. As in one, not several." I smile. "And besides, the one I gave you was damn good."

"And how do *you* know it was good?"

"Because you grabbed my shirt and wouldn't let go. I had to practically pry you off me. I'm surprised you didn't rip my shirt."

I try not to laugh. I know that even now, Jade's still embarrassed by that. We were supposed to be just friends but we shot way past the friend zone with that kiss. She didn't want it to end but I purposely cut it short so she'd come back for more. Unfortunately, that didn't happen and the next day we went back to being just friends.

She's laughing. "Okay, I admit, it was a good kiss but you don't have to be so cocky about it." She gets up from the table, taking her ice cream with her. She only ate a few bites. Then she takes mine and walks away.

"Hey. I was planning on finishing that."

"I'll put it in the freezer. You can finish it later."

I get up from the chair and she appears right in front of me. She slips her hand under my shirt, rubbing it along my abs, just above my belt.

My body instantly reacts. I really hope this is going where I think it's going.

She gives me her flirty smile. "Did I tell you how much I've missed you?"

"I'd rather have you show me." I reach around her waist and pull her into me and kiss her. Her mouth is still cold from the ice cream, but it quickly warms up as I run my tongue over hers. She grabs hold of my hair, keeping me at her lips, her tongue tangling with mine.

We haven't kissed like this for a week, maybe longer. I don't even remember. I know that sounds crazy but she wouldn't let me near her when she was doing her nonstop studying. And then she got sick. So yeah, it's been a while. And the last time we had sex? Who the hell knows? It's been way too fucking long.

I walk her to the bedroom and take her clothes off. I strip my own off as she rips the covers back and lies down on the bed.

"You sure you're up for this?" I hate to even ask because I really don't want her to say no, but I also don't want to do this if she isn't feeling well.

"Are you kidding? I've been waiting all day for this."

I've been waiting *weeks* for this, but I don't tell her that. She knows.

I join her in the bed and run my hand over her smooth legs and kiss her flat stomach. I take a moment to look at her. She's so damn beautiful. Every time I look at her like this, I'm amazed at how beautiful she is. Her body is perfect, at least to me it is. I love every inch of her. I love touching her, sliding my hands over her curves, feeling her soft skin, making her react when I hit certain spots.

I move down, reaching under her and gripping her ass as I lightly kiss the sensitive skin along her lower abs. Her breath catches and I see her smiling, her eyes closed. She loves being kissed here. It totally turns her on. I slowly make my way up her chest and when my lips reach her breast, she arches back, begging for more. She doesn't need to beg. I'm not going anywhere. I could stay here all night. I love her breasts. I love all of her. And I've missed her. Damn, I've missed her.

My mouth remains at her breast, my tongue doing the things I know she loves. Her arms are at her sides, her hands gripping the sheet, her breathing heavy. I know she's getting impatient, wanting to move this along, but I'm not done with her yet. I need to get her close because it's been weeks since we did this and right now, I want to be with her so damn bad that once I'm inside her, I don't know how long I'll last.

I slide my hand down her stomach and keep going, stopping at the spot that makes her moan in pleasure. God, I love that sound. So I keep my hand there, making her do it even more.

"That feels sooo good," she whispers.

I slowly take my hand away and kiss her neck, and then her lips.

"You ready for something else that feels good?" I lower myself over her, letting her feel me between her legs.

She nods, smiling, and opens her legs some more.

I tease her by entering just a little, then pulling out. She sucks in a breath and I know I'm torturing her so I do it again. The more build-up there is, the more turned-on she gets, and I really want to turn her on.

I do it once more. I can tell she can't take it anymore, so I thrust all the way in. And shit. She feels so freaking good. Why the hell did I let us go so long without doing this?

I move in and out slowly, giving her time, but I can't hold out much longer. She grabs my ass, pushing me deeper and making the sounds that mean she's close. I speed my pace and within seconds I feel her releasing. Fuck, that's a good feeling. Between that and one last deep thrust, I get my own release.

As we catch our breath, I gently kiss her shoulder and along her collarbone. She smells fresh and flowery, like she showered right before I got home. The fact that she was waiting for me, thinking about me, wanting me, makes me want to do it again. I love it when she tells me she wants me. And when she tells me she's been waiting for this? Looking forward to it? Preparing for it? It's even hotter.

I hear her softly talking. "If you keep kissing me like that, I'm going to want to do it again."

"Then I'm going to keep kissing you, because I already want to do it again."

"So do I." I look up and see her smiling. "I want to do this all night."

I smile back, then kiss her and roll over on my back, taking her with me. She straddles me and we kiss some more and then do it again. Usually I need more recovery time but it's been so freaking long I have pent-up reserves.

We don't actually do it all night, but we do set a new personal record. And I loved every damn minute of it.

# Chapter 25

**JADE**

*G*arret and I didn't get much sleep last night, but sleep isn't what we needed. Last night, we needed to be together and reconnect. We'd been apart for way too long. So long I can't remember when we'd done it last. It had probably been weeks. And I missed him. Not just the sex, but him.

When we finally got together last night, I didn't want it to end. So it didn't. As soon as we finished, I craved to feel him again. He felt the same away about me. We were completely in sync; our bodies, our minds, everything. And this morning I feel like we're back where we used to be, before everything got so out of control.

"Good morning." I feel Garret kissing the back of my neck. "You tired?"

"I feel okay." I flip over to face him and am met with a view of his naked body; tan, muscular, perfect in every way. "Actually, I feel great. Last night was amazing. It's been so long I'd almost forgotten how good you are at that."

"I won't let that happen again." His warm hand slides over my hip and down my leg than back up between my legs, lightly brushing past the area that aches to feel him yet again.

I glance back at the clock. "We should've got up earlier. We need to get back to having our morning tradition."

"What time is it?"

"Nine. We have to get up. But I'd like to suggest a plan for tonight."

"I'm listening."

"Let's get takeout for dinner, eat out on the deck, then meet back here and do this again."

"I like that plan." His lips are now lightly kissing my neck as his hand moves over my breast, causing a tingling heat to run down my core.

"We should really get out of bed. If we don't, we'll be late for class." I reach down and touch him. "But I can't seem to make myself go."

He flips me on my back and gets on top of me. "Fuck it. We can be late to class."

We're only five minutes late. And my professor didn't even notice me walking in late because he was too busy trying to fix the projector which never seems to work.

This is chem 2 and normally my head hurts during the lecture because I'm always mixing up what I learned in this class with my organic chem class. But now that I don't have organic chem anymore, everything in today's lecture made sense.

After class I sit outside and catch up on the reading that was assigned for my psych class. I'm surprised how much I'm liking that class. I'm learning a lot about how the human brain develops and how much our thoughts and behaviors are affected by our environment from the day we're born.

I've learned that basically everything my mom did while raising me was the complete opposite of what you're supposed to do when raising a kid. Obviously, I knew this, but what I didn't realize is that everything she did affected me in some way and made me who I am today. My fear of getting close to people, my trust issues, my constant disappointment with myself, can all be traced back to how she treated me.

Little kids spend all their time observing the world and those observations teach them to see the world a certain way and react accordingly. As a child, my world was full of fear, uncertainty, disappointment, and sadness. I learned early on that I couldn't depend on my mom for even the most basic stuff, like food and love. I couldn't trust her either. She lied to me all the time. And she told me I was worthless and that everything I did was wrong.

I always tell myself I'm moving past what happened during my childhood but the truth is I'm not. And I know I need to deal with that stuff. I'm not sure how I'm going to do that yet, but it's something I want to work on.

My phone rings. It's Harper.

"Hey, Harper. I tried calling you earlier but you must've been in class."

"No, I met Sean for lunch and forgot my phone."

"How's Sean doing?" I haven't asked her about Sean for a few weeks so I figure now's a good time to get a status update on their relationship.

"He's good. He hates his job, though. His boss is a total jerk. Sean made some special seafood dish the other day and this food critic came in the restaurant and ordered it and loved it and Sean's boss wouldn't even give him credit. He told the food critic that the head chef made it instead of Sean."

"He needs to find a different job."

"I know. I tell him that all the time but he still stays there."

"Has he looked for other jobs?" Maybe I shouldn't ask these questions, but this is getting ridiculous. Sean shouldn't be suffering at that stupid job when he has this great opportunity waiting for him in California.

"There aren't any other good restaurant jobs around here. There's just fast food and diners. And he's too talented to work at some crappy diner."

"Maybe he should look in a different town."

"Yeah, I told him he should try to get a job at one of the fancy restaurants in Manhattan. But he doesn't want the long commute and I don't blame him. It'd be over an hour each way."

"What if he moved there?"

"He can't afford to live in the city. It costs way too much."

"But if he could, would you be mad if he moved?"

"Of course not. This is his career. It's important. He needs to be in a job that has a future. Or a job that will teach him what he needs to know to open his own restaurant someday."

"If he moved, you wouldn't see each other as much. Wouldn't that bother you?"

"Yeah, it would suck. But I love him and I want him to be happy. And right now, he's not. He pretends he's okay working at that place, but I know he hates it. I can tell."

"Aside from the job, how are things going? I mean, how are you and Sean? Are you still unsure about him?"

"I'm not unsure." Her voice changes to a happier tone.

"What does that mean?"

"It means I love him." She says it all slow and dreamy.

I laugh. "I know you love him, but last summer you said you weren't sure if you could see a future with him."

"Yeah, but then I thought about it and I realized that it's my *parents* that can't see us together in the future. Not me. Last summer, I was so focused on making *them* happy that I wasn't able to let *myself* be happy. It's like I had this wall up before and I wouldn't let Sean get past it until my parents approved of him. Well, mostly my dad. I really wanted my dad's approval. Then I realized that it's not going to happen so I need to stop worrying about him and my mom and just be happy. And once I decided that, everything changed. Sean and I are so much closer now."

"So you love him the way I love Garret?"

She laughs. "I don't think anyone has that type of love. You and Garret have that one-in-a-million type of love that nobody believes exists until you actually see it in front of you. I don't know what kind of love Sean and I have. I just know that I really love him and I've never felt this way about anyone else."

"Harper, this is big news. Why haven't you told me this?"

"Because you wouldn't talk to me for weeks. Every time I called, you said you had to study."

"I know, and I'm sorry about that. I dropped my organic chem class so things are getting better now."

"Good, because I was really starting to worry about you."

"So have you and Sean talked about the future at all?"

"Not really. I'm not sure if I'm ready to. I like just being where we are right now. I'm not ready to get married and I'm sure he's not either."

I swear, I do not understand these two. Do they never talk about this? I have to say something. I'm trying not to interfere, but I at least need to drop a hint.

"Now you sound like I did last year."

"What do you mean?"

"Last year you kept telling me that Garret wanted to marry me and I didn't believe you. Now it's my turn to tell you that Sean would marry you tomorrow if you wanted him to. I know he would."

She laughs. "Well, that's not going to happen so don't start shopping for bridesmaid dresses."

"I'm really happy for you, Harper."

"I know you are." She laughs again.

"I'm serious. I'm happy for you. Why are you laughing?"

"Because I know you and Garret are secretly hoping Sean and I get married. And I know for a fact if I don't marry him someday, you'll never speak to me again."

"That's not true."

"Yes it is."

Now I'm laughing, too. "Okay, I admit I'd be annoyed with you but I'd still talk to you. I'd have to. How else would I lecture you on what a huge mistake you made letting Sean go?"

"Yeah, you'd totally do that. But I lectured you about Garret all last year so I guess you owe me."

"I didn't mind your lectures. I needed to hear that stuff."

"Speaking of lectures, you need to get to work on that baby."

"Excuse me?"

"I want to be an aunt, Jade, so hurry up. What's taking so long? You should be pregnant by now. I told you I wanted that baby next summer."

"Well, you're not getting one. I'm only 19. I guess I'll be 20 next week, but I'm not going to get pregnant at 20."

"Why not? You're in good shape. Your eggs are fresh. If you wait too long, your eggs will be old and you don't want to make a baby with old eggs."

We both laugh. "Seriously, Harper. Do not talk about my eggs."

"If you get pregnant, I'll marry Sean."

"There is no way I'm agreeing to that. I'm sure you'll marry Sean long before I get pregnant."

"I don't know about that. As much as you and Garret do it, I think there's a strong possibility I'll get my little niece or nephew before Sean even gives me an engagement ring."

"Can we please change the subject now?"

"Actually, I need to go, but I'll call you later. Tell Garret I said hi."

"Okay, bye."

Now I'm even more confused about the Harper-Sean dilemma. It sounds like she wants to marry him, just not in the near future. So maybe Sean should take the job in California. If she wants to marry him, she's not going to break up with him if he moves. Or maybe she would.

Harper's a touchy-feely type of person who craves physical contact. A phone call isn't enough. She needs to be able to hug Sean and kiss him and everything that comes after that. If he's not around, maybe their relationship wouldn't survive.

"Nice day to be outside." I look over and see Walt sitting next to me on the bench.

Where did *he* come from? I grab my backpack and get up. I don't want to be around this guy. He makes me nervous.

"No need to hurry off," he says. "I could move to a different bench if you'd like. I'm just waiting for a meeting to start in the building behind us."

"I have to go so the bench is all yours."

"I understand why you hid your identity." He's looking down at his phone, swiping the screen.

I'm curious about his comment so I stand there and wait for him to continue.

"You don't want to be a target. Someone with your kind of money is a target for scams. People will try to get close to you. Make their way into your life to get a piece of that money. You never know who your friends are. You never know who you can trust." He puts his phone away and looks at me, and just like the other day, I feel like he's trying to tell me something with his expression and his tone. "It's a shame when you can't trust people, isn't it?"

I don't respond. I don't know where he's taking this. I'm completely confused by this whole conversation.

"Given that Garret grew up in such a wealthy family, I'm surprised he's so trusting. He should know better."

"How do you know if he's trusting?"

"We both know he is." Walt stands up, his dark eyes fixed on me. "That's what made him such an easy target. Isn't that right, Jade?"

"What are you talking about?"

"I need to get to my meeting." He starts walking away.

"Wait. What are you trying to say?"

He stops and turns around. "Secrets and lies tie you down, Jade. Doing the right thing can be very freeing."

And then he just walks off.

What the hell does that mean? He acts like I've done something wrong. *Secrets and lies tie you down?* I'm not keeping secrets. Or lying. Well, technically I *am* doing those things when it comes to hiding the truth about Pearce and his secret society and what he did to Royce.

Shit! Is that what Walt meant? Does he know about Royce? No, that's not possible. Is it? What if Walt isn't a consultant? What if he's a cop or a private investigator? What if he knows something he shouldn't?

It's almost noon and I told Garret I'd meet him at the coffee shop for lunch. He's there when I arrive, at a table near the back.

"How's my beautiful wife?" He kisses me, then holds the chair out for me.

I remain standing. "Remember that guy you met here the other day?"

"You didn't even say hello to me."

"Sorry." I kiss his cheek. "How was class?"

"Good. Can I get a better kiss than that?"

I give him a real kiss, then we sit down. I scoot my chair closer to Garret's and lower my voice. "So I saw that guy, Walt, just now and he said something really strange to me." I retell Garret the story. "What do you think he meant? What secrets and lies? Do you think he knows something?"

"How could he possibly know about that?"

"I have no idea, but I don't know what else he could be talking about. I don't have any other secrets." I check around us to make sure no one's listening. "And what did he mean when he said you're an easy target? An easy target for what?"

"I don't know. Just stop worrying about it, okay? I'll take care of it. Next time you see him here, call me and I'll be right over. I'll talk to him. He won't bother you again."

Sara stops by to take our order. "Do you guys know what you want?"

We give her our order, then before she leaves, I say, "Sara, what else do you know about that Walt guy?"

"Not much. Why? Why do you keep asking about him?"

"I'm just curious. He's in here a lot, right?"

"Usually every day."

"Do you talk to him much?"

"Just about kid stuff. I tell him about Caleb and he tells me about his grandson."

"So you don't ever get a strange vibe from him or anything?"

"No. I think he's a nice man. He leaves me really big tips. I haven't told him I'm a single mom but he's figured it out. He's one of those people who just picks up on stuff, you know?" The bell in the kitchen dings. "I have to get that order. Yours will be out soon."

She leaves and Garret puts his arm around me. "Jade, just forget about that guy and stop asking Sara about him." He leans closer and talks by my ear. "Put your mind on other things, like what I'm going to do to you when we get home tonight."

His lips touch my ear as he talks and it makes me shiver. He proceeds to describe exactly what he'll be doing to me later and I feel my cheeks blushing. I'm so hot for him right now I have the urge to forget lunch and race home quick, but then Sara brings our drinks. The place is packed today so she drops off the drinks and leaves.

"Garret, not here," I tell him.

He sits back and takes a sip of his soda. "I'm just warming you up for later."

"You went way past warming. Way, way past. Now I won't be able to concentrate during class this afternoon."

He laughs. "Then I did my job."

A few minutes later our lunch arrives. As we're eating, Garret checks his phone. "Shit, I forgot I'm supposed to meet with my project group in a few minutes. I have to take this to go." He wraps the rest of his sandwich in a napkin.

"You're leaving me? After what you did to me? I still haven't recovered from that."

His cocky smile appears. "Always leave them wanting more. It's in the guy handbook." He kisses me. "I'll see you after class."

When we get home later, we forget all about dinner. We head straight to the shower and then to the bed for a repeat performance of last night. I know it's a lot, but hey, we're newlyweds and we're making up for all those weeks of not doing it. At least tonight we managed to get a few more hours of sleep.

The alarm goes off at 9 and Garret rolls over and hits the snooze button. "Too early," he mumbles.

"I can sleep all morning. I only have one class today." I yawn and stretch my arms out. "Maybe I'll go for a run."

"Jade, we've already discussed this. You're not running alone."

"I won't go very far." I flip on my side to face him.

"No, it's not safe."

"Why? That burglar is dead and we haven't seen anyone suspicious hanging around here."

"It doesn't matter. I don't want you running alone."

I sigh. "Then what am I going to do all morning? I can't just sit around until class starts. Maybe I shouldn't have dropped organic chem. Now I feel like a loser."

"You're not a loser. You have plenty of things to do."

"Like what?"

"Call Grace. Or Harper. Call Brook and set up a time for the four of us to have dinner. And figure out what you want to do when Frank and Ryan are here next weekend."

"I think I just want to hang out here. Set up chairs on the beach like we did last summer. Do you think you could grill out burgers and hot dogs on Saturday? Or is that too much work?"

"It's not too much work. Decide what else you want. Make a list of what we need. See? You've got all kinds of things to do."

"I think I'm going to tell Frank and Ryan about med school when they're here next week."

"I thought you wanted to wait."

"I did, but now I just want to get it over with."

"Whatever you want to do."

"They're going to be mad, aren't they?"

Garret tucks my hair behind my ear and looks me in the eye. "They are *not* going to be mad. They love you. They want you to be happy."

"I don't like disappointing them."

"I promise you, you will not be disappointing them. They're proud of you. And they were proud of you even before they knew you were considering med school."

"You still think I made the right decision?"

"It's not about what I think. It's about what *you* think. Why do you ask that? Are you having doubts?"

"No. But I still feel like a loser. I had a goal before, and now I have nothing. I don't like not having direction, not knowing what I'm working toward."

"You're working toward finding out what makes you happy. That's not going to happen overnight."

"So you don't think I'm a loser?"

"I would never, ever think that about you. You work your ass off to succeed. You're way more driven than I am. I have no problem slacking off. If I only had three classes, I'd be hanging out on the beach every day or going to the pool. And would you call *me* a loser?"

338

I smile. "No."

"Jade, you've already accomplished so much, and I know you're going to do so much more. You may not know what that is yet, but you're going to kick ass at whatever it is. And I'm going to be here to watch it happen, and be even more amazed by you than I already am."

"I'm not so sure about that."

"You need to stop doubting yourself. You're going to do incredible things in the years ahead. You're going to make a difference in people's lives. I know you are. I can feel it."

"I don't know why you believe in me so much."

"I'll always believe in you. And I'll always support you in whatever you want to do."

I hug him. "I love you."

"Well, you *are* married to me. It's kind of required that you love me."

The alarm goes off again.

This time I reach over and shut it off. "You better get ready. You have class soon."

"Would you call me a loser if I skipped today?"

"No, but I don't think you should skip."

"I'd rather stay in bed with you."

"I'd like that, too, but you should go to class."

He gets out of bed and stands beside it. "Today's Friday which means it's date night. You going out with me?"

"I don't think so." My gaze wanders over his naked body. He's so damn hot. I feel heat rising inside me just looking at him.

"Why not? You got other plans?" He notices me checking him out and leans down to kiss me.

"I want you as my date." I kiss him back. "I just don't want to go out."

"So you want to stay in?" He shoves the covers back and nudges my legs apart with his hand. "And do what?"

He lays over me and I smile as I feel him between my legs, hard and ready. "I thought we were planning our date."

"We are." He says it by my ear as he pushes inside me. "Go ahead."

"I can't now," I say, breathlessly.

He kisses my neck, his hips moving in a slow rhythm. "If we stay in tonight, we'll just end up doing this again."

I'm still smiling. "Then we're definitely staying in."

And that's what we do. But our Friday date night ends up being more than just sex. We order a pizza, watch a movie, and cuddle on the couch. And *then* have sex.

Over the weekend, Garret and I catch up on homework since we both missed classes while I was sick. On Sunday, Garret goes to the gym and the pool to do his shoulder exercises.

His shoulder isn't hurting as much since he started doing physical therapy. I sat in on one of his sessions. It didn't look easy. They had him doing push-ups and resistance training with bands. It made me tired just watching it. After all that, you'd think his shoulder would hurt *more*, not less, but after weeks of doing this, he's in a lot less pain now.

Monday, I start getting excited about my birthday. But then Wednesday morning arrives and I wake up feeling depressed. Every year I tell myself I'm over it and I'm not going to think about it, but then I do. I can't help it.

Today is the anniversary of the day my mom killed herself and no matter how hard I try, I can't get that day out of my head. I just want to erase it from my memory, but I can't. It just remains there, vivid and new, like it just happened, even though it was years ago.

I can still see my mom sitting across from me at breakfast that morning, telling me how she was going to order pizza for my birthday. I remember feeling a twinge of happiness when she said it. I couldn't believe she wanted to do something for my birthday and that she was even acknowledging it.

I went to school that day with this tiny glimmer of hope that maybe my mom was getting better. Maybe something had changed. Maybe I'd come home from school and she'd tell me she'd decided to stop drinking. I don't know why I thought that. I knew better. But for years, I'd held on to this fantasy of her changing into the mom I wanted. The mom I needed. And for whatever reason, on that morning when she promised me pizza, I really believed she was going to change.

Then I got home that afternoon and my fantasy world and my real world came crashing down all at once. When I saw her there on the bathroom floor, I was in total shock. I knew she was dead, but I still screamed and yelled at her to wake up. I was so angry. She couldn't do that to me. She couldn't leave me like that. She hated me and treated me horribly, but she was all that I had. And then she was gone.

I collapsed on the floor and sobbed over her lifeless body. I hugged her and begged her to come back. I would never in a million years tell anyone that. Not even Garret. I don't want anyone to ever know how much I hurt that day and how much of me she took with her when she died.

It was easier, both then and now, to pretend her death had no effect on me. And so at breakfast, when I see Garret giving me that look, I cut him off when he asks how I'm doing.

"I'm not talking about it, Garret, so don't even start." I go to the fridge and take out the jug of orange juice.

"Jade, you can't tell me you don't think about it." He takes the orange juice from me and sets it on the counter, then brings me into his arms for a hug. "I want you to be able to talk to me about this."

"I need to move on." I try to free myself from his hug but he's so strong I can't pull away. "And I can't move on if you keep pushing me to talk about it."

"I'm not pushing you. If you don't want to talk about it, fine. I just want to be here for you." He kisses the top of my head.

"The best thing you could do for me is just to pretend it didn't happen."

He lets me go, but takes my hand and leads me to the table to sit down with him. "But it *did* happen. And I know you think about it, especially today."

"Why would I think about it? Why would I want to remember that? You don't like thinking about the day *your* mom died."

"Of course I don't like thinking about it. But I still do, and I know you do, too. That's why I'm trying to be here for you. You were with *me* last year on the anniversary of my mom's death."

Garret's mom died in a plane crash the day before Thanksgiving when he was just 10 years old. It was a small private plane. Garret said his mom thought they were dangerous so she'd usually only fly in regular planes, but that day she agreed to take the private plane because she was in a hurry to get home to start baking pies for Thanksgiving. She'd been at a fundraiser in Virginia for a senator who was one of Pearce's friends. Pearce had to fly home early for a meeting, but Garret's mom stayed behind to go to a party for the senator. It was his plane that crashed and they were both on it.

Garret and his dad didn't have Thanksgiving that year. And I think that's why Garret's family never has a real Thanksgiving at home. They always take a trip to a tropical island every Thanksgiving. Garret said that was all Katherine's idea but I kind of think it was Pearce's idea, too. He probably likes being far away from home. Far away from anything that would remind him of that day.

November 24th is the day she died, and that year it was the Wednesday before Thanksgiving. But because the date of Thanksgiving changes every year, last year the 24th was on a Sunday. It was the same day I found out my room had been broken into and my mom's letter had been stolen. I was so shocked about the break-in that I wasn't even thinking about that day being the day Garret's mom died. He didn't say anything about it, and it wasn't until that night that I remembered. I felt horrible, because earlier in the day, I'd asked Garret to take me to see his old house where he used to live when his mom was alive. We went to his old neighborhood and walked down the street. I can only imagine how hard that was for him.

When we got back to the dorm, I went up to his room and told him how sorry I was, but he said I didn't need to be. He said going back to his old house was a good way to remember his mom. That night, he insisted I stay with him because he didn't want me to be in my room after it'd been broken into. But I think he also didn't want to be alone. We both needed each other that night.

A few days later was Thanksgiving. We spent the day together at his house and he told me a little about his mom, but he wasn't sad when he talked about her. It was like he chose to focus on the good memories he has of her instead of what happened to her. And I admired him for that. I wish I could be that way and maybe I will once more time has past, although I don't really have any good memories of my mom.

"Last year, you wouldn't even talk about that day," I say to Garret. "We went to your old house and you didn't even mention what day it was."

"I didn't talk about the plane crash but I talked about *her*. That day usually sucks for me. I used to spend it drinking until I passed out. But last year I spent that day with you and I didn't need to drink. I didn't even have the urge to. You made me feel differently about that day. I got through it and yeah, I was sad, but it wasn't the same sadness I felt before. I didn't feel the need to get rid of the sadness by drinking. Instead I just accepted it. And on Thanksgiving I made you the sandwich she used to make me. I always make that sandwich on Thanksgiving in case maybe she's watching. It's my way of remembering her. And I wanted to share that with you."

"It's just that you didn't act sad and depressed on that day so I don't know why you expect me to act that way today."

"I'm not expecting you to act that way. I just want you to feel *something*. Anything."

"Why? What difference does it make?"

"Jade, stop trying to pretend it didn't happen. I know today is hard for you and I just want to help."

His insistence that I talk about this is making me angry. I know he just wants to help but I don't want his help. I don't want anyone's help. I just want to forget about it and make it go away.

"I'm fine. So stop bugging me about this. Besides, you weren't around for me last year on this day and I survived."

I didn't mean to bring that up. Both of us try to forget all those weeks when Garret wouldn't speak to me. I don't know how *he* felt during those weeks, but I was a mess. He had become my best friend and one of the few people I trusted and then he just ditched me and refused to talk to me. He didn't even give me an explanation for why he did it. That was a really bad time for me and sometimes I still feel a little pissed off that he did that to me.

He sighs and looks down at the floor. "I know, and I regret that, Jade. If I'd known, I would've—"

"You would've what? Not stopped being friends with me without even saying why? Not ignored me for all those weeks? Like I really would've wanted you to be nice to me out of pity."

"That's not what I'm saying. And I regret doing that to you last year. Leaving you like that, without an explanation. I hate knowing that last year on this day, you were all alone in your dorm room. That shouldn't have happened. But you shouldn't have waited so long to tell me about this day. Even before we dated, we were friends, Jade. Best friends. We still are, and that's why I wish you'd open up to me about this."

"You're making a big deal out of nothing. Really, Garret. I have nothing to say about it."

His eyes search my face. I can tell he's trying to decide if he should keep pushing this issue or just let it go. Luckily, he lets it go.

"If you change your mind about this, I'm always here for you, okay? Even if it's the middle of class and you decide you want to talk, just text me and I'll be there."

I agree to it, but I know it won't happen. I don't want to talk about it. This is something I deal with in my head and that's where I'm going to keep it.

And by the next day, I've already moved past it, or at least I tell myself that. I focus all my thoughts on my birthday, which is tomorrow. I start quizzing Garret about it. He tells me we're going out to dinner at that crappy diner with the bad pancakes. Obviously, it's a lie but I can't get him to tell me what we're really doing. Whatever it is, I'm sure I'll love it.

Tomorrow is going to be so great. Frank and Ryan will be here and I'll have an actual birthday celebration. Maybe I'll even get a cake with candles. My first real birthday party. This is so exciting!

# Chapter 26

**GARRET**

*I* woke up early this morning and snuck out of bed and went to the bakery. I got two dozen donuts, which is way too many, but I wanted Jade to have her donut smorgasbord and you need at least two dozen for that. Then I stopped at the grocery store and got her a dozen pink roses and three giant helium balloons that say 'Happy Birthday.' I also got a bag of regular balloons. I just finished blowing them up and I feel like I'm going to pass out. I blew up 20 of them, since she's 20 today.

Yesterday between classes, I went to the store and bought birthday-themed paper plates and napkins. They only had ones that are meant for kids so I got some bright pink, princess-themed plates. Jade's so anti-princess that I thought it would be funny. And just to top it off, I bought her a plastic tiara with fake jewels on it.

Once everything's set up, I sneak back into bed and give her a kiss. "Happy Birthday."

She opens her eyes and smiles. "Are you my present?"

"I *can* be, but you have real presents in the other room."

"Really?"

She's so excited. She's even more excited than Lilly gets on her birthday.

"Yes, really. Do you want to go check them out?"

"Can we take a shower first?"

"Whatever you want. It's your day."

The shower includes sex, of course, and as we're getting dressed, Jade says, "Now that's the way to kick off a birthday."

"You ready for more?" I see her smiling and say, "I didn't mean sex. I meant more birthday fun. Although we can certainly have more sex, if that's you want."

She laughs. "I do want more, but not right now. I need some breakfast."

"It's all set up for you." I stand behind her and cover her eyes with my hands.

"What are you doing?"

"Surprising you. Just walk forward toward the kitchen. I'll tell you when to stop."

She takes some steps, with me right behind her, my hands still over her eyes. I almost laugh as I take in the scene; pink and white balloons everywhere, the helium balloons floating above the roses, the giant tray of donuts next to the princess plates. I even hung pink streamers over the kitchen island. The whole thing looks kind of ridiculous but I wanted it to be funny. The real party will be tonight.

"Okay. Open your eyes." I take my hands off her face and pull her back into my chest, kissing the top of her head. "Happy Birthday!"

I'm laughing, but she's really quiet as she looks at everything. And then I feel her shaking a little. I spin her around and see that she's crying. "What's wrong? You don't like it? I know it's kid-like but it was supposed to be—"

"I love it." She smiles, tears running down her face. "Thank you." She hugs me.

"You're welcome." I don't understand why she's crying. It's just some donuts and decorations. "You okay?" I pull back to look at her.

She wipes her face and nods. "Yes. Sorry, I didn't mean to cry. It's just that, as a kid, I always wanted a birthday party with special plates and matching napkins and balloons. I imagined it just like this. Pink and everything."

She's never told me this. She said as a kid, she never even thought about her birthday because her mom just treated it like any other day.

Jade steps up to the counter and picks up one of the princess plates. "Every birthday, I'd wake up thinking that maybe just once I'd come out of my room and my mom would have a balloon or a cake waiting for me. I didn't need presents. I didn't even need a cake. Just one balloon would've made me happy. Just so I'd know she remembered."

I go up to her, taking the plate from her hand and putting my arms around her waist. "Jade, I didn't know—"

"I know you didn't. That's why I was so surprised when I saw all this. I felt like I was a little girl again, except this time I actually got a balloon." She laughs as she looks around at the room. "A lot more than one. How many are there?"

"Twenty." I kiss her. "One for each year that you didn't get one and one for today, when you finally did."

She looks like she's going to cry again. She squeezes her eyes shut and takes a breath. "Okay, no more crying."

I hug her. Sometimes she's so good at hiding the pain from her past that I forget how much of it is still inside her. Little things like a simple balloon can spark a memory and take her back to the dark places in her childhood she tries to pretend don't exist.

It makes me want to do so much more for her. It makes me want to give her the biggest birthday party ever. But that's not what Jade would want. Just something small, like what I've done here this morning, is all it takes to make her happy. I know this about her, but it still amazes me how the smallest things can put a huge smile on her face.

I lift her chin up and kiss her tear-stained cheek. "I love you, birthday girl."

"I love you, too." She eyes the donuts. "Can we have breakfast?"

"Yes. Enjoy your smorgasbord. I got one of each kind they had. You want anything else? I could make some eggs."

"Eggs? No way. I'm pigging out on donuts." She takes a sprinkled donut and sets it on one of the paper plates. "Princess plates." She laughs. "My favorite."

I give her a kiss. "I take care of my little princess."

She rolls her eyes but smiles.

"Oh, and that's not all." I take the tiara off the counter and hand it to her. "You have to wear this. It goes with the theme."

She always says princesses set a bad example for little girls but I guess she thinks it's okay to be one herself because she takes the tiara and says, "I'm totally wearing it." She positions it on her head. "How's it look?"

"It looks good." I take my phone out. "I gotta get a picture of this. Lilly will love it."

"No photos." She hides behind the balloons. "I don't want anyone knowing about this."

"About your hidden desire to be a princess?"

"Yes. I mean, no. I don't have a hidden desire to be—"

I kiss her. "Go with it, Jade. Be a princess for a day, or at least just for breakfast."

"Okay. Go ahead." She smiles for the camera and I take a few shots.

"Grab some donuts and let's eat outside. It's really nice out today."

"Roses!" She runs over to the kitchen table where the roses are sitting in a vase next to some presents.

"Yeah, I thought you saw them earlier."

"No, I didn't even look over here." She hugs me. "Thank you. They're beautiful. They're the same color as the ones we had at our wedding."

"That's why I picked them." My phone starts ringing and Lilly's picture lights up the screen. It's the photo of her from the wedding. She's wearing her flower girl dress and tilting her head as she smiles. It's my favorite picture of her from that day.

My dad got Lilly a new phone so now she calls me whenever she wants. I didn't ask him how he got Katherine to agree to it but I'm guessing my blackmail had something to do with it. She'd never want those videos to be released.

I hand the phone to Jade. "Your sister, and fellow princess, is calling you."

Jade laughs and puts the phone on speaker. "Hi, Lilly. It's Jade."

"Happy birthday! Did you like my present?"

"Um." Jade's looking at me, confused.

"She didn't open it yet," I tell Lilly as I hand Jade the small box.

"Hi, Garret!" Lilly yells it. "I had my swim lesson yesterday."

"What did you work on?"

"Going faster! I'm getting really fast."

Lilly's been taking lessons a few times a week for months now. The teacher comes to the house. My dad said Lilly takes it very seriously and practices all the time in the indoor pool. I love that she's getting into swimming like that. It's good for her and I know she does it because she's trying to be like me.

Katherine doesn't approve of Lilly's swim lessons. She thinks little girls should take ballet lessons, not be interested in sports. And I know Katherine hates that Lilly wants to follow in my footsteps and be on a swim team someday.

"Lilly, I love your present." Jade opened the box. Inside is a picture Lilly drew. My dad had it framed. The picture is of Jade and Lilly at the wedding. Jade's in her wedding dress, holding her flowers and standing in front of the ocean. Lilly's next to her, holding her flower basket. She colored her fingernails bright pink. Katherine didn't know about the painted nails thing so I'm sure she yelled at my dad about it when she saw the picture.

"That's the day you became my sister."

"I know," Jade says. "That was a really good day."

"Are you having a birthday party?"

Jade looks at me. "We're going out to dinner, so it's kind of like a party."

Does she really think we're only having dinner? Wow. I guess I'm good at hiding stuff.

"We're having a princess breakfast right now," I tell Lilly. "Jade even has a tiara. I'll send you a picture."

"You get to be a princess?" Lilly asks.

"Just for breakfast," Jade says.

"Honey, say goodbye." I hear my dad's voice in the background. "You have to get to school."

"I have to go. Bye, Jade. Bye, Garret. I miss you."

"Bye." Jade and I say it at the same time.

Lilly is doing much better at school. She's making friends and having more play dates. She doesn't hang out with crazy Jackie anymore but she does still do stuff with that Max kid, or bow-tie boy as I like to call him. If he ever makes a move on my sister, I'm going to strangle him with that bow tie.

"She only has a half day today," my dad says. "Just the afternoon. Anyway, Happy Birthday, Jade."

"Thank you."

"Did Garret give you the gift I sent?"

"I didn't, but I will right now." I pick up the envelope and hand it to her.

Jade opens it and inside there's a card, signed by my dad and Lilly, and a gift card for Jade's favorite sporting goods store. The store has tons of running gear, which is Jade's favorite thing to buy.

"Thank you! I love this store! This will last me forever."

The card has $1000 on it. That's nothing to my dad, but to Jade it's like a million. Even though she has money now, she still acts like she doesn't.

"You're welcome. I hope you enjoy it. Garret, are you still there?"

"Yeah, I'm here."

"I need to speak with you about something."

"Can we do it later? We're kind of in the middle of a birthday breakfast here."

"Of course. But be sure to call me later."

"Okay. Bye, Dad."

Jade thanks him again for the card before hanging up.

"Did you see this?" She holds the gift card up. "It's for $1000! I can get whatever I want. New running shoes. New shorts. Those cute tank tops that have the sports bra built in."

"Jade, you have money now. You could buy that stuff anyway."

"I know, but it's different when it's a gift from someone. That was really nice of your dad."

"Now that he knows how much you liked it, expect to get a lot more of those. If he knows you like something, he tends to go overboard. You'll probably get one every month now, so you should go online today and start buying stuff."

"This is the best birthday ever!"

"This is just the beginning." I give her a smug smile.

"What do you mean? What else do you have planned?"

Surprises drive Jade crazy. Now that I've hinted about a possible surprise, she'll ask me questions all day trying to find out what it is.

"I don't have anything planned." I lead her over to the donuts.

"Yes, you do. I can tell. So what is it?"

I hand her a princess plate. "Let's eat breakfast. Then I need to get to class."

I'm only going to my morning class. Jade's skipping hers and I'm skipping my afternoon class because Frank and Ryan will be arriving around noon. I won't be here when they arrive. I'm picking up Grace at the airport. Harper and Sean fly in this afternoon and will meet us at the restaurant tonight.

After Jade and I finish breakfast, I get up to leave. "I'll be back around 12:30 and then we'll all go out for lunch."

"Why are you getting home so late? Your class ends at 11:30."

"I have things to do."

"What kinds of—"

"Don't even ask because I'm not going to tell you."

She follows me back inside. "Thanks for breakfast. Those donuts were really good."

I grab my backpack and keys, then give her a kiss. "Bye, Princess." I laugh as I walk out the door.

"Hey! Don't call me that."

"You're wearing a tiara. I call it like I see it."

"It's a hair accessory!" she says as I get in the car.

She stands at the door and watches me leave, the tiara still on her head. I didn't even think she'd try it on, but she not only tried it on, she's had it on all morning. Freaking hilarious.

I get my phone out and call my dad. "Hey, Dad. What did you want to talk about?"

"Hold on. I'm just leaving Lilly's school." I hear him talking to someone, then the sound of the car door closing. "Okay, I'm back."

"Thanks for getting that gift card for Jade. She loved it."

"Good. Maybe I'll send her one every month."

I laugh. "That's funny. I told her you might do that. She thought I was kidding. She would be shocked if you actually did it."

"I just made a note to tell my assistant. Don't tell Jade. We'll make it a surprise."

"So what did you want to talk about?"

"I wanted to know if you've seen or heard anything from that police officer who came to your door after the robbery."

"No. Now that the robber's dead, I'm just trying to forget the whole thing."

"I'm still concerned by the fact that I wasn't able to locate the police report. And as for that officer who came to your door, I've been trying to get information on him, but he's so young that there isn't much—"

"Young? What are you talking about?"

"He's 23."

"Uh, no. I guarantee the guy who came to our door was not 23."

"Officer Trent Daniels. That's his name, right?"

"Yeah, but he wasn't 23. He was more like 55 or 60."

"Officer Daniels is 23. He's been on the force less than a year."

"Then who the hell came to my door?"

My dad sighs. "Someone who was impersonating an officer."

"Why the hell would some guy show up at my house pretending to be a cop?"

"I don't know, but I'll get my guys working on this right away. If that man comes to your door again, don't answer it. And be careful. Keep Jade safe."

"I will."

"I know it's a lot of responsibility, Garret. Are you handling it okay?"

"Yes. I'm fine."

"If you're not, you let me know. We'll talk soon. Goodbye, Garret."

My dad was referring to the responsibility that comes with being a Kensington, specifically my responsibility to keep both Jade and myself safe. I'm out of the organization, but because of what they make my dad and grandfather do, I have to deal with the fallout. My dad has enemies, which means *I* could have enemies and Jade could, too. It comes with being part of this family. My dad's careful when he does stuff, so the chances of someone linking something back to him and wanting revenge are unlikely, but it's always a possibility.

That's the bad side to being a Kensington. I'll always have to be on alert, always looking out for danger, doing everything I can to keep us safe. And I accept that. But I don't want Jade knowing this is what I have to do. I don't want her even thinking about it. It's *my* responsibility, not hers.

The past couple weeks, I've been so busy with school and Jade and dealing with my shoulder that I haven't really worried about our safety. Plus, since we have the security system and the burglar is dead, I felt like Jade and I were safe. But then something like this happens, with the fake cop, and I'm reminded I can't let my guard down.

# Chapter 27

**JADE**

*R*ight at noon, Frank and Ryan arrive in the rental car. I run outside to greet them.

"Happy birthday." Ryan says it first, then Frank.

"Thanks." I give them both a hug. "And thanks for coming. I've missed you guys. Come inside. I'll give you a tour."

"Where's the husband?" Ryan asks.

"At class. He'll be back soon and then we're all going to lunch."

"Did you lose some weight?" Frank asks, concern in his voice. "You look awfully thin."

"I lost weight when I had the flu. My stomach still isn't back to normal. But I had four donuts for breakfast so that should pack on the pounds."

"Garret let you eat donuts?" Ryan asks. "I told him he had to feed you right."

"The donuts are just a birthday treat. Any other day he makes me eat healthy stuff for breakfast." I open the front door for them. "So here it is."

Frank walks in and looks around. "It's very nice."

"Yeah, I like the granite." Ryan's in the kitchen. "Dad's getting granite just like this. He picked it out a couple weeks ago."

Frank's new house is almost finished. He's been sending me photos of it during the construction. The house is all one level with three bedrooms and three bathrooms.

"Do you think the house will be done on time?" I ask Frank.

"Actually, it's ahead of schedule. You're still coming for Thanksgiving, right?"

"Of course. I can't wait. It seems like forever since I was back there."

"That reminds me. Your former algebra teacher gave me this." He pulls an envelope from his pocket and hands it to me.

"What is it?" I rip it open.

"It's an invitation to speak at an event he's involved in. It's scheduled for the weekend you'll be home. He stopped by the house last week and told me about it. He and his wife both volunteer for an organization that helps young women who are struggling because of a difficult past. This group helps them get job training, counseling, whatever they need to move forward."

Inside the envelope is the invitation describing the event, along with a note from Mr. Gatlin, my former teacher, saying he wants me to be a speaker. He wrote down his phone number and email address.

"Why would he want me to speak at this thing?"

Ryan puts his arm around me. "Because you're an inspiration to others." He says it dramatically, like he's kidding.

"Yeah, right."

"It's true. That's what he said. Tell her, Dad."

"Mr. Gatlin said you'd be an excellent role model for these young women."

"What am I supposed to say to them?"

"That's up to you. But I'm assuming he wants you to talk a little about your past and then tell these girls how you became the success that you are today."

Hearing him say that makes me feel like a loser again. I'm not a success. I have no clue what I'm going to do with my life. I need to tell Frank and Ryan my news. I just want to get it over with.

"Can you guys sit down? I need to say something."

Ryan looks at my stomach.

I roll my eyes. "I'm not pregnant, Ryan. Would you stop thinking that every time I say I need to tell you something?"

He shrugs. "One of these times it'll be true."

"Anyway." I take a deep breath and let it out. "I've decided I'm not going to med school."

They both stare at me, not saying anything, then Frank finally says, "Was that it?"

"Well, yeah."

"Oh. Okay. I thought you were going to tell us bad news."

"Yeah, me, too." Ryan gets up and goes to the kitchen. "You should've seen your face, Jade. I thought you were going to say someone died. You got any soda in the fridge?"

"Wait. You're not mad about this? Or disappointed?"

Frank shakes his head. "No. You never acted that excited about med school so I wasn't really sure why you wanted to go."

"Ryan doesn't act excited about med school and he's still going."

"Yeah, but I'm excited about a being a *doctor*," Ryan says. "Nobody's excited about med school. It's a ton of work. So you have to be sure you really want to be a doctor before you suffer through all that."

"Ryan's always wanted to be a doctor," Frank says. "He's been talking about it since he was a kid. He even tried to perform surgery on the neighbor cat."

"I wasn't gonna cut him open," Ryan says, returning to the living room with a can of Coke. "I was just pretending."

"He was 8 at the time," Frank says. "I knew then that he'd either be a veterinarian or a doctor."

Ryan sits next to me. "I just always knew that's what I wanted to do. It's one of those things where you just know."

"Really? I never felt that way about being a doctor. I just wanted to do something to help people."

"You don't have to be a doctor to do that," Frank says.

"I know. I'm just not sure what else to do."

"You'll figure it out. I started college thinking I'd be an engineer. After a year of sitting through classes I had no interest in, I finally changed my major to journalism. My father wasn't happy. He was an engineer so he wanted his son to be an engineer, but it wasn't right for me."

"You never told me that story."

"It was so long ago, I don't even think about it."

"Did you drop some classes?" Ryan asks. "Because if I were you, I'd drop organic chem. I don't know what you were thinking taking that at the same time as chem 2 and advanced calculus."

"Yeah, I dropped it. And the lab. And it's too late to sign up for another class so my schedule's pretty open until next semester."

Ryan's phone rings. It's Chloe calling to wish me a Happy Birthday. And just like that we've moved on from the med school discussion. I worried myself sick all week for nothing. Frank and Ryan weren't even the tiniest bit mad about it. That's a huge relief. Now that I've told them, I can relax and enjoy my birthday.

At 12:30 I hear Garret's car outside. He comes in the front door. "Hi, Frank. Hey, Ryan."

They say hi and Garret motions me to the door. "You have another guest. Come here."

As I walk to the door, Garret moves aside and Grace walks in.

"Grace!" I hug her. "I can't believe you're here!"

"It's your birthday. I *had* to be here."

"You flew all the way out here for my birthday? Grace, you didn't have to do that."

"I wanted to. I missed my—"

"Ryan and Frank are here, too." I had to interrupt her before she called me her granddaughter. Ryan doesn't know she's my grandmother. He just thinks she's a close friend of Garret's family. Last summer we told Ryan that Grace was like a grandmother to Garret growing up and that's why she attended the wedding.

Frank stands up. "Nice to see you again, Grace."

"And you as well." She walks over and says hello to him and sits next to Ryan on the couch.

I stand there, still shocked that the three of them came all this way for my birthday.

"Can I get you anything to drink?" Garret asks.

Grace and Frank both ask for water.

I follow Garret into the kitchen as the three of them talk. "When did Grace tell you she was coming?"

"Last week." He smiles. "Actually, I'm the one who invited her."

"Thank you." I hug him. "I've really missed her."

"I know you have. She'll be here all weekend."

I hug him again as he's trying to pour the water.

"You seem even happier than when I left this morning. Are you on a sugar high from the donuts?"

"I'm just relieved because I told Frank and Ryan I'm not going to med school and they didn't get mad."

"I told you they wouldn't."

"I know, but I didn't believe you."

He shakes his head, then gives me a quick kiss. "Where's your tiara?"

"I'm not wearing that. Are you kidding me?"

"Why won't you wear it? I thought it was just a hair accessory." He smiles, then walks off with the glasses of water.

The five of us sit and talk for a few minutes, then go to lunch at a restaurant Garret picked. He said one of his professors goes there all the time. It has a big outdoor patio with a wood-fired grill where they make pizzas, but the menu has other items as well.

After lunch, everyone goes back to our place and we talk some more out on the deck. Frank doesn't mention his new girlfriend. I'm dying to know more about her but I guess he's not ready to talk about her.

Around 5, Frank and Ryan take Grace back to the hotel where they're all staying. Apparently everyone knows where we're going for dinner except me. And Garret still won't tell me.

I put on a sleeveless red dress. It's short and fitted and a little sexy but still classy. Garret puts on black dress pants and a grayish-blue, button-up shirt. I told him not to wear a suit because it seemed too formal and I want tonight to be casual and fun.

"You look good, Garret." I reach up and kiss him. "Really good. And you smell really good, too. What time do we need to be there?"

He laughs. "We don't have time for sex, Jade. We'll do that later."

I stand back a little. "Do I look okay?"

"You look hot. I love red on you. Actually I love every color on you, but the red is—" He steps back, his eyes sweeping over me, looking like he wants to rip the dress off. "Damn, we need to go."

I slip my black heels on and walk to the dresser. Garret grabs me from behind. "And now you add high heels? We'll never leave."

I turn around and give him a kiss. "I just need my earrings and then we'll go."

"Here." He hands me a small box.

"What's this?"

"A present."

I open it and inside is a pair of diamond earrings.

"These are beautiful, Garret, but you already got me diamond earrings."

He points to the box. "I owed you those. Back on Valentine's Day, when I gave you those diamond earrings, I told you I'd get you ones twice that size if you married me. And you did. So there you go. I keep my word, Jade."

"Thank you." I put them on. "They really are beautiful."

"So are you." He kisses me. "Now let's go, birthday girl."

He takes me to that steakhouse we went to a month ago.

"What do you think?" Garret says as he parks.

"It's great. I love this place." I see Frank's rental car in the parking lot. "Looks like everyone's already here."

"Yeah, everyone's here." Garret laughs a little. He's acting strange.

Inside the restaurant, Garret gives the hostess our name. She leads us to a door on the side of the restaurant. It must be a private dining room. That must be the surprise. Garret rented out a private room that overlooks the ocean.

"You ready?" Garret's smiling.

"Um, okay." I'm not sure what to expect.

He opens the door and Harper's standing there.

"Happy Birthday!" She hugs me.

"Oh my God! Harper, I can't believe you came all the way out here!"

"I couldn't miss your birthday, Jade."

Behind her, I see Sean. "Sean came, too?"

"I go wherever she goes," he kids, as he comes over and gives me a hug. "Happy Birthday."

"Thanks. This is such a huge surprise."

Frank, Ryan, and Grace hug me next.

The room is all decorated. The ceiling lights are dimmed and white twinkling lights are strung all around. There's a table in the back, which has a small stack of presents and a two-layer cake with candles on top. Clear balloons filled with silver sparkly stuff are tied to each chair.

Between the people and the setting I'm overcome with emotion.

"This is amazing. Really. I've never had—" My voice cracks and I can barely get the words out as I try not to cry. "I can't believe everyone came for—" I'm unable to finish. Now I'm crying. Dammit. Why am I crying? "Sorry, I just need a minute."

I race toward the side door which leads to the outdoor patio. Garret and Frank follow me.

"Jade?" Garret stops me, his face full of concern.

I smile at him. "I just need some fresh air."

"Can you give us a minute?" Frank asks Garret.

"Sure." Garret goes back to the party. I hear him talking, encouraging everyone to join him so this isn't so awkward for me.

Frank puts his arm around me and we go out on the patio.

"I know this is a lot for you, Jade."

There's so much meaning behind Frank's words. He's the only one who truly knows what a big deal this is to me. Garret knows about my past, but Frank witnessed it and because of that he knows why my birthday is so hard for me. He knew my mom and he saw how she treated me. He knows I never celebrated anything because of her. Frank was the first person who tried to celebrate my birthday and my mom got mad at him for it. And Frank was there the day she killed herself—two days before my sixteenth birthday. After that, I gave up even trying to celebrate my birthday.

I wipe my face and take some deep breaths.

Frank keeps his arm around me. "It's not just the day, is it? It's all the people."

"Yeah." I don't need to explain it to him. Frank knows exactly what I'm thinking.

It's overwhelming for this many people to show up just for me. Part of me doesn't even understand that people would care enough about me to show up like this. I shouldn't think that way now, but part of me still does. Just a year ago, I couldn't understand why Garret even wanted to be friends with me. Or why Harper wanted to be my friend. And now I have all these people in my life and it almost doesn't seem real.

"Jade, everyone who's here tonight loves you. I hope you know that. And I hope you believe it."

I nod. "I do. I'm just not used to all this attention. I didn't know Garret was planning all this."

"He wanted you to have real birthday. He told me last year you didn't tell anyone about your birthday and that he never would've known about it if he hadn't stopped by your room that night."

"I just didn't feel like celebrating it."

"You need to, Jade. You need to forget about those other birthdays and let this be the start of something new. That room is full of people who love you and we came here tonight because we want to celebrate with you."

"I know. And it's great. It really is. I wish I hadn't reacted that way. I'm so embarrassed."

He leans over like he's telling me a secret. "Don't worry about it. Nobody even noticed."

I smile. "Yes, they did."

He squeezes my shoulder. "Let's go have a party, okay?"

He walks me back inside to Garret, who takes my hand as he continues to talk to Sean and Harper. Ryan and Grace are talking, too. Nobody acts like I'm crazy for breaking down. They just continue to talk.

Harper goes around Sean and wraps her arm in mine, pulling me away from Garret.

"I guess I'll see you later." He keeps hold of my hand and kisses my forehead, then looks at me to make sure I'm okay. I smile and he lets go of my hand.

"You guys are still so in love," Harper says as she takes me aside. "So were you surprised? I made Garret promise not to tell you."

"I was completely shocked. You missed a whole day of class."

"There weren't any classes today, but even if there were I would've come here anyway. I miss my best friend. I hate being so far away."

"You should just move here." I say it jokingly.

"I've thought about it. But don't tell anyone that. I haven't even told Sean."

"You'd really leave Moorhurst?"

She shrugs. "Probably not. I just miss my family and California and you and Garret. Moorhurst isn't the same without you around. I think that's why I get homesick sometimes."

Garret comes up behind me, putting his arms around me.

"Hey, we're still having girl talk here," Harper says, kiddingly.

"What can I say?" Garret leans down and kisses my cheek. "I missed my wife."

Harper laughs. "I swear, you guys are more in love every time I see you."

"I need to thank you for getting the room ready for tonight," Garret says. "It looks great."

"You did all this?" I ask Harper.

"Yeah, I kind of took over the party. You know how much I love to plan stuff like this."

"I always tell her she should be a party planner," Sean says. "And I could do the catering."

She kisses him. "If you keep saying that, I might just do it."

"Are you changing your mind about broadcasting?" Garret asks.

"Maybe. It's such a competitive field that I'll probably end up working as an intern for 10 years. And I don't really want to do that. Plus, I'll have to travel all the time."

Since we're on the topic of careers, I tell them my news about med school. Grace is standing there and she hears the news as well. So now I've told everyone. I can finally stop stressing about it.

We sit down for dinner. Then we have cake and I open my presents.

It's my first real birthday party. And if I count breakfast, I've had two parties today.

After the party, Frank, Ryan, and Grace go back to the hotel, but Sean and Harper insist we stop at a coffee shop that's on the way home. The place has live music on Friday nights. But when we get there, Garret goes home and leaves me with Sean and Harper. He says he forgot something and has to go get it.

An hour later, he's still not back. I call him and he says he had to go to the grocery store to get stuff for tomorrow. I can't figure out why he'd go shopping tonight instead of tomorrow but I don't question him.

The band finishes playing and people start to leave.

"I don't think Garret's coming back here," I say to Harper. "We should go."

She checks her phone and smiles. "Yeah, we can go. We'll drop you off on the way to our hotel."

They drive me home and when I invite them inside, Harper says, "We would, but we're really tired from the trip. We'll see you in the morning."

"Yeah, okay." I go to the door and Garret opens it. "Garret, why didn't you come back to the coffee shop?"

"I was busy." He takes my hand and brings me to the bedroom.

"Busy doing what?"

He flips the light switch on the wall, making the room dark, then flips another switch and a soft blue light glows above us. I look up and see blue lights suspended from the ceiling.

"You seemed to like it last year when I did this for your birthday, so I thought I'd do it again."

"I love it!" I hug him. "It's just like in our dorm rooms."

"Let's check it out." He leads me to the bed and we lie next to each other and hold hands, gazing up at the ceiling. "What do you think? You like this better than the earrings?"

"I like them both."

"You like the lights better. It's okay. You can say it. But I had to get you the earrings. We had a deal."

"I love the earrings and the lights." I flip on my side and hug him. "And I love *you*. Thanks for a great birthday."

"It's not over yet. Everyone's here for the weekend so the party will just keep going. And you still have an hour left of your actual birthday."

"What do you want to do?"

"Get you out of this dress." He reaches around and unzips it.

"And then what?"

"Get out of the dress and I'll show you."

And that's how I end my birthday.

# Chapter 28

**GARRET**

This weekend's been great. On Saturday morning Sean called and asked if I needed help preparing the food. I didn't need help, but I know Sean, and I knew he was asking if he could take over the cooking. He feels most comfortable when he's in the kitchen. He's one of those people who can't sit and relax for very long. He likes to stay busy. So I agreed to let him help and we went to the grocery store and got some meat to put on the grill. Then he got some stuff for side dishes and I loaded up the cart with chips and other snack foods.

Around noon, everyone came over and just hung out on the deck or on the beach. It was exactly what Jade wanted. Just a relaxing day with friends and family.

It's been great having Harper and Sean here. They were at our place until 2:30 this morning. It really sucks having them so far away. Jade still hasn't made any friends here, other than Sara, but they're not close friends. Jade and Harper talk on the phone a lot but it would still be good if Jade had a few more friends. I could use some more, too.

Today everyone arrived at 9 so Jade and I didn't get much sleep, but that's okay. We want to have plenty of time with everyone before they leave.

After lunch, as I'm cleaning up the kitchen, Frank comes in to get some water. Everyone else is outside, so I decide to ask him about Jade. I need to know what happened to her Friday night. When I ask him, it turns out he was wanting to talk to me about it as well.

"Jade struggles this time of year," he says.

"I know she does, but she doesn't like to talk about it."

Frank nods. "It was traumatic for her to find her mother that way. And yet after it happened, she pretended like everything was fine. She went to school the next day, moved her things to my house, and that was it. She didn't even cry at the funeral. The funeral was the day after her birthday. I wanted to wait but she wouldn't let me. She just wanted it over with."

"Maybe I pushed her too much with this party. I just wanted her to have a real birthday this year.

"I'm glad you did this for her, Garret. The party was difficult for her, but she needed it. And I'm glad you invited people to stay for the weekend. It's good for her to be around friends and family, especially this time of year."

"Why was she crying at the party? I haven't asked her about it and she hasn't said anything to me."

Frank sighs. "She couldn't accept the fact that all those people showed up just for her. It didn't make sense to her. I'm sure you learned when you were dating her that Jade has trouble accepting love from people. She doesn't think she deserves it. That's why I was so surprised when she let you into her life the way she did. I knew you two were meant for each other when I saw how good you were with her. You really changed her, Garret. I don't know how you did it."

"It wasn't easy. But I love her. I couldn't give up on her. I never will."

"All the years Jade lived with me, I could never get her to let her guard down. She refused to accept how much I cared for her. I treated her like a daughter but she acted like she was just a houseguest. I remember one day she was making dinner for Ryan and me and she dropped a plate and broke it. She said she was sorry over and over again, then ran to her room and began packing. She thought I'd kick her out of the house for that. As much as I tried to reassure her that would never happen, she didn't believe me. That's why she tried to be perfect all the time. She got perfect grades. She didn't go out. She didn't date much."

"Because she thought you'd kick her out?"

"Yes. She was scared to death of that. Her mother used to get mad at her for every little thing and threaten to kick Jade out of the house. And when Jade was younger, her mother would threaten to leave if Jade made her mad. So now she's afraid people will leave her if she upsets them in any way. On Friday when she told us she wasn't going to med school, she was so nervous. She thought Ryan and I would reject her for that. It's completely irrational but that's how she thinks. So anyway, going back to the party the other night, she just had to remind herself that people actually do care about her."

"That's what I figured was going on. I just wasn't sure. I don't always know what to do for her."

"Just keep doing what you're doing. Jade's finally happy and I credit a lot of that to you. You're able to get through to her in a way nobody else can."

"It doesn't feel like it sometimes."

"Just give her time. You're very patient with her, which is exactly what she needs. Someone who's patient and won't give up on her."

"I won't give up. I'm in this for the long haul."

"You better be. You married her." He smiles. "I'll see you out there."

Frank goes back outside and I finish up cleaning.

That short conversation explained a lot, not just about Friday night, but about a lot of stuff, like why Jade worries so much about school and why she freaks out whenever we fight. Before today, I've never asked Frank about Jade, but I realize he's the only one who really knows her history. And if I'm ever going to help her move forward, I need to know her past.

People start to leave late afternoon, and by evening everyone's gone. Jade and I go to bed early. The weekend was fun but exhausting.

On Monday morning, Jade and I ride to campus together. She only has one class today but she wants to do some research at the library. Before we left, Jade got an email from her advisor asking if she'd like to meet with him today. He knows she dropped a class and usually when students do this, it prompts a meeting with your advisor, at least it does at small schools like this.

"Where are you meeting your advisor?" I ask as I park the car.

"I don't know yet. He said he'll email me later. His office is being renovated so he said he'd have to find a different room."

I go around and open her door. "Call me when you know where you'll be. I'll just meet you over there since we're going home after that."

"Sounds good. Have a good day. Love you."

"Love you, too." I kiss her goodbye.

I go to class, then physical therapy over the lunch hour, then back to class. After my afternoon class I get a message from Jade saying she's meeting her advisor in a building on the south side of campus. It's an old building that isn't used for classes anymore because it needs some repairs. Her advisor must be using one of the rooms for his temporary office.

Jade's meeting is at 4 and it's scheduled for a half hour so I go to the coffee shop to kill some time. Sara is there and sees me when I walk in.

"Hey, Sara."

She comes over to me. "What can I get you?"

"I'll just have coffee." I sit down and set my backpack on the floor.

Sara sits across from me. "Hey, you know that man Jade was asking me about? Walt? Older man, kind of looks like a professor?"

"Yeah, what about him?"

"Jade asked if I got a weird vibe from him. I said I didn't, but then I thought about it some more and, I don't know, maybe there *is* something going on with him."

"What do you mean?"

"I've noticed that he's always in here whenever Jade's in here. I figured they just had similar schedules. But then she dropped those classes and stopped coming here as much and Walt stopped coming here, too. But he still shows up on the other days she's here. At the exact same time. It's like he knows her schedule. Does that seem weird to you or do you think it's just a coincidence?"

I grab my backpack and get up from the chair. "Hey, forget the coffee. I need to go. If Walt shows up here, call me. And if he asks about Jade, don't tell him anything, okay?"

She nods. "Okay."

I race to the door and when I get outside, I call Jade. She doesn't answer. Why isn't she answering? She always answers. I send her a text. She doesn't text back.

Shit. Now I'm getting worried. Why the hell would that guy be tracking Jade's schedule? And showing up at the coffee shop whenever she's there? Is he following her? Who the hell *is* this guy?

What if that email from her advisor wasn't really from him? Now that I think about it, why would her advisor want to meet in a building that's no longer used and needs repairs? There are plenty of open rooms all over campus where they could've met.

This could've all been a setup. That Walt guy could be trying to lure Jade to an isolated area. But why? What does he want with her?

Maybe it's not Walt. Maybe it's that fake cop. He acted like Jade needed protection. Why would he say that?

Or what if the person who shot those guys in the parking lot saw Jade there that day and has been trying to find her? If he found her, he'd kill her. Shit!

I start running to the building. I don't know what room she's in, but I'll check every damn one until I find her.

It's now 4:10 and I'm hoping she's just meeting with her advisor and not answering her phone because he doesn't allow it during his meetings. It makes sense he'd say that, but it pisses me off because I need her to answer her phone!

I shouldn't be freaking out like this. Jade's fine. She's safe. She's with her advisor.

Fuck. Why don't I believe that?

## JADE

That guy, Walt, from the coffee shop, walks in the small room where I'm waiting for my advisor.

"I was supposed to meet my advisor in here," I tell him. "Did you reserve this room? Maybe I'm supposed to be in a different room." I pick my backpack off the floor and get up from the chair.

"You're in the right room. You're not meeting with your advisor. That email was from me." He stands in front of the door, blocking it. "Sit down, Jade."

"I don't understand."

"I sent you that email so I could get you in a private place where we could talk."

"Talk about what?" I slowly sit down, letting my backpack drop to the floor.

"You."

"What about me?"

He looks at his phone and doesn't answer.

"Who are you?" I ask, but again he doesn't answer. "You're not a consultant, are you? And you don't work for the college."

"Actually, I *am* a consultant." He puts his phone away. "But I don't work for the college."

I start to panic, my heart racing. He doesn't work for the college? So he lied to me? Why would he lie? Why would he lure me to this room? Does he know about Royce? Or the organization? Or maybe he's *part* of the organization.

"What are we doing here?" I ask him.

"We're going to have a little chat. And then we'll decide what to do with you."

What does that mean? What is he going to do to me? I search the room for another way out, but there *is* no other way. He's blocking the only exit.

"Who's 'we'?" I ask him.

"I work for someone. He'll be here shortly."

Shit! There's another one? I was thinking I could probably escape from Walt, but I can't get away from *two* men. They'll hold me down or tie my hands or—what if they take me somewhere?

My mind starts imagining all kinds of horrible scenarios just as my phone rings. I reach for my backpack to get it but Walt rushes over and grabs it, then blocks the door again.

"I need your full attention here, Jade."

"Okay, you have my attention." I say it as calmly as possible. I need to appear strong and unaffected by his scare tactics. "Go ahead. Say what you need to say."

"This ends now. All of it. Your relationship with Garret. Your involvement with Grace Sinclair. The money. The car. The lifestyle. It all ends now."

My heart's thumping so hard I can hear it.

"What are you talking about? I don't know what you—" I stop when I see the door behind him swing open.

I hear footsteps as the other man enters the room. He turns to shut the door. I can't see his face, but I can see that he's tall and thin and wearing a dark suit.

Walt steps aside and the other man walks up and stands in front of me.

"Hello, Jade." He stares down at me, his eyes narrowed, his arms crossed over his chest.

I recognize this man. He's from the organization. He's a member.

I've never met him before.

But I know his name.

And I know who he is. I know exactly who he is.

Made in United States
North Haven, CT
24 June 2022

20575688R00232